08X

2.50

THE THIRD WITCH

The
Third
Witch

A NOVEL

REBECCA REISERT

WASHINGTON SQUARE PRESS
PUBLISHED BY POCKET BOOKS
New York   London   Toronto   Sydney   Singapore

This book is a work of fiction. Names, characters, places and incidents are products of the author's imagination or are used fictitiously. Any resemblance to actual events or locales or persons, living or dead, is entirely coincidental.

A WASHINGTON SQUARE PRESS *Original* Publication

 A Washington Square Press Publication of
POCKET BOOKS, a division of Simon & Schuster, Inc.
1230 Avenue of the Americas, New York, NY 10020

Library of Congress Cataloguing-in-Publication Data

Reisert, Rebecca.
    The third witch : a novel / Rebecca Reisert.
        p. cm.
    ISBN 0-7434-1771-2
    1. Macbeth, King of Scotland, 11th cent.—Fiction. 2. Young
    women—Fiction. 3. Scotland—Fiction. 4. Witches—Fiction.
    5. Revenge—Fiction. I. Title.

PS3618.E57 T48 2001
813'.6—dc21   2001034028

First Washington Square Press hardcover printing October 2001

10 9 8 7 6 5 4 3 2 1

WASHINGTON SQUARE PRESS and colophon are
registered trademarks of Simon & Schuster Inc.

For information regarding special discounts for bulk purchases, please
contact Simon & Schuster Special Sales at 1-800-456-6798 or
business@simonandschuster.com

Designed by Jaime Putorti

Printed in the U.S.A.

For my parents, John and Carolyn,
who gave me a love of reading, story, and theatre;
for Courtney, Ian, and Glenn,
who filled my life with joy;
and for my fellow ovarian cancer survivors,
whose stories of courage and grace inspired me
to follow my own childhood dream.

THE THIRD WITCH

O N E

'Tis time to rob the dead."

Nettle kicks me again. I pull my tattered wolfskin closer about my shoulders and curl into a tighter ball, scooting across the packed dirt of the floor to move as near as I dare to the embers in the fire pit.

"Rise up, lass. Stir your lazy bones, or else half the gleanings will be gone before we get there. Do not think to sleep the day away like a princess in a castle."

She kicks me yet again and I open my eyes. Although she is a small woman, she towers above my pallet, her face and shoulders tense as always. If a sorcerer were to bewitch a needle into life, that creature would be Nettle.

Nettle grabs my wolfskin and yanks it from my shoulders. The air is cold and sharp. "Boil a mug of tansy broth for Mad Helga, child, and then we must be off."

"I'm going to the brook first," I announce. "I'll boil the broth when I return." I yank my wolfskin back from her bony fingers.

"There's no time for your foolishness, Gilly. 'Tis already late, and—"

"I'll not take long, Nettle."

"Gilly, there is no time—"

Before she can finish speaking, I'm already out the door of our tumbledown hut, dodging the trees and sucking in the cold, sweet-smelling air.

The brook and woods are still black in the mist of the early dawn. At the edge of the brook, just below the small waterfall, I fling off my wolfskin and shift and plunge into the water. I gasp at its icy touch but duck my head under its surface. As my head emerges, I shake back my heavy shock of wet hair and breathe so deeply that it hurts. After the rank and smoky stench of our hut, the forest air is unbelievably sweet. A doe, drinking a few feet downstream, freezes for a moment. I stare back at her until she recognizes me and resumes drinking.

Since there is no one else around, I kneel so the water comes to my shoulders. Under the water and out of sight, I press my palms together. "Make me a tree," I pray. "Let me spend my life pure and clean in the forest. Let me feel a lifetime of wind and rain against my skin. I swear to cast this whole evil business aside if I can be turned into a tree."

I wait. The woods are silent. Even the doe is still. The only sound is the gurgling of the water.

I jump up, waist-deep in the brook, and fling my arms out like branches. "Change me!" I scream as I close my eyes. *Make me a tree. Make me a tree. I will ask nothing else if only you will make me a tree.*

I hear the doe give a small leap, then run away, brushing through the bushes as softly as a kiss. There is no other answer. I am still a girl standing like a lackwit in the icy water. I begin to laugh and then shiver. For a while I stand there, shivering and laughing like the greatest fool on earth.

I give a quick bow to the sky that is so dark it looks empty. "You are right, old man. I should not be happy as a tree. I would miss running." I add, "But I gave you your chance. You could have stopped all this. Should I take it as your sign of approval, then, that you are willing to have me kill Him?"

I wait for the length of ten heartbeats, but there is still no answer. "Your stars are comely," I call to the sky, "but I do not care for your silence."

Then I step quickly from the water, shaking my body like a wet wolf pup. I pull my shift over my head as I walk back to the hut. As I push the trestle door open, I call, "I'm back, Nettle. I'll brew the tansy broth, and—"

"Do not bother. I did it myself."

"Nettle, I told you that I would just be a moment—"

"I do not approve of this folly, wetting yourself down twice a day. 'Tis madness, it is, Gillyflower, and more than one king has died of it."

I squat by the hearth and scoop up a handful of ashes. I begin to rub them across my cheeks and forehead. "'Tis madness indeed, and folly beyond all imagining, but have you not said time and again that I'm the mad daughter of a mad, mad mother and will come to no good?" I rub the ashes down both arms. "My bathing costs us naught and provides me with much joy." Nettle glowers at me. I soften my voice. "You have your herbs and such, Nettle. Leave me the pleasure of my water."

Nettle turns away. "Mad Helga, if you have finished your broth, 'tis past time we should be gone."

From the shadows of the rear of the hut, Mad Helga totters forth, her long ashwood stick stabbing the ground in angry taps. I am amazed that someone can be as gnarled as she and still be able to move. Mad Helga is nearly bald, yet she scorns the wool cap Nettle knitted for her. A thick scabrous growth covers her right eye, and a scar runs from her left temple to the top of her jaw. Several long hairs grow from her chin. Nettle tries to take her arm to help her walk, but Mad Helga shakes her away. Without looking at either Nettle or me, Mad Helga stumps out of our hut. Nettle shrugs and then picks up two baskets, tossing one to me as she hurries after Mad Helga. I snatch my woven girdle from its peg on the wall, twist it around my waist, and run after the women.

We look the way the wood should look were it to come alive and walking. We move quickly and silently through the trees we know so well. All of us draped in earth-colored tatters, caked with dirt. My hair and Nettle's as jumbled as bird's nests, Mad Helga's pate as bald as a new-laid egg. We look like the wild heart of the wood, but walking. No wonder the villagers fear us. If I didn't study my face in the brook from time to time, I could come to believe that I am not a girl, but simply a wild and untamable bit of the wood.

The battlefield is a good walk away, and dawn is fully risen by the time we reach it. There are already a few other scavengers at work, all looking as shapeless and sexless as we.

"See," hisses Nettle. "I said we should be late."

"Hsst!" I can hiss almost as well as she does. "There's plenty for all."

Under the body of a yellow-haired man in front of me, I spot a glint of gold. I kneel to wrestle his arm from under him. It is heavy and stiff, like a tree limb turned to stone. Nettle crows with delight at the sight of the large gold ring that I tug from his finger.

When I first came to live with Nettle and Mad Helga, it bothered me to glean the battlefields. In truth, during my first gleaning, I cried the entire time and suffered screaming nightmares for weeks afterward. Before the second visit, I fell to my knees, tearfully begging Nettle to excuse me.

Then after the first year, the dead men on the battlefield no longer seemed real. *They are like trees,* I told myself. *When I step over a fallen tree in the wood, I do not cry or dream about it. In a way, these dead men are less important than trees. Trees that fall did not die trying to end the lives of others. Trees that fall do not carry instruments of murder in their hands.*

This day's field is much like the earlier ones. Perhaps a hundred men lie about, like so many hillocks. In fact, that's how I now choose to think of the dead soldiers. It is more satisfying to think of them as hillocks rather than trees because trees once lived, but hillocks are rock and soil without even the faintest spark of life. These things on the battlefield, therefore, are hillocks, just hillocks, and I am the princess, as in the old tales, exploring the hillock to find the dragon's treasure and take it back to the kingdom. In the old tales, princesses never worried whether it was right or wrong to rob the dragon. So why should I worry about robbing hillocks?

Still, it is a blessing that the victorious army always prowls the field immediately after the battle, killing all their wounded enemies and even killing their own companions who are too badly wounded to make it home. In my seven years of gleaning, only twice have I found a soldier who wasn't yet dead. Both times I quickly backed away, fleeing to the opposite side of the field, but sometimes in my dreams I still hear the moans of those dying soldiers.

Oddly enough, it is the smell that still surprises me each time. The smell is always worse than I remember, that stew of drying blood, loosened bowels, and, occasionally—if we arrive late and the sun is high—the stench of rotting meat. Luckily, as this morning goes on, my nose grows more accustomed to the smell, and while it never fades completely, after an hour or so I don't notice it any more.

I tug another pin out of a hillock's draped shoulder cloth. I carefully work it into the weave of my waist girdle, next to the other pins I've plucked from the garments of other hillocks. The baker in the village has six daughters and will always take a few pins in exchange for a loaf of wheaten bread. Wheaten bread makes a nice change from our usual fare, and my mouth waters at the thought of it.

I push another hillock so that it tumbles over. Good fortune is with me this day since clasped in its fingers is the hilt of a dagger. I work it free. I have to hit the fingers over and over with a stone to make them let loose of the prize. The blade of the dagger is chipped. To test if it can still cut, I saw it back and forth across the hillock's tunic. To my delight, the cloth splits in two.

Although it has been a good morning—a ring, a handful of pins, this dagger—it is back-numbing work. I stand and stretch. There are hillocks as far as I can see. *How did they tell each other apart in battle? They all look much the same to me.* A few have more outlandish headdresses than the others, decorated with horns and skulls, but I don't know whether that is the insignia of one side or simply a common soldier fashion. *What did they fight about? Which side won?* A thought hits me, and I shiver.

Is He among them?

I dimly hear Nettle call out, "Child, stay to the edges. You go too close to the heart of the field."

I know it is safer to stay to the edges, but I must find out whether He is there. Every time we glean a field, I'm terrified I might come upon His body among the hillocks.

He doesn't deserve to die in battle! Let Him wait for me. I must be the one to kill Him. He is mine, mine to kill, not the prize of some lucky soldier. Let Him wait for me. I have marked Him, and He is mine.

"Gilly, stay to the edges!"

Then I spot the most marvelous treasure I've ever seen on a battlefield.

T W O

I FALL TO MY KNEES with a little cry, my hands scrabbling through the blood-crusted folds of a plaid cloak till they close on a little book. A book! I hold it up. A book of my own! Riches beyond belief! No matter what, I will not let Nettle trade it. I wipe my hands on the skirt of my shift and carefully press the gilt-patterned leather cover open. It is in Latin, of course. I know some Latin. I studied it in the time *before*. I scan the lines, looking for familiar words. Yes, there is *Deus* and *regnat, stabat* and *mater*. I hug the book to my heart. Something deep within me shines. *I will learn more Latin words until I can read the entire book. Mad Helga knows Latin. Somehow I will persuade her to teach me the words.*

Suddenly from behind, two large rough hands seize me. I cry out and my book tumbles to the ground. I smell the odor of peasants— sweat, onions, turnips, wet wool, and rancid grease. I struggle hard, but the man holding me is as strong as a boulder. Two other men approach, laughing. They wear faded greens and browns and are none too clean and look none too clever. One of them steps on the hand of a dead soldier, and I feel a lightning thrust of pity for all the hillocks. *It is a pity that so many brave lads die, while these great mind-*

less lumps paw over their bodies. Then I cry out again in alarm as one of them steps on my book, not even noticing it beneath the sole of his heavy wooden shoe.

"We've caught us a little battlefield pigeon," says the man holding me. His voice is as thick as pig grease.

"'Tis a scrawny'un," says the shorter of the two lumps in front of me. He spits. "Hardly more'n a mouthful."

The third lump gives a laugh that sounds more like a bleat.

"'Tis a birdie full of spit and fire," says my captor in his thick voice. "It can give us much sport afore we wear it out."

The three lumps laugh and slap their thighs with thick, calloused hands.

I should have listened to Nettle. I knew that it was dangerous to leave the edges of the field. As the sun rises, bands of outlaws arrive. These greedy bands are more dangerous than the soldiers. They find it easier to relieve unprotected women of their store than to do the scavenging themselves.

I squirm to get free. I twist to the side, trying to duck under my captor's arms, but this lump holding me has arms like cudgels and fists like hams. I kick against his knees. He gives a grunt of pain, but the other two lumps just laugh and move closer. I scream, a harsh, bald sound like the shriek of a wounded raven. I thrash and buck like a spooked horse, kicking and trying to bite, twisting, and the whole earth seems to be pounding . . .

And then the head of the shorter lump is gone! Sliced clean from his shoulders, tumbling like a bloody cabbage and bouncing along the ground. There is a horse, a huge black charger, thudding about me, and I am free, and the two other lumps are running, not fast because of their lumpy bodies and lumpy shoes, and the horse is after them. One screams and falls . . . but I see no more because I fall to my knees, grabbing for my book. As I brush the dirt sideways off its cover, I see the short peasant's head in front of me, and I feel sick again.

I raise my head to look at my rescuer.

Then I feel sickest of all.

It is Him.

I haven't seen Him in years, not since I was hardly more than a babe, but I would know Him anywhere. Even in the thickest smoke of hell, I would know Him.

He does not bother to look back at me. I know Him, but He no longer knows me. He has reined his horse to a stop and is surveying the battlefield. He gives us scavengers a look of disgust and then tugs quickly on his horse's reins, and He is gone.

I don't see either of my other attackers. *He must have killed them both.* That doesn't make me sick. I don't feel anything, except panic.

Was that my chance? Was that my only chance? Did I miss it because I was worried about some book that I can't even read?

I feel the broken-edged dagger in my hand. *I will not be a girl, I will not be a woman, I will be a thing, a sexless thing, a thing with short hair, as short as leaves. I will be more tree or rock than woman.*

I begin to hack at my hair.

THREE

So when shall we kill Him?"

Nettle ignores me. It is three days since we were at the battle-field. Now we are harvesting Birnam Wood, looking for nuts and roots and such to sustain us through the fast-approaching winter.

I raise my voice. "Nettle, I asked when shall we kill Him?"

Nettle kneels quickly, wrapping her skinny hand around the top of a wild onion and tugging it from the ground.

"There's little flavor in them," she tells me for the hundredth time, "but boiled with cloth they make a golden brown dye that's second to none."

"Old woman," I shout, "I have asked you three times, and you have not answered me. I will not take another step until you tell me when shall we kill Him?"

Nettle stands and dusts off her skirt. "Then stand there until you turn into stone for I shall not answer such a foolish question." And she takes off through the forest.

I stay behind, hating her.

I will not move. I will stay here forever rather than give her the satisfaction of seeing me trail behind, like a broken-willed hound.

I stand there for a long while, hating her, hating Him, savoring the strong, pungent, onion-sharp taste of hate. I like hating. I feel strong and safe and alive when I hate. If I knew hate songs, I would sing them. Instead I indulge in the pleasure of making up curses and call them out.

"Nettle," I cry. "You are a pockmarked, rickety, toad-bellied, snot-snatching, addle-hag!"

Then I picture myself facing Him.

"You craven snake licker! You son of a ditch drab! Do not dare to stare at me with your eyes of a newt! Do not speak to me with your tongue of a frog! Your hair is the hair of dogs who lie in dung. Your private places are as shriveled as hemlock root. Your soul is more shriveled than a forked mandrake that has lain a sevenday under the eye of the August sun! You eater of babes, may all who follow you in your line learn to hate their father and mother and curse the day they were ever born!"

My maledictions ring out through the wood, sharp as a snapped branch. I love this wood. I love it for itself, but I love it also because the villagers fear it. They believe the wood full of magical creatures who mean them harm.

If they hear me cursing, they will think me an evil spirit of the woods, perhaps a weird woman casting her spells. I chuckle with delight. Then I get an even better idea. I begin to make noises—a low moan, then a shriek to curdle the thickest blood, then a mad cackle, like a queen being turned into a hen.

Perhaps Nettle can hear me. Perhaps she will think, as I stand here so faithfully, an errant wizard has come upon me and is subjecting me to terrible spells. Nettle will blanch with fear and guilt for making me stand stock-still in the middle of this mad wood.

I realize that I am tired of standing here waiting for Nettle to come back. This is how I can tell that she does not care for me, that she raised me only out of pity. Otherwise she would have come back to check on me. The wood is no longer so pleasant. A wind has arisen, dancing in tiny circles about the leaves that bob and twist.

Then I hear the pitter-pat of raindrops. At first they just tap against the leaves, but then one plops down on my neck. I feel another on the top of my head.

Saint Colum's bones, it is enough to drive me mad, this slow, irregular drip-drip-drip of the water. Mad Helga has said this was how some of the Old Ones used to torture their captives, an unsteady drip-drip-drip until they went out of their heads. Water seems so soft, but I have seen the hollows in the hardest stones worn deep by the soft, patient water.

My head jerks up.

I have my answer.

Perhaps I will not wear Nettle down today, but I can ask-ask-ask until she gives in. I am not water, but I can learn the lessons of water.

I hunch my ragged wolfskin about my shoulders and hurry back to the hut.

FOUR

"WHEN SHALL WE kill Him?"

My words fall like a stone into the pool of quiet darkness inside the hut.

Nettle and Mad Helga pause for a moment, then resume their work. All the treasures of the battlefield, except the book, are spread out on the hearth. With the hem of her gown, Nettle cleans and polishes them. Her two wild cats are hunched down at her side—Graymalkin, with his one eye and his three sound legs, and Hecate, with her broken tail. In summer they mostly live in the wood, but as the season of binding approaches, they creep inside to huddle next to the woman who saved them. Every turn of the moon, Mad Helga brings home one or two broken creatures, rocking them in her arms and gibbering at them in a strange language that no one else seems to speak. Despite her attention, most of her wild creatures die. Then as if in some lunatic tribute, she boils their bones until they are clean as Saint John's soul. She piles the boiled bones 'round her bed pallet to use as playthings or prayer beads or conjuring twigs or some such nonsense. This evening Mad Helga kneels at the far side of the hearth, rocking the skeleton of a toad in her cupped hands, her lips moving in the rhythm of a soundless chant.

I stamp my bare foot against the hard-packed earthen floor. "Listen to me! I say we kill Him tomorrow."

The two older women look at each other silently. I hate it when they exchange these silent looks.

"We will leave at dawn," I shout. Instead of the gentle dripping of water, I have become a flood. "Get sleep now, for we must get an early start."

"Women weep and children scream," Mad Helga croons to the tiny skeleton in her gnarled hands. "Paddock sleep and paddock dream. Rockabye, be not shy, we shall all sleep bye and bye."

"Listen to me!" I long to shake the old woman until her jaw rattles.

Suddenly Nettle begins to laugh, a harsh, broken cackle that hurts my ears.

"Stop it!" I shout. I want to shake her, too.

But Nettle cackles on and on.

"Don't laugh at me!"

Nettle shakes her head. "When you are daft, child, then I must laugh. Now we have had enough of your jests. There's barley porridge in the kettle. Fetch your bowl and eat your dinner."

"No!" I hit the frame of the door with my fist. "When I came here, seven years ago, you promised to help me. 'Give us seven years of service,' you said, 'and we shall aid you in fetching your heart's desire.' Seven years of service have I given to you, seven years of faithful service, and now I claim my rights." I take a deep breath. "Three days ago I saw Him, the man that I must kill. For seven years I have made my life an arrow, and He is its target. For seven years I have made my heart a dagger, and He is its sheath. I call to you both. Fulfill your promise. Help me kill Him."

Nettle looks down. Her bony fingers pick up a broken shard of bronze and begin to polish it. "I did not promise—"

"You did! You did! You promised. 'Twas the only reason I stayed with you. Why else would I stay for seven years with two mad old women in this tumbledown hut? The very night I came, you gave me a promise."

Nettle's face darkens. "'Twas only some words, Gilly, said to soothe a frightened child."

"But what you said was a promise."

We continue to quarrel until I slam out of the room and stomp down to the pool in the stream. In the spilled light of the fat moon, I study my face in the water. My hacked hair, outlined by the moonlight, looks like stubble in a barley field after the final winnowing.

"Water," I beg, "teach me your ways. Teach me the way to wear Nettle down."

I sit for a long time and listen to the water.

Then hunger nudges me back to the hut.

AUTUMN BLEEDS into winter.

Past All Hallows, through Advent, all through the dark days, I wear away at Nettle with my words, my sulks, my anger. It is not a pleasant winter, the three of us either huddling in our hut that reeks of smoke and sour, unwashed linen or shivering in the outside air that is as sharp as an iced blade. No, it is not a happy winter for any of us. I hate the way I sound when I open my mouth, but I cannot stop my bleating.

There is little for us to do in winter. I often see Nettle studying our food store and then counting on her fingers the days until the middle of spring. Mad Helga seldom stirs from her trash heap of rags and bones by the fire, except to totter out to relieve herself. I go for long solitary walks, my wolfskin tight around my bony shoulders. I often wish Nettle would join me, but I am too proud to ask her. From time to time, one of the villagers appears at our door, begging for a potion to cure a cough, a plaster for a phlegmy chest, or a poultice for chapped fingers and shins. Villagers shun us in health and fortune, but when they are weakened by disease or heartbreak, they come creeping to Nettle and her herbs.

Many days I sit in front of the hut wrapped tightly in my wolf-skin in the thin light of the afternoon trying to decipher words in my book. I do not ask Mad Helga to teach me Latin. I will request nothing from her except her help with the murder.

Some days I sit in the pale dribbles of winter sunlight and let myself dream of revenge. I do not picture His dying, but I picture Him dead. I see myself towering over His lifeless body, a knife or torch or flask of poison in my hand and my face as serene and saintly as Judith's when she hammered a spike into the head of her foe. Other times I amuse myself by picturing His face just before I kill Him, and in my mind I practice the words I will say. Perhaps *Now the score is evened* or *Thus my promise is fulfilled.* Sometimes I compose a long, lofty speech in which I make clear how He has wronged me, but at other times I imagine myself merely giving Him a long, cold, scornful look. A handful of times I imagine Him lying in a silent castle with all His servants dead around Him, and once I let myself envison the slut that He loved kneeling at His side, but this frightens me so much that I vow to imagine for Him a solitary death.

In winter we do not glean the dead. We hear that this year there are battles all through the winter, but Nettle doubts this. "Most warriors," she tells me, "go home for the harvest and stay snug at home through the spring planting. Then, in the late spring after Beltane, when they have naught to do at home, they grow restless and fight wars until harvest calls them home again."

Lent comes, the emptiest days of the year. Now we take care to avoid the villagers. In Lent, all but the invalids and babes eat only one meal a day. Hunger makes everyone spiteful.

One frosty afternoon when the light is as thin as a graybeard's spittle, I carry a basket of herbs over to the holy sisters at Cree. Fat Sister Grisel slips me two fresh-baked oatcakes and a warning to take special care. "Between this war and the hard winter, our country grows more dangerous. They say that even some of our good Scottish lords have turned traitor and now swear fealty to the king from the north. I wonder at Nettle's letting you come here alone. 'Tis not safe for a girl to go about on her own."

"I am not a girl," I say, but I cannot tell whether the feeling in my heart is pride or sadness or both. "I am neither lass nor lad. I am a thing of the wood, and things of the wood have no sex at all."

Her mouth frowns, but her eyes are kind. "Remind Nettle that 'tis not safe for any of you to go about much until after Easter Sunday. Remind her that more people are hanged as witches during this season when folk are hungry and holy than at any other time of the year."

So like three angry mice corked in a bottle, we stay close to the hut.

Although even I have grown tired of my demands, I do not stop. "When Lent is over, will you help me kill Him?"

Nettle is sharpening our knife on a whetstone. As usual, she ignores me, but Mad Helga joins our conversation. Her tone is unusually sensible, even though her cupped right hand cradles the skeleton of the mouse she strokes with her gnarled left fingers.

"And just how will we kill him, girl?"

FIVE

Eagerly I turn to Mad Helga. I have been thinking about this for a long time. "We can use magic—yours and Nettle's—to kill Him. We will lay an enchantment on Him."

For a moment there is silence. I hear the hiss of the fire. Then Nettle begins to cackle wildly, rocking back and forth with cruel laughter. I want to put my hands over my ears to shut out that ugly, broken sound, but I don't want to give Nettle the satisfaction of seeing how much her laughter hurts me.

Mad Helga's calm voice, however, cuts through Nettle's jagged laughing.

"And how, child, do we employ this magic?"

"All I ask you to do is to cast a spell to bring about His death. A painful, lingering death." I warm to my subject, delighted at last to be able to give details. "A death so horrible that it will be talked about for generations. A death—"

Nettle slams the whetstone against the table. "You are almost a woman now, Gilly. Do not speak like a silly child. Surely we have had our fill of your foolishness, so—"

"Nettle, I claim my due."

"Gilly, I have told you and told you, there was no prom—"

"'Tis not fair!"

"'Tis a foul thing to wish a man's death, Gilly. Even if I wished—"

"You gave me your word. Is your word of so little account?"

"A promise to a child, my lass, is not a prom—"

"Hsst!" There is a surprising edge of steel in Mad Helga's voice, but her face looks as vacant as ever. "Gilly, the man you speak of, did he not save your life on the battlefield one morning during harvest time?"

My face hardens. "No," I say loudly. "He did not."

Nettle shrieks like a stoat with a foot caught by a trap. "Who lies now?" she says with a trill of triumph in her voice. "Whose words are now false? You twist-tongued prevaricator, did I not see with these very eyes that man you speak of save you from those three peasants—"

"I did not ask Him to save me. Given enough time, I should have saved myself." My breath quickens. "Anyway, it makes no difference. I have made my life an arrow, and He is my home. I have made my heart a dagger, and His heart is my—"

Mad Helga says, "'Tis a serious business, child, to kill a man who saved you. Whether he saved you asked or saved you unasked, it matters not."

"Mad Helga," I say, "should He save the entire world, it makes not a whit of difference to me. Should He save God and Jesus and the whole stable of shining saints, I will kill Him. With your aid or without it."

Nettle shrugs. "I do not like such foolish prattle. We will do naught to aid your foolish plan."

"Then I will kill Him myself. I will find Him, and I will—"

Nettle's cackle cuts off my words. "Just dance up to him and say, 'God save the mark, sire, and begging your pardon, but I have come to kill you, so if you will kindly take off your shirt of mail, I shall—'"

"Do not laugh at me!" Oh, to be Samson and be able to pull the poles of this hut down, burying Nettle and her mockery in the rubble.

Mad Helga holds up her hands. The skeleton of the mouse, unheeded, tumbles to the hearth. The tiny bones scatter. "We cannot cast a spell, child, unless we have aught of our victim."

All at once, my heart jigs with joy. At last my revenge begins to take real shape. "What do we need? Things like bits of His hair and fingernail parings? Threads of His clothes and—"

Mad Helga ignores my words. "If you desire his doom, lass, 'twill not be a free gift. Doom is costly, more costly than love."

"I have given you seven years of service."

Mad Helga snorts in seeming disgust. "Seven years of service is a mere trifle. Less than a trifle. Doom demands heart, hands, and blood. At most seven years of service buys your right to *ask* to buy the spell. It does not buy the spell itself."

Nettle shoots an angry look at Mad Helga. "Old woman," she says, "shut your mouth. Your wits are as scattered as those silly bones on the hearth stones. We'll have no more of this foolish talk."

"'Tis not foolish talk," I say. "I do God's work, Nettle."

She quickly makes the sign of the cross. "Hush! We'll have no blaspheming here, girl. Do not try to hide your selfish desires under the cloak of our Lord. To cure your own flea bite, you want to burn down a hut. Can you not see your own madness?"

"'Tis but justice I seek. With all your second sight, can you not see that? Did He not slaughter all my family, all those I loved?"

"All save one, Gilly."

"And that one is just as dead to me." How dare Nettle try to stop me? "Nettle, I will kill you rather than let you stop me now." I feel a quiver of fear because I may be speaking the truth. Out of the pouch at my side, I pull the broken dagger from the battlefield. "I will stab you in the heart with this dagger, Nettle, rather than abandon my plan."

Nettle studies me for a moment, her mouth tight and hard. I hear the sputter of the fire and Nettle's angry breathing. Then a branch in the fire snaps. Nettle stands. "So you would use that bit of blade that butchered your hair to kill the woman who raised you?" Her voice shakes. "Please yourself, then. Both of you. Mad old woman and mad, mad child. I shall not be part of this dangerous folly." She walks to the door. Her stride is unsteady. "I shall go out for a bit, and when I return, I will hear no more of this mad talk." She fumbles her cloak off its peg and wraps it around her knobby shoulders.

She turns back to glare at me. "But before I go, Gilly, I give you two warnings. Heed them well. First, know that 'tis easier than anything—easier than breathing, easier even than death—to find that you yourself have become the very thing you hate most. It happens quicker than a body can reckon." She closes her eyes briefly, as if she feels a twinge of pain, and then opens them. Her eyes look sad. "And second, child, as you well know, against my will, I have the gift of second sight. So I warn you both now, no good will come of this plan. The doom in the plan is not for him alone. That doom will also find us out and bring death to our very door."

Then she stalks out of the hut, her skirts twitching like the fur on an angry cat.

SIX

*N*ETTLE HATES THE WOOD *at night. She must be angry indeed to seek out peace in the wild wood.* Although I will not admit it, Nettle's words frighten me. She does indeed have second sight. *Am I willing to doom all of us just to pull Him down?* I push that thought away as firmly as a mother would push away a babe with sticky hands. *I cannot afford to think these things. If I soften, I am lost. A tree must not yearn to become a feather, nor can a stone afford to long to become a bubble. I am not a girl but a thing, a thing made only of revenge, hate, and a fierce, wild will. My hunger for blood will burn out any thread of softness in my soul. If doom were to walk, it would wear my face. Doom will not find me. I myself am doom.*

Mad Helga's trembling, gnarled fingers gather up the mouse bones, one by one.

I ask, "With what coin, then, shall I buy my revenge?"

"Once was wrecked," Mad Helga sings in her creaky voice, "now made whole. Spend the life but save the soul."

The old fool! Swiftly I bend down to sweep the remaining bones up into one hand. With my other, I grab Mad Helga's cupped hand and dump my handful of the bones into hers. "Take your blasted bones, old woman. Now answer my question plainly. I've had enough of your riddles."

"Haste makes waste, slow the pace." Mad Helga's fingers moved lightly across the tiny heap of bones on her palm, flicking them one by one into a pattern. "Fleetest feet can lose the race."

I seize Mad Helga's shoulders and twist the old woman to face me. "I do not want these silly rhymes! Answer my question, hag, or I will shake you until your bones are as loose as the ones in your hand."

Mad Helga grins. Her one good eye seems to twinkle. "Spells and charms can ne'er come free. Your heart and courage is the fee. Now fetch his things, one, two, three."

"What do you mean? Do you mean that I must seek Him out and steal three things from Him? Will you then cast the spell to kill Him?"

"Through the world, a child must roam. Spells need things from heart and home."

Impatience rises in me like a bloody tide. "Should I seek Him out on the battlefield? Or must I go to His castle?"

Mad Helga only chuckles. With one thick fingernail she flicks a bone into its place.

"You daft old bat," I say, "speak plainly!"

Mad Helga holds up a tiny bone. The lower part dangles, broken. "See what your impatience has wrought? Once broken, never fully mended."

"I shall break *your* bones, old woman, if you do not answer me."

Mad Helga's eye continues to twinkle. With the dangling end of the bone, she draws a faint pattern in the ashes on the hearth.

"Heed well, Gilly. These curls here, this is our own wood, Birnam." Her voice is suddenly as sane as a tax collector's. "For two days you will travel through it. Until midday on the first day, travel due north. Then turn west for a day and a half. Partway through the morning of the third day, you must leave the wood and take to the road that folk call Old Grapius Road. Follow that road through the hills and mountains. 'Twill not be an easy journey through the mountains, girl, but the road will lead you through the best passes.

Finally you will come to a long silver loch. Travel north past its northernmost shore till you come at last to the castle of Inverness, his northern castle, perched high on a ridge above the firth where he can guard against attack from the loch, river, or sea."

I study the map of ashes, tracing its outlines onto my heart and searing its curves into my memory. Finally I look up. "Helga, I do not remember much of castles and their ways. How shall I gain admittance?"

Mad Helga's hands thrust out suddenly, spilling the bones into the ashes. Her fingers flash about till the map is erased and the bones soiled and buried in the ashes. "'Tis your revenge, not mine, lass. I neither know nor care whether you be admitted to his castle or no." She begins to rock back and forth, singing, "Graymalkin shall not stalk your rest, nor Ulfling seize your—"

I close my fingers around her wrists. "Stay with me, Mad Helga, just a moment more. Tell me, I beg you, once I gain admittance to the castle, what must I take to bring to you?"

For a long time Mad Helga is silent. She sits so still that I snake my thumb to the underside of her wrist and press to feel the throb of her pulse to make certain she is still alive.

Then she says, "Bring me three pieces of his heart."

Try as I might, I cannot get Mad Helga to say more about the spell.

After a long time, Nettle returns. I give her my most triumphant look. "Mad Helga has promised to aid me," I say. "You were false, but Mad Helga is my true friend. On the morrow I set off to His castle to fetch what is needful for the spell of destruction."

Nettle opens her mouth as if to protest, and then closes it without a word. She presses her lips together tightly. She turns toward Mad Helga, but the old woman continues to kneel by the fire, rocking back and forth to music that neither Nettle nor I can hear. Using the bottom of her skirt as a pan holder, Nettle picks up the small iron cauldron. "Gilly, do you want this porridge or shall I scrape it into the leavings bucket for tomorrow's stew?"

Even though I feel pinch-gutted, I say, "Scrape it." No matter the cost, I will look strong to Nettle. I announce, "I feed on hope!" Instead of sounding defiant, my words merely sound silly, so I quickly add, "I'm off at daybreak, Nettle."

"I heard you the first time." With a piece of broken bark, Nettle carefully scrapes the sticky gray mess of porridge into the brown clay pot.

"I shall need food for my journey."

Nettle scrapes the bark back and forth across the mouth of the pot, trying to save every bit of porridge so naught will go to waste. "You well know where we keep our store of food, Gilly. I trust you to take your fair share. Just have a care to take naught from my store of herb mixtures. Some of those are dangerous and could cause you much harm."

At Nettle's words, I feel a prickling at the back of my eyes. The prickling is not tears, because I never cry. At the back of my breath, I feel a flutter that cannot be fear because I will not be afraid.

But I dare stay no longer in our hut. For seven years, this hut has been the only home I have known. For seven years, these two women have been my only family. *They risked their lives, taking me in. If He had found me, they too would be dead.* And while I do not love the hut or the women—since I am a thing of revenge without even a sliver of space inside me for love—I am still a little worried that if I stay in the hut with them much longer, the prickling in my eyes might be tricked into becoming tears and the flutter behind my breathing might be bewitched into becoming something too close to fear. I gather my wolfskin and hold it tightly in front of my chest the way a warrior holds a shield.

"I'll sleep out of doors this night."

Nettle frowns. "You'll do no such thing. 'Tis bitter cold."

" 'Twill be good practice for my journey."

" 'Tis foolish to freeze afore you have to, Gilly."

But I cannot afford to listen to her.

My life is an arrow, and I am finally headed home.

SEVEN

THE NEXT DAY I travel west.

Just as I am born into my new life, the earth gives birth to spring. I feel powerful, striding across this tender, shy, awakening world. Pale green blades poke their tips through a dusting of snow that looks like flour sprinkled on a malt loaf. The birches and oaks are beaded with dots of green. Only the pines are still in their winter dress, the tips of their sweet-smelling needles as sharp as Nettle's tongue.

I will not let myself think of Nettle . . . or of the girl I was before I was reborn as an instrument of darkness.

I am a wanderer who prowls alone.

Twice, during the first morning, I hide from wild beasts, holding as still as a stone until they pass. The first is a wolf, gaunt and swift-moving, fierce on the scent of some other prey. The second is more deadly—a wild boar. But she does not heed me as she wheezes and snuffles her way along a little path she has made.

Although Nettle does not like the wood, she has taught me its ways, showing me how to treat each animal with courtesy. I know never to look in the eyes of wild dogs, and that old boars will leave you alone if you do not venture too close, but that young boars—like newly dubbed knights—will pick fights to prove their mettle. Thus old boars are more deadly, but young ones are more dangerous.

Nettle herself is rather like an old boar.

After the boar passes, I seek out a walking stick. I find a fine one, near as tall as I, with only two gnarls. A good walking stick is your best possible companion for a journey. You feel less lonely with something in your hands, and it is a grand protector if you encounter danger. I know that warriors name their swords, so I call my walking stick Fangmore.

Three times that day I hear the sounds of people traveling. I melt into the trees until they go past. During these times of war, only a noddycock would risk meeting strangers.

I know I should feel naught but joy now that I am on my way to the revenge I have dreamed of for seven years, but to my surprise, I do not feel joy. Instead I am filled with worries. *What if I cannot find a way into His castle? What if I cannot find a way to get close enough to kill Him? What if He kills me first?* I shiver. Despite my fine words, I truly do not want to die. Finally, just as I shut my mind to all memories of my time *before,* I shut my mind to these cowardly thoughts and concentrate on looking for any green shoots of lion's tooth that might be poking up from the ground. After our winter diet of dried grain, the fresh, stringy, bitter leaves taste better than honey cake.

At the edge of the first afternoon, when day turns the corner to dark, I hear the barking of hounds, shouts and squeals, and a crashing through the undergrowth. *What can it be?* It is too near spring to be a boar hunt, and I cannot think of any other reason that such a large company of folk would come into the wood during the burnt ends of Lent. I consider climbing a tree, but I do not wish to be treed by their hounds. So instead I run to a bramble thicket. I poke it with Fangmore to make sure no boar or badger or bear dwells within. When there is no response to my poking, I pull my wolfskin over my head and shoulders and wriggle into the heart of the thicket. Brambles claw me fiercely, but my wolfskin affords me some protection. Crouching, I peer out.

In a moment, a boy bursts into view. He is small, perhaps half my size, and in a sorry state. The wood has pulled and scratched his tunic until it is little more than rags, and his skin is filthy with sweat-streaked dirt. He is crying as he stumbles along. The boy's head jerks from side to side, like a trapped and baited bear cub's, unable to decide which way to run. He pulls along with him an equally ragged woman. The woman does not run well. She lurches and staggers. I see that she has an injured foot.

About two tree lengths from where I hide, the woman falls to the ground with a small cry.

I slide my hands into the pouch at my waist and slip out my broken dagger.

These folk may bring trouble upon me.

"Go on, my partridge," the woman says, tugging to pull her hand away from the boy's. "Get thee gone. Run ahead, and I will follow."

How like a mother. As soon as there is trouble, she sends her child away. For even in this brief glimpse I can tell these folk are not canny about the wood and its ways. If he runs ahead, she will never find him. Her bad leg will never allow her to catch up. With that leg and her ignorance of woodlore, if the hunters do not finish her off, the animals will. The wood has no kindness for those who are ignorant.

"I c-c-c-cannot," he blubbers like a babe in arms. "I will not leave you, Momma."

"Hie thee hence, lad," she cries out again. "For both our sakes, do not let the Witch Hunters find thee."

I do not know whether it is mention of the Witch Hunters or a feeling for one cast off by his mother that makes me act so foolishly. Without thinking, I wriggle out of my thicket and grab hold of the boy's sticky hand.

"Come," I say. I pull him away from his mother and begin to run across the small clearing, back into the trees.

"Momma!" he screams like a spear-stuck bear cub.

The crashing grows louder in the wood behind us.

"The Witch Hunters are coming!" she screams, as loud as he. "Run, lad, run!"

"Run!" I scream, louder than both.

The mother and I both keep screaming, "Run, run!" louder and louder and shriller.

The boy and I run.

EIGHT

W<small>E RUN</small> for a long time. I hold Fangmore out in front of us to
keep branches from slapping us in the face. For a long while the boy
sobs, and for a longer while he makes no sound except grunts.

I make the same sound.

When we finally come to a small brook, I judge we have run far
enough. I let go of his hand.

"Drink," I wheeze. "Rest."

I fall to my knees by the brook. My breath sounds like a torn
thing, like cloth ripped by a savage wind. I make my hands into a
cup and drink two handfuls of the sweet, icy water. Then I splash the
water all over my head. I fall to the ground and lie on my back, panting, looking up into the branches and the sword-colored sky
beyond. I cannot believe my foolhardiness. To risk a band of Witch
Hunters for this unknown boy . . . sometimes, even as old as I am, I
still wake sweating and whimpering from nightmares about Witch
Hunters and what they do to their prey.

Only as my breath returns to normal do I realize that the boy
is huddled in a heap where I dropped hold of his hand. He is
crying again.

Let him cry. But I roll over with a groan, and push myself to my hands and knees. I crawl to him. I take his hands and pull them away from his face.

"Hsst. Stop that blubbering. We have run far, and by the looks of you, lad, you have run farther. Drink some water."

"Momma," he sobs. "I want my momma."

"Your momma did not want you," I say. "Now cease your blubbering and drink some water. We still have a ways to go before dark."

He does not stop crying completely, but he does make a gallant try to swallow his sobs. Obediently he crawls to the brook. His first drink of water is slow, but then he drinks his second handful eagerly, and then two more. I stop him when he reaches for a fifth.

"Wait. Too much cold water, especially after running, will give you belly cramps. Wait a spell."

I dip the ends of my tunic in the water and wipe the sweat off my face. After a moment, since my hem is already dirty with my grime, I do the same for the boy.

"Lie on your back and snatch a moment's rest," I tell him.

He lies down. To my amazement, in a moment I hear a familiar pattern of breathing.

The boy has fallen fast asleep!

I study him as he sleeps. Although he is sturdy of body, he is younger than I first thought. He looks to be about the age of a boy toward the start of his service as a page, perhaps eight or nine turns of the year.

What a fool, to fall asleep in the midst of all this danger. I think back to all that has befallen me these past two days. *What a fool I am to saddle myself with this strange boy.* Yet part of me is strangely satisfied. *Is it because I am no longer alone in the wood?* That is not it. *Is it because Nettle and Mad Helga rescued me, and now I have paid my debt by rescuing another child and need no longer be beholden?* This is not it either.

What I do know is that I will have to tell him about mothers, about how they cannot be trusted, but I will wait a few days.

I think back over our escape. My blood still chills at the memory of the mother's screaming at her son to run away into the wood. Surely she could tell that her son could not survive without her. I remember grabbing him and our dash away. I can hear again her screams at him to run. As we ran away, I thought I heard her call out something different. I seemed to hear the woman cry, "God bless thee, lass, for our good angel and savior." But no, this must have been a trick of my memory, the voice of my wishes rather than the voice of truth.

I turn my head to look at the sleeping boy. *What shall I do with him?* And then, into my head, comes a funny idea. *I could give up my revenge. I could instead haunt the towns and villages. Wherever I see a child who is not wanted by his mother, I could steal that child. The Old Folk steal children and leave a stone in their place. I could do the same. It would be blamed on the Old Folk. We could all turn outlaw, like Rob o' the Green, and I would be queen of the band of unwanted children. We would steal our food and live in a hut in the wood, all together . . . and then I see the walls of the red castle. They loom high above. I am tiny. Too tiny even to reach the knocking-brass on the studded gates. In the dying light of the dying sun, the top of the walls glow golden. Perched on the top of the walls I see an angel. He is coming to rescue me. He leaps into the air, his wings streaming out behind him, his wings made of light. . .*

I wake with a start. I am shaking. I have not had that dream for a long time. I force myself to sit up. My bones feel like frozen rocks. It is dark and and my body is stiff. The witch boy is rolled into a ball like a hedge pig. He shivers, but he sleeps on. I shake him awake.

His eyes jerk open. "Momma!" he cries.

"She is not here," I tell him. I fish an oatcake out of my pouch and break it in two. I hand one half to him.

He stares at it a moment as if he does not recognize it, then he stuffs it greedily into his mouth, making one bite of the whole thing.

"Are you hungry?" I ask.

He nods.

I silently hand him the other half of the oatcake. He bolts it in a single bite.

"Where is my momma?" he asks.

I stare at him without answering.

"Will my momma be coming soon?" he asks.

"I do not think your momma will be coming," I say cautiously. His lip starts to tremble. I quickly add, "Leastways, not for a while."

He stares down at the ground, biting his bottom lip. I think about offering him another oatcake, but with two of us I need to be stingy with our store of food.

"Why were people chasing you?" I ask.

He fixes his big blue eyes on me. He has a pleasing enough countenance, although his nose is shaped too much like a turnip for his face to be considered handsome.

"The granary burned down to the ground. You know. Old Peterkin's granary."

I have no idea who Old Peterkin is, but I nod.

"Momma"—he swallows hard before continuing—"said it was 'cause of Old Peterkin's dadda who likes to carry live coals in a little stone box in his pouch, but Old Peterkin started saying it was because of Momma and how she had had a baby and no husband and how that baby was born a lackwit. At first nobody listened, but then everyone in the village began to get hungrier and hungrier, and Old Peterkin and his dadda started saying it more and more, and how Momma was a witch and her lackwit son was the spawn of Satan"—his voice, when he says these things, unconsciously takes on the tone of a cranky old man—"and then the miller's house was set ablaze, and Momma said that was done by Jack Cabbage-Nose, who is a mean boy and only looks for the chance to do mischief, only nobody believed 'twas Jack after he claimed he was out tracking March hares. More and more folk started to look at us funny, and then Molly Bailiff's baby was born dead, and she started to scream it was witches had done it, and me and Momma went home, but Granny Truag came to our house this morning and told us to be gone from the village because they was going to hunt us with dogs and hang us to rid the village of the curse, and Momma wanted to pack a few things, only Granny said begone now, there's no time to fritter away, so Momma wrapped us up in our outdoor things and we took off through the wood, but we got lost and then we heared the dogs and started running, and Momma fell and broke her foot, and—" His lip begins to tremble again.

"Drink some water," I command, to take his mind off his troubles. He crawls to the brook and drinks two handfuls.

He crawls back. "I'm cold. Can I sit close to you?"

I can think of no reason not to let him, so he snuggles up next to me like a puppy. If he were a puppy, I would put my arms around him, but since he is human, I do not.

"Where are we going?" he asks.

"To a castle."

"Are you a princess?" he asks in an awed tone.

I laugh at this. "Lad, we go to the castle to find work."

He gets very still.

After a while I ask him, "What's wrong?"

He snuggles closer. "I do not think I will like to work in a castle."

"A strong boy like you! Are you lazy? Or are—"

"No!" He sits up, but he looks away. "I do not like being among folk. I am not clever. Folk mock me."

I can well believe this to be true. In our village we have a lad called Tom Halfwit. The other boys follow him and mock him and pelt him with stones and dirt clods and bits of dung, treating him as rudely as they treat me.

Nonetheless, I cannot turn back now. And although I do not know why, I cannot abandon this boy on the road. He could never take care of himself. I wrap an end of my wolfskin around his shivering shoulders.

"How will Momma find us in the castle?" he asks. "Momma has never been to a castle. How will she know where to look?"

It is growing very cold now. I decide to risk a bit of fire. While I find two good oak sticks, I direct the lad to gather up branches and bits of kindling. I let him keep the wolfskin tucked around him. I am used to being cold.

"Bring as many holly branches as you can," I tell him. Holly burns well, even if the branches are green, and its embers last a long time. It will give us warmth without a lot of flame.

With my dagger I scoop out a tiny bowl in one stick, just wide enough to hug the end of the other stick. Then I twirl the long stick back and forth till its spark hops out onto the tinder, and I can puff softly on the kindling to coax it into a small flame.

"How will Momma find us?" he asks again as we warm our cold, stiff fingers at the wee flame.

I cannot think of an answer to that, so I say, "I will go back and leave her a letter where she will be sure to find it."

"What is a letter?"

"'Tis a bit of writing that tells a body something."

He looks at me scornfully. "Momma cannot read writing."

I consider that for a moment, and then I say, "I will leave her a letter with pictures instead of writing. She can read that."

He frowns. "What kind of pictures?"

"I will draw a castle, and I will draw a lass and a wee lad walking to it."

He thinks this over and then nods. "'Tis a right good notion."

"You wait by the fire," I tell him. "Snuggle close to stay warm. I must borrow the wolf pelt for a spell." He obediently wriggles out from under it, and I pull it close about me and slip away.

I figure I will fool him. I will go a few paces into the wood, and then I will return and tell him I left the letter of pictures. But after I walk a little way, I become curious about the woman. Could she be where we left her?

I doubt my ability to find my way back to where we left the woman, but there is an almost full moon, and my years of roaming the forest have given me a talent for discovering a path. I decide not to think but to follow my hunches. Still I take careful note so I can find the boy and the fire again.

I travel for a long while. Finally I come upon a fallen tree that looks like one I leaped over a few paces from the clearing. I fall to my hands and knees, crouching behind it, listening. All seems quiet. I crawl forward . . . a few creepings and then freeze, like a wary deer. I still see nothing. A few more creepings and I am at the edge of the clearing. Even in the darkness I can see the ground has been much trampled. I drop belly-flat on the ground. I fumble in my girdle for my broken dagger. I wait a long while, but no living creature stirs. I stand up, and something stiff, cold, and heavy brushes against my face. Startled, I jump back and cast a glance at it.

A heavy dark form hangs from a limb high in a tree. At first I think it is the carcass of a butchered deer.

Then I realize what hangs from the tree is the gutted body of the boy's momma.

DAWN IS ALREADY BLEACHING the sky when I reach the boy again. He is asleep, shivering, curled in a tight ball next to an almost extinguished fire. Fresh tears have left tracks on his face. I am glad that he did not see the cowardly way I ran from the body of his mother, fearful that sprites or bogies might come chasing me and hang me up next to her. I did not even think to search her for gleanings.

Again I shake the boy awake.

"Come," I say.

"Did you leave the letter with the pictures for Momma to find?"

"I left the letter," I lie. "Now 'tis time to go to the castle."

NINE

THE CASTLE HUNCHES like a sick beast on the crest of its hill, brooding over the river in front of it and the sea to its back. Its stones are dark, black as the wood of a burned-down house, black as cinders, black as rotting teeth.

At the gates stands a group of ragged lads, shifting about nervously, punching and shoving each other. I have seen that sort of horseplay among some of the lads of my village. Their jabs are mean-spirited, but when challenged, they bare their teeth in a predator's grin and whine, "'Tis but a joke."

When we are about twenty paces from the gates, the small witch's boy grabs my hand.

"I do not want to go there," he says, and his voice shakes from fear.

I do not know whether he, too, has seen that sort of vicious horseplay in his own village—doubtless as the butt of it—and fears it, or whether he simply fears all packs of human beings. I do not tell him that I, too, do not want to go there. *Would it be so awful after all if we turned back now?* Nettle and Mad Helga would take this boy in as they have taken in other lost creatures, and he could help around the hut, doing the chores and such that I did at his age. There is still time for me to turn away and forget this scheme. No one, in truth, could expect a lone lass to fight the greatest warrior in the land. No one but me sees any need for revenge at all . . . yet no one but me has seen what I have seen. What I saw seven years ago was evil, evil in a form as pure as truth. Even if I lacked my own motive for revenge, it would be the greatest sin in creation for me to allow that evil to continue to wander about the world. *I have made myself an arrow, and His heart is my home. I have made my life a dagger, and His death is my sheath.*

"Don't be silly," I tell the boy. I clutch his hand a little tighter. "There are two of us. They will not hurt us."

"I do not want to go there," he says, twisting my hand.

I stop and study the group on the drawbridge. I see there are no other girls. This could be a problem. Perplexed, I scratch my head, trying to think what to do. The feel of my stubbly hair against my fingers gives me an idea.

"Stay here," I command the boy. I take a few steps away and squat behind a rock. With my dagger I slash at my skirt, just above the knee. I tear off a length of it and then step out and put my hands on the boy's shoulders.

"I am a lad," I say. His hand gropes for mine, but he just nods, as if he is not surprised.

I draw myself up like a great lord and walk with firm steps to the gates, since I know from experience that lads who form packs are more likely to hurt the weak than the strong, to torment the lowly rather than the high. Inside I am afraid, but on the outside I take pride in my calm, confident stride.

Almost immediately one of the lads sees us. He elbows his neighbor. They begin to jeer at us.

"Ragpickers!" one cries.

"Stablegrunts!" cries another.

The whole company joins in the cries, sounding like crows and flinging jeers like small pebbles. The boy beside me trembles, but I

stand firm, although my heart flops and flips like a trout on the
banks of a stream. Even in my fear I note that their insults lack
imagination. When the tallest lad starts toward me, I hold out
Fangmore like a magic staff.

"Stop!" I cry in my most terrible voice.

The lad stops. None of them has a stick.

To take their minds off the attack, I swiftly ask, "Why do you
gather here?"

For several moments, no one answers. I wait. I know that if I
wait long enough, one of the pack, overcome by the temptation to
show off his superior knowledge, will answer.

Sure enough, one of the larger lads finally says, "The lord has
sent a messenger ahead to those who work in the castle to say that
his people arrive today to prepare the castle for his arrival, perhaps as
soon as the end of the week."

It is a sign! Chance has bestowed upon me a good omen. *Blessed
be Mad Helga!* It had not occurred to me that He might be at
another of His castles. He could have stayed at His other castles for
years and years, never coming north, but now the day I arrive, His
arrival is announced. *Surely this is a sign that my revenge is favored by
Heaven if He and I arrive almost at the same time.* I straighten my
shoulders.

I show, however, no outward sign of joy at this news. I make my
voice as scornful as possible. "Are you so schooled to worship this
great lord that you gather at His gates just to cheer the arrival of His
servants?"

"No," says another lad, eager to show off *his* knowledge. "But
they will be hiring lads to work in the kitchens and stables and such,
and we hope—"

"Here they come!" another lad shouts. He points down the road.

I turn around. I see the dust of approaching wagons. I drag the
witch's boy with me to join the crowd at the gates. *Another favorable
sign! Just when I need a way into the castle, help appears.* I mouth a
thank-you to the sky.

The huge oaken castle gates nudge open. The filthiest man I have ever seen steps out. He is an ox of a man with a face that is too flat, as if his mother had set a cauldron upon his baby face until it smashed his nose and forehead smack into the planes of his skull. He also stinks more than anyone I have ever encountered. Several of the lads reel back from his stench. Even at the far edge of the group I catch a whiff of his reek, a compound of sweat, onions, leeks, garlic, sour wine, bad teeth, unwashed linen, and other things too nasty to mention.

"Get out of the road," he bellows. His voice, too, is like an ox's. "Ye sorry collection of droppings from the divil's dark hole, ye balls of snot from Satan's snout, clear the way for your betters."

One of the lads gives a shout and points down the road. Out of a whirlwind of dust, a line of carts appears. We step to the side of the road as they clatter across the drawbridge and into the castle yard. The carts are heaped perilously high with barrels and butts of wine, great baskets and bales, crates and mountains of folded linen bound with twine. It is a long time since I have seen so many things gathered together in one place. Then the gates creak shut again. There is a long period in which nothing happens. I grow hungry, but I do not dare take out any food because I know it will be snatched away by one of the ragged waiting lads.

When the sun is within a hand's span of the horizon, the gates push open again. A bevy of grown-ups in fine, unpatched clothes stand there. A round-gutted man in a fancy linen robe the color of a wooded loch steps forward. He carries a polished staff in his hand. He holds himself as stiff as if the staff were up his backside. It makes me want to laugh.

"I am Seyton the Steward. I seek a few able-bodied lads to help with the work inside the castle. With me are Master Stableman, Master Cook—" and he names a handful of other masters of the castle.

The lads start leaping with eagerness, showing off their strength and energy.

"Choose me!" they cry. "I will serve you well."

"Stand still!" thunders Seyton the Steward.

Abashed, the lads stop moving.

Seyton the Steward moves among us. He flicks his staff at three of the lads, three of the biggest. They swell with pride and follow him into the castle yard.

Seyton the Steward does not so much as glance at me or the boy with me.

Master Stableman chooses next, and then Master Smith. As Masters Bottler, Huntsman, Chandler, Tailor, and Poulterer select assistants, our numbers dwindle, but no one has even let his eyes rest on me. I edge forward.

This is my chance to get into the castle. To get three pieces of His heart. If I do not get in as a worker, then I do not know how else I can get past that foul-tempered porter. Desperation starts to rise in me like a Noah tide.

Master Cook is the last to choose. He is a tall man whose sinews seem a little too tightly strung. Both his skin and hair are shiny as if he rubs them with goose grease.

"I need some pretty lads to aid me in the kitchen." His voice is soft and sticky, like milkpod fluff dipped in honey.

He takes longer than the others to examine each lad. Where the others just looked at the lads to select their assistants, Master Cook has to examine each candidate with his hands. He runs his grease-shiny fingers up and down the arms of each lad he examines. "To see if you are strong enough to lift a haunch of venison or set up the dining trestles," he says. He makes each lad open his mouth. "I'll have none but sweet breath blow across my sweet victuals," he says.

He lifts each lad's hands and studies them, front and back. He rubs his thumb across each palm. "Soft hands make soft doughs." I make my face a mask, smooth as a nun's wimple, as I stand there, hating him.

He comes over to me. I do not want him to touch me, but I will myself to stand still. *If this is the way into the castle, then I will take it.*

He fondles my arms, my hands. I do not let myself think of his touch. *This is a dream. Master Cook touches my skin, but he does not touch me. I am not my skin.* I turn my thoughts to my enemy, the lord of the castle. *I am an arrow, and His heart is my home.*

Master Cook makes me open my mouth to test my breath. *I am a dagger, and His death is my end.*

Then he strokes my cheek with his pointer finger. "Pretty lad," he says. "With cheeks as round as a girl's."

He smells of almonds and spice. Up close I see that his mouth is too large with lips as soft as sausages.

"I vow," says the sticky voice, "you are the prettiest of all the lads here."

And in spite of myself, I jerk back from his fingers.

TEN

His face hardens and his breath escapes in a puff. He turns to the witch's small boy beside me.

Suddenly I cannot bear the thought of Master Cook touching that little boy either.

But before I can say or do anything, the smallest of the remaining lads speaks up.

"Great sir," he says, "that one is a mooncalf." He points to my companion. "Great sir, you do not want a lackwit in a fine kitchen like yours."

Master Cook swells up like an opened peacock tail.

" 'Tis true," he says. "My kitchen is a fine kitchen. Perhaps I do not choose to ape the cooking of Paris like some I can name. Perhaps I do not choose to baa like a sheep and learn my cooking from cookery books like those Frenchmen who call themselves cooks. For all that, my food is finer than theirs. My cookery is more worthy than theirs of being written down in books."

Without touching the lad who spoke up, he snaps his fingers at him, and turns to go back inside.

No more masters wait by the gates. As I watch my last chance walk away, desperation goads me.

"Sir Cook," I cry out. I am ready to grovel in the dust of the road. I would eat rat droppings. I will do anything to get inside the castle gates.

He hesitates. I sense he cannot decide which would be the greater act of pride, to continue walking or to turn and watch me beg.

"I am sure your recipes are worthy of being written down, Sir Cook," I call out. "But for a busy man like you, I am sure, Sir Cook, that you have no time to write them down with all the work you must do." His back is still to me. "Sir Cook, I can write."

Wonder ripples through the handful of waiting lads. Master Cook turns around to stare. Had I pulled up my tunic to reveal goat legs sprouting from my hips I could have occasioned no greater amazement. "I can write down your recipes for you. I can put your cooking in a book that will dazzle folk for centuries hence. I can write about your cooking so fair and sweet that those false cooks in Paris would turn as green as new peas with envy."

He hesitates. "How can I know you can write?"

With Fangmore I draw a letter in the dirt of the road. "There's an A." I draw another letter. "That's B."

"Let me see you write a word. Write"—he thinks for a moment—"write *frumenty.*"

Carefully I write f-r-u-m-e-n-t-y across the road. He comes to stand on the other side. He looks down at my word. His eyes flicker as if he is nervous.

After a bit, he nods. "That's it." He looks around and announces to the porter, "That's *frumenty.*"

He's looking at it upside down. He does not know that words have upsides and upside-downs. I understand at once. *He cannot read.* I am careful to give no outward sign of my sudden knowledge.

Still he hesitates.

"Sir Cook," I say, "I did not mean to insult you when I pulled away from your hand. But, Sir Cook, I knew my face is dirty. I did not want your fine, fair hand to be soiled."

What a huge lie, a lie bigger than Jonah's whale. It is a stupid thing to say, but I cannot think of anything else. *Unless the man is a moon-born fool, he will see through that lie. My hands are dirtier than my face, but I did not pull away when he touched my hands.* In despair, I cast about in my mind for another way to get into the castle, but my head is empty of all ideas.

"Come with me," he finally says. He turns and heads into the castle yard.

Relief washes over me. I start to follow him.

I'm stopped by the grasp of the witch's boy's hand.

"What about me?" he asks. He looks at me with huge, frightened eyes. "What will happen to me?"

My mind races. I cannot give up this chance. Master Cook has reached the gates.

"Boy," he calls. "Boy who can write! Are you coming or no?"

"Sir Cook," I cry, "I cannot leave my brother. Please let me bring him, too. He is a good worker and does not eat much."

"I will have no lackwits working under me." He signals to the porter, and the gates start to stutter shut.

I look back and forth between the frightened boy and the gates. Then I drop Fangmore. I tear the large pouch from my belt and thrust it into the boy's hands.

"There are oatcakes in there, and a good twig to clean your teeth."

I break away from him and run to the gates.

I hear him wailing behind me, "Come back, come back."

The gates stop, the width of two people, and I slip through. Master Cook is already halfway across the castle yard. A woman of about Nettle's age, but plump as risen dough, catches my arm as I go past. She is dressed in a woven gown the color of dried wheat with a mustard-brown wimple set firmly on her head.

"Will you leave your brother, just like that? For shame, a big boy like you." She speaks with a soft accent as if she has come from a distant place.

"We need the work, lady," I whine. "He can go back to our village." *I must be inside the castle for my plan to succeed.* "Our auntie will look after him there," I desperately lie. *The boy will be fine. He is nothing to me. He found me to help him. He will find someone else.*

I can still hear him wailing outside the gates. I hear the other abandoned boys taunting him, calling him "Crybaby!" and "Weeping Will!" and "Leaky!"

The woman calls out to Master Cook, "A word, Master Aswald!" At the same time she waves a hand at the porter, who stops pushing the gates and leans against them.

Master Cook turns to her. "Yes, Mistress?"

"As you know, I am not as spry as I used to be. May I choose a boy to be my legs, to fetch the flour and such?"

He inclines his head, gracious as a king, then continues on into the castle proper.

She lets loose my arm. "Run and fetch your brother, lad."

I hesitate. "He is not clever, lady. He is a good boy, but—"

"Bless you, my little cabbage leaf, that matters not. My third child, he was a moonling, too, but he was as good a boy as ever breathed. Me, I would rather have a moonling than some clever, sly m'sieur that must be watched every moment so he does not steal the raisins or torment the cat. Now run to your brother."

I race out to the teary witch's boy. "I have persuaded Master Cook to let you come with me," I tell him. His face lights up. "But you must say you are my brother."

He nods solemnly and repeats, "I am your brother."

"And not a word about your momma, understand? If folk think you are from witch stock, they will cast us both out."

He tugs at my sleeve. "You left a picture letter for my momma and told her to come for me at the castle, remember?"

I suddenly see how this can be used to my advantage.

"If you say or do anything wrong, they will throw us out of the castle. If you forget to say I am your brother, they will throw us out. If you are lazy or fail to do everything you are asked, they will throw us out. And if they throw us out, your momma will never find you and will die of grief."

His face turns white.

I put my hand on his shoulder. "If we are to be brothers, boy, I must know your name."

"Pod." His eyes begin to fill with tears. "Momma called me her little pea pod 'cause—"

"We'll have no talk of mothers here!"

He stares wide-eyed and then lowers his head like a lamb to the slaughter and trudges into the castle yard. I follow.

The gates of His castle thunder shut behind us.

I smile.

I am in His stronghold. My plan is ripe. By the end of the week, He will be dead.

ELEVEN

I HATE the world of the kitchen.

Even though the kitchen is easily ten times as big as Nettle's hut, there are so many people bustling about that I am always bumping into someone. Since everyone else but the witch's boy outranks me, I am sore from their cuffs and kicks.

My worst tormentor is the apprentice to Master Cook, a tall, slender boy called Brude. He is supple as a whip and as sly as a serpent. His face is as soft-featured as any lass's, and his eyelashes are the longest I've ever seen. But his fair face hides a foul heart. When Master Cook leads me, the witch boy, and the ragged lad in, Brude minces over to examine us and pinches his nose with his fingers.

"Paugh, paugh!" he cries out to Master Cook. "Master Aswald, surely these are the stable lads who have followed you by mistake. These filthy ragamuffins will never do justice to your fine kitchen."

Master Cook sighs and shakes his head.

Brude adds, "Two of these lads look too pisley to give full service. Should we not go to the village and trade them for larger beasts?"

Then Brude and Master Cook titter and wink at each other and roll their eyes around.

"I would be glad to go for you," Brude offers.

I find out later that Brude will do anything to get out of the kitchen. When Master Cook is nigh, Brude fawns and makes much of him, but as soon as Master Cook is out of sight, Brude finds an excuse to creep out and flirt with the laundry maids. Still, in the afternoon, Master Cook does let Brude go to the village to hire two more lads.

We new hires are put to work fetching and hauling so the masters can set up the kitchen in preparation for the lord's arrival. Master Cook takes delight in cursing and calling us names when we set things down in the wrong place. He swears more when Master Baker, Master Steward, and Master Bottler are nigh—as if the oaths and insults are meant more to impress them than to chastise us.

He swears most at the witch's boy, who begins to breathe even harder and rush around even faster. After he is called a puddle-puffin, tears well up in the boy's eyes. I pull him aside and in his ear I whisper a rhyme that Nettle used to chant when the village children mocked me:

> *Ye may break my bones*
> *With sticks and stones*
> *And clods of dirt,*
> *But names do no hurt.*

I see the plump, gray-haired woman watching us out of the corner of her eye. After a few moments, she goes over to Master Cook and whispers in his ear. He pouts, but he grabs the witch's boy by the neck of his tunic. "You lazy lumpkin, you should be helping Mistress Lisette and not getting under the feet of my kitchen lads." He gives the witch's boy a little shove toward the plump lady, and she sets him to work piling bowls and such on some low shelves.

By the time the sun sets, everything has been unpacked. Master

Cook directs a ragged village lad and me to set up a trestle table in the courtyard, and we pile it high with day-old bread, green cheese, and buckets of ale. From all over the castle come other servants— men and boys from the stable, the poulterer and his assistant, the laundry maids, Master Steward, the tailor, the alewife, Master Smith and his sweaty helpers, the stinking porter, and all the other workers. Brude arrives in time for supper, followed by two large village lads. It makes me dizzy to see so many folk about. They ignore me, which makes me glad. This way I can study them and learn their ways and customs. The witch's boy stands close to me, his chin pressed against my arm. We all eat standing up, taking turns sipping from a ladle of ale. I notice that folk talk only with those who work with them—kitchen folk talk only with other kitchen folk, stable-men talk only among themselves, and so forth. Many of the men make eyes at the laundry maids, the only young women about, and most of the laundry maids peep back at them. The witch's boy and I eat silently.

The food is good and we are allowed to eat our fill.

BY THE END of my first day, I learn that the kitchen staff occupies the next to lowest rank of servants in the castle. Only the stable lads who shovel out the stalls are lower than we. It is clear that the village lads, the witch's boy, and I are the lowest ranking of the kitchen staff.

After supper, Brude sets us to gathering up the scraps, taking down the trestle table, and cleaning the ale buckets and the bread knives in the scullery shed. I learn that the small ragged boy who was hired with us at the gates is called Mungo. He talks a lot and is never still, as if ants have nested just under his skin. One of the new boys from the village has a huge body but a young, gentle face. His hands are as big as chickens, but he is clever with his fingers. His name is Ban. Alpen, the other new lad, is lanky and dark. He is always chewing on something—an oat straw, the top of a knuckle, a thumbnail. He seems overwhelmed by the size of the castle and company, and he speaks only when he is asked a question.

None of them know when the lord is to arrive.

After we finish our tasks, it is full dark, and so we return to the kitchen. All the household masters are gathered around the biggest table, throwing dice. In the corner, all the apprentices except Brude also throw dice. The gray-haired lady is seated on a low stool by the far corner of the fire hearth. The witch's boy sits on the floor next to her. Both of them are polishing pewter ladles.

The village lads creep over to a shadowy corner where a pile of hempen sacks can serve as their couch, but I join the lady by the fire.

"I am called Lisette," she says, looking up at me, not breaking the rhythm of her polishing. "I am the wafer maker."

Master Cook glances her way and sniffs. "Wafers!" He sniffs again. "A French notion if ever I heard one. Good Scottish fare is not good enough for our lady. Oh, no, she must ape the ways of Paris! She—"

He shoots an angry glance at me, and then, as if embarrassed at saying too much, struts over to shout at Mungo, who is examining a barrel of boardlike cod.

Lisette rolls her eyes as if she has heard this many times.

"Master Aswald cannot forgive me for being French," she says softly. "Even though my husband—Lord keep his soul—was born and bred in this land, and both my sons are Scots through and through."

"What are wafers?" the witch's boy asks.

"Bits of pastry," she tells us. "Sometimes sweet, sometimes spicy or savory or salty." She shows us her wafer press, which is made of two flat stones. "I mix up batter no thicker than spring cream, and I brush it on this stone after I have heated it to just the right hotness. Then I press this stone atop it for just the right spell. I lift off the top stone and peel off the thin baked dough. *Voilà!* A wafer!" She chuckles. "Master Aswald is always waspish at the talk of wafers because he cannot master their art. No one in the kitchen can master it but me." Her tone is one of simple pride. "Press one too long, and it crumbles when you try to take it off the griddle stone. Press it too short, and you have a mess of string. Heat the stone too hot, and the wafer chars. Heat it too little, and the wafer is naught but tough saddle leather. There is magic in the making." She winks at me and Pod. "'Tis true."

The boy listens to her, gape-mouthed. I nudge him to shut his mouth, but instead my touch startles him into speech.

"Can you teach me, lady, to make the wafers?"

Before I can explain that if Master Cook cannot master the art, then he certainly cannot, Lisette says, "My little marrow bud, had I the time, that I could do. I taught it to my Jimmie, my third child who is like thee, and now he can make a fine living at any place he pleases." The witch's boy's face lights up with a joy so bright that it hurts me to see.

Lisette hands the boy a tankard. "Now be a good lad and run out to the well and fill this with sweet water so we all may have a good drink." The boy wrinkles his brow. "You remember the well," she says in a gentle tone. "We passed it as we walked in, about three paces from the kitchen door."

Joy flashes back into the boy's face.

"I will go," he cries out and runs off in his wobbling way.

Lisette pulls me closer. She smells of lavender and sweet-spice. "While your brother is gone, I thought we might have a bit of a chat."

I swallow nervously.

"I meant what I said," she adds. "It takes patience more than anything else to master the art of the wafer. Moonlings, poor lambs, may not have the brains of Master Aswald, but often they beat him all hollow for patience. Could this lad learn to make wafers, he would have a trade to keep him in fine style all his life. 'Tis true, many of the lords and ladies like to ape the ways of France and England and such, and so they like to have a wafer maker in their holdings." She sighs. Her breath gusts like a March wind, and there is the scent of cloves in it. "If I were younger, I would teach wafer-making to your little brother as I taught it to my own Jimmie. It took me three years and more to teach my Jimmie, but learn he did. And learn your brother could, too, I have no doubts."

"Then will you teach him, lady?"

She shakes her head till her mustard brown wimple wobbles. "But no, my child. I am too old. My bones ache like a miller's gate. Come Twelfth Night—or Midsummer's Eve at the very latest—and I will serve his lordship no more. Both my sons and my married daughter have offered me a home at their fireside. Within these next few months, I will accept their offer, and then I will make wafers no more." She sighs again her clove-scented sigh. "Your brother seems steady and faithful of heart. Could you but find a good and patient wafer master to teach him . . . ."

Her soft voice trails off. She looks down at her plump hands with the small calluses on their fingertips. I cannot blame her for not meeting my eye. We both know that good and patient masters are hard to find in this harsh world.

A log cracks in the fireplace. The dice players cheer a throw. Lisette raises her eyes to mine. Her eyes are soft like a flower, like brown heart's ease. "But tell me, young one, what is your name?"

"Gilly."

Her eyebrows shoot up. "'Tis a queer name for a lad."

Inwardly I curse my inattention. I have forgot that I am now a lad and not a lass. I cast about in my mind for an explanation to satisfy her.

Before I can think of aught, Master Baker calls out, "Hereabouts, Mistress Lisette, *ghillie* is another word for servant."

"'Tis a fitting name for this one," crows Master Cook. All the masters hoot with laughter and return to their dice.

Just then Pod comes trotting back, both hands closed tightly around the tankard, which slops sprinkles of water onto the floor with each wobbling step. He thrusts it forward to Lisette as if it were the very Holy Grail itself.

She drinks and hands it back with a long "Ahhhhhhhhh." He holds it out to me with the same reverence, an anxious expression on his face. I drink and nod to him. He smiles suddenly, and then he finishes off the rest in a long, gurgling swallow.

Lisette says, "Good work, my pretty lambkin," and the boy beams. Then she asks, "What is your name, my little one?"

"My name is Pod," he says, proud as can be.

Lisette laughs. "As odd a pair of names as I ever heard tell. Were your folks gardeners that they named you after a vegetable?"

Pod shoots me a frightened look. I'm glad to see that he knows better than to talk of his momma. To my relief, Lisette does not wait for an answer. She pats his shoulder. "'Tis a sweet name for all that."

Soon it is time to sleep. I learn that most servants in the castle take their pallets to the Great Hall in the keep and sleep on its floor, but those of us who toil in the kitchen find places to sleep down here. The masters take the tables for their beds. The apprentices make themselves nests out of the sacks of grain. Lisette tells us she prefers to sleep in the ale shed with the alewife each night. Mungo, Ban, and Alpen curl up by the hearth, but I use some soiled table linen to make a bed for Pod and for me. I glare at the sleepers on the tables, envying how being up high can keep them away from the bugs and beasties that creep about the night-time floor. I find two long-handled roasting forks and hand one to Pod. We drift off to sleep, clutching the forks in our hands in case we have to beat away the mice and rats.

The kitchen is blessedly warm. In my mind I sing a lullaby I have made up:

> *Lullaby,*
> *Time is nigh,*
> *He will die,*
> *He will die,*
> *He will die.*

TWELVE

THE NEXT MORNING, Master Cook formally presents all the new kitchen staff to Seyton the Steward. He is a large man with a broad chest above his round gut and a broad, bumpy, pockmarked face. When he talks, he sways back and forth. His eyes are a little unfocused, as if he is listening to voices inside his head, voices the rest of us cannot hear. We follow him across the kitchen courtyard to the keep, a tower atop a swell of ground in the middle of the castle enclosure. Pod stays as close to me as if we were stitched together. We clatter up a set of wooden stairs to the Great Hall. Brude, as pretty and scornful as ever, trails behind, running his fingers through his yellow curls, listening and watching us.

"You need to be swift, moving back and forth from the kitchen and up the stairs," Master Steward informs us, swaying back and forth. "When his lordship is in attendance, I do not expect to see any of you moving at a pace less than a run."

"When does His Lordship get here?" I ask.

Master Steward looks down his broad nose at me but does not answer. Instead he shows us where the planks and trestles are stored and makes us practice setting up the long wooden tables and the benches. There are a great many tables, but they do not completely fill the room, which is the biggest room I have ever seen. Even the fireplace is huge. If I were to stand in the middle of it and stretch out both arms, my fingertips would not even reach the sides.

Master Steward climbs to the dais at the far end of the room. He waves his hand back and forth over the raised platform. "The lord and lady and highest-ranking guests sit up here."

On the dais stand two large chairs with the heads of dragons carved at the end of each armrest. "The first table you set up will be the one on the dais," he says.

"I'll do it!" I flail my arms about, hoping to catch Master Steward's notice. *This can give me a way to reach Him.*

He stares down his nose at me again, sways, and then snaps his fingers at Ban and Alpen, the newest lads. "You two will set up the dais table."

He next shows us the wooden chest in which the long, snowy white cloths are kept to be spread over the tables.

"Before each meal you must cover the tables with these cloths." He shows us how to place three across the dais table—one longways and then two across the ends. He looks speculatively at restless little Mungo, who is jiggling from foot to foot. Then he turns to me. "This will be your task."

He adds, "But on the tables on the floor, use only a single cloth each."

He leads us to a barrel. "Before every meal, you will sprinkle the rushes on the floor with this sweet-smelling mixture." I sniff it. My nose makes out lavender, bee balm, moth bane, dragon's tongue, woodruff, and pine needles.

He shows us another chest in which the goblets are kept.

"You will give each person at the high table up on the dais a goblet. To the people in the middle tables, the warriors and such, you will give one goblet to every two people. At these tables in the back, the servants and foot soldiers will share one goblet among every four people."

He explains that the first meal of the day is served at nones, the ninth bell after daybreak. "Each meal is served in two shifts." At the first meal, the principal servants will eat after the lord, the lady, the guests, and the men at arms have finished. "Then you will clean up the cloths and wash the dishes." The last meal of the day is served just after sunset. "The servants will eat first at day's end. After they finish, you will tidy the tables and set them with the cloths for the warriors and high-born folk. You need put down no cloths for the servants."

"Please, Sir Steward," Mungo pipes up, his fingers jiggling against his leg, "will we be eating with the servants?"

"You kitchen folk must eat catch as catch can."

I grow impatient with all these boring details. "Where are His Lordship's chambers?" I ask.

Again Master Steward ignores me. His unfocused eyes slide over the tops of our heads. "All of you must learn to set up the tables as quickly as you can. If you are not nimble and quick, I will whip you myself."

He assigns special duties. The biggest lads, Ban and Alpen, are to hand out the goblets as well as set up the dais. Little Mungo is given the easy task of scattering rushes and herbs. All of us must set up the trestle tables. Master Cook tells Ban and me to set out the trenchers.

"What be trenchers?" Ban asks.

Brude snorts with laughter. "What a pinchbrain!" he jeers. He wallops big Ban across the back of the head. "Empty as a witch's heart!" he calls out, and the rest of them jeer and laugh.

Master Steward frowns at our merriment. "After you set up the tables, you will run to Master Baker. He will have a basket of slices of bread from the day before. You will run back here and portion them out in the same manner as the goblets." He frowns at Brude, who is making faces at us. "When we return to the kitchen, Master Baker will show you how to slice the round loaves into the square trenchers."

"Where do we find the knives to give the guests?" I ask.

*Perhaps I can find a better knife than the broken-blade dagger tucked
in my girdle.*

He tells us that we need not bother with knives. "Each guest will
bring his own."

He stresses that we are to run everywhere. "If the food grows
cold, I will whip you."

My eyes keep slipping back to the bigger of the two chairs on the
dais.

"If you drop even a morsel, I will whip you," Master Steward
says.

I can picture Him there. *In just a handful of days, I will be beside
Him. How easy it will be in my guise as a scullery lad to step in from
behind, my dagger in hand, and—*

"Please, Master Steward, " I blurt out, "I will be glad to serve at
the high table."

Master Steward gives a bark of sound followed by several more.
It takes me a moment to understand that he is laughing at me. He
reaches out his long arm and hits me on the left ear. He turns to
the lads.

"This boy thinks he can wait on the high table." The tone of his
voice invites them to laugh. They all do, all except Pod, who has
been silent the whole time.

I hate them all. If I were a true witch, I would turn them all into
slimy creeping things.

"Boy!" Master Steward grabs both my shoulders. He shakes me
till my teeth chatter. "You will have naught to do with the high table
or any table. Scullery lads are lower than the lowliest dung beetle in
the castle." He releases me. Over the ringing in my ears, I hear the
sound of Brude's snickering. Master Steward says, "Lads who are
training to be men at arms will serve at the tables. We have a lad
who is being fostered who will serve at the high table." He sways
back and forth silently for a moment, as if mustering strength to
train such a hopeless band of servers.

"You kitchen lads will carry the dishes up the stairs to the doorway to the hall," Master Steward continues. "They will be taken from you there by the serving boys. If you drop a morsel, I will whip your legs with a willow wand so they ache for a week."

Then we are put to work scrubbing out the Great Hall. I do not know which is harder, scrubbing so long it wears your knees to pulp or running up and down the stairs with buckets of water so heavy they near pull your arms from their sockets.

There is no proper supper that night, just bread, green cheese, and ale. This night's bread is fresh and hot. Lisette motions us over to a corner of the kitchen, far from the fire but cozy enough, where she has a pile of crusts and a bowl of broth. We take turns dipping the crusts into the fragrant broth, while Lisette tells us about her three living children—Jimmie, the wafer maker, Donal, the ship's master, and Doatha, the mother of six fine sons. "For many years they have begged me to make my home with them, but I have always preferred the bustle of a castle to the peace of a village. Of late, however, I have felt the desire to be among my kin."

Although my head is thick with sleepiness, I force myself to keep awake because it feels so good to be warm and have a belly full of food. My ears grow just as full of Lisette's tales about her good children, especially wild, impish, good-natured Donal, who is quick with the jokes and even quicker to protect his mother and little brother and sister. As I listen I try to imagine what it would be like to grow up with a mother like Lisette in a home full of wafers and broth.

THIRTEEN

The next morning Master Cook clangs pots together to rouse us. We grab crusts from a heap on a table, and as we gnaw on them, Brude struts about, assigning tasks. I hope to be working today as a scribe, but Master Cook is grinding some roots into a pulp and ignores me.

" 'Tis a good two days at least till his lordship reaches us," Brude says, tossing back his pretty curls. "So Master Cook has offered his kitchen lads to help out elsewhere."

Brude's smile is tinged with poison. "Ban and Alpen will assist Master Poulterer by mucking out the poultry yard." I rejoice at my escape. Brude turns to me. "I have a special task for you, Gilly."

I do not like the look of his cold eyes above his smiling rosebud mouth. "Gilly, you and your brother are such little muck-babies, I find it fitting to send you both to shovel out the night soil from the latrine pit."

I press my lips together, not letting out the refusal I long to spit in his smug, pretty face.

My life is an arrow, and His heart is my home. Let me say nothing, do nothing, that will remove me from my destiny. I am too close to my target to risk being cast out now. My chance, once squandered, may never come again.

The backside of the castle squats at the edge of a cliff looking toward the mouth of the sea. We servants relieve ourselves in a closet along the northernmost castle wall. The hole of that closet's shaft is directly over the waters of the firth. When I sit in that latrine, I seem to hear the panting of the sea beneath us. The high-born folk find it too long a walk from the keep to the back castle wall, so the masons built them a latrine closet in the back corner of the Great Hall. The shaft of the closet is atop the mound at the rear of the keep.

Brude tells Pod and me to get shovels and sacks. "No dinner for you until you finish the task. I think 'twill suit the talents of you both."

I hate him.

Pod and I tie scraps of cloth about our noses and mouths to keep out the smell. All morning, we wrestle with the unwieldy shovels, lifting out shovel after shovel of the foul-smelling stuff and empty-ing it into the sacks. Pod works hard, the tip of his tongue some-times poking out of his lips, his brows knitted in concentration. He keeps peeking over at me and struggles with his big shovel as he tries to use it just the same way I use mine. To pass the time, I teach him some of the songs I learned as a child. He is not quick at picking up the words, but he bobs his head in time to the tune, and whenever I stop, he begs me to keep singing. His favorite is the ballad about the knight and the wizard's cat. He has me sing it five times.

Although the spring air is chill, the work keeps us from feeling cold, and the night soil itself is warm like banked embers. Partway through the morning, Lisette bustles over.

"My little cabbages, this will help against the smell." She has strung bay leaves on threads, and she ties a garland about each of our throats. It makes the work a little less smelly . . . but only a little.

The one good side to the messy business is that we are out of sight of the other workers, especially Brude. Halfway through the morning, I have an idea.

"Keep working," I tell Pod. "I must go to relieve myself."

He nods. I must say, although the boy is not clever, he is as fine and faithful a worker as I have ever seen.

I nip round the keep. No one from the kitchen is in sight. I start up the stairway to the Great Hall. I hear steps coming down. I begin to flee, but then I decide to brazen it out.

A strong-bodied gray-haired man appears, perhaps a guard or an armorer. He carries a long dagger in his belt. He snatches the dagger out of his belt and holds it in front of him. His nose wrinkles as he smells me.

"Where do you think you are going, sprout?" His voice is scornful, but his eyes are wary.

I make my voice soft and humble. "My brother and I, we're mucking out the garderobe. I've been sent to run up to the top to look down and check that we've made it all clean and sweet."

After a splinter of time, he says, "Then do not dally. Up and do the business and nip right down again."

As I dash past him, he presses himself against the wall so I will not soil his clothes. He calls after me, "'Tis not safe for lads to wander about the castle. You are lucky indeed that I did not mistake you for an enemy spy come here to scout out the castle."

Instead of stopping at the Great Hall, I climb up another floor. *Surely this must be where His chamber is.* My heart stops for a moment when I reach the top of the stair.

Although the first chamber is empty of any furniture, my blood begins to quiver. *I am come so close.* But I know that no one as important as a lord would lodge in the outermost chamber, so I move to the next. Almost in an enchantment, I wander from chamber to chamber. *In one of these chambers, He will lie.* I can picture myself, my broken dagger in hand, wandering to find Him late at night.

"Hey!"

Another man approaches, twig broom in hand.

"Lad, you have no business up here!" He looks at me closely. "Are you one of the cook's lads? I need to warn him that his lads should never—"

I turn and gallop down the stairs. I hear the man thundering behind me, but I am too fleet for him. I run back to Pod.

My heart sings. *How easy it will be.*

However, as Nettle says, what is woven under the sun unravels under the moon. It is not as easy as I imagined.

Supper that night is bread, cheese, and a sticky porridge flavored with almonds. Lisette makes us saffron wafers and peels them off her griddlestone, one by one, and tosses them to those of us who crowd before her, clamoring for a treat. Each eager prize winner must juggle the wafer from hand to hand for a minute or so, letting it cool before taking a bite. Mungo gets too eager and chomps down on his as soon as he catches it. He gives a wail and rushes to the water bucket to plunge his whole head down into the water. The folk roar with mirth. As soon as he lifts his dripping head out of the water, he takes a second bite of the fresh wafer and a smile cracks his face.

Midway through, I notice Pod is not in the crowd. I slip outside. "Pod?" I call. "Pod, there are treats."

I find him sitting on the side of the well, looking very small in the huge purple shadows of the falling night.

"Pod, what are you doing out here all alone? Lisette is making wafers."

He sighs, sounding more like a tired old man than a young boy. "I don't like it here, Gilly. When do you think Momma will come for me?"

In spite of myself, my heart flies out to him. I well know what it is like to be abandoned and small. Yet I am angry at him for feeling this. It's fatal for me to divide my heart now. *No. I will be single-hearted or I will be nothing.*

So when I answer, my voice is edged like the small stone axes I find from time to time in the wood. "Boy, well you know that your momma has a hurt foot. 'Twill take her a goodly while to reach this castle. I doubt not but she will need to rest along the way and baby her foot so it can carry her the entire journey."

To my horror, his lip begins to tremble and tears roll down his cheeks. God's blood, but he is a tender shoot. "What ails you now, boy?"

He ducks his head low and whispers, "I do not like to think of Momma out there hurt and all alone."

My breath escapes in an impatient puff. "You found someone to take care of you. Your momma will find someone to tend to her along the way."

He looks up eagerly, his face like a May Day sky breaking through the rain. "I had not thought of that. But it could happen. It could, could it not, Gilly?" Before I can answer, he begins to cloud up again. "But what if—"

Tongs of the devil but I am weary of his questions. To distract him, I quickly say, "Lisette is making wafers in the kitchen. She will be sad if you do not eat some."

His face is sunshine again. "She says that I could learn to make wafers."

She also said she does not have the time to teach you. It is a foul thing to raise this hope in you and then refuse to teach you. But I do not say these words to him. The words that come from my mouth are "There are many good things about living in a castle."

To my surprise he gives a little snort and rolls his eyes as I have seen Lisette do. It tickles me to see such spunk in him. I keep my voice as grave as an untithed parson's. "Think, Pod. Here we are safe from both beast and outlaw."

Except for the great beast and outlaw who must soon arrive!

"But," he says, "not from that mean lad, Brude, or that bad man in the kitchen."

"Here we are warm."

He considers this for a moment, then nods.

I press on. "Here we have good, plentiful food."

He nods again. In a solemn tone he says, "When I have become a maker of wafers, I will live with my momma in a castle."

I look at him, little and brave and alone, and in my heart I make a new vow. *I will find a way to make Lisette agree to train you as a wafer maker.*

I must do this quickly, for despite my fine boastings, I do not really expect to survive my battle with Him.

TWO DAYS LATER, He comes with all His retinue.

Once He is spotted on the road, the castle throbs with excitement. The bell begins to ring wildly, and Mungo comes clattering into the kitchen, screaming, "The guards in the tower see the lord and his party approaching. They say he comes with more men at arms than an abbot has prayers." There is more shouting and running and twitching of garments than I could ever imagine. Like spit on a hot griddle, I jump this way and that with excitement and nerves, desperation and fear.

In no time at all, I hear the sound of the gates shuddering open, but when I start to run out to join the others to watch the approach, the alewife grabs me by the neck of my gown.

"Not so fast, laddie." She thrusts a paddle in my hand. "His lordship will want a welcome cup. I have set the ale and the spices to warm o'er the fire. Set yourself to stir them until his lady sends for the cup."

No! He is supposed to be alone. She cannot be with Him. I swallow hard and make my voice deliberately casual.

"His lady. He has a wife?"

She looks surprised by my ignorance.

I plunge on, steeling myself against her answer. "What is she like, this wife of His?" I dare not ask her name, but I concentrate fiercely on willing the alewife to say it.

"Keep stirring." The alewife pokes me in my side. Once the wooden paddle is making brisk circles, she adds, "She is a fair and noble lady, the woman to whom he is married." *Tell me her name.*

"When you look at them, you can see they adore each other." *Her name*. "Some folk reckon the finest lady in all our land is the lady Roah."

No! I slam my mind shut against the image of His wife, that whore that He wed. *I have enough to worry about. I will not let myself imagine her.* But unbidden, a vision of her slips into my mind. *No!* Anytime I start to picture her, I will replace it with the image of Him lying dead. If I let myself think about the harlot He took to His bed, then I will be lost. My revenge must be as hard as obsidian, not a lump of butter on a hot oatcake.

Despite my resolve, I hear myself asking, "Do they have any children?"

Let there be no children. If there is any divine justice, then no children will have come from their mating.

The alewife pokes me again. "Stir." She makes a clucking sound. "Alas, our lord has not seen fit to bless them with offspring."

I close my eyes in relief. *Thank you, God, for giving them no children.*

"Stir."

To MY DISMAY, for the next week, I can find no way even to catch a glimpse of Him. We live in the same castle, but as far as I am concerned, He is as far away as the moon.

We kitchen lads are set to a great deal of work. We turn spits over the fire to roast the great haunches of venison and the whole boars, spending hour after hour at this shoulder-numbing task. We stir great pots—big as lye tubs—with paddles near as tall as me, mixing batters and doughs until I wonder if it would be pleasanter to hack off my arms with the big cleaver and have done with it. Then there is a fury of slicing and peeling and scrubbings of pots, after which we boil table linens and rub them with heated stones so they can look smooth as water. We spend hour upon hour scouring cauldrons and griddles with sand in the cold scullery shed.

Most evenings, a soldier or two—the older ones who have seen more than their fair portion of fighting—wander into the kitchen to sit before the fire and turn the faces of the kitchen lads pale with tales of blood-soaked battlefields and men cleaved in half. Too often for my taste, the talk turns to the brave deeds of the lord of the castle. "Never has Scotland seen such a warrior as your lord," the soldiers say in their hoarse voices. I leave the kitchen and go sit by the well. I will not stay and hear that monster praised.

For several nights as I sit scrunched like a gargoyle next to the well, I dream about sneaking to the enemy camp to offer my help in smuggling some of their soldiers into this castle. How He would hate that humiliation—to be killed by the soldiers of the northern king within His own castle! *I pay you back in your own coin,* I would scream at him triumphantly. *A treacherous death for a traitor!* But I worry that Lisette and Pod and the other innocent castle folk will also be killed by those frost-eyed Northmen, and I regretfully abandon this scheme.

I am squeezed by the need to make Lisette take Pod as her apprentice. I must be ready to seize my chance to kill Him, whene'er that chance comes, and I see that there may be only one chance. Pod is a boulder tied round my feet. If I can coax Lisette to take him, then he will no longer hobble me. So whenever I work near her, I praise Pod as a hard and loyal worker and tell her it would mean the world to Pod could he learn to make wafers.

She shakes her head. "In a year or so, I will leave this castle. I have not the time to train him, Gilly. Good as he is, 'twill take more than a year to train him."

"I know that he can learn in less than a year," I lie. If only I can get her to take him, she will not cast him off at the end of the year.

But each time she just turns away, and after several days, she says, "No more, Gilly. Speak of this matter one time more, and I will have Master Cook cast you both out."

From time to time kitchen folk catch glimpses of Him and they report on His doings. By Saint Colum's tongue, it makes me angry to hear them prate about Him as if He were the Savior Himself, but I press my lips together and go about my work.

Brude the bully orders us about as if he were the lord of the castle. One day he calls to Pod, who is plucking geese on the far side of
the kitchen, and commands him to fetch a roasting pan that is no
more than five steps away from where Brude himself stands. When
Pod starts after it, Brude jeers, "Learn to walk, draggletail!"

I am about to answer back, but his cruel words make me take a
close look at Pod. I do not want to admit it, but Pod is, in truth, a
draggletail indeed—raggedy clothes, hair as matted as a lost sheep's,
fingernails and toenails solid black crescent moons. *Perhaps if I make
him sweet and clean, Lisette will take him off my hands.*

That night, after we scrub the kitchen flagstones so they glow
like a polished plum, I tell Pod to follow me. I lead him to the laundry shed. After I make sure no one is around, I say, "Take off your
clothes."

I turn my back and begin to ladle water from one of the rain barrels into a tub.

He taps me on the shoulder. He has not even started to take off
his filthy clothes. "Pod," I say, and my voice crackles like a cat's fur in
winter. "I told you to—"

He gives me a puzzled look.

"Have you never had a bath, lad?"

His brows pull together. " 'Tis not Midsummer," he says firmly.

"Midsummer or no, Pod, you need a bath now."

He looks as scandal-struck as if I had suggested going to the castle's chapel and stripping the statues of the saints stark naked and
painting them scarlet. I make my face and voice stern. "Take off your
clothes, boy, and climb in this tub, or I will wallop you within an
inch of your life."

He gulps and pulls off his tunic. There is a bruise on his chest
that I do not like the looks of, but I do not ask about it. He peels off
the rest and steps into the water. He shivers. " 'Tis cold, Gilly."

"Hush." I shave off a sliver from the big brown cake of soap on
the trestle table in the corner. There is a brush next to it which I use
to scrub him. Soon the water is gray with scum floating on the sur-

face. I scrub his hair, too, and then I have him straddle the draining trough as I ladle fresh rainwater over his little body.

Next I pick up his tunic. It is so raggedy that I fear it might dissolve to a handful of threads should I wash it. It would be very heaven to give him some new clothes, but new clothes are hard to come by. So I sigh and soak the tunic in a fresh tub of water. I rub the soap in with my hand and then squeeze the water through it, over and over, careful not to pull at the worn and tired cloth.

"Gilly, why aren't you a girl anymore?"

Startled, I bang my elbow on the rim of the tub. I whirl around to face him. He is standing in the middle of the floor, his arms wrapped around his body, looking small, clean, damp, and puzzled.

"Pod," I say with all the intensity I can muster, "you must never say that. You must not let anyone know I am a girl. Never. You must forget that ever I was a girl."

I dare not think what punishment might await us both should the truth be told. For all I know, in this witch-mad country, it might be seen as a form of witchcraft. At the very least, I would be whipped. It is entirely possible that my transformation would be seen by the church as one of those sins deserving of death. God's bread, but I have not come this far to be betrayed by the thoughtless prattling of this boy. "Say anything about it, Pod, and I will turn you over to the Witch Hunters myself."

For a while there is no sound but the swish-spurt of water through his tunic and my angry breathing.

Then he asks, "Are you still a girl, Gilly, or are you just a boy now?"

"Pod—"

"I will not tell anyone, but I would like to know."

I rub harder against the cloth. "I am all boy now, Pod. The girl I was is dead."

After a while he says, "I'm cold."

"Let me rinse out your tunic, and we will go over to the fire."

As soon as the tunic is rinsed, I lead him next door to the drying room. We weave through the drying racks to the fire. Sheets hang from the tallest racks, making magical cloth walls like the sides of huge white tents. The room smells of lavender from the bundles of drying flowers hung from the rafters. On the lower racks are several men's tunics, and I toy with the idea of stealing one and cutting it down for Pod. *What a fool you are to risk your mission for a little witch-boy.* Besides, it is certain that someone would recognize the tunic should Pod wear it, and he would be punished as a thief.

We sit near the fire between two racks of small clothes, white and fragrant. It is like snuggling in a nest of ruffles. I sit cross-legged facing Pod, and with my broken-blade dagger, I scrape most of the dirt out from under his finger- and toenails. I am pleased to see his clean hair drying into pale little curls around his face. When Pod is clean, he is a handsome little lad. *Surely Lisette's heart will melt like goose grease when she sees him.*

He gestures toward a pale gold gown draped across a drying rack. "That would look pretty on Momma." Then he jerks his chin toward a white linen night dress whose sleeves and bodice are woven of Flemish lace. It is a lovely trifle. "You would look pretty in that one, Gilly."

"Pod," I frown, "I told you not to say—"

"But I did not say you were a girl. I did not, Gilly. You know I did not. I just said that you would look pretty in it."

My stomach tightens. *God help me, both my quest and my safety depend on the silence of this lackwit who does not even understand when he misspeaks.* I feel all pushed and pulled. To calm down, I scramble to my feet and walk away from him. I find myself in front of the lacework gown. It is lovely indeed, one of the loveliest gowns I have ever seen. I stroke the lace, and my rough hand rasps across its surface. The gown is faintly warm from the fire, and its white cloth glows like an eggshell lit by a candle. Before I know what I am doing, I lift it off the rack. It is surprisingly heavy in my hands. Then quicker than you can say Peter Pumblekins, the gown is over my head and falling down my body. O, how wondrous it would be to wear such a lovely thing. It fits me smoothly as if it were made for me, exactly the right length and width about the shoulders and arms.

I give Pod a shamefaced grin, but he is staring at me open-mouthed.

"Gilly," he breathes, "you look like a princess."

There must be enchantment in the gown, for suddenly I feel giddy. I lift the skirts and sweep him a deep bow. "In sooth, Lord Peapod, I am the Princess Moth, empress of all butterflies and shape shifters. I am the queen of confections." Just as a clever cook can fashion a banquet trifle in which a pastry castle can enclose a fondant swan, which in turn encases a marchpane egg, so I am a girl dressed as a boy dressed as a girl. "I am the regent of riddles," I call out laughing. I do not know why I laugh. "I am the princess of puzzles, the duchess of disguise." I hold out my hand. "Lord Peapod, come dance with me."

He does not look as though he understands my foolery, but he laughs, doubtless because I laugh. He puts his hot little hand in mine, and we begin to weave in and out through the panels of drying sheets, footing it in our own fashion, part jiggle and part hop. I feel carefree and as light as a soap bubble.

FOURTEEN

I BEGIN TO DREAD the two mealtimes of the day. The rush to set up the trestles. The mad dashes up and down the stairs, carrying platters and kettles so heavy that my arms and legs battle to see which aches more. Each time I carry something to the Great Hall, I bob and weave, trying to catch a glimpse of Him at the high table, but the bottler's apprentice takes the platter from my hands before I can even get a sight of the high table. He kicks me and curses me, watching to make sure that I disappear from view. Twice I try a ruse. I pretend to go down the stairs, then turn around and tiptoe back up, but there is always a man at arms to keep watch near the top of the stairs, and once he serves me such a cuff that I tumble down a dozen steps or more. When I pick myself up, I see nothing is broken, but I ache from the bruises for the next two days.

Each day I grow angrier and angrier. God, the Divine Cat, has made me his plaything, amusing himself in batting me about like a lame mouse.

Then Lisette causes everything to change.

Toward the end of the week, she sends Pod up to the Great Hall with a tray of fresh wafers.

"Is that wise?" I whisper to her. "Pod is nervous around great groups of folk." *This is my chance.* "Let me take them instead."

"No," she says, giving Pod a fond look. "Now that he is so pretty and clean, 'twill do him good to master this task."

"I will do it, Lisette." I reach for the tray.

But Lisette slaps my hands away. "Pod is longing for a glimpse of the lord and his company. He has told me many times that he has never seen a lord before." She glances at Pod proudly as he carefully places the wafers on the tray.

Even I do not have the heart to gainsay him. He is so proud to be chosen for this task. He has scrubbed his face until it is as pink as a piglet's, and he has had me scrape under his nails with a knife until they are as white as moons. Before he leaves the kitchen, he wets down his hair and smooths it back from his face.

"You look as comely as a coin," Lisette tells him, and when he looks anxiously at me, I nod and smile. So proud and heedful he looks as he walks slowly out of the kitchen, the carrying board held tightly in both his hands. I do not have the heart even to feel jealous. In a hand's span of time, though, he is back in the kitchen, his face soggy with tears.

"One of the men at arms called me names and knocked my tray out of my hands," he wails.

Lisette turns pale. She clutches the front of her apron as if she were squeezing her heart. "The wafers?"

"They all tumbled down the stairs and broke," he wails. "The serving boys, they went diving for them and stuffed them in their mouths and belt pouches."

In less than a moment, Master Steward storms into the kitchen, his face like thunder over Dead Moor.

"Where is the lad who dropped all the wafers?"

I try to shove Pod under the table, but he is too slow. Master Steward whacks him over and over with his polished staff. I am shouting and trying to push Pod under the table, and Lisette is crying, and Pod is squealing, and the other kitchen workers are roaring out opinions, and the dogs out in the yard start to bark. It is all fury and thunder, and yet there is a tiny part of me that wants to laugh at this comical disorder. All at once, Master Steward recalls his dignity and pulls himself up as tall as he can, points at Pod (who is safely under the table) with his staff, and states in a voice like a pope, "Never let that lad carry the wafers again."

He struts to the door, and I firmly seal my mouth against my laughter at the silliness of this scene.

Just before Master Steward leaves, he whirls around and points his staff at me. "I understand this one was caught trying to sneak into the rooms above the Great Hall. I do not want him found up there again." He glares at Master Cook who has come over and is wiping his hands on his apron. "'Twill be your place, Cook, if either of these lads comes near the upper chambers."

Then Master Cook says, "You and your brother will leave the castle at first light."

FIFTEEN

N o," I CALL OUT.

I cannot leave so close to my target. This cannot be happening. Never again will I get such a chance.

Master Cook's face draws tight with anger. "If I say you are to go—"

"Please, great sir, give me one more chance. 'Twill not happen again." His face does not soften. "Please." Although it sickens me with disgust, I fall to my knees. "I beg of you."

Lisette speaks up. "I fancy, Master Aswald, 'twas naught but ignorance and a desire to gawk at the castle." His face remains stiff, so she adds shrewdly, "And Master Aswald, you have already trained these two lads in the ways of the castle. Do you really wish to bring in two untrained louts now that the lord is home?"

He still looks unconvinced.

I crawl to him like a fawning spaniel. *I will do anything, anything to reach my goal.* I reach up and paw his arm. "Please, great master. I will be good. I will do whatever you wish. Besides, we still have your recipes to write into a book so your art of cookery will not be lost to the world." I force myself to kiss the top of his shoes.

Never, never have I lowered myself like this. Never have I felt such humiliation. But I must do it. My life will be worth naught should he turn me out-of-doors.

I feel his hand stroking my hair. His hand strays down to my neck, and his thumb caresses my skin in little circles. My stomach lurches, but I do not let myself move.

"One more chance," he says. "But just one more."

That night, after all the castle is asleep, I draw a bucket of water from the well. I scrub and scrub till my neck tingles with cold and rawness, but I cannot wash myself clean.

STILL, TRY AS I MIGHT, I find no way to come near Him.

In the meantime, to my shame, I develop a new, odd, secretive habit.

One morning when I am polishing the cutlery, I catch a glimpse of a sliver of the face of a servant boy who looks familiar. With a jolt, I realize the boy is me. I peer more closely at the reflection in the blade and feel a clutch of fear. *Where did Gilly the girl go? Who am I now?* It is as if a spell has been placed on me and I have changed completely into something unknown and strange, as if I have become a boy indeed.

As soon as I can snatch the chance, I creep off to the chapel to study my reflection in one of the windows there. I stare and stare, but I see nothing of the girl in my face or stature. I examine my hands. The fingers are tapered, but the hands are so marred with calluses and half-healed cuts and cracked fingernails that 'tis more the hands of a boy than of a lady. From all the running and kitchen work, my arms and legs are hard with muscles. Finally, desperate to find some trace of the girl in me, I smooth my hands down the front of my tunic, only slightly relieved to feel the small swell of my breasts. *Yes, there is still something of the girl about me,* but then I hear a noise and jerk around. The old priest totters into the chapel. I whip my hands behind my back. I cannot afford ever to be caught smoothing my tunic to reveal the girl-shape underneath. *If I am found out*—I dare not even imagine the punishment that might be mine if anyone sees beneath my disguise.

"Can I help you, my lad?" the priest pipes up in his quavery old man's voice.

I decide to risk it since it is well known that this priest's wits are as addled as a shaken egg. "Father, I have a question. What would happen if a lad in the castle were found to be really a lass in disguise?"

His voice is surprisingly strong in his response. "Thou shalt not suffer a witch to live!"

"Father, I do not talk of witchcraft. Just a simple disguise—"

"Such things be shape-shifting and thus are the work of the devil. Thou shalt not suffer a witch to live!"

That should have ended the matter, but to my disgust, I became obsessed with catching glimpses of myself, trying to puzzle out my girl-self in my eyes or manner. I am like a drunkard rooting out his next tankard, only instead of ale, I seek any surface that can cast me back a reflection of myself. I catch myself preening in front of polished metal platters, buckets of water, even puddles in the courtyard after a rain. Each time I vow I will stop, and yet I do not stop.

During the second week after His return, as I wait to carry up the basket of wafers, I complain to Lisette that I have not even caught a glimpse of the lord and lady.

Lisette, patiently pressing a sugar wafer for supper, clucks sympathetically. "There's no rush, little peaseblossom. I hope you will be a long time in his service. I hope to secure a place for you and your brother even after his lordship quits the castle. Be patient, Gilly. You will see him one day."

She peels off a beautiful wafer, thin and lacy. She scrapes off a drop of fried batter with her little fingernail. "Open your mouth." When I do, she flicks that tidbit of sweetness in. But for all its sweetness, it fails to sweeten my temper.

"I want to see Him now!"

Lisette just laughs. I could strangle her, no matter all her kindness to me and Pod.

I snatch up the basket of wafers and stomp over to the door.

A strange boy is standing there. He is smaller than me by a head and shoulders. "Out of the way!" I order him.

He glances up at me, but he does not move. I see that he is dressed in fine clothes, perhaps the son of a nobleman. I know I should fall to my knees and beg pardon for addressing him in that tone, but I feel grumpy, so I grumble, "Is it not enough that we cannot go in the Great Hall, but we must have those of the Great Hall crowding into our kitchen?"

The boy looks at me reproachfully. I see he is undergrown for his age. He has delicate bones, like a bird's, but there is nothing girlish about his looks. He is just finely drawn. His tiny hands fumble with the hem of his tunic, as if he is nervous about being here. His hands have the quick motions of squirrel paws. He looks from side to side, turning his whole head and not just his eyes, just like a squirrel.

"I seek the cook," he says. He has a funny voice, both high and fierce, like a mouse's squeak scraped across an asp.

Brude steps up. "Master Cook is out, but I am his apprentice. Can I help you, young master?" I am disgusted by his oily, fawning tone.

"My lady's gentlewoman has an ache in her head, and I have read that an infusion of cowslip leaves is effective in relieving the pain."

I blurt out, "A better potion is equal parts hen's tooth, ground ivy, tiger's stomach, and slippery elm."

The eyebrows of the squirrel boy shoot up. "You're gammoning me. Hens do not have teeth, and we have no tigers in these parts."

I fish in my mind for the other names of the herbs. "Hen's tooth is garlic—we have it here in the kitchen. The curve of the garlic bud looks like the beak of a hen. Some people call it dog's toe. And tiger's stomach—that's blackthorn, but I don't know why it has that name. Perhaps the prickly thorns are like tiger claws."

The squirrel boy looks at me closely. "It sounds as if you know herb lore, lad."

My mind flickers back to Nettle and her years of teaching. I smile.

"I know herbs."

THE NEXT MORNING, the squirrel boy appears again in the kitchen. I am turning a mutton haunch on the spit, a hot, dull task. He lowers himself to the hearth beside me and stares down at the flame.

"I am trying to unravel a riddle of natural science," he says. I struggle not to laugh at such a squeaky-growly voice from such a small boy.

In spite of myself, I ask, "What riddle would that be?"

The boy tucks his feet under his crossed legs and settles in, apparently for a long chat. I do not care. It breaks the boredom of turning the spit. I welcome Tuesdays, Thursdays, and Sundays—the fasting days of the week when no one can eat meat. There are no spits to be turned on those days.

"Aristotle," he says, "writes that all the matter of the universe is compounded of the four elements. Do you know what those elements are?"

I shake my head.

"Fire," he says, "water, air, and earth. Four thousand years ago, at the beginning of time, these were the only four things that existed. Everything else in the world was made of a blending of these four elements. And each of these original elements longs to join with its own kind. You can see it here." He points his tiny finger at the fire. "The source of fire is in the heavens. Thus fire burns up, not down, because it longs to join with the absolute fire."

I nod. It makes sense.

"But rain falls *down*, do you see? The source of water is our lochs and the sea, so rain longs to join with the water in the sea."

I nod again.

He continues his lesson. "If we were to go outside and take a clod of earth and hurl it up, 'twould not fly to the heavens because earth wants to rejoin earth, so it falls back to the ground."

"So what is the riddle?"

"This." He points to the huge bread trencher set next to the hearth to warm the rising dough. "As I understand it, you mix our bread of wheat—which is a thing of earth—and salt—which is also of earth. You add water. Yet all these things of earth and water start to rise—which they should not do. If Aristotle is right, they should fall back to earth. Yet when you then put the pans of dough into the fire—whose movement is upward—the dough stops rising. It makes no sense to me, and as far as I can tell, Aristotle did not address it. Have you any ideas why this should be so?"

"I have never thought about it—"

"But I have." He scoots closer, his eyes bright and excited. "I have thought about it a great deal. That is why I decided to come to the kitchens to watch this sensation for myself. Oftentimes the best discoveries are made by observing a thing until it reveals its true nature."

"Are you very interested in Aristotle?"

"I am very interested in the sciences." Although his tone is proud, a flush rises in his cheek. "Before I die, I want to understand everything about the world, what it is made of, what makes it work." He scoots a little closer. I notice that all the others in the kitchen are looking at us. Brude is practically falling off his wooden stool to listen to our exchange. In a corner Pod silently oils griddle stones and watches us with a jealous look in his eye. The squirrel boy continues, "I was excited when my father sent me to foster here. I have never before been so close to the sea, and I wish to determine for myself if it is true, as Bede the Englishman writes, that tides follow the moon."

I am tickled by this small, serious lad and wish to keep him talking, so I say, "But that makes no sense. Why would water follow the moon?"

"It might be," he says in a confiding tone, "that the foam on the waves looks like the light of the moon and so tries to rise to the moon, and when the foam rises, it pulls the rest of the tide along with it. I do not know yet. I have not had a chance to watch. But Bede writes that the size of the moon determines the size of the tide, so I am making a chart. Each night I will go to the ramparts and write down the phase of the moon, and then I will look north to the tide and describe it. I wish to see for myself if Bede is correct."

He looks up at me. "I am also interested in plants and their properties. I have a book about herbs, but I would also like to hear from you what you know about them. Then I can compare what you know with what it says in the book."

I hear a man's voice bellow, "Fleance! Fleance! Drat your eyes, boy, where are you now?"

The boy flinches.

"A good hidey hole," I say to no one in particular, "would be behind those barrels of cod over in the far corner."

Quick as a hare, the boy leaps behind the barrels. In two breaths, a huge man in warrior garb lumbers into the kitchen. I recognize the one-eyed Master of Arms.

"I'm looking for a boy!"

The other kitchen lads glance nervously at the cod barrels, but they say nothing. Brude opens his mouth, looks at the barrels, then closes his mouth without speaking.

"There are lots of boys around here," I say in my most innocent voice. In her corner I hear Lisette cluck her tongue, but I ignore her.

"Not a serving boy! A boy of gentle birth. He is supposed to be training in swordsmanship out in the courtyard. One of the grooms thought he saw him come in here."

"We do not get many of the gentry down in these—"

But before I can finish, the arms master snarls and lumbers out the door.

The boy, Fleance, creeps back to me.

"'Twas nobly done of you to help me like that." He fumbles in his pouch for a coin, but I shake my head. He puzzles a bit, apparently trying to think of another way to reward me, and then his face lights up.

"As a kitchen lad, I daresay you do not know much about the sciences."

"'Tis a safe enough guess."

He beams. "Then I can teach you! Right after luncheon."

I laugh at his nonsense. "Right after luncheon I need to pluck the doves for tonight's dinner."

"Can you not pluck them later?"

"'Tis messy work if they are not plucked when they are fresh-killed."

"Oh." For a moment he looks crestfallen, and then his face lights up again. "We can start tomorrow." He sighs. "You have no idea how delightful it is to learn all that the sciences have to teach us. When I am grown, I intend to go to Rome and Padua and talk with the great scientists there. My only fear is that they will have discovered everything there is to discover by the time I join them." He draws his small body up proud and tall as a gatepost. "I hope to be a great discoverer."

"Lord Fleance," I say, snatching the nearest excuse, "I do not think the kitchen will be a good classroom for—"

"True." He looks around for a moment. "And we will not want to meet in the courtyard for fear of the Master of Arms . . . and my father."

"Your father would not like you to be teaching a scullery boy?"

"My father does not like my interest in science." He looks down at his fingers, which are paddling against each other like a squirrel twisting a nut. "My father is a great warrior, and he would prefer that his son be a great warrior, too."

Mother of our Lord and Savior, do not let this fierce, funny little boy be His son. My mouth goes so dry I can hardly croak out, "Who is your father?"

"Banquo. I am Fleance, his son and heir."

Relief makes me weak. I like this odd boy. I would not wish to be the murderer of his father.

I open my mouth to tell him that it is not a good idea for us to study the sciences together, but he says something that stops me cold.

"No," he says. " 'Twill not do for us to study in the kitchen. You must come to my chamber up above the Great Hall. We can study there." He gives a shy grin. "I can show you my astrolabe, a wondrous instrument for surveying the skies. I hope one day to locate the exact position of Heaven."

An invitation to the chambers above the Great Hall. My hand slides to my dagger.

I now have a way to reach Him.

Soon, soon I will carve out three pieces of His heart.

SIXTEEN

THE NEXT AFTERNOON, as soon as I finish scouring the last cauldron, I bang it into its place on the shelf and announce, "I'm off."

Master Cook looks up from the carp he is stuffing with chestnuts and raisins. "You're no such thing. You will grind the dried blaeberries for this sauce."

"Lord Fleance has ordered me to come to his chamber."

Master Cook looks disbelieving, but Lisette chimes in, "'Tis true, Master Aswald. Young Lord Fleance has come to the kitchen two days running, and I heard him order young Gilly to his chamber." Pod, who sits next to her, chopping nutmeats, looks at me with wide eyes. He frowns. I glare at him. *What right has he to rain on my haymaking? Have I not scrubbed him and do I not thrust him at Lisette at every turn of opportunity? Have I not done more than enough to secure his future?* But at the same time, I feel a little ashamed. I well know what it is to be shut out. *When I can grab some time, I will tutor him in the ways of a gentleman. Perhaps then Lisette will wish to keep him.* A voice in my head says, *You could take him back to Nettle. She and Mad Helga will give him a home.* But I shut my mind to the voice.

"Master Cook," I say, "Lord Fleance will have it so."

Keeping his eye on me, Master Cook says, "Brude, do you know aught of this?"

I'm pleased to see Brude scowl. He does not dare lie. " 'Tis true," he confirms in a sulky voice. "Lord Fleance did invite this ragpicker to his chambers."

But his eyes are as cold as a frozen snake's.

"I come to see Lord Fleance!"

What power those words hold! The grim-faced, brawny-armed, giant-tall guard steps aside when I say those magic words. I give a jaunty flip to my shoulder as I walk past this man at arms who guards the upper chambers, showing off, no doubt, but it feels grand for once not to be the lowest of all in the pecking order of the castle.

The grim-faced guard directs me to young Fleance's chamber. "Go up the winding stairs above the buttery. Go all the way through the first four chambers. Each bedchamber leads directly into the next."

As I pass from chamber to chamber, I study each room with care, hoping to find His quarters, but none looks grand enough to be the private apartments of the lord of the castle. My heart sinks as I go farther into the warren of bed chambers. Each grows smaller than the last. It is clear His chamber is not in this warren. It must be up the stairs at some other end of the Great Hall. My disappointment feels as thick as phlegm.

Finally I come to the last room, a small room where the wee pale lad, Fleance, is hunched on the floor.

"Are you sick?" I ask.

"One moment," he says, not looking at me. I stand by the door, but soon grow bored so I crouch down with him. He is watching an ant nudge a crumb of bread across the floor.

I laugh. "A great lad like you, have you never seen an ant before that you must gape and gawk?"

He looks at me, frowning. "This day I have read in Pliny that there is a creature called the ant-lion, part ant and part lion. It is the child of a mating between the lion and the ant." He shakes his head. "No matter how close I look at the ant, though, I cannot fathom how it is able to mate with a lion." With an impatient hand, he pushes his hair off his forehead. "Not that I have yet seen a lion. Perhaps when I see a lion, all shall come clear." A sweet smile flits across his small face. "Still and all, 'tis glad I am that you have come, even if you cannot unravel the ant-lion mystery for me."

I laugh, too. He is so young and so serious. I start to stretch my hand out to ruffle his hair, but I pull back just in time. A lord's son would not accept such familiarity from a kitchen lad. *I am a kitchen lad,* I remind myself. I feel a twinge of fright. *I am a lad.* It is not the way of lads to ruffle a younger boy's hair. I must learn to be rough, to punch, push, and pound.

Fleance shows me about his room. *How Pod would marvel at all these sights.* Fleance ignores one corner in which is heaped a small sword, a saddle, and other things befitting a lad training to be a knight. Instead he shows me first his precious astrolabe, a small wooden circle, with tick marks all around its edges.

"If I point this bar here at the sun, I can figure out exactly what time of the day it is," he explains, his eyes shining.

He shows me his other treasures—rule sticks to measure distance, scales, lenses, and vials. All the while, I listen with only half a mind, as I try to lead the conversation round to Him. In truth, I am also a little worried about being found here. Would a noble punish me for daring to befriend a boy of high rank? But Fleance's tongue moves faster than the devil's mare, fluttering with delight at having someone listening to its prattle.

As he shows me his pile of books, his door flies open and hits the wall with a great crack.

A big man stands there, brawny like a bear. At first glance, he looks soft and round, but under the cream-and-gold-striped cloak he wears, I can see the power in his massive arms and huge chest. He looks like the kind of man who could pick up a cart with one hand and pick his teeth with the other. Yet he has the same eyes as

Fleance's, the mottled gray of a misty sky. I have no doubt that this is Fleance's father.

Behind him stands the one-eyed Master of Arms I encountered yesterday.

Wee Fleance ducks behind me.

"Fleance," thunders the bear man in the striped cloak, "step out and face me like a man."

Fleance steps out. I can see he is trembling. He hunches his shoulders up about his ears.

"Boy," the bear man continues, "the Master of Arms here tells me this is the second day straight that you have failed to show up for your lesson. Does he speak true?"

Fleance pulls himself up to his full height. I can sense his fear, but he does not let it show. "Sir, I do not like his lessons."

"Silence!" thunders his father, but I sense bewilderment and even sadness behind his anger. "Do I ask whether you like the lessons?"

Fleance hangs his head. "No, sir."

"Then answer what I asked. Have you or have you not failed to show for your lessons for two days running?"

"Yes, sir." Fleance's voice is barely loud enough for me to hear, and I am standing right next to him.

His father steps to him and puts his hands on the boy's shoulders. "This is not acceptable, son."

"But, sir, I do not wish to learn about arms. I do not wish to be a soldier."

Fleance's father rolls his head back and forth like that of a bear with his paw caught in a boar hole. "Such talk is mad, child. You have no choice. You are my son and heir, and as such, you must learn to fight. Such is the way of the world."

To my surprise, Fleance roars back at him, his voice tiny but strong. "I wish to be a scholar, sir. I shall study the sciences and make grand discoveries that will change the ways of the world. I wish to go to France to live with my mother's people and—"

"No!"

"I will make but a poor warrior, but I can be a great scientist."

"No! No, no, and again no!"

Fleance breaks free of his father's grip and runs over to the narrow window. His back is to us, but I wonder if he is crying.

"The other boys who study with the Master of Arms are much bigger than I. They mock me, sir, they trip me and push me into the mud, they hit me with their swords and laugh when I cannot hit—"

"Silence! I allow no man in my service to tattle, and I will have no talebearer as a son."

For several heartbeats, no one makes a sound. I long for magic powers so I can fade out of sight, disappear into the kitchen, but I figure my best chance of avoiding trouble is to stand stark still and hope I am not noticed. While part of me wants to jeer at Fleance and call him "Crybaby," another part aches for the boy. He is just the sort of small, pale, nervous lad that the bigger oafs do delight in tormenting.

His father steps back, and I hear him whisper to the Master of Arms, "Is it true the tale that my lad tells?"

The Master of Arms sighs. "I try to stop the lads, my lord, but you know lads spoiling to be great knights. Lord Fleance is about half the size of the next-smallest boy. There is little chance he can overcome any of them in a struggle of arms or strength. In fact, my lord, I am surprised you have sent him to foster here, small as he is. Most lads his age are still at home with their mothers."

Fleance gives a little hiccup, and I suspect he, too, is listening to this.

Fleance's father says, "My wife spoils him. She's as pale and scrawny as he, a great one for reading and writing and silly tales of romance. She fills the lad's head with her nonsense." He sighs. "As you know, these are hard times. There has been no end to the battles and skirmishes these past years. A lad must grow up fast in times like these. Scotland is not safe for the weak." His voice hardens like dried sap. "I will not have a son who runs away when he is attacked."

"Send me and my mother to Grandpapa's castle, sir, if you wish us to be safe," Fleance pipes up. I admire his spunk.

His father shakes his head. "You are the son of a Scottish lord, and your place is here. Your mother has married into this land, and in this land she must stay." He turns to the Master of Arms. "While my son is small like his mother, he is of sufficient age to train as a warrior. Many lads scarcely older than he are already made knights."

Then, to my horror, I realize that Fleance's father is studying me. I stand without moving, feeling his eyes move up and down my ragged, dirty frame.

"So you have befriended my son, have you? Are you, too, besotted with sciences and learning?"

His voice is not unkind, but still my cheeks grow hot as I stammer, "No, sir . . . not . . . I mean to say I do like learning . . . but about the sciences I know little . . . I mean—"

He holds up his hand, mercifully, to stop my babyish ramblings. *Idiot! Fool! Your tongue is as flabby as the bladder of a hag. Can you not speak with a spoonful of sense when asked a simple question? How can such a foolish girl hope to bring down a warrior?*

Fleance's father turns to the Master of Arms. "School Fleance at a different time from the other lads. I will have you teach this lad, this friend of his, along with my son." He jabs his thumb toward me. My mouth falls open in shock. Fleance's father continues, "Perchance 'twill be easier for my son to learn without those other louts about him." He jerks his chin toward Fleance. "What say you to that, boy?"

Fleance trots over, the smudges of tears on his cheek. "You mean that, sir?"

The Master of Arms shoots a frowning glance at me then says, "But this is a scullery lad, sir."

"So? Did you not say that there were no well-born lads of my son's size—"

"But, Lord Banquo—"

"Scullery lad or no," Fleance's father shouts, "I will have him learn with my son. Be glad 'tis but a scullery lad. If 'twould help my son learn the arts of war, I would have you train a dog or pig alongside him."

"You mistake my meaning, Lord Banquo," the Master of Arms says. "My only worry is that the cook may not like releasing one of his scullery lads to us when he needs his help in the kitchen."

Fleance's father throws back his head and laughs. I like the sound of his laugh. It is loose and generous and seems to fill his whole body.

"Leave it to me," he says. "I will talk to the lord of the castle. I can safely promise you that you can have these lads to school together."

He pats Fleance's cheek with one thick finger. "'Tis past time I should be back with the other warriors, my son. Learn the arts of war. Learn them quickly. For me."

SEVENTEEN

Master Cook is not pleased. "Had I known you would be so much trouble, I should have left you outside the gates," he screams at me. "Be prepared, boy, to work late into the night so I can make certain you have done your share. Should you not finish all the work I set for you, then out of the castle you go!"

I am outraged, but Lisette comforts me. "Do not fret, Gilly. He dares not throw you out. To tell the truth, my bramble bud, I know not why, but 'tis true what folk say—cooks are often bad-tempered. Many folks say 'tis because they work so near the fires. Just as the fires of hell sour the temper of Satan and his minions, the kitchen fires give cooks the devil's own temper." She sighs. "But I fear you have made enemies of Master Cook and the other lads. They will not be much pleased that you are to spend your time training in the ways of a knight. They will feel, my little pipkin, and perhaps rightly so, that you reach above your station." And she gives me a share of a broken wafer to sweeten the harshness of her words.

Pod looks frightened. "Will you spend all your time with that noble lad, Gilly? Will you no longer care for me?" His eyes are sad and his lower lip starts to tremble. I want to shake him. I want to scream at him and ask did I ever say that I would care for him and take time for him? I want to scream at him, *Do not trust me, I cannot be responsible for the protection of others.* Instead I ruffle his hair with my rough hand and keep whispering, *My life is an arrow,* over and over, until the fire inside me dies away.

Lisette is right. The other lads are jealous and resentful. Brude huddles with Alpen, Mungo, Ban, and the other apprentices. They shoot me cold looks and make no attempts to hide their sullen wrath.

But I do not let this stop me. *Surely by staying close to Fleance I can soon find a way to come close to Him.* Near three weeks have passed since I came to the castle, and I am still far distant from my revenge. I do not know what is happening with the war, but I do know that He cannot stay much longer at His castle. Doubtless 'twill soon be time for Him to return and fight. In fact, I marvel that He has remained this long.

I quickly learn that I do not enjoy the warrior training. Every day I am sore and bruised from our work with the Master of Arms. Every day my muscles ache, for all that I am stronger and fleeter than Fleance. When he goes to supper, I must plod back to the kitchen where I am given the worst tasks. Whenever I must carry a platter to the Great Hall, Master Cook heaps it so high that my arms tremble from the weight. When I must take a basin of soup, he fills it so full that I must walk heel to toe so that I do not spill a drop. I notice he uses more bowls, knives, ladles, plates, and such than ever before. I suspect he does it to provide me more work. Many a night, when all the castle has gone to sleep, I work alone in the scullery shed, scouring and rinsing. Pod keeps me company, prattling of the little things that went on in the kitchen while I was at my training, although oftentimes he struggles so hard to stifle his yawns that his eyes fill with tears. I have made up my mind to teach Pod the ways of castle folk, but I am too tired. Each night I vow I will do it the next day, but that day never seems to come. Some nights when I tumble into my makeshift bed, I am too tired even to think of my revenge.

And yet, some small parts of the training are fun. We play at fox and hounds, for instance, because the Master says this will make our legs and wits strong. Fleance does not make a very satisfactory fox. When he is the fox, I can tag him within a few steps.

"Use your size," the Master of Arms bellows at him. "Since you are small, learn to be nimble. You can duck and turn much quicker than this kitchen lout." But Fleance does not heed him, so most of the time I am the fox and not the hound. I do love being a fox. Most of the time I take joy in running. It makes me feel fleet and free, for all that it makes my legs ache afterward, especially when I am later running to and from the Great Hall with great heavy platters of food in my hands.

To my surprise, the Master of Arms is a passing good teacher. His speech is filled with hard oaths, and he is prone to shouting, but he is patient and explains things well. In spite of myself, I feel a thrill when I take the wooden training sword in hand.

"A true broadsword, a warrior's broadsword," he warns us, "can weigh as much as a full-grown pig."

To build up our strength in our arms and hands, he makes us carry small grinding stones from one end of the courtyard to the other. As I wheeze my way along, Brude and the other kitchen lads line up to watch me and snicker.

Unfortunately, there is never much time for talking with Fleance. I always arrive first, and the Master of Arms shows me different ways to handle the sword until finally Fleance's sad, dragging footsteps are heard. Sometimes Fleance's father comes to watch. He, too, is patient, and shouts out encouragement to the boy as he struggles to lift the small wooden sword. At times other warriors stop by on their way to and from the stable. They often laugh at our mishaps, but their laughter is not unkind. Sometimes they regale us with stories about their early days as pages and squires. A few of them swear to Fleance that they were just as pisley and flap-armed as he when they were young. But to my frustration, He is never among the warriors who show up to cheer us on.

Every afternoon the Master gives us one short break to draw a bucket of water to drink and to pour over our heads to cool us down.

One afternoon, during our break from training, I ask Fleance why he is there.

"I am being fostered," he says, and his mouth turns down.

"I do not know what that means."

"Those of us who are noble born—the boys—are sent to other men's castles to learn to be warriors and noblemen. We are trained at arms and horsemanship. We serve at table so we can learn manners." He looks reflective. "I suppose 'tis thought that other men can teach a lad easier than his own father. I don't really understand why it must be done."

Wordlessly I offer him the last of the water in the bucket, but he shakes his head.

"If you could have any wish, would you choose to be at home with your mother?"

He shakes his head again. "I would choose to be in Rome or Paris or someplace to the south where learned men congregate and there are books aplenty. I am going to be a great man of science, you see. I love my mother, but our home is just as drab as this place."

As the days pass, I am pleased to note that Pod continues to keep himself fresh and clean. Brude and the other kitchen lads give him a wide passage when I am near, but I suspect they are often unkind to him when Lisette and I are elsewhere. I praise Pod lavishly to Lisette, but I cannot soften her heart. She only shakes her head sadly, and once, when I remark how Pod loves to please her, she says, "The little one is your brother, lad. 'Tis your duty, not mine, to care for your own kin. You cannot pass this off to others just to buy the freedom to live your own life lightly."

You do not know, old woman, you do not understand that I am near broken under the yoke of duty. Not one day in my whole life have I lived lightly. And Pod is not my duty. You would gawk if you knew how much I have done already for this lad who is no charge of mine. But of course I cannot say that to her, nor can I risk angering her. So no matter how foul I feel, I keep my face as pleasant as a posy.

I will wash my hands of Pod and this whole matter, I vow, but that night as I scrape trenchers and watch Pod, who keeps me company, fight his yawns so I will not have to work all alone, I reconsider. *If He kills me, what will become of Pod? Surely Lisette will soften. But perhaps not. Perhaps things are pinched in her children's households and they cannot spare a crust for a mouth that is not kin. Even if they could feed Pod, it is doubtful that Lisette would have coin enough to buy the fancy stuff needed to make wafers just so she could teach Pod the trade.* I worry that he will not survive in the kitchen with Lisette and me both gone. Besides, I would not leave him with Master Cook with his devil's temper and hungry eyes, his love of bullying and tendency to pat and pinch and stroke the kitchen lads. He does not touch me, not since I pulled back from him, and he does not touch Pod, but I do not like the way his hands play about the shoulders and faces of both the kitchen lads and the littlest laundry maids who are sent to the kitchen for ashes and bowls of grease. Even less do I like the way that Brude returns Master Cook's pats, speaking honey words to his face and spitting out vinegar behind his back. *No. Anything but that for Pod.*

I will toughen him up. Surely Fleance will need a manservant, and perhaps after Pod is a little bolder and knows more of the ways of castle folk, perhaps Fleance would take him on as his serving man.

So even though I feel hewed from toe to crown with tiredness, I say to Pod, "Stand up."

He looks puzzled, but he obeys.

"You know I am in training?" I say.

He nods.

" 'Tis time you go into training, too."

He looks alarmed. "Gilly, I do not think I can lift a sword."

"You will not need to lift a sword, lad. But we both must harden a bit if we wish to survive. We will start with your walk."

He looks even more puzzled. "I know how to walk, Gilly."

When you walk, you wobble like a gallywoggle. But I do not say these words. Instead I say, "Stand behind me. Walk just the way I do."

We march about the scullery shed like a mama duck and her lone duckling. Was there ever such a comedy? Here am I, a girl, teaching a boy how to walk like a boy. From time to time, I stand back and watch him. "No, Pod. Step firmly like you know the earth is yours by right. That's the way warriors tread. Pull your shoulders wide. Take up as much space as you can."

We work for a long time till we are both far too weary to move one inch more. Pod will never be mistaken for a warrior, but he moves with a little more power.

Then I teach him how to stand, to sit, to clean his teeth, and how to eat with castle manners.

For all the time I spend with him, I know that I will throw him over in a snail's breath as soon as I find a way to come to Him. Life crushes small lads like Pod all the time. Everyone knows that a lord is worth hundreds of peasants. It's sad but it's the way of the world. It's not my lot to reform life. My lot is to commit one murder and nothing more.

As spring drains into summer, I train daily with Fleance. And daily I grow angrier and angrier that I am no nearer my goal.

When at last I learn the location of His chamber, the lesson takes place in the kitchen and not the arms yard.

Master Cook continues to be spiteful about my warrior lessons with Fleance. I grow frustrated. *He picked me to work in the castle because I was a scribe, but he does not give me any writing to do.*

"Perhaps he cannot come by any parchment," Lisette consoles me when I complain to her. "Or perhaps, for all his lofty talk, he fears to begin."

"What can he fear?"

"My brave little radish, 'tis a hard thing to start something new, and it grows harder as a body grows older. If Master Aswald has never had a scribe write down one of his recipes, perhaps he is fearful to start."

That gives me something to think about indeed. I munch on the handful of parched peas that Lisette slips me and contemplate her words. During the next few days I study Master Cook. Can it be true that behind the swagger and bluster hides a man who is afraid of having his words written down?

Still and all, he piles up the work on me, saving me all the nastiest chores. I am ordered to gut most of the game and often find myself up to my elbows in blood and steaming entrails. I turn the spit at least three times a week, standing and turning for hour upon hour. Pod usually sits nearby, but I am often too tired to talk. One time he asks me to sing for him, but I am fearful of the mockery of the other kitchen lads, so I quickly shush him.

One evening Lisette is summoned to the Great Hall. When she returns, her face is pink and her eyes sparkle. "The lady herself complimented me on my wafers."

The kitchen folk cheer. I am pleased to see Master Cook stalk out angrily. No one has summoned him to the Great Hall.

Later that night, when Lisette and I are cracking almonds to soak in milk for the next day's wafers, I ask, "What was the lady like?"

"Very beautiful, very elegant. But what impressed me most is how his lordship keeps his eyes on her. Like a falcon on a rabbit."

I lean forward, trying to keep the excitement out of my voice. "As if He suspects her of something and wants to catch her in the wrongdoing?"

Lisette's laughter shakes her whole body. "No, my little innocent. He watches her because he is still in love with her. 'Tis as good as a ballad to see a man so in love with a woman, especially after so many years."

I snort in disgust. "'Tis indecent to think of Him at His age still panting after her like a hound in heat. It disgusts me."

Lisette laughs again. "Have you never had a sweetheart, Gilly?"

I jerk back in disgust. "I will never love! I have seen what love can do. I have seen too much death in the service of love, so there will be no love in my life."

Lisette looks shocked. I know I am saying too much, but the words keep spilling out of me like grain from an upturned sack. "Those who love are fools indeed. There will be no love in my life."

Then from across the courtyard, I hear Pod's voice.

"I did not do it," he wails.

"Hush," a lad says, and I hear Pod give a yelp as if he has been hit.

I dash out.

On the far side of the dovecote stand Mungo, Alpen, Ban, and Brude, all in a ring with six or seven stable lads. I am surprised to see the kitchen lads mixing with the lads from the stables, for always before the stable lads have been our sworn enemies. But now, united in purpose, they are shoving something back and forth, like lads in a game of tumble-push. I catch a glimpse in the space between them of what they are shoving.

It is Pod.

EIGHTEEN

In the center of the band of boys cowers Pod, his hands clutching his chest. Goo and bits of shells from broken eggs drip down the front of his tunic.

"I did not do it!" he wails again.

"Hush, mooncalf!" And the biggest stable lad shoves Pod to his hands and knees in the courtyard mud.

Brude whispers in a mocking tone, "Doesn't a little pig boy like you know that his lordship's eggs are valuable?"

"I did not do it! You made me break the eggs!"

"'Twould be a sin to waste his lordship's good food this way." The biggest stable lad pushes his huge, mucky foot into the small of Pod's back. "Lackwit, lick up your mess and then we may let you live."

"I did not—"

"Lick!" With his foot, the lad shoves Pod's face into the dirt.

In the soft tone of enemy drums heard from far away, the other boys begin to chant "Lick, lick, lick," but quicker than my thinking, I grab a broken fence stake lying on the trash heap, and I am in the center of the circle, whirling the stake like a sword, knocking the scullery lads aside, leaping and twisting. My heart sings as I see them fall. I feel like the archangel Michael, and for the first time in my life I feel the glory of fighting. A couple of them also grab broken stakes, but they are no match for me. I scream like a ghost of death, and in next to no time, they all run.

Panting, I stagger to Pod. He is curled up like a hedge pig, all in a little frightened ball.

"'Tis safe now," I gasp out, drawing in huge gulps of breath.

Then I hear a deep voice say, "Well done, lad."

I whirl around.

There He stands, the man I hate most in all the world and time, gloved and booted as if He has just returned from riding. His red hair flames across his head, the color of a dying sun.

My mouth drops open. I glance at the stake in my hand. *Move swiftly, Gilly, and stab the stake into His black heart.* But immediately I realize that my stake would be hacked to bits by the sword that hangs from His belt long before it would even touch His chest. *There is no glory in dying for a cause if I fail to accomplish my goal. It would be a waste.* And yet my brain screams, *Do something! Do something!*

But I stand frozen as a fire-spooked horse, just gawking at Him.

He is tall, taller than most of the men in the castle. I did not remember His hair as being so bright, but it is fitting since everyone knows the devil marks his special children with red hair.

"He is the lad who trains with my son." I see Fleance's father standing beside Him, both of them dark shapes like standing stones against the fading light.

Then He nods at me. "You have a good heart, fighting for one who cannot fight for himself. In a few years, when you have a little more muscle on that body, if you want to train as a warrior, come see me."

Then He is gone.

I stand, numb.

A second chance, and I do nothing.

I am a gapeseed, a strutting hobbledee horse, full of fury and threats but able to do nothing but playact. I have prayed for another chance, and for a second time, I do nothing. *My life is an arrow . . .*

To my shame, my eyes fill with tears.

Pod uncurls and rises to his feet. He puts an arm around my shoulders. "Don't cry, Gilly. You saved me. Don't cry."

And so we stay for a long time in the growing dusk while egg yolk drips down his front and a few traitor tears drip down my cheeks.

I do not know who is the greater loony.

NINETEEN

WHEN WE FINALLY GO back into the kitchen, Master Cook begins to shout, but Lisette takes one look at the two of us and silences him. "I followed Gilly out," she says, "and our lord himself told Gilly well done. Would you countersay what our lord has spoken?"

Master Cook presses his lips tight together and stamps away. Lisette sits us both down on stools by the fire and uses her apron to wipe off Pod's shirt and my face.

"I did not do it," he tells Lisette. "I did not drop the eggs. They made me."

"'Tis all right, my mustardseed. I know you are a good worker and you do not drop the things you are sent to fetch." She hugs Pod to her plump bosom, and she stretches out her free hand toward me, but I move away. I have failed a second time, and I do not deserve a kind touch.

That evening, Master Cook is summoned to the Great Hall. He glitters with joy.

"No doubt 'twas my dish of Mawmenny," he tells us, shiny with expectation. His fat little mouth purses into a smile. "I used both minced pork and chopped mutton, and then I flavored my sauce with juniper berries. In France I hear they color the dish indigo, but I think the red color I use shows the dish off to better advantage." With his best paring knife he begins to scrape under his fingernails. "For ten years I have toiled faithfully for our thane. Tonight all my work will be rewarded."

He is even jovial to me. "Gilly, tomorrow you shall begin writing down my recipes for all to see."

The other masters gather around the hearth, speculating on how big the reward will be.

"I vow he will bring back a sackful of gold," says Master Baker.

"Nay," says the red-faced alewife. "Them that rule is often ungenerous. They think their notice and their soft words are reward enough for the likes of us."

Finally the kitchen folk decide that Master Cook will be given a purse of silver coins.

"I will use one coin to buy sweetmeats for all who work in the kitchen," Master Cook announces as he follows Master Steward's man up to the Great Hall.

"Could it be true?" Pod whispers to me with shining eyes. I nudge his shoulder with mine in a friendly fashion, but I do not return any other answer. I am too heartsick with failure to speak.

When Master Cook storms back into the kitchen, it is clear that he did not receive a reward. He stalks over to where I sit by the fire.

"Not only," he announces in a shrill voice to us all, "did I not receive even a word of praise, but I had to listen to praises of this lazy, greedy shirkwork!" All of a sudden he backhands me across the face. I am not expecting it, so I tumble sideways off my stool. I feel his handprint burn on my cheek.

"Ten years," he says, "I have worked faithfully for him. Ten years of hard, hot toil, and then this moorsnipe knocks a few lads down with a stick, and his lordship is all atwitter with delight. In front of the whole hall, he asks me what kind of worker this lad is. 'I hate to bear tales, sire,' said I, 'but young Gilly is not one of the best.' What does he do then but throw his head back and laugh. 'A warrior's place is not in the kitchen,' said he. 'If the lad is not so good, send him along to me. We'll train him as a page.'"

Pod gasps. He clutches my sleeve as if I were about to go that instant. His eyes are wide with fright. But I pull away from him. Inside my heart shouts with joy. I am to be a page! I will be near Him all the time! *My life is a dagger, and it is headed to—*

A whack to the top of my head brings my attention back to the present. Master Cook glowers at me. "Page, indeed! We can see who has dreams far above his station." He raises his hand to hit me again, but I scoot out of his way.

Master Cook's plump lips tremble. "Gilly, do not be puffing yourself up with fine airs just yet! 'Sire,' said I, 'even though young Gilly is not so good a worker, I can ill spare him at present. We have barely enough hands to get the work done as 'tis,' said I. So what does he do? What does he do, I ask you, but tell me, 'Next time you go to the village you must hire a lad to take the young fighter's place.'" Master Cook stomps to the corner in which the garden goods are piled. He yanks up a sack and stomps to a table where he spills out the turnips. He grabs the biggest cleaver and begins whacking it down, hacking the vegetables into thick slices. I am sure he would prefer it to be my head that he is hacking to bits. "Next time I go to the village! Hah! 'Twill be a frozen day in June before I go to the village and hire a lad to take the place of this pig's ear who thinks himself a prince."

Most of the others are slinking out of the kitchen. I make a motion to follow, but Master Cook grabs a nearby earthenware pot and flings it at me. He misses. Instead it hits an edge of the hearth stone and shatters, sprinkling its contents of dried peas over the ashes.

"Pick the peas out of the ashes, Gilly, and be quick about it."

I open my mouth to answer, but out of the corner of my eye I see Lisette press a single finger to her mouth in a warning signal, and so I am silent. She puts an arm around Pod, who is crying, and leads him from the kitchen. I kneel on the far side of the hearth. Keeping a wary eye on Master Cook, I let my fingers dart into the ashes and roll out the dried peas, one by one.

Master Cook continues to talk. "Ten years have I served him. Ten years, day and night, with no grumbling or complaint. Ten no-account years, all because of a grubby scullery lad who thinks he's so grand because he knows how to read. Next thing I know, our lord will be adopting this lad to be his son. 'Twould be hard to pick between them as to which has his nose stuck highest in the air. Too proud to notice his faithful cook is his lordship. Always wanting the best food, but too proud to give any mind to where it comes from or who works like a serf to provide it. Too proud to say a thank-you. Too proud even to relieve himself with the rest of us. Has to have his own private night closet does his lordship and his lady wife."

Desperately, recklessly, I seize the opportunity. "How can that be?" I try to sound as young and as innocent as possible. "Are His private chambers away from the rest?"

For a few heartbeats Master Cook regards me with wild eyes, then he resumes his hacking away at the turnips. "Oh, Lordy, yes! Too proud is he to live cheek to jowl with his guests. No, his lordship and his lady wife must have their private chambers with its own private latrine, up their private stair at the far end of the Great Hall. He is even too proud to let his nightsoil mingle with that of the other nobles."

Tomorrow I can search out His chambers, now that I know where to start. I can—

Another blow makes my head ring like a dropped kettle. Master Cook towers above me, and I can see he is crying.

"Do not be thinking you can just stroll up there and demand an audience with him, no matter how well he admires your gutter fighting. We are at war, and day and night one of his men at arms stands guard over the steps to his chamber. Even though his lordship favors you, his men at arms will not let a filthy kitchen snipe near his master."

He throws the cleaver back onto the table amid the mangled corpses of turnips.

"After you finish sorting the peas, clean up this mess." He strides to the door. Just before he goes out, he stops and stands still for the space of several breaths. Then he looks at me with narrowed eyes. "You may be in his favor now, but he does not have a long memory. I daresay the next time he sees you, he will not know you at all."

Nonetheless, the next morning, as soon as I reckon all the sleepers have left the Great Hall, I sneak out of the kitchen. *His lordship and His lady wife have their private chambers, up a private stair at the far end of the Great Hall.* Of course! When I had visited Fleance, I went up the stairway at the near end. Yet I have never seen any other stair. Now I creep to the dais at the far end of the hall. I still see no stairway, only three woven tapestries with pictures of battles I do not recognize. I lift a corner of each tapestry. Behind the last one is a small spiraling stairway. I start up these new stairs, but at the top stands a man at arms, a sword in his fist.

"You have no business here," the guard says, his fingers tight on the handle of his sword.

"His lordship favored me last night with—"

"Be gone, boy! You have no business here."

"I want to thank His lordship for his fine compliments sent to me through Master Cook—"

His free arm swings out and knocks me to the ground. My elbow smashes hard against a corner of a step, and I cry out with pain.

"You have no business here," he repeats, and he moves toward me. I scoot backward and fall to the next step.

"His lordship is leaving for the battlefield tomorrow. If I catch you trying to bother him again before we leave, I will cut off your hand!"

He jabs his sword toward me and laughs. I scuttle awkwardly like a crab down the remaining stairs.

Leaving tomorrow! My stomach drops like a stone in a well. *If only I had more time. . . .*

At my lesson in arms, I am inattentive. I'm frantic that He is leaving so soon. To his delight, Fleance twice knocks the small sword out of my hand.

"Hurrah!" he cries, and struts about the arms yard like a thin banty rooster.

My next blow of the day comes from the Master of Arms who, after witnessing Fleance's triumph, thumps me across the shoulders with a long pole. "Wake up," he says. "Do not be woolgathering, lad."

But all at once excitement explodes inside me. I suddenly understand that Master Cook has told me exactly the way to reach His chamber.

TWENTY

Had I not known it was there, I might have missed it.

It is cleverly constructed, barely a shoulder span wide and flush along the far side of the motte, the small hill from which the keep rises.

Dirt has been heaped against the wooden panel that serves as a tiny door to His private night shaft. With my fingernails, I scrape around the corners until I can lift the panel open.

The smell tells me I have found what I seek. The shaft to His private night closet.

I wonder why this latrine is constructed different from the other one. But all I can think of is that perhaps they were built at different times.

Then I wonder why I'm delaying. *Get on with it.*

I tear handfuls of grasses from the motte and scatter them over the bottom of the hole until there is a fine carpet.

Still I hesitate.

"Fool," I chide myself. "Clodpole, blockhead! Have you come this close to abandon it now because your nose cannot accommodate a little stink?"

If I am caught, what will be done to me? I am not fool enough to imagine I would escape with a mere beating. This is a time of war, and not even the most tender-hearted holy sister would have a smidgeon of mercy for one who sneaks into the lord's private chambers armed with a knife, even if the knife is a worn-out dagger with a broken blade. My own traitor heart keeps screaming, *You do not want to die, you do not want to die.* And death would not be the worst thing about being caught. There would be torture, too. I am sore afraid that I lack the strength to endure torture valiantly. And should I die the slow death of a tortured coward, sniveling and begging Him to kill me quick and free me from my pain, then would I betray those I loved a second time.

Stop these horrible imaginings! All you need do is climb into that narrow darkness. Soldiers have done as much when they have captured enemy castles. You have more reason than they to be stouthearted. Your cause is just. Climb!

And still I do not climb.

I have made my life an arrow . . .

But you do not shoot arrows into darkness.

I have made my life a dagger . . .

I do not climb.

Perhaps it is all a lie. Perhaps, Gilly, it is nothing more than a nursery story to frighten bogies away. Perhaps you do not want to kill Him at all, perhaps He did you and yours no wrong, perhaps it is all baby-play to you and your life has no meaning. Admit that you are a coward and He is all courage and might, that you—

And I begin to climb.

It is a long, thankless climb up the shaft of the latrine. The very narrowness of the shaft is all that makes the climbing possible. A grown man would fit too tight in it, like a cork in the mouth of a bottle. A child like Pod or Fleance would be too small to reach from wall to wall. But I fit snugly enough, as if the very size of this rank place has been fashioned just for me. *It is another sign that God approves of my course of action. This shaft was made so I could climb it to my revenge.*

As I inch upward, I pray that neither He nor His lady will need to use this latrine.

It takes a long, long time to creep upward. Every few inches I pause and listen hard. *Is that the sound of someone up above?* My heart pounds loud as a battledrum. Although out in the air the day is cool, inside the shaft I am too warm. Halfway up, a stone falls loose and I start to slide. I scrabble madly and push my hands hard against the wall and press hard with my feet. If I were to fall now, I would break my bones—perhaps even my neck. But for once luck is on my side, and I slide no more. I let myself hang there until I have mastered my breath.

I do not let myself think about what my hands and feet are touching.

Soon a faint, water-gray light begins to seep in from above. The air grows less clotted with stink. I hold still for a few breaths, listening, but I hear no sound from the chamber above me. I inch up silently until the top of my head brushes against the underside of a wooden lid. I balance carefully and use one hand to push up the lid. I then hold very still.

No sound.

I push the lid all the way up. It makes a soft slap when it hits against the wall. I hold still and listen.

No sound.

My arms snake through the hole, and I scrabble up till I can roll onto the floor. I curl up like a clenched fist and listen.

Silence . . . except for my breath.

My arms ache. My brow is sweaty. I am afraid the stink I smell is not just the night filth from the latrine but on my clothes as well. After a little while, I uncurl and look around.

This is His world, His private world, and I am in it.

Bring me three pieces of His heart, Mad Helga told me. I have puzzled over this but I have not been able to determine what Mad Helga meant. She cannot mean for me to kill Him because my reward for bringing the pieces of His heart is to be her help in bringing about His death.

Could the heart of a buck have done just as well? Suddenly I feel very silly. *Perhaps I could have taken the heart of a buck to Mad Helga and pretended it was His. Then I need not have endured all that I have endured here at the castle.*

Nonetheless, since I am here, I decide to look around. Perhaps something here will help me unravel Mad Helga's riddle.

If not, I will take the heart of a buck to Mad Helga.

I am in a small room, the garderobe. A basket filled with straw sits nearby on the floor. It is meant to be used to clean oneself after using the latrine.

I chuckle. *I could surely use some cleaning.* I grab a handful of the sweet, scratchy straw and scrape it back and forth on one hand, then the other, then drop it down the shaft. With another handful I scour my legs. Another handful scrubs my feet. I scour my face with one last handful. I know it is daft to waste my time cleaning up, but still I do it.

Why do you still delay, girl? Could it be that you are afraid to do what you have come to do? Your life is an arrow . . .

On my hands and knees, I crawl to the door and nudge it open.

On the other side is a grand chamber, the grandest that I have ever seen.

In the center stands a bed near as big as Nettle's whole hut. It stands high off the floor, like a ship with a carved pole at each corner. A frame of carved poles sits atop the poles, just the same width and length as the top of the bed. Fine woven blue cloth drapes across it, making a bed-roof like an upside-down sea, and blue curtains hang from the frame, falling down each pole like a silken waterfall. At night, I reckon, they can be pulled so that the whole bed is hidden behind the curtains.

A lot of things seem hidden in this castle.

On top of the bed itself lies a thick bearskin, looking so soft and warm that I long to curl up in it and take a nap. Several wolfskins are scattered across the floor as rugs, so finely tanned and silky that my old wolfskin seems but a snot rag. At one end of the chamber is a huge fireplace, big enough for me to stand in without my head's touching the top. The stone around it and on the mantel is carved with vines and leaves. In front of the fireplace are two oaken benches, one with a carved wooden back and one without. At the foot of the bed is a wooden chest, near as wide as the bed. Its lid also is carved with vines and flowers, which have been painted red, green, and yellow. Underneath the narrow window there is a smaller chest that looks to be made of carved ivory or a fine, smooth white stone.

Pounded into the far wall are several pegs for clothing. From one hangs a gown of heavy silk, as red as holly berries or fresh blood. Its sleeves, bodice, and hem are embroidered with green and gold vines all twisted and wound round each other in a beautiful dance of pattern and color. From the shoulders hang loose oversleeves of silver, no heavier than a whisper and as transparent as frost on a brook. They are like wings of a magical moth, although they are boneless and could never fly. I am drawn to that wondrous gown just like a moth to rushlight. Before I realize it, I am stroking the gown with my rough, dirty hand, and then I have plucked it from its peg and am holding it to the front of my body. For an instant it transforms me from a warrior—a thing of revenge and hate—into a princess who is leading a dance in a torch-lit Great Hall. How Pod would stare could he see me in this bit of fancy.

Go to the looking glass, I order myself. *Look into it and see how monstrous you look, stubble-head, peacocking about in—*

I cannot bear to see my matted hair and boy's face peeking out above this enchantment of silk and broidery. *I will shut this gown up in the long chest so it does not call to me.* I bundle it up in my arms and move quickly to the chest by the bed. I lift the lid—which is very heavy—to drop the bewitched gown inside.

Then I hear voices and approaching footfalls.

TWENTY-ONE

QUICK AS A FINCH'S WHISTLE, I tumble into the large chest and ease the lid back down. I am lying on top of the silk gown. The inside of the chest smells of lavender, woodruff, golden cat's paw, and oak. To my relief, the weight of my body presses the gown and the cloth beneath it flat enough so that the lid shuts entirely. *Should I be discovered, I will be killed.* I am stiff and scared.

"Must you indeed leave so soon, my lord?"

At the sound of her voice, I begin to shiver. My muscles pull so tight they shake. My stomach twists within me like a wrung-out dish clout. *Focus, Gilly. Think of your revenge.*

A deep voice answers. His voice.

"Aye, lady, I must. I have stayed here more than three weeks. 'Tis past the time I should be gone. Now near Fife, the messenger tells me, the rebel army gathers."

Her tone is scornful. "Then let the Thane of Fife deal with the traitor who camps in his pasture." Her voice softens. I hate her seductive tone. "You have been away at war so much during the past few years, my love. Stay with me. Fife can handle Fife."

"Fife!" The word is more the snarl of a beast than the speech of a man. "I am told Fife has come to the north."

"Indeed? I had not thought him to be a coward."

"He claims he has come north only to visit his wife and his brood of children, who have sought sanctuary in her brother's castle. He says he will return to the south once he has seen to them."

"If Fife can neglect this war to see to the well-being and pleasure of his wife, cannot the lord of Glamis do as much?"

"Fife holds his duty to the king as lightly as milkpod fluff. He is a silly light-minded man—"

"But if he cares so little about the enemy in his own lands, then there is no cause for you to leave. I say again, let Fife deal with Fife."

"My dearest love, 'tis not the enemy at Fife that draws me. There are also battles to the east."

I wonder briefly if Nettle and Mad Helga have begun again to glean the battlefields. *Focus!*

His voice grows harsh. "Today I receive tidings that Macdonald has marched an army of Irish mercenaries toward the camp of our king. My place is there, my love, defending good King Duncan, not passing my days here in luxury and idleness. I am not Fife."

"Am I luxury? Am I idleness?" Although her voice is soft and clear, I am shocked by the hunger underneath her words. "Let all of Scotland melt into the Western Sea and let good King Duncan rot to dust! I am your place. Stay with me."

He, too, seems to hear her hunger speaking, for He is silent. After a while, I hear her light steps tapping angrily over to the fireplace. There is a pause in which I fear my jagged breath will give away my hiding place. Then I hear His heavy footsteps lumbering over to her.

When at last she speaks, her voice is a bowstring pulled too taut. "You play me false, my lord. Before God you do. You claim to love me, yet you love war more than you love me. I have sacrificed all for you—I have given you everything—and yet you leave me for your true mistress, the true love of your heart—"

"God help me, lady, but 'tis true, I do love battle. And even should I not love fighting, I owe fealty to my king—"

Swift as a falcon, she swoops down on his words. "Your king! King Duncan! What right has that white-livered upstart to claim to be King of Scotland?"

"Of the Scots, my love, not of Scotland. The land is free, but we Scots—we loyal Scots—serve the high king."

"You are better fitted to be king than the silken-spined Duncan. *Your* blood is as royal as his. *My* blood is more royal. My poor, dead babe whose little body molders in the ground—even the blood of my babe—gnawed by worms and other crawling things of the darkness is more royal than our greedy king's."

"Lady, for all that, he is our king—"

"*Your* king, not mine!" Her voice rises higher and higher like a wind in a gale.

I want to put my hands over my ears, I want to shut out her voice, her witch's voice, a voice that seems sweet at first hearing but grows more and more deadly the more you listen. *Can I squirm my dagger out of its pouch, can I spring out of the chest and drive my dagger into His heart now, can I have as my ally the element of surprise, and could I kill Him now, but now, in this instant of time?* If I could know that with one blow I would drain Him of His life, I'd risk eternal damnation.

But even as I think this, I know it is a fool's thought. He is the greatest warrior in all Scotland. Thus far my finest feat of arms was to frighten some village louts with a fence post. I can climb a latrine shaft well enough, but I doubt not that He would overcome me in any contest. He could crush me like a beetle, the breaking of my bones no more to him than the faint crack of a crushed beetle's shell.

Still her voice whines on and on, a harp whose strings are tuned too tight. ". . . He is a poor excuse for a high king, never setting so much as his little toe onto a battlefield for *his* crown, *his* kingdom, but asking that you risk *your* life and *your* fortune, no, nor sending his sons neither—"

"They are but lads!"

"Lads big enough, I whit, to be learning how to be men. At your age, my lord, tell me, did you not wield the sword? Did you not shoulder the battle ax?"

"They say the king's lads are scholars, not warriors—"

"Scotland needs a warrior king, not some mewling scholars. You have a better claim to the throne than Duncan's cubs. I have a better claim. My dead babe—"

I wriggle my hands to cover my ears, but I can still hear her screeching. "—my dead babe's blood is more royal than that of the king's pair of cubs."

Again there is a little silence before He speaks. When He does, His voice is slow and reluctant like the steps of a beaten ox being dragged to harness.

"What would you have of me, lady? I have sworn fealty to my king."

"Aye, lord, that you have. And even now you fail to understand how ill you have used me. I give up everything for you, but you love your fighting and your king and I know not how much else more than you do me. You give them the high hall of your heart, and you cast me in some dark chamber, better fitted for—"

"No!" His voice thunders. I wonder if it can be heard down in the Great Hall. "'Tis not the king I love, although he is a good man—for all his weakness—who has borne himself both meek and mild. But I love that I have never forsworn my oath nor word. I love that the strength of my word is as strong as the strength of my arm."

Liar. Will you lie even to the she-wolf you wed?

I expect her to thunder back at him, but when she speaks, her voice is the coo of a well-fed dove. "Oaths, kings, but you say nothing of your love for your wife. Where do I rank, lord, in the heraldry of your loves?"

His answer comes quick and strong.

"Wife, there is nothing in this world or the next that I love so much as you."

She laughs in her throat, low and soft and secret . So would a serpent laugh if it could laugh. "Then, lord, do I still sit in the seat of honor in your heart?"

His voice is so tender that my stomach twists. "Lady, you do not have the seat of honor because you are no guest but the very ruler of my heart itself. 'Twould give you a moment of pleasure, I would tear my heart from my chest and offer it to you on a golden platter."

She laughs again. But I lie there, swaddled in hatred for both of them, as they continue to prattle on about the details of his parting—who will go with Him and when to plant which field and such.

Yet I pay this talk little mind for now I know how to get my revenge.

TWENTY-TWO

As soon as the chamber is empty again, I am down the latrine shaft as quick as a cat. My heart sings. *I have what I need to destroy Him.* I am drunk with impatience to be gone, to take my treasure back to Mad Helga. When I reach the courtyard, it is nearly time for the castle gates to be shut for the night. *If I am not gone at once, then I must wait till the gates open again at dawn.* I will go mad if I have to wait the night through, so I dart into the kitchen where the bustle to prepare supper has begun.

Master Cook glares at me. "Gilly, get yourself—" and then he staggers back from the stink I give off. "Out of my kitchen! Wash yourself, clodpole, and then march back in here fast as can be. I'll deal with you then."

I grab a sack of nuts and cast my eyes about the kitchen, but I do not see Pod or Lisette. Ignoring Master Cook's outraged screams, I dart back out to the courtyard. I wish I had time to get more food for the journey, but I must be out the gates before they close.

What about Pod? If he were handy, I would take him with me, even though he would slow me down, but if I take time to look for him, I will lose my chance to be out the gates and on my way this very night. *He will be fine. No doubt this is all for the best, for surely Lisette will take him on as her apprentice now that I am out of the way. Indeed, my departure will be the best possible thing to happen to him. In fact, my leaving will be a gift. Staying here, I cannot change Lisette's mind, but by sneaking away, I assure him of a fine future.* I begin to feel puffed up with virtue, but there is a nagging bit inside that makes me feel guilty for not even bidding him farewell. *He has gotten over his mother's leaving just fine,* I tell that nagging voice, *and he will have no trouble getting over me. It will do him good to toughen up. Let him learn to be a man. He cannot always stay a helpless child. My leaving will be good for him.*

Then I am out the castle gates and on my way home.

I BURST INTO THE HUT, filthy, exhausted from my days of traveling, my skin scratched by thorns and brambles, with twigs in my hair. But I am elated, too.

There is no sign of Nettle. Mad Helga cowers behind the churn as if she is expecting the armies of Scotland to arrest her and drag her to her execution.

"I have the three pieces of His heart."

Mad Helga stares at me for a moment. Her face is as blank as new cheese. Then she hobbles back to her old place by the fire hearth, singing a wordless little tune to the tiny bones in her bony hand.

I shriek like a drowning sailor, "Did you not hear me, old woman! I have them."

When she still fails to respond, I stomp over to her and jerk her chin up so I can stare into her good eye.

"Mad Helga, I have what you asked me to get."

I let go of her chin and stand there, triumphant as God on the seventh day of creation. To my frustration, she looks back down to her handful of bones and shakes them back and forth, singing in a reedy voice:

> *Dragon's blood, revenge, and the heart of stone—*
> *These are things best left alone.*
> *Seek high-low,*
> *But if you go—*

I stamp my foot and screech, "Leave off, old woman! Bring me the three pieces of His heart, you said. Bring them and I will give you the means to destroy Him, you said. I have done my part of that dark bargain. "Tis your hour now."

From behind me I hear Nettle's voice. "'Tis you who should leave off, Gilly. Stop plaguing Mad Helga." Her voice sounds tired.

I whirl around. Nettle stands at the door of the hut. On her arm is a basket filled with weeds and herbs. "Gone for more than three spans of the moon," she says. "Now no word of greeting, but—"

"Leave off!" I shout. "When I have risked my life, sacrificed my dignity—humbled myself in the kitchens—letting a pullet paddler scold and shame me, when I have endured the jeers and japes of a rabble of unwashed bullies, when I have crawled through filth and worse than filth, when I have endured every foul thing—and now you dare tell me to leave off! Do you know what you ask, Nettle?"

Nettle sighs and moves past me to set her basket down in the corner. "Do you know what *you* ask, Gilly?"

I nod so hard my head rattles. "I know what I ask. My birthright!"

Nettle lowers herself to the floor. She puts the basket on her lap and starts to sort out its contents, putting each herb and grass in a different pile. I move angrily to stand in front of her. When she takes no notice of me, I knock the basket out of her hands.

"My *earned* birthright. I have made my life an arrow, and I shall not relax the bowstring now that I've pulled it taut."

Nettle looks up at me. "Child, be you as single-eyed as a mountain troll and as brain-empty as a drunken parson's hen that you fail to see that to carry out this mad dream would make you not a jot better than him you seek to destroy?"

"I do not want to be better. Let me be worse than the foulest demon in the bowels of hell—only let me destroy Him."

Nettle quickly makes a sign to ward off the evil eye.

I kneel beside her, crushing some of the herbs beneath my legs. "Nettle, I ask nothing of you but that you fulfill your promise."

We lock eyes. For a moment both our eyes are hard. Then Nettle's face softens. She takes my rough hand in her even rougher one. "Gilly, you know that I have the double sight. And I hoped never to tell you this, child, but if you pursue this mad revenge, death waits for one that you love."

"I love no one!"

She continues as if she does not hear me. "Not only that, but I see Gilly herself disappearing. I have seen it, and my double sight never lies." She gives my hand a little squeeze. "'Tis Gilly, child, not him that will vanish in your revenge."

Never before have I heard her voice so afraid. For the length of several heartbeats, I too am frightened. Then I make my face hard, but, to my surprise, my voice comes out as a whisper. "Then let Gilly die. But, Nettle, better a destroyed life than no life at all, and I can have no life while He lives and flourishes." She tries to let go of my hand, but I squeeze hers tightly. "Nettle, death comes for us all. I would rather live briefly as a burning castle than for long years as a muddy stream."

"You say that only because you are young—you do not know—"

I am a dagger . . . and a dagger has nothing soft and kind about it. I choose to be cruel, so I select words meant to wound. "Would you have me lead a life like yours, Nettle—an ugly, scrawny woman, old before her time—hiding in a tumbledown hut with a witless hag, scorned and jeered at by the villagers, eking out an existence gathering weeds and robbing battlefields? Is this the glory you would have me live? No, a thousand times, no. Give me blazing, give me the glory and high drama of the flame, make me the daughter of fire— anything but this."

Mad Helga says, "The child is right, Nettle."

Amazed, both Nettle and I snap our heads to look at Mad Helga. Her face is tranquil as that of the mother of Jesus.

"We did promise her," Mad Helga says.

"You," says Nettle. "Not I. 'Twas you made this mad promise."

Mad Helga nods. "And I need your help to keep it."

Nettle moves to Mad Helga and kneels before her as if she is confessing to the parson.

"Mad Helga, in the water, I have seen it, in the earth I have read it, I have found it in the smoke—if she pursues this mad revenge, our Gilly will be no more." Her low voice drops even lower. "Helga, I see all life wiped from our hut if Gilly persists in her wild scheme." She presses her hand against her forehead. "There has been enough death already."

Mad Helga touches her free hand to Nettle's cheek. "I will keep the promise, Nettle, with or without your help. I cannot read water or earth or smoke, but I do know that without your help, Gilly will have no chance whatsoever to outrun her fate."

After a moment, Nettle drops her head in resignation.

Mad Helga looks at me. "Give me the three pieces of his heart."

TWENTY-THREE

I TELL THEM what I discovered when I was entombed in the chest in His chamber. "The first piece of His heart is His loyalty to His king."

Nettle opens her mouth, but Mad Helga holds up a bony hand and silences her.

I continue. "The second piece is His besottedness for the harlot He calls His wife. I do not use the word love—His passion is more sickness than sacrament."

Mad Helga nods.

"And the third piece," I say, my voice larded with triumph, "is His secret longing to be king."

In a startled voice, Nettle asks, "He said that?"

"He did not say that," I admit. "I do not think He even knows He fosters that desire. But the desire lurked in His tone if not His words—like a dragon who bides his time in the caves beneath a castle. From my earliest memories of Him, I know that He is ambitious. I know He covets what is not rightfully His. I know the laws of God and man mean less to Him that the hunger in His heart." My voice shakes with my passion. "I know Him. His face may be as fair as a flower, but a snake lies coiled in its leaves."

Mad Helga and Nettle look at each other for a long moment. *Help me*, I beg inside my head. *You must help me. I have no other place to turn. I cannot do it all alone.* Then Nettle lowers her head, as if she heard my thoughts. She whispers in a voice soft as prayer, "Tomorrow, then, let it begin."

Mad Helga gives the shaky sigh of an old woman. "'Tis not enough, Nettle."

Nettle draws her breath in sharply. Her face is pale and frightened and lost. Into my mind flashes the tale she told me of how she came to live in the forest. How her father had betrothed her to a man as a gambling debt and how, at the altar when the debtor first set eyes on young Nettle, he had roared he would not be leg-shackled to such an ugly hag, no, not for all the money in Christendom. That night when her drunken father had thrown her out-of-doors to fend for herself, she must have looked just as pale and frightened and lost as now.

"You must talk with the Old Ones," Mad Helga says gently.

The Old Ones? What can Mad Helga mean?

I had not thought it possible, but Nettle's face grows even whiter.

"You know I do not like to let them in," she whispers. "Someday I will not be strong enough to control them, and then what will become of us?"

Mad Helga sighs again. "We must give Gilly a chance," she says. "Do it quickly."

Nettle staggers to her feet, as if she is even older than Mad Helga, and totters to the corner in which she keeps her store of herbs. She pokes through them, untwisting several packets to dribble pinches of their contents onto her leathery palm. Then she totters back to the fire and eases herself down. She twists her head to look at me. "Go outside, Gilly. There is no need for you to see this."

How dare she try to get rid of me! "No! 'Tis my revenge, and—"

"Go outside, I say!"

"I will not go. I have the right—"

"Gilly—"

Mad Helga's voice breaks in. "She is old enough, Nettle, to witness what you do for her."

Nettle opens her mouth to reply, then presses her lips tightly shut. I feel triumph . . . and fear. What am I about to see? Who are the Old Ones?

"Douse the light," Mad Helga says.

I plunge the lighted rush into the bucket of loose dirt and pebbles. Its light goes out, leaving the flickering orange light of the fire pit surrounded by a moat of shadows.

Nettle shakes her hand over the fire like a farmer sowing spring wheat, scattering herbs. Some of the herbs make a little popping sound as they hit the flames. The hut fills with the smell of charred leaves and something vinegary sharp that puckers my nose. I hear Nettle's heavy, ragged breathing.

Suddenly the room plunges into a bitter coldness—cold as quick and painful as if the hut itself had tumbled into an icy stream. I blink and look, but the fire continues to burn although it does nothing to beat back this terrible chill. My teeth begin to chatter. Then just as suddenly, the room fills with a wave of smell, an odor both sweet and foul, like the stench of a body six days dead. I cover my nose with my hand, but the smell is just as strong. I have to fight against gagging. What is happening? I don't understand it. I look to Nettle, and I see that her lips are moving. Then I hear a voice coming out of her mouth, but it is not her voice. It is a voice I have never heard before, a voice that is gnarled and twisted and dry like the root of an ancient oak.

"You will find what you seek two leagues from Forres." The voice cracks and grates against the cold and hurts my ears. I move my hands to my ears, but the voice is just as loud and just as painful. "Go north to Forres. Find the seven sisters of the north. And there you will find him, too." Then the voice crashes into a blizzard of sound that mixes laughter, pigs' grunts, donkey brays, and the screams of dying horses.

Without warning, Nettle falls forward as if a rope holding her up was suddenly cut. Her head misses the fire by less than a hand's width. I quickly pull her to a safer distance. Then I notice that the room has grown warm again and the smell is gone.

"The Old Ones have spoken," says Mad Helga.

THE FOLLOWING MORNING, I lead them north, following the route I took with Pod. Oftentimes my mind strays backward to early spring when he and I traveled this route. But then I imagine how frightened his little face must have looked when he learned I had left the castle. *No. Pod is neither kith nor kin. I am not his keeper. There is not rhyme nor reason for me to feel guilty. He is safer in the castle than in the woods with the Witch Hunters seeking him. Did I not try with all my might to make Lisette apprentice him? He is nothing to me, and it is not my fault that the world is a cold place. I did not design it, and I cannot change it.* But before my eyes is the fantasy of Pod's pinched, white, woebegone face shooting reproachful looks at me. So as quick as wind can blow mist off the surface of water, I push the vision of his face from my mind.

The three of us travel more slowly than Pod and I did. For the first few days, Nettle is especially tired. Her face is drawn and she walks stiffly and often stops to rest. Whenever I try to question her about what went on in the hut, she ignores me. Finally even Mad Helga tells me to hush and speak of it no more. But I continue to puzzle over the scene by the fire and the strange voice and mention of the Old Ones. I can make no sense of it, and it makes me angry to be left out of knowing. Did Nettle let spirits into the room? Is she indeed the witch that the villagers call her? They call me a witch, too, but I have no powers at all. I have always known that Nettle has double sight, but so do many people, and I know that Nettle has skill in herb lore, but herb lore is something that can be learned like weaving or swordsmanship. What if Nettle is truly a witch? I do not like this thought. We women who live alone in the wood are vulnerable to attack and accusation, but if Nettle is a witch in truth— No, I do not want her to be killed. There is no safe place on earth for one who is a real witch. Try as I might, I cannot put my thoughts in order, so on the fifth day I decide to shut the doors of my mind against all these matters. Over the years I have grown skillful at shutting out notions and memories I do not want to face.

On the eighth day we veer to the east. All Nettle will say is "This is the way we must go."

On the tenth day we find ourselves in a wood that is more rocky and barren than our wood at Birnam. We fight our way through a heavy mist. We stay close together, wrapped in lengths of cloth whose color is a little darker than the mist and a little paler than the earth. We dare not stray from each other's sight, for it would be a simple matter to disappear from view. Long lengths of the cloth also cover our heads in a vain attempt to keep us dry. A ghostly world surrounds us. Shapes loom up suddenly like apparitions, twitch into view to reveal themselves for the space of a heartbeat as trees or boulders, then disappear just as quickly into the broth of fog. We cannot see our way, but Nettle leads by using her double sight, although it seems that she is listening to an invisible voice rather than leading by her eyes.

After a long span of walking—or rather swimming on our feet—through the mist, Nettle stops and holds up her hand for us to stop, too. Although I am eager to reach Him, I am grateful for a few minutes of rest. Mad Helga—who has been panting and wheezing like a badger—can also use a break. Only Nettle, her shoulders as tense as ever, now seems to need no respite from this driven pace.

"Nettle," I say, "I had not thought—"

"Hsst," she hushes me. She stretches out a hand, a skinny finger pointing. *What does she mean?*

Then I hear the hooves of several horses, the sound of their approach muffled by the woolly mist.

They travel slowly because of the mist, but I can tell from the sound that these are horses of men at arms, not the ponies of wealthy peasants or the donkeys of the good brothers.

"It begins," Nettle says.

She takes a few steps forward. I follow. I can tell by the feel of the earth under my feet that we have stepped onto a road. The mist thins out a little as we stand there so we can see several body-lengths farther.

The hoofbeats grow louder. Suddenly five or six armed men appear. They pull their horses up short at the sight of us. One horse rears, and its rider pulls its reins sharply.

One of the men beckons to us. "You there. Come closer."

Nettle and I move to his horse. Nettle keeps her head lowered, but I look up at him. His face is shadowed by his hood, but on his cheek I see a blade-scar in the shape of a cross.

"Can you help us?" he asks. "We seek two travelers, two captains and thanes. One lives not half a day's ride from here—you may know him by sight. The Thane of Glamis."

'Tis the title of the very man I seek. My breath catches in my chest, but the rider does not notice. "Have you seen him?" he asks.

Another rider guides his horse up close to us. "We have word he will be traveling along this road today, but this blasted mist is so thick we have thrice gone astray since we set out."

Without raising her eyes, Nettle says, "We have seen no one but you this day, my gracious lords."

The first rider nods. "I feared as much. I thank you for the information, my good—" He stops a moment, then continues, "This blasted mist! I cannot even tell whether you be men or women."

He makes a signal to the men, and they rein to the side to walk their horses past us. Before they have gone more than a couple of paces, Mad Helga steps into the road.

"Will these two thanes welcome you, my lords?" she calls out, bold as a saint on the day after judgment.

The riders wheel their horses around, startled.

"You dare question your betters?" the second rider asks, and his tone is sharpened steel.

Mad Helga swiftly lowers her head and raises her hands in a placating gesture. Her voice sounds humble. "I mean only, good sires, if we see these thanes, shall we tell them you seek them, or would you rather have us keep our silence?"

The first rider asks, "What is your meaning, old one?"

The second rider says, "Lord Ross, these peasants seek to buy our silence with a few coins shaken loose from your purse." He leans down to Mad Helga. "Is that not so, old fox?"

"Silver has power to make one forget one's own name," Mad Helga says. She holds her hand up suggestively.

I am confused. What can she mean by this? Never have I seen her act in this fawning, begging manner. I feel ashamed of her.

The first rider laughs. His laughter pulls his scar sideways across his cheek. "You will get naught from us today, old one. The news we bring is joyful."

Mad Helga says, "Joyful to you, perhaps, but will the Thane of Glamis find it equally joyful? A spider spins a joyful web, but the fly does not rejoice."

The first rider laughs again. "In faith, old one, even the fly will rejoice this time. Our good King Duncan has added the fiefdom of Cawdor to Glamis's holdings."

Nettle steps forward and asks, "But what of the present Thane of Cawdor? Does he fling away his title and lands so carelessly?"

The riders exchange looks, and their hands move to the hilts of their swords. The second one asks, "How come you to know so much of the Thane of Cawdor?"

Nettle says, "I saw him once—not so many years since—when he and his retinue passed through the countryside. He looked to be a young and lusty gentleman."

"He was a traitor!" snaps the second rider in a bitter tone.

The first rider says, "Should you wish to see what remains of this young and lusty gentleman, you might travel to King Duncan's castle at Forres. There you may see the former Thane of Cawdor face to face. His head is impaled on a pole on the battlements." All the riders laugh.

"The king punishes traitors," says the second rider, "but he is generous in rewarding those who are true to him. Thus he sends us to find the Thane of Glamis to reward his honorable service in this last war by presenting him with Cawdor's holdings as well."

I cannot bear to hear these lies. I blurt, "He is not hon—"

Both Nettle and Mad Helga say, "Hush!"

The second rider leans down. "What does this one say?"

Nettle gives me a warning look, and already I regret my outburst. *A sword that is drawn too soon will give a plan away.*

"Please, great lord," I say in my most humble voice, "I mean to say only that the man you seek is not on this road—at least not on the part of the road on which we journeyed."

A third rider dances his horse closer to us. "Lord Ross, we lose time. Let us away, or we will never find Glamis."

The first rider nods. He raises his hand, and all the riders flap their reins. The horses trot away into the white darkness.

Once the sound of their hoofbeats has died away, I demand, "Mad Helga, what was all that talk about the spider and fly?"

Mad Helga smiles to herself but says nothing.

"Tell me!" I say. I do not like to be kept once more out of the knowing. *Annoying old woman!* Why will she not explain her meaning? It is not right to keep me in the dark about this plan.

Nettle pulls her wrapping more tightly against the chill of the day. "What we now know, Gillyflower, is that the Old Ones spoke true. The man you seek is on his way to the king's court." She looks at me for a moment, then adds, "There is yet time to turn away from this, child. 'Twould be the wisest course."

I say, "If we do not get moving, we shall miss Him entirely."

As we trudge along, the mist grows even thicker. Nettle leads us through the wood for a long time till we finally reach another road. Walking is a little easier once we travel along this path. After a while, I raise the subject again. "Mad Helga, I still fail to understand what you meant about the spider and fly."

Mad Helga, who is softly singing a tune without any sensible words or melody, pays no attention to my question.

Nettle gives a sharp sigh. "She meant nothing at all."

Mad Helga glances at her and smiles to herself, still crooning her strange little tune.

I am tired of their riddles. I make my voice sharp. "Come along!"

There is no way to tell time in the mist. When we reach a narrow clearing at the side of the road, it feels as if we have been traveling more than half the day. There are large boulders scattered close together, and the clearing is ringed by seven standing stones, all but one of them taller than I can reach even by standing on tiptoe and stretching up my hand. Mad Helga and Nettle sink down on two nearby boulders to rest, leaning their backs against two standing stones, but I am too impatient to sit.

"Rest," Nettle commands.

"But I—"

"Rest, Gilly!"

I am losing faith in Nettle's sight and the knowledge of the Old Ones. *Could all this be but a wild chase after the will-o'-the-wisp?* Finally I plop down on a nearby boulder. After we rest for a long time, I ask, "Should we not be doing something?"

"We are," Nettle says. "We are waiting."

I mutter, "I do not like waiting."

As the day drones on, Mad Helga dozes and Nettle huddles in her swaddling cloths, trying to get warm. I find a supple branch and pass the time by pulling strips of bark from it. After a while, I use it to whip a nearby stump. I hit it over and over.

"Gilly!" says Nettle.

I stop whipping and look at her, expecting a scolding. Instead she just shakes her head and sinks back down into her wrappings. I throw the peeled branch away, but after many minutes I go collect it again. I sit on a rock, digging patterns in the soft wood with my fingernail.

Finally I say, "Should we not discuss what we will do when we see Him?"

Nettle says, "'Twill come to us."

I say, "We should plan—"

"Till I see him, Gilly, I cannot know what is needed. God willing, my double sight will give me guidance. All you need do, child, is follow my lead."

I do not like the sound of this. "I do not think—"

Nettle says, "Settle down, child."

I shout back, "I do not know what to do."

"Helga and I know," says Nettle. "Follow us, whate'er we do."

"Nothing will come of this. 'Tis all show. You do not wish me to—"

"Hush!"

"But I do not—"

"Hush!"

I stalk over to one of the standing stones and kick it.

Just then Nettle stands up. She walks over and puts a hand on Mad Helga's shoulder. "'Tis time."

Without opening her good eye, Mad Helga nods. *It is about to start.* I take a deep breath and put a hand on my belly to steady myself. I feel both cold and hot, shivery with both fear and elation.

Then two men walk into the clearing, leading their horses. It is hard to make out more than their shapes. The taller one stops, steadying himself with a hand against the tallest standing stone.

It's Him.

TWENTY-FOUR

He does not see us. He turns to the shape that is His companion and says, "So foul and fair a day I have not seen."

I gasp at the sound of His voice. Quicker than lightning, swords appear in both men's hands. I throw my hands up to show I am not armed.

The other man steps forward. I recognize his striped cloak that glitters gold and cream in the mist. It is Fleance's father, Lord Banquo. I lower my head and pull the cloth of my wrappings low over my forehead so he will not recognize me.

Lord Banquo asks me, "How far is it to Forres?"

I am frozen into silence. The man I have come to meet makes an impatient clucking in His throat, sheaths His sword, and turns to go. *I cannot lose Him now,* but I can think of no way to keep Him. *I have made my life—*

Mad Helga steps into His view. She presses her finger to her lip. "Hsst," she says.

Nettle steps out of the mist, her finger to her lips. "Hsst."

I snap back to life. I imitate their gesture. "Hsst."

Lord Banquo moves close to Mad Helga. She keeps her finger

to her lips, her one eye flickering back and forth like an adder's tongue between the two warriors. Lord Banquo looks at her closely.

"Are you fantastical, or do you live?"

"Hsst," says Mad Helga again.

"Are you aught that a man may question?"

"Hsst," says Mad Helga for the third time.

He gives a little laugh, but he sounds uneasy. He glances to his companion, my enemy, who seems as frozen as I was. Then Lord Banquo looks back at the three of us. "You seem to understand me. But what are you? Who are you?" He brings his face close to Mad Helga's. She does not move.

Then He steps close, His fingers drumming against His sword's hilt. He regards us for a moment, and then His fingers tighten around the hilt. "Speak if you can!" His voice is pitched a little too loud. I feel a thrill of power. *He is afraid. He is afraid of us.* I have made Him feel fear! I am giddy with delight.

Then, to my dismay, He turns to go. "Time grows short. 'Tis clear these creatures are short in their wits, and we must—"

Swiftly, despite her age and creaking bones, Mad Helga kneels in front of Him. "All hail, Macbeth! Hail to thee, Thane of Glamis!"

Swiftly Nettle kneels. "All hail, Macbeth. Hail to thee, Thane of Cawdor!"

Clever of her! She has used her private knowledge to—

And I know just what to say.

I kneel, disguising my voice so that it is rough and low. "All hail, Macbeth. You shall be king hereafter!"

At that His head jerks up as if He has been bitten by a serpent. He exhales quickly, as if He is about to choke, and He takes several agitated steps backward. I start to rise, but Nettle's hand on my tunic pulls me down again.

Lord Banquo looks at Him. "Good sir, why do you start and seem to fear things that sound so fair?"

But He takes several steps away till He is just a blurred shape in the clearing. He turns His back on us, leaning a shoulder against one of the standing stones.

We have frightened Him. I do not know why, but we have frightened Him! I want to leap to my feet and do a little jig. I like this power to frighten people.

Lord Banquo studies Him for a moment and then turns back to us. "Are you fantastical, or are you just what you seem?" He reaches into his purse and tosses some coins on the ground. "You foretell great things for my partner. Now look into the seeds of time and say what fortune you see for me?"

Mad Helga says, "Hail."

"Hail," says Nettle.

I repeat, "Hail."

"Lesser than Macbeth and greater," says Mad Helga, speaking in her familiar riddling way.

"Not so happy yet much happier," says Nettle.

I glance at Him standing by the great stone, and I pitch my voice loud enough for Him to hear, even though I direct my words to Lord Banquo. "You shall father kings, though you will not be one."

At these words, He jerks around and stares at me. In the pale shadows of the mist, I cannot make out His expression, but His body is stiff and tight as an archer's arm. Clearly He does not want Lord Banquo to father kings.

Mad Helga says, "So all hail, Macbeth and Banquo."

"Banquo and Macbeth, all hail."

As they speak, He strides across the clearing till He is right beside me. *I am your death,* I think, *and you know it not.* Yet I still do not know how I am to kill Him. Is this the moment for me to snake the dagger out of my girdle? Surely not—He is safe in His armor. But—

He shakes my shoulders so that my head flops back and forth. "Stop, you imperfect speakers. Tell me more! Since my father's death, I am indeed Thane of Glamis. But the Thane of Cawdor is still living, a healthy gentleman. And to be king is no more believable than 'tis for me to be Thane of Cawdor."

I give a nervous laugh, and He pushes me away. I collapse to the ground, and He takes a step back as if He is looking at something foul. "Tell me," He thunders, "from what power do you get this strange knowledge?"

Out of the corner of my eye, I see Mad Helga melting back into the mist. Nettle makes a little beckoning hand gesture to me, and then she, too, begins to fade backward out of sight.

His voice grows louder. "Tell me why in this deserted place do you stop us to pour the wine of strange prophecy into our ears?"

Lord Banquo says, "My lord—"

As soon as He turns to look at Lord Banquo, I scrabble to my feet and bolt like a hare back into the cover of the trees. The mist erases all sight, but I can hear the voices of the two men like lost souls.

"Tell me!" He shouts. "I command you to tell me!"

I hear Lord Banquo's soothing tones. "The earth has bubbles just as the water does, and these creatures are those earth bubbles."

A hand falls on my shoulder, and I leap, stifling a shriek. It is Nettle. "'Tis time to go," she whispers.

I am stunned. "Go? But we've done nothing. We mumble a few words, and then we fade into the trees? Nettle, 'tis not the revenge I intended. We have not even struck one blow—"

"We have struck a blow," she whispers. "The spell has begun— the spell that will lead to His death."

His death . . . and mine.

TWENTY-FIVE

THEN WE HEAR mist-muffled hoofbeats, and we melt farther back into the trees. I want to creep back and spy, but Nettle warns me that this could unravel what we have done. "Leave it, child. The baker who checks his cakes too often in the oven will end up with naught but flatbread. Spells need time to ferment and grow."

"But, Nettle, I don't understand. How will this all work to destroy—"

"Leave it, Gilly. Press too much, and you will crumble our gains."

I am not sure I believe her, but 'twould be foolish to take the chance.

"So what do we do now?" I ask.

"We go home," Nettle says.

"Home!" *Home? Creep home like thwarted grave robbers? Like whipped hounds?* I am outraged. "If we go home, we will not see the spell unfold."

" 'Twill matter not a jot whether we see it or no. The spell will unwind just the same. Dawn comes for both the sleeper and watcher alike. We need not be its witness."

"But I want to witness it," I protest. "'Tis my revenge. 'Twill matter little if I am not there to see it."

"Leave it, girl!" Nettle blows out her breath in a cross little puff. "All has been set in motion. You need do no more. So let us go home. There is plenty at home that needs our tending."

"No! This is my revenge, and I must bear witness."

"Listen to yourself, Gilly! You wanted him destroyed. What we have done will destroy him—'less your future meddling gets in the way of our spell."

"'Tis not enough for it to happen unseen. I must see it with my own eyes."

"'Tis a sickness, 'tis, child. Leave it be."

"No! If this middle-mash that we just muttered is indeed revenge, then 'twill not come full circle until I witness all. Unless I am present, His destruction will be incomplete."

We argue for a long time, until Nettle finally throws up her hands. "'Tis a fiend I have nursed in my hut and not a human child. Always I have had my suspicions that you have no heart, and now—"

"Let her go," Mad Helga says. "She has bewitched herself with her dreams of revenge, and there is naught you can do to break the spell."

Nettle does not looked pleased. "Go, then, you changeling, you unnatural child. Your revenge sickness is much beyond my arts to cure."

My heart warbles with joy. *I can see the spell run out. I can see His destruction.* And so it is decided. Nettle and Mad Helga will return to their hut while I return to His castle.

"Go due west," Mad Helga instructs me. "You will pass through this forest and find yourself at the sea. Follow the shore for the better part of a day, and you will arrive just to the northeast of Inverness Castle."

As we part, it hurts my heart to see how small and thin the two women look as they disappear into the swirls of mist, more like twigs wrapped in rags than living women.

But I am drawn back to Him like a starving stoat who smells the blood of a dying pig. As I travel westwards, however, the voice of doubt begins to chatter in my ear. I begin to lose faith in Nettle's spell. *Was that a true spell, or just a show to quiet me and make me leave off my quest? Why did I ever trust those women? Indeed, it was no spell at all. He comes into our grasp, and all we do is mumble nonsense as if all our wits had gone begging.*

Though it is now nearing summer, the air is chilly. I pull my wrappings tightly around me. *My life is an arrow, and its target is his death. My life is an arrow—*

Then I stumble over a rock and find myself face-to-face with the sea.

This is, of course, not my first glimpse of the sea. At Inverness when the wind blew south, I could hear the sea calling, and from the top of the castle walls I could spot its broad gray waters. But the sea at Inverness is just the mouth of the sea, not these wild, roiling waves. The air here smells of salt and dampness and a dark, vegetable smell that I cannot name. The beat of the waters against the shore is like the beat of my heart.

Awestruck, I sit down and watch.

AFTER A WHILE, I force myself to stand up and walk along the shore. I cannot peel my eyes away from the marvel that is the sea. How wondrous it would be to ride a ship far out on those unknown waters. I do think that in this afternoon if a ship were to sail up and invite me to board, I would cast aside this whole revenge business.

Coward! I chide myself. *Hen-heart! Faithless of purpose!*

No, I will follow my course to its bloody end . . . But it would have been glorious to sail across the sea.

I fear I might come to His castle too late to witness His death, so I keep walking well past the coming of the dark, even though dark comes late in the summertime. My belly aches from hunger, and my body aches from tiredness. My eyes feel scratchy, but I will not let myself rest. At one point I fall asleep walking and topple to the ground. I lie for a moment, longing to stay there, but then I take a deep breath and push myself upward.

I continue to plod onward, although my steps grow slower and slower. I start to weave and stagger like one who has sipped too much ale.

Then at about the fifth hour of the night, I see a fire ahead.

It is not safe to seek out that fire. I must stay far away from strangers. Strangers mean danger or even death.

But something within me whispers, *Still, it would be good to be warm.*

Castle life has made me too soft. *I will not move toward that fire. I will not move toward the fire—*

Yet my traitor feet keep carrying me nearer and nearer.

Then someone grabs my arm, and a knife blade is pressed to my throat.

A man's voice asks, "Where do you fancy you are going, peasant boy?"

I make my voice meek. "Please, great lord, please, don't hurt a peasant boy. What harm can a peasant boy do to your—"

Then as soon as I feel him loosen his grip, I push clear of his grasp and run. He grabs my wrap, and I twist free of it. A piece of sea-drift wood lies on the ground, and I pick it up to fight with. The teachings of the Master of Arms come back into my head, and I thrust and parry. I see my opponent is a peasant, and I pray he is not trained in swordcraft.

I soon see he is indeed skillful, but I am younger and smaller, which makes me more agile. I silently thank the Master of Arms for teaching me so many stratagems and countermoves. I hold my own, but I begin to lose faith that I can get out of this fight without hurt. This man is a much tougher opponent than young Fleance.

A crowd begins to grow around us. They know the man who fights with me, and they toss out good-natured taunts at him.

"Be you getting soft, Padric, that you cannot overcome this wisp of a boy?"

"Padric, do you need to give over and have us send a serving maid in to finish off this intruder?"

"Padric, 'stead of taking you to battle with him, our lord might do better putting you in charge of fighting off kitty cats and such if this be all the better you can fight."

Fortunately their jokes and japes makes him increasingly angry. As he grows more angry, he gets clumsy. Now not only do I hold my own, but I begin to show off a little, using some of the fancier moves that I learned.

Then a man's voice, used to command, breaks through the jeers and teasing of the crowd. "Enough!"

Instantly the crowd pulls back, and my opponent drops his knife and steps back. A sturdy man with dark curly hair steps between us. He is dressed like a noble. "What is this coil?" he demands. "You have awakened my children and my wife."

My opponent drops to one knee before him. "I beg pardon, sire. This peasant lad was sneaking up on us."

The curly-haired man looks me over, then says in a tone that contains a thread of amusement, "I do not think a single peasant lad can do us much harm." He takes a step closer to me, but I will not kneel. "Can you, young cub? Do you intend us harm?"

"I can knock this fat fool to the ground!" I announce. I swipe my stick at the peasant. Startled, my opponent topples over onto the sand. The crowd roars with laughter.

But I have no time to savor my triumph. Before I know what is happening, my stick is snatched from my grip and I find myself on my back on the ground, a sword tip pressing against my chest. The curly-haired man stands over me. "Sometimes 'tis necessary to cuff cubs for their own good. Call peace, lad, and let us have no more fighting."

I grumble, "I could have beaten him."

The curly-haired man laughs. "In faith, I think you could have, young wolf cub. So we owe you a forfeit. Come to the fire and have some mutton stew. Let that and a warm place by the fire be your forfeit tonight."

The man I fought starts to speak, but the curly-haired man waves him aside.

I stumble to my feet. "I should not tarry. I must reach Inverness Castle . . ." My voice trails to silence as I cast a longing look toward the fire. The thought of food sends a mating call to my traitor stomach. I try not to think of how good hot stew would taste.

"Cub, so must I, but you will never reach the castle tonight. The mist grows as thick as the vapor from hell's mouth, and the stars are blown out. Stay here tonight, and tomorrow you may ride with me and my men to Inverness."

I look at him with more interest, knowing he is headed to His castle. I cannot make out this man's features in the dark, but he seems no more than thirty. Surely he is not one of the castle's men at arms—he seems a great lord in his own right. I ask, "What business have you there" —I quickly add— "sire?"

"A strange peasant boy—to quiz a lord."

I am torn between my need to make my peasant guise believable and my desire to find out the information. I hesitate, unsure of what to do.

But the man says, "And a strange peasant boy to be out in the wood so late at night. I thought all peasants were snug in their cottages by vespers. Let me pose the question—what are you doing out abroad so untimely?"

I cast about in my mind for an answer, but I am saved by a lady's voice.

"Let the lad be, my lord." A young woman appears. She is small—shorter than I—and slender as a wand except for her swollen belly. Her hair falls down to her waist without the covering usually worn by married noble ladies. Her voice is sweet and gentle. "The poor lad looks as starved as a wizard's cat. I warrant his tongue will flap more readily after he has a good measure of mutton stew in his belly. Come to the fire, lad. I've already ladled up your portion."

I follow her to the fire. The members of the crowd drift back to their bedding, leaving me alone with the lady and the lord. In the light of the fire, I see that she is only in her late teens or early twenties. She has a dainty fairy quality about her, like a willow wand turned into a princess. I have never seen such a delicate lady, all spun sugar and silk, except for her great lump of a belly that bulges with a child soon to be born. Never have I felt so scruffy and awkward.

" 'Tis best you begin with some broth. Drink this, and then I will fill the bowl with the good meat." She hands me a bowl of stew, and I begin to sip the savory, thick broth. The curly-haired man gives her shoulders a little squeeze, and then he settles down by the fire and begins to polish a dagger. She sinks down on a pile of skins beside him. They both watch me eat. Then I see we are not alone at the fire. A boy of perhaps six summers clings to the lady's skirts. In the flicker of the firelight, next to her feet, a pile of sheepskins are made into a bed. Snuggled together like sleeping fledglings in that cozy nest are a little girl of about four, a boy a little younger, and a baby too small to be walking.

"No one will hurt you here, lad," the lady says. "Eat your fill."

I finish my bowl and shyly hold it out for more. She ladles up another portion, this one rich with bits of onion and meat, but before I start to eat it, she takes my chin in her hand and turns my face up to hers. She studies it as if it were a map to a secret treasure. She hands the bowl to me, but looks troubled.

"Eat, child, and then I think we should have a talk."

I try to eat daintily, but after a few bites, I start wolfing the food. Out of the corner of my eye, I see the lady whisper to the man, and they stroll down to the sea, her hand wrapped around his arm.

As I slurp down the hot stew, a child's voice pipes up, "You eat like our dog Trey."

The oldest little boy is staring at me in the peculiar way small children stare.

His voice is not critical, but I feel myself flush.

He adds, "Do you always eat like that, or are you just very, very hungry?"

"I am very hungry," I say.

He nods, pleased to be right. "We are on our way home. We have been staying with my mother's brother, but a messenger from my father came to say that our home is safe again, so we rode to meet my father. We are camping here tonight. Tomorrow my father must go to wait upon the king, and my mother and brothers and sister and I will go home. It will take us four days."

I nod, my mouth full of food. He smiles at me. "You must be very brave to travel by yourself through the woods. My little sister would be too frightened to travel through the woods by herself, but I daresay I would be able to do it. Mother doesn't let me travel anywhere by myself, but if she did, I would be brave enough to travel through the woods as you have done. I think my mother would be frightened as well, but I would protect her."

I nod again.

He says, "I saw you fighting with old Padric. I would like to learn to fight with a stick the way you did. Can you teach me?"

My belly feels full, and I smile at him. "It takes a lot of practice."

"I am very good at practicing. Will you teach me?"

My smile grows broader. "I do not think there is time to teach it tonight."

The lad draws himself tall with offended dignity. "I did not mean tonight. But you will be coming with us, will you not?"

The lady walks back up to the fire and stands behind the small boy. Her fingers ruffle his curls. "Has my little orator been chewing your ears off?" She bends awkwardly—because of her swelling belly—and plants a quick kiss on the top of his head.

The boy says indignantly, "I do not chew ears!"

She smiles fondly. "Run to Papa, my little monkey." To me she says, "Would you care for another bowl of stew?"

I look longingly toward the cauldron on the fire, but I do not want to seem greedy.

The boy says, "We were having a very good talk, this boy and I. I do not wish to run to Papa."

"Ninian, there are sweetmeats in my satchel by the fire. I thought perhaps you would take one to your papa—and have one yourself. But if you would rather that I wake your sister and send them with her—"

The boy stands up. "I believe this boy and I have finished our conversation. I also believe Papa is longing for a sweetmeat." He bows to me. "We will talk again later, you and I." He gives me a hard look as if we share a secret.

His mother holds out three sweetmeats. "Give one to our guest, Ninian." He takes them and carefully hands one to me. I bite into it, a chewy cloud with a faint flavor of almonds. Then Ninian races off into the darkness beyond the fire. The lady watches him go with a fond expression on her face. When he is out of sight, she turns to me.

"He is a bright lad, is he not? Already Father Ralf has taught him some of his letters. His father and I—we cannot read. My lord has no interest in such matters—monk's broth, he calls it. As for me, my father believed that teaching a girl to read was like teaching a pig to dance. But my son is so quick. When his sister is a little older, she will be taught to read, too." She smiles at her sleeping daughter, then looks at me. "Can you read?"

Her words catch me off guard. I answer cautiously, "Yes, I—I mean—a bit. I have picked up a bit of—"

"So your father did not object to a girl's learning to read?"

"No, he—" I catch myself and change my course. "I mean, since I was a lad—am a lad—I am sure he—"

"My girl," she says softly, "we need to have a talk."

TWENTY-SIX

I DO NOT KNOW what to say. No one else has seen through my disguise. *How can she tell I am a girl?* I feel unprotected. I blurt out, "My lady, this is foolish talk. I am not a girl. I am—"

The lady puts a hand on the small of her back and stretches. "May I sit down? This little one inside me will be a warrior like his father—he kicks and pulls so." She lowers herself awkwardly to sit next to me. "My favorite sister, Nerida—the eldest of us all—she wanted to be a boy. 'Boys have a better time of it,' she said. 'Boys get to see the world.' Poor Nerida. She was married at twelve to a lord who had already survived three wives and sixty summers. Then in less than two years, she died in childbirth."

I say nothing but continue to regard her, transfixed. Could I see myself, I am certain I look like a frozen rabbit.

She continues in her soft voice. "Me, I am quite content to be a woman. I like fine dresses and having my hair combed and threaded with jewels. I was so happy to be married—and to be married to the finest man in all Scotland. After Nerida's death, my father was afraid that his daughters might be poor breeding stock, but I am a few days short of my twentieth year and all four of my children have lived."

She gives a little laugh. "Sometimes I believe I am the most fortunate of all women. Oh, I pout when my lord has to go off to one of these endless wars, but he always brings me a pretty gift when he comes home, so I have no cause for complaint."

I say bitterly, "Then you have indeed been fortunate, lady."

She catches my tone, and she lowers her eyes. "Indeed, 'tis true." She lowers her voice. "I know I am a silly woman, but even I can understand that 'tis safer for a girl alone in the world to wear the weeds of a man. Especially a woman of gentle birth."

I am uneasy, but I choose to bluff it through. "I do not take your meaning, lady. While I agree that it might be a hard life for a girl alone—"

She pats my hand. "I will not reveal your secret, if that is your wish."

I cannot decide if it is safe to trust her, but I do not have any other choice.

"Only," she says, "I must tell my lord. I never have secrets from him. But will tell no one else."

I quickly ask, "Who will your lord tell?"

She laughs, a light trilling laugh like a southern bird. "My lord is the most silent of men when it comes to talk of other folk. When he returns home from King Duncan's court, I beg him to tell me what this lady was wearing and how that lord fared. But my lord merely wrinkles his brow and tries to remember if these folk were even there. My lord will talk of his children and battles, his land and his king, but he has no conversation beyond these four subjects."

For several minutes we sit silent, watching the fire. Then I ask, "How did you know, lady?"

"To say true, I am not quite sure how I know. But I am sure of what I know." She sighs. " I was very fond of my sister, Nerida. She had the heart of an eagle." She pushes her hair back from her face. "Sometimes I wish she had indeed disguised herself in male garb and run away the night before her wedding. Perhaps she would be alive today." She sighs again and shakes her hair back. "But 'tis foolish to question God's will. Nevertheless, there are times I miss her fiercely." She smiles at me. "There is something about you that reminds me of Nerida."

This lady is indeed silly. She is pampered and soft, but still I find I like her. I ask, "Will you keep my secret?"

"If 'tis your wish, I will keep it to the grave."

She interrupts my thanks with "But be wary of disguises, lass. A person begins by wearing the disguise, but far too soon 'tis disguise that begins to wear the person."

All I can think to say in reply is, "My condolences, lady, on the loss of your sister."

She looks up at the sky. The wind has blown the mist so that a few patches of stars appear. "'Tis very late. I must bring my son and my husband back to the fire so they can get some sleep. 'Twill be hard to see my lord leave again, but I know he will soon be home with us."

I eye her rounded belly and offer to fetch them for her.

She thanks me, but adds, "In return for my promise to keep your secret, I would ask something of you."

I tense myself against her request, but it takes me by surprise.

"Come with me to Fife," she begs.

"Fife?" I cast about in my mind, trying to discover where I have heard mention of Fife.

She nods. "Fife. My husband's home."

Then I remember. Back at His castle, He talked of Fife and its feckless lord when I was curled in the chest. *So this is the wife of that man who stayed away from the war, even when it threatened his own lands.*

The lady continues, "I will give you fine gowns, and you can be a girl again. Fife is the loveliest place on earth. So many beautiful trees and flowers—my lord has made me a swing in the orchard and you can swing nearly up to the sky. My nurse is old, so she would be glad of help with the children. Since you can read, you can tutor my sons and daughter. You and I can talk and play music, and when my lord is at home, we will have such dances and revelry. I will find you a fine, strong young husband." She smiles mischievously, and a dimple dances in her cheek. "If you wish, you can even teach my son to fight with a stick."

A picture swims unbidden into my mind. I see myself at Fife— wearing a fine blue silken dress. My hair is long and hangs down my back. The lady's children scamper around my legs, and we play together. Then the lady, carrying a fifth babe, walks up and joins us. We all stroll through a beautiful garden to a tree in an orchard. The lady motions for me to sit in the swing. The oldest boy starts to push the swing, and I swoop higher and higher. Suddenly my swing is seized and lowered to the ground. I turn around. A handsome young lord stands there. He helps me rise to my feet, and then he seizes me in an intense embrace. And then I pull back to smile at him—

The face of the handsome young lord dissolves into the face of Him, the man I seek to destroy.

"I cannot, lady."

"Can Not is the brother to Will Not," the lady replies.

I make my voice as hard as granite. "Then I *will* not."

The lady lifts a hand to silence me. "You are tired. Do not answer yet. We are both tired. Tomorrow, when the mist has lifted, give me your answer."

We hear her son and husband approaching. The little boy is prat-tling about a large spider he saw at his uncle's castle. The lady leans toward me and says, "Quickly, before my husband gets here, will you not tell me your true name?"

"My name is Gilly."

"Is that your true name?"

I repeat, "My name is Gilly."

She attacks from another direction. "I know you are not a peas-ant. Will you not—at the least—tell me your station?"

I shake my head.

Then her lord runs up and pulls her to her feet. He sweeps her into his arms and gives her a fierce hug. Their son dances around them, laughing, and his laughter wakes up his sister, who sleepily demands to know what is going on.

Envy twists my belly so much that it aches.

I slip away, down to the servants' fire, and find a place to lie down. I close my eyes and try to sleep. *I am at the end of my plan,* I tell myself. *Soon He will be destroyed.*

But my brain, like Judas in a castle, whispers, *You can turn back. These schemes of revenge are but the play-dreams of an angry child. In this world of flesh and stone, there is no way that one lone lass can bring down the most powerful warrior in all Scotland.*

My heart, too, sings out its longings to go with the lady to Fife and be a girl again. I'll have naught to worry about other than simple, homely amusements.

It takes all of my willpower to hush my brain and heart. *I must take my revenge,* I whisper over and over as I wait to fall asleep. *I will take my revenge. I have made my life an arrow. . . .*

But when I finally sleep I dream I am swinging back and forth in a soft, green, flowered land.

TWENTY-SEVEN

In the morning the lady asks me again to join her at her castle at Fife.

"I cannot," I say. "There is something I must do first."

"Join us after you have finished your task," she says.

I do not tell her that I do not expect to survive my task.

Her husband is anxious to be off. "Do not wake the little chicks, my lovely hen," he tells the lady. "'Twill break my heart to say farewell to them. Let me kiss them as they sleep."

After he kisses each babe, he holds his lady tight and whispers to her. I stand with the five or six men at arms who will be riding with us. The rest of the company is to travel with the lady and her babes to their home at Fife.

Finally the curly-haired man pulls apart from his wife. "Would that I did not have to go to my king. I have been away so long of late that I would not desert you now."

"Go," she says laughing, but there are tears in her eyes. "The sooner you go, the sooner you will return to us."

He signals us to mount our horses, and we ride away. I see that his eyes, too, are filled with tears.

It is a marvel how swiftly the miles fly by when you travel on horseback. I had forgotten how free and glorious it feels to fly across the countryside when you're perched atop a horse. The men talk among themselves, and I ride behind them and listen. I learn that the curly-haired man in charge is Lord Macduff. Once or twice he throws me looks brimful of amusement, and I gather his lady has revealed my secret to him, but he says naught about it.

I soon adjust to the bumping of the horse ride, and my mind begins to worry about my plan for revenge.

I do not see how our spell can work, but since I have no other plan, I try to put my faith in it. It is true that Nettle and Mad Helga have never lied to me. *So let their spell work. Let their spell work.*

For all that, my new longings are wasps that flit in and out of my mind. I keep seeing myself in a red silk gown, sweeping up and down the corridors of a castle, a handsome warrior at my side, his strong warm fingers resting on my waist.

I have made my life an arrow—

I see myself playing hide and seek with the laughing children—

I have made my life a dagger—

—or picking apples while a strong, handsome warrior holds my ladder steady.

No!

I wipe these pictures from my mind. I force myself to see Him—to see sword after sword being thrust into His body. I picture myself watching, and then I picture myself picking up a sword and moving toward Him—the blood from the other wounds spattering my face and tunic—

I click my heels into the horse and gallop toward Inverness Castle.

On the way, I decide that the Lord of Fife, Macduff, is a good match for his openhearted lady. He seems friendly and as transparent as water. In the middle of the afternoon we finally reach Inverness. Lord Macduff parts from me at the gates of the castle, explaining that he and his men do not come into the castle with me.

They are to lodge at a nearby abbey to leave room for the king and his great company in the castle chambers.

The gates are closed, so I bang the heavy knocker until they jerk open. The unkempt, stinking porter stands there, barring my way. "Why, 'tis the sore-licking, donkey-breath, castle-fleeing slug-heart of a brother to the leak-eyed halfwit who helps in the kitchen. Come to lap tongue 'gainst the shoes of the king, did you?" The breath that pours out from his huge mouth feels as black as the stubs of his few rotting teeth.

"I have returned. I must go to the kitchen."

He roars with laughter till he chokes. Only after he has coughed up a mouthful of black bile does he say, "So you think you can just amble up, pretty as you please, and I will let you in? You pox-riddled pup, is that your game?"

"I need to enter." *By the bones of all the saints, I did not come this far to be turned away at the gates.*

His eyes glitter like pools of blood in the moonlight. "'Twill make Master Cook as angry as a tipsy hornet to have you return." He spits. "'Tis a fair thought. Now that the nation is at peace, let us have battle in the kitchen. So enter, miscreant. Brew us some discord along with your soups."

He steps aside, and I run through the courtyard to the kitchen.

Never have I seen such a bustle in the kitchen. Many lads I have never seen before hop about with bowls and pitchers. I see Brude hunched over a table, stuffing dried dates and apricots into a half-roasted goose. Master Cook stands stirring a cauldron over the fire, his face anxious. The room is filled with the smells of roasted meat and spices.

I see Pod sitting on a sack, plucking the feathers from a swan. There is a trickle of blood running down the swan's neck onto his legs. The blood against the white feathers is an ugly sight. I feel such a rush of fondness toward him that I am almost dizzy.

Pod looks up. He sees me. At first he looks stunned, and then joy spreads across his face like melted butter.

"Gilly! Gilly! You've come back!"

He lets the swan tumble to the earthen floor and runs to me and hugs me so tight I can barely breathe. I feel uncomfortable. It is not safe to care this much about him. Still I thump him on the back a few times, and then stand there, waiting for him to let go. His shouts attract the attention of the workers in the kitchen. The other workers look up at us and start to whisper among themselves. Master Cook sees me. He looks more oily than ever with fat drops of sweat on his forehead and cheeks. He hands his spoon to a nearby lad, and then he marches over to where I stand by the door.

"So the prodigal son comes home, no doubt expecting us to kill the fatted calf for him." He calls out, "Brude! Brude!"

Brude looks up and grins. His grin is not pleasant. "Yes, sir?"

"Fetch the fatted calf! Gilly has deigned to come back to us."

I feel my cheeks grow red, but I stand my ground.

"Nay, why stop at a calf? Fetch the whole herd! This filthy urchin that I took in from the goodness in my heart, from my unquenchable font of human kindness—what does he do to repay my generosity? Does he not take off without so much as a by your leave, without so much as a begging your pardon—"

"Sir, I do beg your—"

"Too late! Too late!" He puts his hands on his hip. "So why have you come, swine? Surely you do not expect us to take you back. Even our Savior would not expect such forgiveness—"

Then I see Lisette move from the fireplace to stand next to Master Cook. I want to run to her, to hug her, to smell the scent of sugar and spices that cling to her clothes. But I stay back. I was wrong to leave her without a word. She probably hates me now. I don't want to meet her eyes, but I force my chin to raise up, and I study her face but I cannot read her reaction. For a moment she studies me, as if deciding how to respond to my return, and then she turns to Master Cook. "Ah, Master Aswald," she says in her warm voice with its thread of an accent, "of a certainty, this little one was wrong to go without taking leave of you. That much is certain. But I gave him permission to go."

My eyes open wide in amazement. She is lying. I told no one when I left. She seems to be helping me, but I do not understand. I have done nothing to earn this kindness. Can it be that she still cares for me, even after I have betrayed her trust?

Lisette wipes her hands on her apron. "Master Aswald, there was a problem in the family, and Gilly had to depart quickly."

Master Cook frowns. "I thought he had no family except this brother here."

I say quickly, " 'Twas an uncle on my father's side."

Master Cook looks unconvinced so I add, "Twice removed!"

Master Cook continues to look unconvinced.

" 'Twas an accident with an oxcart," I say.

"I do not think—" Master Cook begins.

Lisette interrupts him. "Yes, the lad was wrong, very wrong, but this can be sorted out later. With the preparations for tonight's feast, we have much to do, and this naughty boy knows his way around the kitchen and is quick with his hands. Let him help out tonight, and in the morning you can take him to task. The more able workers you have, the more you can do to show off your very great art."

Master Cook bites his lip, considering her words. Then he glares at me and shouts, "You can begin by scrubbing out those pots."

He gestures to a mountain of filthy pots, platters, and serving ware.

Brude says, "You are not going to take that gangly-legged village snipe—"

"Do not question my authority!" Master Cook thunders. He gives Brude a clout on the head. The other kitchen lads elbow each other and snicker. Master Cook shoots me a poisonous look. "And you, goose grease that you are, if you have indeed come back to work, get to work."

I fill my arms with a pile of crockery and stalk out to the scullery shed.

As THE AFTERNOON PASSES, I cannot get ahead in my work. Every time I finish an armload of pots, I return to the kitchen to find two armloads waiting. I use sand on the roasting pans, but I draw bucket after bucket of water from the well in which to dunk the bowls and pitchers. The day grows unpleasantly warm. My tunic is soaked with sweat and dishwater, and my arms and legs grow spattered with grease. Once Pod sneaks out to help me, but Brude comes looking for him and marches him back to the kitchen to peel onions. Partway through the afternoon, Lisette wanders in and hands me a tankard of ale. I feel very shy around her. I am ashamed of leaving her the way I did, and I am eager to make her like me again.

"Thank you," I say.

Lisette snorts. "You—I have not forgiven. I have no respect for you. But that little one in the kitchen, your little brother—for him I would do much. And he loves you. Each night you were gone, he cried himself to sleep. Your behavior has been abominable. Of a certainty, you are a child of the devil. But that little one, he is an angel child, and so I convince Master Aswald to take you back."

I will not let her see how much I care about her opinion of me. In this world, caring makes you weak. So I keep my voice light. "Still, I say 'twas kind of—"

Lisette leans close. Her look is threatening. "But should you leave again like that—farewell. Adieu! I will not take you back again." I can tell she means this.

She starts to leave. I call out quickly, "Lisette—wait!"

She turns back. She folds her arms across her broad chest. "I have much work to do."

"Lisette, I—I heard talk—when I was traveling. I heard"—I fumble for acceptable words—"a prediction that his lordship is poised on the edge of ruin. And yet the king comes here—but if He is facing His ruin—"

Lisette gives a snort. "Then you heard lies, for his lordship has never been more honored than he is tonight."

She leaves. I am so confused and angry. *I go to all the trouble to bring Mad Helga three pieces of His heart, we travel for more than a seven-night to confront Him with our strange babble, Nettle says she sees His doom, and what is the outcome? Our king rewards Him and honors*

Him with a visit. I bang my hand against a bucket until my hand is sore. "God rot them! Damn them! May their souls rot in hell."

BY THE END of the afternoon, my fingers are raw from the work. My head keeps drumming the refrain, *It can't be. We cast a spell, and He ends up with more honor than before.*

I picture Nettle and Mad Helga gasping with thirst, and I stand there with a pitcher of water, refusing to give them a drink. I picture them starving, reaching their skinny arms toward me, imploring food, and I hold the haunch of roasted pork just out of their reach. I picture them drowning in the brook, begging me to save them, and I stand on the bank and laugh.

The dreadful notion hits me: *I must think of a new plan.*

I slip my fingers into my girdle to touch my dagger to give me courage, and my fingers pull out a small packet of ground herbs securely wrapped in a scrap of cloth. For a moment I cannot think what this is, and then I remember. The night before we left the hut to go north, I filched this mixture from Nettle's store of herbs. Nettle kept this particular compound in a small sealed clay jar. She used it only for those who were mad and had strange visions. "Sometimes," she used to say, "when a soul is far gone in madness and naught else can work, this concoction can bring that soul home again." I reached out a finger to sample the powder, but Nettle slapped my finger away. "'Tis not for the sensible. For one who is not mad, in small doses, these herbs play strange tricks on the mind. In larger doses, belly cramps and convulsions and screams that the devils are eating you alive."

An idea begins to curl around my brain. *Perhaps I can find a way to drop these herbs into His food. Surely, if He begins to rant and roll on the ground with belly cramps in the presence of the king, surely this will lead to His disgrace. Can there be a way,* I wonder, *to sneak into the banquet hall tonight and sprinkle some in his soup or sauce—*

"I crave your pardon!"

My mouth falls open in surprise.

TWENTY-EIGHT

A YOUNG NOBLEMAN stands in the doorway to the scullery shed. He is the most handsome young man I have ever seen. He is tall and slender and dressed in silken clothes of deep green and gold. His hair, too, is silken, the color of a roasted chestnut. His beautiful head is large for his body, but it has a finely drawn face with heavy-lidded eyes and a rosy mouth. It is a face that would not look amiss on the neck of Saint John in an illuminated gospel. I suddenly long to run my fingers across those heavy eyelids, to stroke that soft mouth. What would it be like to kiss that mouth? With a start, I jerk my thoughts back to the moment. I reckon the young man's age at the border of twenty. I wonder if the fine ladies at court are mad for his eyes and tender lips.

He laughs. "I throw myself on your mercy, lad. I pray you, come to my aid."

Although the sight of him makes me a little breathless—and very aware of my filthy appearance—I tilt my chin up boldly and make my voice stern. "And what business does a fine lord like yourself have in the kitchen quarters? Do you need me to carry a message for you?"

He laughs again. "'Tis just my stomach is devilishly empty. I was hoping to beg some bread, a slice of cheese or dried meat—anything."

"This is the scullery, sire. Not the pantry. Not the kitchen. Those are the places to find food." I frown. "I do not know why you seek food now. There will be a huge feast tonight—for the king, you know."

The corners of his mouth turn down, but his eyes continue to laugh. "I told my stomach as much, but it—cheeky beggar that it is—whines that it cannot wait that long."

I want to smile back, but I will my face to stay stern. "In any case, I cannot help you here. Go to the kitchen if you wish to find food."

He gives a loud sigh—so loud that I suspect him of playacting. "I did venture as far as the kitchen door, but inside was such a fury of cooking that I did not have the courage to proceed." He shakes his head. More playacting. "In this last war I learned that I do not fear to face armed soldiers, but to face an angry cook—that heroic feat is beyond me."

I refuse to respond to his foolery, although something deep inside me is laughing. "The kitchen workers have been toiling since sunup to prepare the feast. There's no one free to fix you a private meal."

I make a great show of emptying a bucket of dirty water out the door. He goes down on one knee. "Lad, I throw myself on your mercy. I do not ask that anyone wait on me. Just point me to a loaf of bread or a wheel of cheese." He pulls a knife out of his sheath. "See. I have my carving knife all whetted and ready. Surely you would not deny a starving man!"

My smile—a traitor to my will—shows itself on my face.

He smiles back. "I ask only that you guide me through the labyrinth of the kitchen to the grail of cheese at its center."

Now I make a great show of sighing loudly. "I must fetch more water at the well. Since we'll be right by the kitchen door, 'twill be not a very hard task for me to show you where the cheese is kept. But mind you, do not get in the way of the cooks."

"You are a veritable prince among the kitchen boys." He picks up the second bucket. "At least I can work for my food."

I thereupon hold out the first bucket to him. He looks surprised, and then he takes it with a laugh. "Lad, you are a hard taskmaster."

After directing him to leave the buckets by the well, I lead him to where the cheese is kept. I fold the cloth back enough for him to cut himself a wedge, and while he does so, I filch a small warm loaf off the baking tray. I toss it to him, and he catches it with one hand.

Several workers glance at us curiously, but no one says anything. The pace is feverish and tense in the kitchen. Already huge platters have been heaped with all manner of wondrous confections. I grow dizzy at the smell and sight of so much food, but the young man does not even notice the great bounty.

He holds his knife above the wheel of cheese. "Shall I cut you some?" he asks.

I would dearly love some cheese, but I dare not try the temper of Master Cook so I shake my head and leave the kitchen. To my surprise, the beautiful young nobleman follows me out. As I fill my buckets at the well, he munches away.

"Did you come with the king's party?" I ask him.

"That I did." He takes a bite of the bread, chews it, swallows, then says, "In fact, I follow him everywhere."

"He must have great trust in you."

He smiles as if I have said something comical. "I have been led to believe that is so." Then his face grows serious. "And I hope ever to repay that trust."

I toy with the notion of asking this young man's aid to get close enough to Him to drop my mixture of herbs in His dish, but I cannot think of how to broach my request. So I say, "You are young to be a close companion to the king. Has he known you long?"

"Since my birth."

I pick up the buckets. "Then is your father some great personage at court?"

He laughs so loud that I fear someone from the kitchen will come out to investigate. "He is indeed," he finally says.

I begin to walk back to the scullery shed. He follows me. "Is your father also here?" I ask.

He nods and takes another bite.

"Is he also close to the king?"

He nods again. "No man is closer to the king than my father."

I suspect him of boasting and exaggerating his connections in order to impress a simple kitchen lad, but before I can ask any more questions, another lord bustles up to us. He is finely dressed, although not quite as finely dressed as the young man with me. This new lord is older, perhaps Nettle's age. To my astonishment, he dips his head down and up in a bow before he speaks. "My lord, your father craves a word with you before dinner. He is in the garden with the lady of the castle. If you will follow me, Prince Malcolm, I will escort you to him."

Prince Malcolm! The king's son! I turn to him with accusation in my eye. He had no right to make sport of me that way.

Clearly unrepentant, he winks at me. "I thank you for saving my life," he says. Then he follows the other lord across the courtyard, still munching his bread and cheese.

To MY CHAGRIN, because I am in such disgrace, I am not allowed to help with serving the great feast—not even with running the platters of food to the entrance of the Great Hall. Instead I am condemned to the inferno of the scullery shed, washing and scouring through the night.

JUDGING FROM THE SOUNDS I HEAR, the feast is a merry one. And the workers in the kitchen seem jubilant about their results. After a long while, the sounds start to die down. Lisette and Pod appear in the doorway.

"I saved you some food!" Pod announces, a broad smile on his face. He holds out a napkin filled with bits of roasted meat. "I could not bring you any of the sauces. Lisette said she did not think the napkin would take kindly to them, but the meat is very good even on its own." He lays the napkin down on the table on which the clean dishware is stacked. I am touched by his thoughtfulness.

Lisette whisks two speckled buns and a handful of broken wafers out of her pocket and places this bounty next to the napkin.

"Not even Master Aswald would forbid you from eating."

I doubt her, but later that evening, when Master Cook peeks in on me, it is clear that he is giddy with success and wine.

"They praised my cooking! Even the king himself—the king, Gilly! He said that none of his cooks can touch my way with a savory sauce! Finish the washing, lad, and tomorrow you shall begin to write down my recipes. Perhaps when I complete this, I will present a copy to the king himself!"

It is rising midnight when I finish the last dish. All is hushed in the castle. From the door of the scullery shed, I do not see any candles alight. The only light in the courtyard is my small grease lamp. I have saved Lisette's wafers and one of the buns to eat when I finish, so I perch on a tabletop and start to nibble. I am so tired I almost fall asleep in mid-bite. I wonder where I am to sleep for the fragment of night that remains. But I console myself with the thought that anyplace will serve since the night is warm although mist has been pouring into the courtyard like smoke from a green chip fire.

Then I hear a noise outside the shed.

I slide to my feet and pull out my dagger. The wafers slip to the ground, and I regret their departure. I place an upside down bowl over my lamp to cut the light and wait, my body tense. No one should be creeping around the courtyard this late at night.

A small shape appears in the door to the shed.

Fleance.

"Gilly," he whispers. "Are you indeed here?"

"I am," I whisper back and then wonder why we need to whisper.

He hobbles in. Even in the darkness I can see that one foot is bandaged with a leg splint on its shin. I lift the bowl off the lamp, and in the flickers of light I see his face and arm are bruised on the same side.

"You've come back! You've come back!" I am startled by his obvious joy. "One of the older boys spotted you crossing the courtyard, and I asked the Master of Arms, and he said he thought 'twas you! I'm so glad you've come back."

Before I can speak, he says, "Come with me to the ramparts. I need to fill in this night's information on my charts about the tides. You can help me."

He hobbles away and I am hard-pressed to keep up with the small fellow.

Perhaps Fleance is the very person to help bring me near Him so I can try Nettle's mixture of herbs.

He limps up the stairs so quickly that I am panting and wheezing by the time we reach the top.

"How long does the king stay here?" I gasp out.

He shrugs, indifferent to the doings of the people in the castle. From his belt he takes out a rolled piece of parchment.

"Find some stones to hold it down," he commands me.

I find a handful of pebbles at the base of the wall, and we anchor down the paper.

"What is this?" I ask.

He draws himself up tall and looks at me, seeming amazed. "'Tis my chart," he says. When I say nothing, he adds, "My chart of the tides."

"Chart of the tides?"

"Do you not recall?" He sounds outraged, his squeaky-growling voice more comical than ever. "I told you about it. I said that I liked being near the sea because I can note the state of the moon— whether 'tis waxing or waning, full or dark, and then I can note the state of the tides. Thus we see whether indeed the moon draws the tides or not."

He makes a little clucking sound. "'Tis a pity that the sea just over the wall is only a bay and not the sea full strength, but there is movement in the water, so—"

"Do you know Prince Malcolm?" I ask, making my voice careless.

"The king's son?" His voice does not hold much interest. "Malcolm's the one he named Prince of Cumberland, is he not?" He cranes his head back and looks at the sky. "A pox upon it! I know 'tis a cloudy night, but I had hoped that by coming up here to a higher place perhaps there would not be so many clouds. I cannot make out the moon, can you, Gilly?"

I look up, but the moon seems well shrouded against our peering eyes.

"Fleance, what does that mean, Prince of Cumberland?"

"Oh, Malcolm is to become king when his father dies, or some such nonsense. Gilly, do you think if we were to light a torch, the moon might be drawn to the light and so show herself?"

Now I am the one to lose interest. "I do not know." Then I ask, "What happened to your foot and leg?"

His gruff little voice is impatient. "The sword-stick lessons did not go well after you left." He chuckles. "But 'tis for the best. The Master of Arms says that I may not come to the lessons until I am healed. I do hope that I will be a good long time in the healing." He chuckles again. "If I had known 'twas so simple to get out of the lessons in soldiering, I would have bribed those bigger boys to beat me up many weeks since."

Suddenly he waves his arms about rapidly, then stops. "Do you think 'twill get rid of the mist if we wave our arms around?"

"No."

He gives an exasperated groan. "I hate this northern country with its eternal fogs. How will I ever figure out the patterns of moon and tide if so many nights the moon is hidden in the mist?"

"Tell me, Fleance, why does it matter, these patterns in sea and sky?"

He sounds shocked. "There are patterns in everything, Gilly. If we are to know life and understand it, we must find out the patterns beneath everything."

"But what are they good for, these patterns of yours?"

"Good for?"

"Yes, what use are they?"

"Truth does not need to be useful!" he says indignantly. "It only need be truth to matter." He lifts his head up to study the sky. "Do you think 'tis clearing up?"

Fleance has not asked where I was or what I was doing. It hits me that he is interested in the big truths, but he cares little for the small truths of individual lives. Now I do not give a peeled twig for the big truths, but the small ones interest me greatly. My present small truth is that I am damp and tired and long to go to bed.

"Give it over, lad. 'Tis impossible to spot any of your patterns in this fog that has blown up. Even the stars have been blown out. And even if there were no fog, 'tis so late that I fear the moon is down. Let's to sleep."

"Do you know, Gilly," he says, as if he is settling in for a great chat, "the Venerable Bede writes that the earth is surrounded with seven heavens? There is our world, the world of matter, surrounded by water that separates us from the heavens which is the world of spirit—"

"Right now all I care about is the world of sleep, Fleance, and that is a realm I must soon visit, else—"

"Is it not amazing, Gilly, that the seven heavens and our world are all composed out of four elements, just as you mix up foods down in the kitchen—"

"I also sleep down in the kitchen. Fleance, 'tis late and—"

"When I am a man, I shall become an alchemist and study how to put these elements together to cook up matter—how much of each element is needed, for example, to make a tree or to make gold. Then I shall write it down for all to know. I shall write the cookery book of God himself."

"Hush!" I say. "These words are dangerous. They smack of blasphemy. You could be burned as a heretic."

He hunches smaller. "'Tis true," he says in a tiny voice. "The Church of Rome does not like for us to explore such things. I have heard tell that some alchemists have been burned as witches." He sits up a little straighter. "But I do not understand why God gave us a mind if he did not—"

Heavy footfalls on the stairs make us both jump. Fleance rapidly rolls up his chart and stuffs it under his shirt.

I see the shape of a man at the top of the stairs.

"Fleance?" he calls out.

It is Lord Banquo. The pale stripes of his cloak stand out like a faint light against the darkness. I am amused by this mark of vanity in such a plain man. I drop to one knee and lower my head, praying he will not recognize me as one of the seers, the one who predicted he will father kings. I roll my eyes to the top of their sockets so I can peek out at him and Fleance.

"Not yet abed, son?"

"No, sir."

"Does your leg trouble you, boy?"

Fleance's head jerks up as if he is astonished by his father asking after him. "No, sir."

Fleance's father moves around restlessly, as if he is troubled. I do not think it is worry about his son that preys on his mind. He sighs, and then he looks all around the ramparts.

"How goes the night, boy?"

"The moon is down." I can tell he does not want his father to know about his charting and his science. Fleance continues, "I have not heard the clock."

Lord Banquo says, "The moon goes down at twelve."

"I take it 'tis later, sir," says Fleance. I can hardly believe they are father and son—they are so very different from each other.

Fleance's father pulls his sword from its sheath and tosses it to his son. "Take my sword." Fleance buckles from the weight of the great sword, and his father seems to wince. Fleance's father looks up at the sky and sighs again. "Heaven is a frugal houseman tonight, son. He has blown out all his candles." He pulls out his dagger. "Take that, too." He tosses it to Fleance, who looks lost and awkward trying to balance the two weapons. "I know your leg troubles you, but show me some of the passes the Master of Arms has taught you."

Fleance makes a few weak passes with the sword. I long to reach out and straighten his arm, but I keep my place.

Then we hear more footsteps.

"Give me my sword!"

Fleance's father moves in front of Fleance and me, his sword held out in a menacing manner. Fleance looks down at his father's dagger which is still in his hands and tosses it to the floor as if he is afraid that if he is caught with it, he will have to fight.

"Who's there?" calls out Fleance's father.

"A friend," says a heavy voice.

And then He appears at the top of the stairs.

TWENTY-NINE

HE IS CARRYING a huge silver goblet in his hand. He moves like someone who has traveled a great distance and still has many miles to go before he can take his rest.

Fleance's father says, "What, sir, not yet abed?"

Sighing, He sets his wine goblet on the stone wall of the ramparts, not half a body length from where I kneel. Then He steps away, over toward Fleance's father. My heart leaps up! God has given me this opportunity—I must not waste it. Stealthily I edge my fingers to the packet of herbs in my girdle. *Let me sprinkle this mixture into His goblet.* While these herbs will not kill Him, it will warm my heart to know I have caused Him discomfort.

The two men continue to talk. I edge myself forward ever so slowly, my eyes focused on His cup. I work the packet of herbs free, and with one hand I unwind their wrapping. I pray that night will serve as my cover and cloak my actions from view. I maneuver my body into place, right below the goblet, and let my body shield my right hand, which begins to inch up the stone wall, when the words of Fleance's father cause me to freeze. "I dreamed last night of the three weird sisters. To you they have shown some truth."

Goose bumps pop out on my arms. *They talk of me and the women.* Perhaps the tide has indeed begun to turn my way. *Please,* I pray, *please let there be some long-lasting effect. Please let our spell unfold, trickery though it be. Please, please—*

But when He responds, His words dash all my hopes.

"I think not of them," He says.

Then, to my horror, He reaches an arm out for his goblet although He continues to talk to Fleance's father. I dart my arm out quickly and shake it over His goblet, but the herb packet goes tumbling over the wall. I cannot be sure even the smallest pinch of my herbs has fallen into His drink. I fold my fingers around the goblet and offer it to Him, bending on one knee like a good serving lad. He takes it without even looking at me.

Please let some of the herb mixture have fallen in His goblet. Please let one of my schemes bear fruit. I grind my teeth together in my impatience. *Am I God's fool or plaything? Does he make sport with our hopes and lives, just for a laugh?*

Then I hear Him wish Fleance and his father good repose. They clatter down the stairs, and I am left alone with Him.

To my amazement, I feel as calm as a nun at communion. It has been so long since I first knew Him, and yet He is still as familiar as if it has been less than seven days and not more than seven years since He was last part of my life. He looks just the same—tall and strong with a loose-limbed warrior grace. He smells just the same way He used to smell on banquet days in the time before. I remember liking His smell with its hints of civet and cinnamon. If I am honest, I must admit that He has a pleasing shape, but well I know that the devil is partial to assuming attractive forms. This man beside me is worse than the devil, for the devil has no choice but to do evil, and what He did was a matter of cold-hearted choice. I study Him silently. I have no fear that He will recognize me as one of the three prophets upon the heath. He does not look at underlings. So I wait for Him to drink the doctored potion. *Please, please, let a few flakes of Nettle's herbs be floating on His wine.* Oh, it will be a banquet to my soul to see Him mad. It will be paradise indeed when I behold Him dead.

To my dismay, He sets the goblet down again on the stone battlements, not taking so much as a sip.

Then He turns to me. He says, "Go bid your mistress—when my drink is ready—she strike upon the bell."

How fate toys with me! All the trouble I took to doctor the goblet He holds in His fingers, and now He wants a different drink instead. *It is not fair! I will not let this come to pass!*

I pick up the goblet again and again go down on one knee, offering it to Him. I school my face not to show the disgust and hatred I feel, offering Him the face of spring when there is a devil in the undergrowth in my heart. "My lord, there is yet drink here. Should you not finish this one before you require another?"

He accepts the goblet and looks at it in surprise, as if He had forgotten He had brought it up with Him.

For a moment all is still. He stares at me without moving. Then He tilts His goblet to His mouth, drinking it all the way down.

My heart is a bird that takes flight—all the way through Fleance's seven heavens.

"Get to bed!" He commands me.

And I can think of no excuse to stay.

It is not until I am clattering down the stairs that I realize I will never know if the herbs have an effect, but even the thought that they *may* cause Him discomfort kindles a warming fire of hope in my breast. I float down the stairs to the kitchen. All the good sleeping places are taken, but I do not care. There is a stool by the door and I sink down beside it, folding my arms across the seat to make me a pillow. And quicker than thought, I am asleep.

I AWAKE when the stool is kicked out from under me. I fall to the floor. Master Cook towers over me.

I blink in the darkness. It is not yet dawn—it is the hour of the wolf and the other beasts that roam the night, their final hour to hunt the earth for prey. My body is stiff and sore from hunching over the stool.

"'Tis night still," I protest.

"Get you up," Master Cook says, "or you will do naught but scullery duty for the next ten years."

"'Tis not yet day."

"Our king is leaving at first light. Last night, Master Steward commanded that the king and his two chamber guards are to have tankards of ale and some cold fish upon rising." He gestures with his thumb toward the barrel of white herring. "Take it up to them."

As I puzzle out whether it is an honor or a punishment to be sent on this errand, Master Cook gives me a push toward the fish barrel. "You will do what I say, insect! Take up the food or you will be out the castle gates at first light, looking for another station in life."

I make a face but pull out a tray. Master Cook yawns loudly and settles back onto the table on which he sleeps. In the flicker of an eyelash, his snores join the chorus of snores and night noises that rumble through the kitchen. I fill three tankards with ale and plunk them down on the tray. From the barrel of white herring, I scoop out three plump fish. I pass to the bake kitchen where the loaves of bread are rising for this day's meals. I find a round loaf from last night's feast and hack off three fat slices. I plop a pickled herring on the top of each slice of bread and, balancing the tray against my hip, I light a taper from the fire. I cross the dark courtyard and climb the stairs to the Great Hall. I wind my way among the sleeping men at arms and upper servants.

As I travel, I amuse myself by imagining what might have happened when He drank the wine with the herbs that cause dark fantasies. By my reckoning, nothing much happened or else the men at arms would not be sleeping so peacefully. As far as I can tell, it has been a calm night at the castle. *But perhaps there were small madnesses of which I know naught. Perhaps He tore off all his clothing and ran round and round the ramparts, howling at the moon. At the very least, perhaps He tossed all night, tangled in knotty dreams of demons and trolls come to gnaw on His soul.*

I climb the stairs. Should I continue in a straight path, I would come to Fleance's chamber, but I veer to the side to a small bed-chamber on the left. It is an antechamber beyond which lies the largest of the guest chambers. I am sure that this is where the king sleeps.

I confess I am curious to see the king. I chuckle to think that our king takes breakfast. The noblemen and men at arms at our castle scorn breakfast, calling it a custom fit only for babes and servants. But if the king chooses to break his fast—

At the door of the antechamber, I step on an arm.

I jump back. Ale sloshes out of the tankards and onto my tray. I am worried it will soften the bread. I must deliver my food quickly or the bread will be too soggy to eat.

Now I can make out in the dim light that one of the guards lies across the doorway to the antechamber. I am surprised that he is taking his duty as guard so seriously that he feels he must sleep crossways across the threshold. I smile in spite of myself. *The fool! He takes all the trouble to sleep across the door, and then he falls so deeply asleep that anyone could sneak past him.*

I clear my throat, but the guard does not move.

With my toe I nudge his arm.

He does not move.

I toe him again and say in a soft voice, "Get you up, slugabed. I have food and drink for the king."

He does not move. I kick him with more force. "Rise, I say!"

He mutters something I cannot make out, and he rolls to the side. I smell the stale reek of old spiced wine. *He is drunk.* I know better than to try to rouse a sot. I step over him and go into the antechamber. The other guard is slumped against the far wall, his legs splayed out at odd angles. He too is soundly asleep.

"I have fish and bread for the king," I say in a loud whisper.

This second guard does not move. It is strange these sleeping guards show so little concern for their king. I nudge him with my foot. Then I kick harder.

I chuckle to myself. *Nettle must have felt this way those mornings when she could not get me out of bed in a timely fashion.*

The upper body of the second guard slides the rest of the way down the wall.

How odd these guards are so sound asleep, even if they are drunk. Odder still for both guards to be drunk on duty, even if the war is over. I feel the little hairs rise up on my arms. *Could this be a prank that Master Cook is playing on me?* As soon as I think this, I throw away the notion. Master Cook is not a man to enjoy a jest.

I step over the second guard into the main chamber. I can make out nothing but a man's shape on the bed.

"Sire?" I call out. "I am from the kitchens. I have the fish and bread you requested."

There is no answer.

I see the king lying in his bed, turned on his side. I take the liberty of moving closer. *Do not let him grow angry with me. Do not let him order me to be beaten for daring to approach too near.* The king, too, sleeps so soundly that I wonder if I should slip away without waking him. *The company feasted and drank till late into the night. It is no marvel that he plays the slugabed this morn.*

But should I slip away without delivering the breakfast, perhaps he would order me beaten for not following his commands. I wish there were someone else here to tell me what to do.

"Sire? My lord? Your majesty?"

I wrinkle my brow, considering what best to do. Then I balance the tray in one hand. With my other hand, I touch his arm.

"Your majesty?"

He still does not wake, so I give his arm a little shake.

The body of the king rolls over toward me.

The front of his nightshirt is soaked with wet blood.

THIRTY

Mᴏ ʜᴀɴᴅ ɪꜱ ɴᴏᴡ ꜱᴛɪᴄᴋʏ with blood.

My tray goes clattering to the ground. I hear the hollow ring of the tankards against the floor. My hand flies up to cover my mouth, and I feel the sticky blood on my mouth. I smell its rusty metallic odor. I jerk my hand away, and blood drips from my fingers onto the bed.

Just then I hear the sound of distant knocking.

I jerk, stumble over one of the dropped tankards, and slip on a puddle of blood, skidding to the floor. I grab the bed cover and pull myself up, making little whimpering sounds. *This cannot be happening. This is not real. Of a certainty, this is a dream and this knocking will awaken me.* But I do not wake up, and the knocking continues. I scramble out of the room, stumbling over the unconscious body of the guard at the doorway, and again falling, this time banging my knee.

I run down the stairs, through the Great Hall, dodging the sleepers there. A few of them mutter and roll over, disturbed either by the endless knocking or my running, but no one seems to wake. Then I am clattering down the stairs from the Great Hall and dashing through the courtyard to the kitchen well.

I draw up a bucket of water. I splash it onto my face, down my chest. I keep splashing my face with water until the pail is empty. Then I draw up another. This time I plunge my hands into the clean water and begin scrubbing one hand against the other, rubbing, rubbing so hard it hurts. I scrub and scrub, determined to get my hands clean of every bit of blood.

The king is dead. Someone murdered the king as he slept. And I am stained with his blood. I feel frantic with fear so I scrub harder. *Why did his guards not wake?* I empty the bucket of water. In the darkness I cannot see its color, but I am sure that the water has turned dark red with blood. I draw a third bucket. *But this is the safest castle in all Scotland. The lord of the castle is the most skillful warrior in all the country, and—*

I turn white with horror.

The king was well guarded. Who could have come so close as to stab him? My head aches, but I push my thoughts hard to squeeze sense out of them. *Few could have come here—but the lord of the castle could have. It is clear—plainer than the shine on a bald priest's pate. I know that He longs to be king. What way could bring it to pass more quickly than to kill the king when he comes visiting? But what would have made Him choose last night for His murder?*

Then my stomach flops over and I press my lips tightly together so I will not be sick. *What if it was the herbs that I put in the wine? What if the herbs turned Him into a murderer? That would mean that it was I who caused the murder of the king!* No! I did not do it. Nettle said that all the herbs will do is bring strange fantasies. *They could not make a hero a murderer and drive him to kill the king. No, they could not. Surely there is no way that the death of this poor man was my fault. Besides, He was a murderer long before He killed the king . . . if He was indeed the man who did the killing.*

I cannot bear it. All I want is to destroy Him, but the nearer I come, the farther I seem to slip away. Have I destroyed the king instead?

Then I remember that my legs slid about in the blood on the

floor, and I pour the water in the bucket over them. I rip off a corner from my tunic to use as a scrubbing cloth. I rub up and down my leg till the skin grows raw.

No, the wind blew the herbs away. The packet tumbled over the side of the ramparts. None of them fell into His cup. This is not my fault. It is not my fault. It is not . . .

A loud bell clangs somewhere in the castle, but I continue to scrub my legs like a mad thing. All about me folk go running to the Great Hall. They do not spare me a glance. I draw up a fourth bucket of water, and I scrub my hands with the torn cloth.

After a while I lose count of how many buckets of water I draw to use as my washing water. I smell burning bread. Master Baker and his apprentice and his lads must have been among the folk to run to the Great Hall. As dawn seeps in, I see that my hands and legs are still bloody, but now it is my own blood from my flesh scrubbed raw. I know it is folly, yet I continue to scrub.

I hear shouts and the clatter of feet running down the stairs. Shouts and then the thunder of many horses' hooves. No one seems to be coming back to the kitchen. Then the noise of the crowd fades away. I begin to scrub my mouth.

"Kitchen lad!"

I look around, wet and sore and frightened. Prince Malcolm steps out of the shadows. His clothes are all jumbled as if he threw them on by guesswork, and he is pale. I am heavy with guilt that through my herb craft I may have set things in motion for the murder of his father, and I do not dare meet his eyes.

"Help me," he says.

I do not know what to say.

"Kitchen lad," he says, "I need your help again. Help me now. Without your aid I fear I will perish in earnest."

I hide my hands behind my back as if I fear that he will see his father's blood on my skin.

"The king is dead," he says. I begin to shake. "My life depends on you."

I gather the courage to glance up at him. He stands there, running his hands through his hair, making it stand straight up on his head. He says, "My father has been killed."

Into my mind flashes the picture of his father's bloody body, lying on the bed.

The prince says, "I do not know who did the murder. If anywhere in the world should be safe, this is the place. Surrounded by his most loyal nobles—and yet my father was slaughtered like a trussed goat."

The gates of my mind split open. Other memories flood in, other deaths, and all those bodies I have not let myself picture for so many years, all those people I have not let myself mourn—and with all my inner strength, I slam the gates shut again. I dare not think of the past. I cannot afford a misstep, a slip of the tongue.

The prince is still speaking. "The war has ended. This is no time or place for my father to die."

"What do his chamber guards say?" I ask. Behind my back my hands continue to twist around each other as if one is washing the other. *It was not my fault. It was not my fault.*

The prince looks at me with a puzzled expression. "Nothing."

"You are the king's son. Make them talk!"

"Not even the king's son has that power, boy."

"You lack faith in your position, sire. You do have the power to make them talk.

The prince shakes his head. "Only God has that power now. They are dead."

"No!" I say, alarmed. "They do but sleep. They sleep soundly, perhaps, drunk or drugged with some potion. But they were alive when—"

Malcolm's chin jerks up. "When? You said, 'Alive when—'"

I think of a quick lie. "When I took them a nightcup last evening."

Does he believe what I said? From under my lashes I look at him. But I am confused. This tale outruns its sense. Something is out of joint.

"The guards *were* alive," he says, "right after the murder. But the lord of the castle, in his fury and great grief over the death of my father, slaughtered them before they could tell their tale."

I gasp in surprise. "What?"

"Yes, carried away by his sorrow—"

So He knows! It is as plain as my thumb—He did not kill His king in an herb trance. I know Him well, and He does not kill in a mindless frenzy. Some warriors kill in a blood-red heat, but He is a cold killer, a killer of ice and deliberation. No, it is as clear as a cloudless morn. He killed the guards deliberately to cover His own trail. I feel sick with relief. *I did not cause the death of the king.* "'Tis a great pity you cannot question the guards," I tell the prince. "I doubt not but they would have quite a tale to tell. His lordship has done a foul thing to murder them before they could talk."

"He killed them in a rage of grief," the prince says. "He was out of his head with sorrow. He didn't know what he was doing."

"'Tis a handy excuse," I say.

The prince rubs his forehead with the back of his hand as if he is clearing away cobwebs. "What do you mean?"

I look from side to side, making double sure that there is no one to overhear us. "Who killed your father?" I ask. My voice is tight and hard.

His voice is just as tight and hard. "They say 'twas the chamber guards. Blood dabbled their hands, and—"

I pull my hands out from behind my back and look at them. "'Tis easy to be blood-dabbled." I hold out my hands, dotted with my own blood from my vigorous hand scrubbing.

The prince looks at them in confusion. Then he draws his sword and points it at me. His hand is not quite steady.

"Are you saying that you are the one who killed my—"

I snap, "Put down the sword! I had naught to do with your father's death. All I say is that 'tis easy to spatter blood where you please."

We hear footsteps on the stairs to the Great Hall. We both duck behind the well. Lisette, the alewife, and the laundrywife walk past us, talking excitedly of the murder of the king.

Prince Malcolm says, "I'm not safe here. Whoever murdered my father can murder me. 'Tis my duty—I owe it to my father and family to get away safe. 'Tis the only way I can bring his assassin to justice. My brother is hardly more then a child. If I die here, there will be no men left to right his death." He clasps his hand on my shoulder. "Help me get safe out of the castle and on the road to England."

"England?"

"Aye. My brother goes to Ireland, but I was fostered down in England at the castle of my uncle Siward, my mother's kinsman. He will aid me. Help me get clear of this place. My life is in your hands."

I hesitate. *Why should I risk my neck for this unknown prince, no matter how handsome he is? He is a rich man. Let him fend for himself.*

Then I remember my packet of herbs.

"I will help you, sire," I say. "Do you have a mount?"

"My horse is in the stable," he says. "Come."

Hunkering low, we run to the stables. His horse is the only one left in there. "'Tis the work of a few minutes only to saddle the beast."

"'Twill be safer to lead the creature out of the gates and hold the riding until you are out of this castle," I say. "'Tis hard to hide when you are on the back of the horse."

We cross the far end of the courtyard. The gates stand wide open, and we lead the horse through it. To my relief, no one is in sight, so we hurry through the gates.

"Mount quickly," I tell him. "And ride like the wind across the clearing. Head for the trees."

He scrambles into his saddle, but instead of taking off, he sticks his hand down. I wonder at first if I am to kiss it or such, but then he says, "Grab hold, lad, and let me swing you up behind me."

And in the blink of an eye, I am seated on the horse behind him. I wrap my arms around his waist, holding tight, as we gallop toward the trees. His body is thin, but nonetheless strong and hard. Before we slip into the wood, the prince reins in and turns his horse about so he can take a final look at the castle. I see the shape of a woman standing on the battlements—His wife. My heart flops like a landed fish. She is staring across the countryside in our direction.

The going is slower once we are in the wood. I direct him which way to go, but the horse steps slowly to avoid holes and stumps and such.

I want to understand as much as possible about the king's death. Partly, it is true, to clear my conscience. So I ask in an innocent voice, "Why would the guards murder your father?" *I know that they did not do it—they were too drowned in drink to do aught, even to protect their master. But I must find a way to twist our conversation around so the prince can discover for himself the truth I know in my heart and bones.*

"They say the guards were bribed—" he begins.

"Who benefits most from the death of the king?"

I feel him stiffen beneath my hands. "I am his heir. But if you are trying to suggest that I was his killer, before God I will run you through with my sword, and—"

"You fool! 'Tis not what I'm saying."

A branch snaps nearby, and the prince reins his horse to a stop. We sit motionless for several minutes, but we hear nothing else, so we resume our journey. We do not talk. We both know well that somewhere out there is a heartless killer who doubtless would love to murder the prince and would not balk at slaughtering a mere kitchen lad. As we pick our way through the wood, I puzzle about how to tell him all I know of this history of the lord of the castle and why He is never to be trusted, but I am not sure how to begin.

We reach a clearing that is up a little hill.

We hear voices. I slide from the horse and pull Prince Malcolm to the ground after me.

"Hide," I whisper in his ear.

Quickly we climb behind a bramble thicket, coaxing the horse after us. We wait. A crowd of ten or twelve castle lads crash through the clearing, chattering excitedly about what they will do with the king-killing traitor once they lay hands on him.

"They say our lord has offered a reward beyond all imaginings to anyone who captures the man who killed the king!"

"More than that! Should we find the traitor and beat him to death with our clubs, we would surely be called the saviors of all Scotland!"

"They would make us all knights!"

"We would have our pick of women!"

The lads cheer and stumble on more quickly, never realizing that all the noise they make would give even a deaf assassin ample warning to hide. The prince and I wait until all sound of them has faded away before we come out from the thicket.

He remounts his horse, but I shake my head at the sight.

"What is amiss?" he asks.

"Wait."

I wrestle a branch from the nearest tree and hand it to him.

"Why do you give me—"

"Wait."

I snap off several other branches. I lace them around the saddle and across the horse's mane.

"What are you doing?" he asks. "Are you mad?" He starts to let go of the big, leafy branch I gave him, but I push it back into his hand.

"What are you thinking of?" he asks.

"Your safety, my lord! 'Twill fool no one up close, but at a distance you will seem part of the wood and shadow your progress from any who might be watching for you. With luck these branches will hide you from view." *Without luck, they will see the tree seem to move, but we will be in the depths of the wood before any watchers can figure out what they saw.* I climb up again behind him, scooting behind the cloak of branches.

By the top of the morning, we reach the road. I tell him to stop.

I slide off the back of the horse and step around to its head. As I talk, I give the horse's nose a pat. "Follow this road," I say, "till you have passed two waterfalls. Then at the next crossroads, take the arm that leads to the south. 'Tis a road that will lead you to Perth. After that I can tell you naught, but the folk at Perth can direct you to the England road. Have you any money?"

The prince holds up a bag of gold. I nod. I am relieved to see that he has enough for his journey.

"Get you gone," I say. "And God be with you."

"Thank you, my lad." He holds his hand out again. This time I understand what he wants, and I clasp his hand warmly. "When I return as king," he says, "I shall not forget this kindness."

His fingers go to his money pouch, but I frown. He hesitates, then lets his hand drop. He understands that I do not want money. I have noticed that he is quick to understand things. "I wish I could give you some sort of thanks now," he says, but I interrupt him.

"Before you go, sire, think! Who would wish you harm?"

He lets fall the reins. His horse tosses its head up and down, making a little snorting noise. Prince Malcolm pets the animal's neck, soothing it. To me he says, "'Tis that very thing that puzzles me."

"I am still surprised that your brother has deserted you."

He shakes his head. "'Twas my idea. Separated, we shall be the safer. That way one assassin may not—with a single visit—eliminate the House of Duncan." His horse twitches, and Prince Malcolm takes up the reins. "Farewell, lad. You have done me much service. Thanks to you, the heir to the throne of Scotland is not cold with death."

I grab the reins. "My lord, you must think. Who would wish harm to you and your family?" *Fleance would be proud of me could he hear how I press the prince to think.* "Probe deep, sire. Who gains benefit from the death of the king—besides you and your brother?"

Prince Malcolm's face looks bruised and blank.

"If you are gone to England," I press him, "who will be king?"

"Surely there will be no king until I return."

We hear a sound in the nearby underbrush. We stiffen, and then a deer bolts out of the undergrowth. We relax.

"I must be gone." He draws a ragged breath. "This very night you have saved the life of your king, lad. When I am—"

"Reward me later. Go now, your highness. But as you ride, think. Think hard. The answer stares you in the eyes. 'Tis not a safe time for willful blindness. My prince, in these dark days, 'tis not enough to be innocent. Innocence can be the same thing as stupidity. And in this dangerous time, if you choose to be stupid, then you are choosing to die. Ride hard, my lord, and ponder hard as you ride." I step back. "And may God walk with you, Prince Malcolm, all the days of your life."

I give the horse a hard pat on its rump. It gives a little jump. Then the prince is off through the undergrowth, holding his branch to hide him from his pursuers.

I trudge back to the castle.

T H I R T Y - O N E

It is long past mid-day when I slink into the kitchen, dirty and disheveled. I pass no one in the courtyards, but as I walked back from the wood from time to time I caught glimpses of the men searching for the murderers, some riding wildly and others—in packs—dashing about on foot. All seemed to be making far too much noise—they were sure to give warning to their prey. *Who are they searching for? They had said that the guards had killed the king, and the prince told me the guards were dead. How would they know the murderers if they found them?* It seems to me that they are more caught up in the chase than in the results of the chase.

In the kitchen Lisette is brewing a fragrant drink over the fire. Pod is seated on a stool beside her, sipping from a cup. As I pass him, I give his shoulders a little squeeze. I am glad he is safe in the castle. He leans against me and I wrap my arms around him. Things are moving so rapidly. I do not know what to do.

As if she can read my mind, Lisette says, "Things have gone mad, have they not?"

I blink at Lisette, bewildered. I cannot put the pieces together to complete the puzzle of sense. I feel off balance, fearful, dizzy. It is as if my brain has dried to sawdust. Lisette's face softens like cheese in the sun.

"Here, my little one." She pours some of the hot drink into another cup. "Take a cup of something to warm your soul. You look done to a shadow."

"Gilly," Pod says, bouncing up and down. "Gilly, did you hear? The king has been killed."

I take a sip. The drink is spicy, sweet, and good. "I know, lad."

Lisette folds her arms across her chest. "Though why every jack-anapes and rogue in this castle had to take off after the scent of the murderer, it passes understanding. Not a lick of work is getting done today. The poor cows have been bawling their heads off to be milked till finally Eda from the laundry went out and milked them."

"We had milk and bread for dinner!" Pod says. "All the milk we could drink!"

Lisette says, "Even most of the laundry maids have taken off on this wild hen hunt."

I say, "They have the blood scent in their noses."

Toward dusk the folk straggle back to the castle after a splendid day of hunting, their outrage providing that extra bit of spice to make the dish savory. One man killed a peasant who looked at him cross-eyed, claiming that he had the sneaky look of a man who might know aught about the murder of a king. Afterward he found out that the peasant's eyes had been crossed from birth. Three of the swordsmen, traveling together, killed two travelers, arguing that since they weren't from these parts, that made them suspicious in times like these. The castle stable lads used the excuse of the king's death to beat up their sworn enemies, the swineherd's sons in the nearby village.

But no one truly seems to believe that these digressions have done aught toward punishing the killers of the king.

As the sun slips down toward the horizon, the hunters begin to fill the Great Hall.

Lisette sends Pod and me up with tray after tray piled high with red herrings, dried apples, and wheels of cheese. Since Master Baker joined the chase, there is no bread. We just heap the food on a couple of tables we hastily set up and let the weary hunters help themselves. The Master Bottler, limping from the hunt, commands us to help three of the youngest stable lads carry up jugs of honey wine from the cellar. But Lisette stops us and whispers, "Water it first. They'll all be too tired to know the difference. There have been ugly doings aplenty today. The good Lord knows that we have no need of drunkards this night."

Lisette herself has been brewing a thick stew in the biggest cauldron, one near as tall as Pod. "After blood work, men crave strong tastes—meat and onions and strong spices." When Brude drifts in, she puts him in charge of transporting the huge cauldron to the Great Hall. He is too weary to protest.

As the evening unspools itself toward the emptiness of night, the men in the hall trade tales of great derring-do. In his own mind, each one triumphed over great challenges in his quest to apprehend the murderers. At the far end of the Great Hall, He sits watching the company from His carved chair on the dais. His eyes are cautious, His body tense. Only when it is quite dark does He order torches in the Great Hall lit.

Lisette, Pod, and I stay close to the fire, ladling out the fragrant stew. Pod keeps dipping his fingers into it to pull out raisins, and I keep slapping his fingers. Fleance nods to me when he comes to fill his bowl, his little face looking tired and wan. His father is with him, so he does not talk to me, but he jerks his chin upward several times. I take it that we are to meet up on the ramparts later to chart the moon and tides. As the night unwinds toward midnight, talk grows rougher and voices rise in anger.

Then His lady enters. Amid this travel-stained company, she looks as cool, elegant, and removed as the Virgin in a church. Like the Virgin, she is robed in spotless blue and white. Beneath her veil, her hair hangs long and shining. *She looks as beautiful as ever. What the parson preaches is true—evil can look as fair as an angel.* I catch myself fingering the dirty stubble on my own head.

The company falls silent as she moves to stand next to Him. Then one horseman calls out, "What news, my lord?"

"Has aught been learned of the identity of the murderers?" Lord

Macduff, the curly-headed lord who gave me shelter by the sea and rode with me to the castle, stands, his dark ringlets reflecting the torchlight in tiny halos on his head. He looks ill at ease.

The crowd rumbles in support of his question.

Immediately He glances toward His lady.

She pitches her voice so that even though it seems soft, it seeps into every corner of the Great Hall. "I know I have but a woman's understanding, but I thought 'twas the king's guards that did this bloody deed."

"But they did not work on their own!" Fleance's father leaps to his feet, his bearlike body quivering with outrage. "They were bribed!"

The company shouts in agreement.

She continues smoothly, "We must find those behind the guards. They are the more guilty!"

The company shouts again in agreement. I think I see a small smile lapping like a cat at the corners of the lady's mouth. She turns toward Him and inclines her chin, signaling Him to speak.

At His lady's urging, He steps to the edge of the dais and raises His hands over the company like a parson giving a blessing. "Although you have searched faithfully and well, we have naught to report."

The company grumbles.

Again He looks toward His elegant lady. She nods, then tilts her chin toward those of us out in the Great Hall. It is clear that she wants Him to speak some more. But He shakes His head. He looks weary, lost, and confused. She studies Him for a moment, and then she steps forward. She raises her small white hands and the company grows silent.

"And—in a sense, my lords and all—this is good news indeed."

Every face turns toward her, questions in every eye.

A man calls out, "What means your ladyship?"

Lord Macduff calls, "How can this be good news, lady?"

From the corner of her eye, the lady glances at Him, but He stands still as a rock. She continues, "Not good for our hearts heavy with sorrow for our great loss, that much is true. But this unnatural murder is good for our heads, for 'tis clear that 'twas no enemy who came by stealth and robbed us of our saintly leader, the good King Duncan. No, I have heard you talk among yourselves, and I know that many of you have come now to agree that he was killed by an enemy from within his own household."

I am shocked by the boldness of her lie. *She has not been near any of these men today. She cannot have heard a thing they said.* More than that, I have been in the hall among all the men, and I have heard no one say any such thing. But the company in the hall does not seem to realize this. Their faces are puzzled but trusting.

"Like many of you," she says in a voice as sweet and clear as honey, "I have resisted the thought, but your wisdom has persuaded me that it must have been the king's own sons who masterminded this murder."

Her audacity stuns me. The company, too, is shocked. They leap to their feet and burst into speech, some low mutterings, some gasps, and many people call out, their words overlapping each other and blurring the words. Then I hear Lord Macduff call out, "This cannot be right."

"True, true, true," she says over and over like a mother soothing a fretful child until the company grows silent again. "Yes, that is what I said when you first argued your case to me. This cannot be true. Prince Malcolm—to look at him is to see such an innocent flower of young manhood. But you have convinced me that underneath the bloom of that fair young man is coiled the most treacherous serpent ever to be found in Scotland."

She lies! She has stitched this fantasy out of whole cloth!

Lord Macduff calls out again, "This cannot be."

A few people nod, but their nods now seem uncertain.

She goes on as if he had not spoken. "Like all of you, I would fain be persuaded otherwise. Let us invite Prince Malcolm and Prince Danelbain to step forth. 'Twould be unfair not to allow them to defend themselves."

Someone cries out, "Bring Malcolm forth." A few voices echo that, and then most of the company begins to call out for Malcolm.

THIRTY-TWO

You witch! You saw Malcolm depart. You know he cannot step forward. I remember how the prince and I looked back to see her outlined against the sky. At the time I failed to realize that if we could see her, she could see us. *She watched us as we crept out of the castle gates.* I long to scream out my accusation, but I fear to bring attention to myself. Doubtless she would brand me as one of the king's killers, and the mood of this crowd would certainly bring about my instant death.

She gestures the crowd to be still. "Perhaps there is some reason why Malcolm and his brother are not here with their father's loyal subjects."

"Yes!" shouts the Master of Arms. "The reason is that they killed their father! And fearing the wrath of us honest men, they have taken themselves off!"

The company cheers. I glance to Lord Macduff. His jaw tightens.

The voice of the lady rises about the noise like a banner above a field of battle. "That gives us another reason to mourn. We have lost not just our king, but we have lost the hopes of the future which were planted in these two poisonous young princes."

The hall grows quiet, attentive. The lady looks to her husband, but He stands dumb. She looks back at us.

"Our grief-stricken hearts know that what has been so foully taken can never be restored."

Next to me, one serving man—bulky as a Northman—wipes his eyes.

"So now," she says, "we must turn to the cold comfort that is the crust offered all who mourn. Although our precious loss cannot be restored, we must find a way to replace it."

Someone calls out, "That cannot be."

She nods. "You speak the truth. For Duncan was a noble king, a good man, a virtuous man—more a saint than a man of flesh and blood."

The listeners murmur agreement.

She says, "I do not agree with those among you who argue that this very virtue made him more suitable for a monastery than for a country racked by war."

I see several people look at each other in confusion. *Will no one shut her up?* But even Lord Macduff seems caught in the spell of her soft voice. I have heard of wizards who can talk to snakes in such a way as to render them motionless, but in front of me now is the serpent itself casting a spell on its listeners. Oh, how I long to leap to the top of a table, shriek out the truth about her, but right now everyone in this hall would tear me apart rather than hear a word spoken against this creature who has bewitched them.

Her face grows sweet and sad. "'Tis true—who can deny it?—the king's very saintliness allowed him to see only the good in others. We all praised our dear king for this. 'Tis also true, this pure and holy virtue kept him from seeing that the former Thane of Cawdor was plotting to betray him. Because good King Duncan refused to see the evil side of this lord he loved, our country was plunged into war, ransacked by northern forces, and thousands of our loyal countrymen lost their lives. I know that 'tis said that many of our loved ones would be alive had this king been less saintly and more attuned to the discord in his country. But we do not grumble about these small misfortunes because we know that they are the inevitable result of the wonderful virtue of our king."

She is false! Can no one see that this is all playacting? She is twisting their minds. She is twisting the facts.

Yet still she goes on. "Yes, I heartily agree with those of you who say our recent woes were largely due to the saintly Duncan's blindness to the treachery of the former Thane of Cawdor whose title now adorns my husband, one of King Duncan's most loyal subjects. Duncan's virtue, like the wimple of a nun, did not let him see the Thane of Cawdor's treachery first sprout. Duncan's holiness, like his private cloister, shut him away and prevented him from plucking out the evil roots before this treachery grew and flowered and cost the deaths of so many fine men in this last war. Should we not say that the loss of so many men was a small price when we had such a good king?"

The crowd mutters. It is clear that they are beginning to question the virtue of King Duncan. I look at Lord Macduff. I see a muscle tighten in his jaw, but he says nothing.

"I am only a weak woman," she says gently, "yet even I understand that kings must be chosen to fit the tune of the times. None among us would deny that when Duncan was chosen as king, our country had need of a good, meek man. But I can see in your faces what you are thinking tonight. Your faces say that our present time calls for a very different sort of king. Duncan came to the throne during a time of peace. But now we still stagger under the weight of this last war. We are crippled by the treachery of Duncan's own sons—two more villains in whose evil natures the good Duncan could see naught but good." She looks around the hall. The company stares at her hungrily, as if the Virgin incarnate stands on the dais. "Your faces betray your secret fear that the Norwegian king, learning of the death of our good Duncan, may see us as weak and leaderless, and come once more to smash us, steal our lands and riches, make slaves of our wives and children, and destroy all we hold dear."

People cry out, "Never! No!"

She nods. "You are right, all of you, when you argue that our next king must be a warrior, a man of great strength and courage. We need a man who has proven his worth against the Northmen, a man of great loyalty and heart."

The company cheers.

She smiles. "Then you say I have heard you aright?"

"Yes," they shout. "Yes!"

Her smile fades. "Or should we scour the monasteries for a good, mild man, and leave the fate of Scotland to God?"

"We need a warrior!" someone calls out.

"Give us a warrior!" someone else calls.

The crowd picks up this cry and repeats, "Give us a warrior!"

The lady looks again at her husband. This time He meets her eye, and now He nods for her to continue. She holds up her slender white hands, and slowly the crowd quiets down. "Since I am but a weak woman, I cannot fight as you do for our beloved country. But women are sometimes given the skill to look deep into the hearts and minds of men and give word to their private thoughts. I see one more thought tonight—that to save this country from the lack of leadership that could lead to war, you would choose our next king this very night."

"Yes!" the company in the hall cries out. They cheer her. "Yes! She speaks aright! Yes!"

"Why should we wait while we have here the very cream of Scotland? Now King Duncan himself chose to honor my husband, his captain in war, by holding his court here. Surely among this fine assembly we can find a king suitable to replace our good Duncan."

The company cheers again.

"But who would Duncan himself have chosen?"

Silence falls. I can see by the expression on their confused faces that they are trying to work this out.

Finally one man shouts, "We need a strong leader."

The crowd shouts assent.

Another man shouts, "A military leader!" and the crowd cheers.

The Master Steward calls out, "A captain of war!"

The crowd cheers.

The Master of Arms shouts, "Macbeth and Banquo, they were the generals most beloved by Duncan."

Some in the crowd begin to shout "Macbeth!" and others shout "Banquo!"

The lady holds up her hands. Again the crowd grows silent, but now they seem to be a wolfhound straining at the leash, barely under her control. "'Tis true," she says, "the man most honored by Duncan in this last war was my husband. Duncan gave my lord the title abandoned by the treacherous Thane of Cawdor. Duncan honored my lord above all other lords of Scotland by choosing to spend his first night off the battlefield in our humble castle. My lord has indeed been showered above all others with favors from the dead king."

"Macbeth!" the crowd shouts. "Let Macbeth be king!"

"He was Duncan's favorite!" someone shouts out. I think the voice belongs to the Master Cook. *Indeed, it would fluff his pinfeathers if he should be Master Cook to the king himself.*

The lady cries out, "You would have my husband as king?"

"Aye!" roars the crowd.

"'Tis true," she cries, "no man loves Scotland more than my lord. He has given all he has to the service of this land. Would you in truth ask him to shoulder one more responsibility?"

"Yes!" shouts the crowd.

Lord Macduff's voice rises above the din. "Listen to me. Listen to me."

The crowd quiets.

He says, "My lady, you speak truth. Your husband has given much to Scotland already. Therefore 'twould not be fair to ask him to do more."

A few people cheer and then stop, seemingly confused by what they are cheering.

Lord Macduff continues, "Banquo would make a goodly king."

I cannot spot Lord Banquo in the crowd, but voices begin to chant, "Banquo, Banquo, Banquo!"

I am amazed to hear the lady cry out, "Yes, Banquo would make a fine king!"

The crowd cheers.

"Yes," she says, "our noble Banquo also has given much in this late war. And for the length of this war he has not been home to see his wife or his small children. Indeed, he has been so occupied with this war, he has not even found the time to journey home to see his newest son. Good Banquo has lands that were ravaged by war, and there has been no leisure for him to set his own lands in order. Thus we must ask ourselves, are we being fair to this good man? Is it possible to ask too much of him?"

The crowd again seems confused.

"I know what you are thinking—your thoughts shine forth in your face. You are right. Lord Banquo has earned the privilege of attending to his own family."

A few listeners cheer.

She sighs. "I can see you thinking that my lord and I have no children."

Thank God that there are no offspring to this union of monsters, that this mother from hell has whelped no brats of His.

"I see you thinking also that if my husband were king, unlike Duncan, my lord has no children to betray him and bring about his downfall, no children to put our beloved country into peril. Were I a man, no doubt I could think of a clever answer to your assertion, but as a weak woman, all I can do is agree with you."

How must Fleance feel to hear her suggest that one day he might be a traitor? At the same time, I know that if he were son to the king, his dreams of traveling south to study would become even harder to bring to pass.

The lady's voice interrupts my thoughts. "So is it your desire that my husband become your next king?"

"Yes!" thunders the crowd. "Yes!"

She stretches both arms up as if she is receiving heavenly blessing. "Will nothing persuade you to change your mind?"

"No!" they cry. "No!"

She kneels to her husband. "My lord, you hear the people. They would have you for their king, to lead them through this perilous time. What is your will?"

"Say yes!" cries the Master of Arms.

The crowd repeats, "Say yes!"

The lady stretches out her hand to her lord. He stares at her for a moment, His face as empty as a clean slate. Then He steps to her, takes her hand, and raises her to her feet. He looks hard at her, then turns to the crowd.

"You have asked me to be your king," He cries out, His voice as slick as a blade, "and I will say yes!"

The crowd goes mad with excitement, crying out "Hurrah!" and "Long live King Macbeth!" Lord Macduff silently shoulders his way to the door and departs. I cannot believe my ears and eyes. *Is this the spell? I wish to destroy Him, and He ends up king?* How could things go so horribly wrong?

I see the lady cover her mouth as if she is surprised, but beneath her hand I see her satisfied smile.

THIRTY-THREE

So BEGINS the worst time of all.

It is as if we are at war again, only this time the enemy is our king Himself. Hired kerns, savage mercenary warriors, are brought from Ireland to be the king's special guards. Spies are placed throughout the land as thick as nuts in a ladycake, set to keep an eye on all that goes on. Anyone suspected of being the king's enemy is thrown into a dungeon with no trial and no hope of ever leaving. Even neighbors begin to spy on one another. It is as if all joy and laughter were buried along with the old king.

We move south, to the castle of Dunsinane. Most local lads are left at His northern castle, but Lisette demands that Pod and I be taken with the court, so we travel south with her, Master Cook, and Master Baker.

The night before we leave, I find Pod sitting out in the dark with his back to the wall, his arms wrapped around his knees.

"What ails you?" I ask.

"Momma," he whispers. "When Momma comes to look for me, she will not know where to find me."

"Yes, she will. She will come to this castle, and the porter at the gates will tell her where we have gone."

"She will not know how to find her way to our new place in the south."

I sit down next to him and put my arms awkwardly around his shoulders. "Yes, she will. She will ask people, and they will tell her how to find us." He looks away. "Pod, 'tis not hard to find your way to the king."

We sit in silence for a few minutes, and then he says, "Momma is not going to come for me, is she?" I tighten my arm around him. I do not know what to say.

He lowers his head onto his knees.

We sit for a long time without speaking.

IT IS ODD to be at Dunsinane Castle. Here I am no more than half a day's journey from Nettle and Mad Helga, but I am still angry with them for betraying me. Their spell and all that business in the wood near Forres did not bring doom upon Him. On the contrary, it seems our meeting there has done naught but advance His cause. I hate Nettle and Mad Helga. *They gave me hope, and then they, too, betrayed me.* I know that only a fool will trust someone else, but it is a lonely way to live. Sometimes I forget that I hate Nettle and Mad Helga and wish they were near to talk to. But then I lash my armor back around my heart. *I have made my life an arrow....*

Even in these bad times, there are some good things. Dunsinane is a much larger castle than Inverness. The Great Hall is large enough for the kitchen folk to sleep on pallets near the rest of the household servants.

Since Mungo, Ban, Alpen, and the other Inverness kitchen lads do not come south with us, there are fewer folk to torment me. In fact, my position improves among the new southern lads who are hired to work in the kitchen. I am seen as someone of importance, someone who has served the king awhile.

Master Cook finally begins to dictate his recipes to me. We spend time together each afternoon, he talking and I writing. I do not find his recipes clear, but I write them just as he tells them to me. At least, sometimes I write them just as he tells them. At other times I take delight in changing what he says. When I read them back, I give back the words he says, but inside I chuckle because when other folk try to follow his cooking, they will say, "What dreadful food this is."

"For roasted quail," he says, "pound one handful of juniper berries until they are soft as stewed pears."

I write, "Peel a whole pail of juniper berries until they are raw as an eyeball."

This will teach him to treat me badly.

Fleance's lame foot heals, and we resume our lessons with the Master of Arms. I learn to fight with short swords and double sticks. Fleance continues to dream of going to Rome to learn about science. Many days Pod watches us, his face moony and sad. I think he would like to be learning to fight, too, but he is awkward and would not be able to master it. He never speaks of Fleance, but I suspect he is jealous of the time I spend with the young nobleman. I am a little annoyed by this, but if I say truth, I must also admit it is a little heady to have someone—even a small boy like Pod—care enough for me to be jealous of my other . . . friend. It is passing strange. Never before have I used that word about myself. Yet in this dark time, I seem to have two friends.

One day in early summer, we castle folk travel to the Stone of Destiny to see Him named king. We are all given new clothes to wear to the ceremony. I receive a blue tunic and yellow trews. The cloth of the tunic is so finely woven that I think I could fold it and pass it through the eye of a needle. The tunic is as soft as a cloud on my skin. It is the most elegant thing I have worn in many years.

Pod has a splendid new outfit of forest green. "You are as pretty as a skylark," I tell him, and his smile almost splits his face in two. Lisette, too, looks pretty in her new gown of red and brown. I wish Nettle and Mad Helga could see me looking so fair.

I do not let myself think that this gift came from Him.

"Why does He have to travel to that particular stone to be crowned?" I ask Lisette.

"Little peaseblossom, 'tis a very special stone. Do you recall Jacob in the Good Book?"

I nod, but Pod shakes his head.

"One night," Lisette says in her storytelling voice, "the good Jacob lay himself down to sleep. In the night a ladder appeared with an angel on it. Jacob grabbed hold of the angel, and he would not let the angel go—no matter how much he struggled—until the angel promised to bless Jacob."

Pod's eyes were round with amazement.

"What has this to do with aught?" I demand of her.

"This Stone of Destiny," she says, "is that very stone that was used as Jacob's pillow when the angel came to his side. I'm told that every king of Scotland is crowned at this stone."

AT THE CEREMONY, the lords of the land each pour a shoeful of dirt onto the stone.

"What are they doing?" I whisper to Lisette.

She presses a chubby finger to her lips, but afterward she tells me, "Each lord of Scotland brings a shoeful of the earth of his lands and pours it in offering to the new king. Then, when our king puts his foot on top of the earth on the stone, it shows his sovereignty over all his subjects."

Or it shows that He intends to crush his subjects. "But 'twas not all the lords," I say. "Lord Macduff of Fife did not come to the crowning."

Lisette looks worried, but she does not answer.

In these times, He is never alone. He keeps His kerns, His specially hired Irish bodyguards, at the doors of each room He is in. They are arrogant, and they treat the servants at the castle with contempt. One night when we bring supper to them, one of them takes a bite and spits it out. "'Tis pig swill," he calls out in his funny accent. Then he dumps all his food on the floor. Quick as a hiccup, the other bodyguards dump their food on the floor. We kitchen lads are sent in to clean it up, and the men at arms kick us and laugh.

When they see Pod is frightened of them, they begin to throw more and more food on the floor for him to clean up, laughing at his red, troubled face.

After that Lisette does not let Pod help in the Great Hall. "'Tis not safe for that little one," she tells me one day after she has sent Pod out to gather eggs. "When I was a young bride, come with my husband to the first castle in which I worked, there was a lad like your brother. Only he was not right in his head, and the lord of the castle made him his fool. One night the drunken young warriors there decided to play kick-the-ball. Not having a ball, they used the poor lad. They kicked him to death."

From time to time I catch glimpses of the she-devil of the castle, her face hard and shiny with triumph at her new position as queen. She is still beautiful, but she is as cold as a dagger frozen in a block of ice.

Then the executions begin.

The first one takes place on a fine June day. The sky is blue and as hard as an agate. The sun is so bright that even the dark stones of the castle seem lit from within. It is strange to believe that anyone at all could die on a day of such clean beauty. But as Lisette, Pod, and I are sieving petals for rosewater to flavor sweet wafers, the bell tolls thrice, the signal for the castle folk to assemble in the courtyard.

In the center is a new platform, and on it stands a gallows with two noosed ropes dangling from the cross-brace. At the front of the platform stands the Captain of the Guard, an ugly Irishman with a snaggletooth and a thick, muscle-broad badger's body. Behind him, with their hands tied behind their backs, are two boys who have just turned the corner to manhood. One of them has a chin covered with the soft down of a lad who is trying to grow his first beard. They are dressed in peasant garb, and both look confused and frightened.

"Ye are assembled here," bellows the Captain of the Guard in his thick Irish accent, "to bear witness to the fair and just execution of two traitors to the high king. These two ruffians did try to assassinate our king, and so must pay the price of their misdeed."

"No," shouts the taller of the two lads, the one with the start of a beard. "We did not try to do aught of the kind. We did but approach him to ask him a favor. Our old granny had her house taken away by the landlord, and we ran up to the king's horse to ask him would he give her the house back again."

"Silence!" The Captain of the Guard backhands the boy and knocks him to the floor of the platform. The other lad begins to shake and cry.

Then the Captain of the Guard signals his men to slip the nooses over the boys' necks, and the boys are hoisted just a few feet into the air. They kick their legs about. Then we see the most awful sight of all. Some soldiers hold the boys' legs still, while two other soldiers slit open their bellies and pull out their guts. Still the boys are not dead. We are made to stand there and watch for a long time until the two boys finally stop kicking.

All through this, I can see Him standing with Master Steward at a window, watching the boys die. When their bellies are slit open, I turn away to stare at Him. He smiles the slow satisfied smile of a man who has just finished a good dinner.

Someone must stop Him. It is as plain as day, these lads did not try to assassinate the king. They should not have died! I must find someone to kill Him and so prevent Him from killing more innocent folk. Think, think of a plan!

The boys hang in the courtyard all afternoon. Toward evening they are cut down. *Thank God, I need see them no more.* But then their heads are cut off and stuck on long pike staffs and placed up on the ramparts of the castle. I see them every time I cross the courtyard. Even though the ravens peck out their eyes, they seem always to be watching me.

Two days later, there is another execution. This time it is a man, his wife, and their son, who looks to be a lad of nine summers or so. The Captain of the Guard claims that they offered the king poisoned water when he stopped to drink at their well.

After that, every week or so brings more executions. The walls of our castle grow thick with heads. To my shame, as my heart hardens even more against Him, each time I pass the heads I think, *If He catches you or even suspects what is in your heart, He will do the same to you as He did to these poor folk.*

Still, whenever I pass through the courtyard, I make a silent promise to all these dead folk. *I will kill the man who killed you. I have not come up with a plan, but I will, I will, I will.* I practice picturing myself going through an execution, picture my head on the pike, so that when my time comes to die, I will die bravely. I cannot forget Nettle's prophecy: *As a result of the revenge, Gilly will cease to be.* Each day I pray, *Let me die well.*

Finally the summer begins its slide toward autumn. While I rack my wits to think of a way to kill Him, in the meantime I do my best to make Him suffer. When no one is looking, I spit in food that might be going to the high table. Sometimes I sprinkle dirt in the stew pots instead of pepper. Once I squeeze a blister on my finger and let the ooze drip into the white, creamy blancmange. It is a foolish revenge, I know. But, as Nettle says, the weak must use whatever splinters they can find to build their walls. At present it is the best I can do.

At Lammastide, I think of Nettle and the herbs she would be gathering—colt's foot, adder's tongue, bat's wool, and babe's finger. I wonder if her double sight has told her that I am but half a day's walk away.

One hot autumn afternoon as I shuffle my way back to the kitchen after finishing my lesson at sword-fighting with Fleance, I see Pod sitting on the side of the well. He is crying.

I am tired of his boo-hooing, and I reckon I can slip behind him without his seeing me. I start to do this, but as I do, my heart feels as heavy as a boot dropped in a lake so I go over and sit next to him.

He takes no notice of me, so I bump my hip against his in a friendly sort of way. Again he ignores me. I bump him again, but to no avail.

When he snuffles, I offer him the end of the sash round my

waist. He looks bewildered, so I mop his cheeks and hold it to his nose.

"Blow!"

He gives an enormous honker of a blow. I scrape my sash end against the rocks of the well to clean off the snot, and then I ask, "What's wrong?"

His voice is as shaky as a twig in a stream. "I don't like it here. Let's go back and find Momma."

Just then one of His enormous Irish guards strides up to the well. I quickly fall to my knees behind it, but Pod is slow in getting out of the way. The guard puts his huge foot against Pod's rear end and gives him a shove. Pod sprawls across the flagstones, and the guard laughs.

When he is gone, Pod says, "I don't like it here."

I cast about in my mind for something to say, but I can't think of anything comforting.

Pod raises his arm to wipe his eyes, and his sleeve falls away, disclosing a horrible mess of scrapes and bruises. I take his arm and look at it. Then I dip the other end of my sash into the puddle of water that the guard spilled when he drew a bucket. I press my damp sash gently against the mottled mess, hoping to give him comfort.

"The other kitchen lads?" I ask.

Pod stares straight ahead without speaking.

"The guards?" I ask.

Pod starts to cry again. I hug him to me. I am so sorry for the little fellow that my heart feels like a bruised fist.

"Gilly," he sobs, "please don't make us stay here."

I hug him tighter. "Come back to the kitchen. I'll make a poultice for your arm. 'Twill take some of the sting out of the pain."

In the kitchen, Pod sits on a stool while I mash herbs together in a pestle to make a compress. One of the younger kitchen lads starts over to see what I am making, but I glare at him, and he moves back to a group chopping greens by the door.

Lisette bustles in, her arms filled with clean linens. She sees

Pod's arm stretched out on the table, and she hurries over, clicking with concern. She looks hard at me.

"'Tis not your work, surely, Gilly?" Still, there is a question in her eyes.

I shake my head.

Lisette takes Pod's chin in her hand and looks at him. He won't meet her eyes. She strokes his hair.

"Little one, little cabbage," she croons, "tell old Lisette who did this to you."

Pod just looks down at his chubby hands.

"Oh, my little dumpling," Lisette says, "how can we help you if you will not talk to us?"

Again tears begin to trickle down Pod's face and splash onto his lap. Lisette fumbles at her waist for a key then hands it to Pod.

"Little cabbage, run to that brown chest and bring us back three sweetmeats."

Pod nods, without much joy, and toddles off. Lisette looks after him, her face puckered and concerned.

"If he will not tell us who is hurting him, Lisette, we can do naught to make his life better."

Lisette clucks. "The little one is not happy here. I try to keep him under my wings, but I cannot be with him all the time."

My voice is defensive. "I look out for him, too."

Lisette opens her mouth. I know she will contradict me, but I do not care. In truth, I look forward to it. A good quarrel will make me feel much better. But then Lisette shuts her mouth and presses her lips together as if to keep angry words from flying out. I wrap up the poultice. I feel guilty, even though there is no reason for me to do so. *I did not hurt the lad. Besides, he needs to toughen up. It is a cruel world, and he must learn to defend himself. It is no service to him to let him go boo-hooing whenever some little thing happens to displease him.* Still angry, Lisette snaps the linens onto the shelf, one by one. Finally she blows her breath out in a sigh and says, "Me, I do not like the things that are happening here now."

"If Pod would just tell me which of the guards or servants—"

"Then what? What would you do, Gilly?"

"I would make them stop," I say quickly. "I would fight them."

"Fight them with sticks? You might triumph for the moment over any servants who bully him, but then they would come back when you are not around and hurt the little one even worse. If 'twas the king's guards that hurt him—hurt him for sport—what would you do then?"

I feel ready to burst with frustration. I no longer like Lisette. She is as cantankerous as Nettle. She does not care enough about Pod to 'prentice him. *How dare she look down on me?* "Something," I say. "There would be something to do." A thought pops in my brain. "I would tell the sword master!"

Lisette makes a face. "Ah, yes, of a certainty the sword master would take the word of a kitchen lad over the word of one of the king's guards."

"'Tis not my fault! I can't be with him all the time." I no longer like Pod either. I hate them both. I hate them for making me feel guilty and helpless.

"Just how much are you with our little one?" Lisette asks.

I look away, not meeting her eyes. She begins to set out her flour and such to make her wafers. "'Tis a hard world, Lisette. He needs to toughen up, to learn to survive."

Lisette snorts. She begins to bang her foodstuffs against the tabletop.

"If he would just fight back," I say, "they would not hurt him so."

"No," she says softly, "they might kill him instead."

I shout, "'Tis not my fault." *I do not want to think about such things!* The room goes silent. I see everyone looking at me. I drop my voice to a whisper. "You have no right to scold me. You could take Pod as your apprentice and teach him to make a living, but you will not, so—"

Lisette sighs. "If we could find a small place of our own . . . and just a few gold coins. Then I would take him as an apprentice. If needs be, my children can wait a year or two. In a town we could set up a shop of our own—I could make wafers and other confections—we could live like a family, we three, and our little one could be kept safe until he learned the trade, and—"

For a moment my heart sings, and then a dark thought hits me. "The king would never let you go!" I say.

Lisette's face falls.

My voice is as hard and cold as the blade of a knife. "I did not ask to be his protector!"

To my surprise, Lisette pats my cheek. "We seldom ask for the people we love, but we love them all the same."

I stamp my foot. "I do not love anyone! I do not love you or Pod or—"

Then I see Pod standing in the doorway, listening. I expect him to cry again, but he does not. But his face looks tired and old—like the face of an old, old man. I thrust the poultice into Lisette's hands.

"Here. Bind this to his arm, and 'twill not hurt him so."

I stalk out of the room, stiff and straight as the tail of an angry cat. When I pass Pod, I tell him, "I do not love you, lad. Do not tie your wagon to a star."

I am no more than half a dozen steps into the courtyard when I am stopped by Master Cook.

"Since you have naught to do this afternoon, Gilly, Master Steward has ordered us to scrub down the flagstones in the hall. The queen's nose is offended by the stink." He thrusts a scrub brush into my hands. "'Tis to be finished by supper."

When I reach the Great Hall with my bucket of water, a group of castle servants are scooping up the last of the rushes. They clunk off, grunting under the weight of the baskets. I begin to scrub.

The afternoon is endless. I am haunted by the memory of Pod's sad little face. My shoulders are tight with all the sadness and guilt I feel about him. *It was for his good. It would be wrong of me not to toughen him up. This cruel world gobbles up any soft or tender children.* My knees hurt, my skin scraped raw between my bones and the hard stone floor. My hands are red and sting from the harsh lye soap. I trudge up and down the stairs, carrying out a pail of dirty water and carrying in a pail of clean water until my shoulders ache. Sweat rolls down my brow.

In spite of myself, I wish Pod were here with me. The afternoon would pass much more quickly could I talk with him as I work.

I do not love him, I tell myself. *I will not love him. Or anyone.* I feel as cross as a cat with its tail caught in a door. I scrub the floor as hard and furious as if I want to rub it to dust. After a while, the scrubbing starts to make me feel better.

Perhaps an hour before the time of setting up the tables, I reach the far end of the hall. I think about skipping the section of the floor that is hidden behind the hangings, but it will be easier to scrub that last strip of floor than to bear the scolding of Master Steward should he see that I failed to clean the last bit. I lift up the hangings and crawl behind them. It is pleasant there, like a peaceful woven cave. I wriggle around and sit with my back against the wall, enjoying a few moments of rest.

Then I hear His voice.

THIRTY-FOUR

BRING THEM IN HERE," He commands.

A moment of silence, then footsteps scruff across the flagstones of the hall. A rough voice says, "My lord."

I peek out and see two coarse-looking men kneeling in front of Him. One has the thick and lumpy shoulder muscles of a bear. The other is smaller with a pointed weasel face and ginger-colored hair.

With a wave of His hand, He dismisses Master Steward, who bows and leaves.

I duck back behind the tapestry to listen. I dare not let myself think of what He would do should He find me there.

"Was it yesterday that we talked together?" He asks.

"It was, my lord," says one of the others. He has a low rumbly voice. From his accent I reckon he is perhaps a soldier or a small land-holder. His voice is a little more refined than that of a peasant, but much too uncouth to be that of a noble. From the depth of the tone, I presume that the speaker is the man with the bear-broad chest.

"Have you thought more of the matter?" He asks.

"We could think of little else," says the other man in a reed-thin voice that makes a faint whistling sound on the word *else*.

"So both of you now understand that Banquo is your enemy?" He asks.

"Aye, my good lord," says the low voice, and the thin voice echoes, "Aye."

"You both understand," He asks, "that 'twas Banquo who caused your misfortune?"

The low voice says, "We were foolish to think that you, my lord, were the one who took our lands and clapped us in prison."

"Forgive us, my lord," says the thin voice, "for suspecting you."

I hold my lower lip between my teeth so I will not cry out, *You fools! Are you so dazzled by His title that you cannot tell that it was surely the king Himself who cast you down, not Lord Banquo? Don't you see He's playing with your mind as a cat might play with a mole just before it kills it?*

The low voice says, "We thank you for making it plain to us that Banquo was the one who robbed us of our homes and dignity."

How can they be such fools?

But He continues, "And now that I have freed you from your imprisonment, now that you know that 'twas Banquo who destroyed your lives, how do you plan to use this knowledge?"

My stomach turns in sick horror as if I had swallowed a worm the size of a hedge pig as I understand what He intends.

The low voice answers, "I don't know, my lord."

"Perhaps, like a good Christian, you will forgive Banquo and pray for the soul of this man who stole from you all that you value," He says.

Both men chorus, "Never, my lord."

"Or perhaps," He says, "like a dog or beaten horse, you will lie there and accept anything that Banquo wishes to give."

"Never!" they chorus again like trained ravens.

"Or perhaps," He says, "like men, you will rise up and demand justice!"

"Yes, my lord!"

"Perhaps you will reclaim your dignity as men by punishing him who wronged you!"

"Yes, my lord!" Their voices are bold as brass trumpets.

There is a pause. I want to look out again, but I fear He might see me. Finally He says in a surprisingly gentle tone, "Then it must be done tonight—before Banquo is out of your reach."

I was right. He has tricked these fools into killing Lord Banquo. *Why does He want Lord Banquo dead? Lord Banquo is His friend.* All the recent executions bear proof that He is going mad with suspicions, willing to slaughter the innocent willy-nilly just to protect Himself from any imagined attack. Then an awful memory lurches into my brain. *On the heath, I predicted that Banquo's descendants would be the kings of Scotland.* Shivers run up and down my spine. *Oh, no. Not that. Please God, do not let it be my careless words that set Him off to murder Fleance's father.* Quickly I press my hands against my mouth so I do not moan in fear and dread.

Just then, as if He senses my presence, He says, "'Tis not safe to talk here. Come with me."

"Aye, my lord."

I hear their footsteps clip-clop across the floor—the working men in heavy wooden shoes and Him in His leather boots. Above their footsteps I hear Him say, "Fleance, his son, must also embrace the fate of this dark hour."

As soon as I judge it safe, I wriggle out of my hiding place. Right now it does not matter why He wants Lord Banquo and Fleance killed. What matters is what I must do. I can ponder all this later. Right now I must warn Fleance.

I run to the stairway to the upper chambers, but a guard stands there.

"I need to see Master Fleance."

The guard looks at me, frowns, and then bursts into ugly gobs of laughter.

"What does a kitchen lad have to do with his betters?" He pinches his nose between his fingers. "Laddie, you stink to the skies. Run away, and do not ask for access to your betters."

I stomp my foot in frustration. "I must see him now."

The guard draws his sword from his sheath. "Be gone, goose, and do not bother me again."

I toy with the notion of telling him the truth, but if he reports to the king, it would be my death and would avail Fleance naught. I cull my brains for an idea but can think of nothing clever. So I turn and race out of the keep, running to the armory. I stand there, shouting for the Master of Arms.

At last he hobbles in. "I must see Fleance. Immediately," I blurt out.

He narrows his one good eye, perplexed by my haste and irritated by my intrusion, but all he says is, "There is no lesson today."

"I must see him," I repeat, my breath coming harsh and fast.

I want to tell him about His plan, but the Master of Arms is the king's man, and I need his help. I feel too small and frail to handle all this bother alone. I long for Nettle to help me—she would know what to do.

The Master of Arms jerks his chin upward. "No doubt the lad is closeted with one of his books up in his chamber."

"The guard will not let me up the stairs to see."

The Master of Arms rubs the back of one wrist against his forehead. "'Tis not easy to see your betters. Best wait until supper."

I blink in disbelief, and then I run out into the courtyard. Foolish old man. He may be good at arms, but he is no use now when danger truly threatens.

I dash to the kitchen. Pod is squatting next to Lisette, waiting for the griddle to heat up. She nods, and he leans over and spits. His spittle makes a loud sizzle against the stones.

"'Tis ready," she says. He pours a ladle of thin blond batter onto the hot surface.

"Pod," I say. "I need your help."

Lisette frowns at me. "We make a batter for cheese wafers. 'Twill not keep."

"Pod! Come!" I bark.

He looks back and forth, his brow creased in confusion, unable to decide what to do.

"Gilly!" shouts Master Cook. "If you have finished with scrubbing the Great Hall, come scrub these turnips for—"

"Lisette, please," I plead in lowered tones, "I will never ask you for aught else, but a life depends on what I must do."

She looks at me for a moment and then she gives Pod a little push. "Go with your brother," she says.

His face lights up in relief, and he hurries to me.

"Gilly," calls Master Cook, "come here and—"

But I do not hear the rest because I have Pod's hand in mine and am pulling him out the door.

I stop him at the top of the stairs to the Great Hall.

"I need your help," I tell him. "If you do not help me, Fleance will die."

His eyes grow as wide as trenchers.

"I must get past the guard at the stairs," I say. "So listen to what I say and do exactly as I tell you."

He gives a little shiver, but he listens carefully.

ONCE INSIDE THE GREAT HALL, I give him a little push. He falls to the floor and begins to scream. Even I am impressed.

Scream with all your might. Pretend your momma is being hanged as a witch, and you must scream to attract help before she dies. Scream and scream until the guard comes to you. Then tell him that you are having a fit. Tell him that it is often thus.

Pod keeps screaming and rolling about. Even I could not do better.

I wait till the guard moves toward Pod, and then I slip up the stairs. I clatter around a bend—

I see His lady running down.

"What has happened?" she asks. Her face is pale.

Face-to-face with her, I can say nothing. My tongue is as dead as a mouse in a trap. There are no words in my brain. I stare at her in shock.

"Has my husband done something?" she asks. Her voice sounds afraid.

As if I am under a spell, I cannot even shake my head. Finally she brushes past me and is down the stairs before I manage to whisper, "I am only a lad from the kitchen."

I stand there for a few moments, waiting for the beating of my heart to slow and my breath to steady. I am unnerved, seeing her so close. *I did not want to see her.* Then I pull my wits together. *I must save Fleance.* I run the rest of the way up the stairs.

Fleance is not in his room. I run to the ramparts where he has his experiments and his study of the tides. It is possible he is working on that. But he is not on the ramparts. I am panting and have a stitch in my side. I lean against the wall to catch my breath. Then, down in the courtyard, I see Fleance and his father on horseback. They trot out through the castle's gates.

I run down the stairs and back through the Great Hall. Pod is gone. Clever lad, I think, to do my bidding and find a way to get away so quickly. I race to the stables. Perhaps I can filch a horse and ride after Fleance and his father and warn them.

"Where did Lord Banquo go?" I demand of a stable boy.

He looks me up and down, his nose wrinkled in distaste. "Out of my stable, kitchen waste!" He makes a face at me.

I grab a pitchfork and quickly knock him to the ground.

I make my voice as threatening as possible. "Do you wish to give me a different answer?"

"Lord Banquo's gone riding. He and his son."

I brandish my pitchfork in a menacing manner. "Where do they ride to?"

"I don't know." He keeps his eye on the pitchfork. "They are to return at nightfall in time for supper."

I see several of the other stable lads start over to us. They look eager to avenge the wrong done to the lad in front of me, and I doubt I will be a match for the whole group. With regret, I let go of my idea about filching a horse. I will have to go on foot.

As I run across the courtyard toward the gates, I bump into someone and sit down with an *oof!*

"Careful, lad," says a low growly voice. Above me stands one of the coarse men who were talking with Him just now in the Great Hall. A thick bearlike hand lifts me to my feet. "Look where you are going, lad." The weasely ginger-headed man stands next to him.

"My good sirs," I stammer, "who . . . I have not seen you about the castle before."

The men exchange looks.

The weasel-faced one says, "Take care who you run down. If we had more time, we would give you a lesson." His voice gives a little whistle on the final word.

I must keep them from leaving. I blurt out, "This castle, my good men, prides itself on its hospitality. Surely you are hungry. If you will come with me to the kitchen—we have some good venison on the spit and—"

The eyes of the weasel-man light up. "Surely our business can wait a few moments more—"

"Nay!" says the other. "Would you sell your birthright as a man for a mouthful of roasted meat? Come along—"

"There is a dish of stewed pigeons and a table of jellies," I say desperately, "and sugared almonds and—"

"Come along!" says the bear-man, pushing past me.

The men stride toward the gates. I hesitate for a moment, biting my lip and considering what to do. Then I dart back to the kitchen, looking about wildly. The place is a flurry of activity. I see a cloak hanging on a peg by the door. It apparently belongs to a beefy soldier who is sitting by the fire, beguiling the kitchen boys with tales of his travels up to the Orkney Islands.

Lisette beckons to me. "Gilly, my lad. If you are finished with the hall, come lend a hand and stir the batter. We are behindhand preparing the feast for Lord Banquo—"

I snatch the cloak and am out the door.

It is up to me to save Fleance and his father.

THIRTY-FIVE

I FOLLOW THE TWO ASSASSINS out the gates and across the fields to the edge of the wood, the soldier's cloak wrapped well around me so my shape is smudged. I keep well behind so that in the fading light I am but a shadow. The raspy crush of the drying grasses under my feet sounds loud in my ears, but the two men do not notice. I feel safer when we reach the wood. Of course it is easier to hide from view there, but more than that, the wood is my home even though it has been a long time since I have been in it. Above my head the trees loom like twisted ghosts. The wind rises and the dead autumn leaves twitter dryly like hoarse gossips. In the cracks between the branches, I can see gray, swag-bellied clouds begin to clot the sky, and the air smells heavy and thick. I hope I will not be drenched in the coming storm.

For a short while the men follow the road, but at the first bend, they step into the trees.

The bear-shouldered man grunts, "We will wait for them here, for they surely must pass through this glade to return to the castle."

I must slip past them. If I go past them, out of their sight, and then run as fast as I can, perhaps I can stop Fleance and his father before they ride into this ambush. I move from tree to tree, holding my breath, but I concentrate too hard upon what I want to do and not enough on what I am doing. A twig snaps under my feet. The two men leap across the ground till they stand on each side of me, their swords drawn. I fling up my hands to show I am harmless, but I keep my head bent so my hood hangs low over my face.

With the point of his sword, the bearlike man jabs against my chest. "Who be you?"

"Why be you here?" demands his weasel-faced companion.

I pitch my voice low. "The king sent me."

I wait. My heart pounds almost painfully, but I do not let myself move. *Look confident. Show no fear.* I wait to see if they will take my bait. *Come to my trap, you fools. You fell for His lies. Now listen to mine.*

The men exchange looks through the dusk. Then the bearlike man says, "He needs not mistrust us."

"You know the plan?" asks the other.

I nod. The hood of the cloak sloshes back and forth, but I do not let it fall away from my face.

"Then stand over close by me," says the first.

"Have you weapons?" asks weasel-face.

I shake my head. All the while, I strain my ears to hear the approach of horse hooves. *What shall I do when the time comes? What can I do?*

I have a sudden vision of Fleance's small, thin, earnest face and my knees grow weak with worry.

Bear-man is talking. "Then grab the leads of the horses. Hold the horses while we do the deed."

There must be a way I can stop them. But although they are stupid, they are much larger than I. And they have weapons while I have none. I try to think of a way to outwit them, but my brains feel as if they have turned to watered porridge. *Think, girl, think!*

The bear-man says, "There's a fallen log over here. Help move it across the road. 'Twill slow them down."

I can think of no way to avoid this, so I help the men lug the heavy log across the path. *Surely their horses can leap over the log. Surely the log will alert them that something is amiss.*

I clear my throat. "Perhaps 'twould be good if I go forward to scout out if—"

The weasel-faced man gives a twist, and suddenly his blade is pressed against my throat. The metal feels cold and hard. "We will do the plan my way!"

Then I hear horses.

The weasel-faced man pushes me to the ground. I see two horses pull up short at the fallen log. Fleance and his father.

"Have a care, son," Fleance's father says.

The fingers of the weasel-faced man dig into my shoulder. He squats beside me, shadowed by the trees. I see his knife in his other hand. *Can I make a lunge for it and get it away from him?* I calculate the distance and what I need to do.

I glance at Fleance and his father, trying to guess how much time I have.

Lord Banquo cranes his head to see the patch of sky between the trees. "'Twill be rain tonight."

"Then let the rain fall!" shouts the bear-man.

In a blur of activity, the two men dash out with swords flashing. Fleance's father tries to pull his sword out, but the bear-man pins it against the flank of the horse.

I sprint to Fleance's horse, which rears, startled by all our motion. Weasel-face snatches the reins and thrusts them into my hand.

"Hold the sprat here!"

Fleance tugs to free the reins. "Stop! Let me go!"

"Get away from him!" Fleance's father shouts. "Leave my son alone!"

I toss the reins to Fleance. Then I slap the rump of his horse.

"Fly!" I whisper. "Go as fast as you can."

"But my father needs—" Fleance begins.

His father cries, "Fly, Fleance! Fly! Live and avenge—"

The two assassins pull Lord Banquo to the ground. I snatch a branch off the ground and, with all my strength, whack it against the side of Fleance's horse. It rears up, knocking my hood off my head. I slap it again, and it gives a scream. "Fly!" I shout so loudly that my throat hurts.

I see Fleance's frightened face. His eyes seem to widen, but then his horse takes off, leaping over the fallen log and racing down the road.

I turn. The two men are standing over Lord Banquo's body. Lord Banquo is not moving. Even in the dusk I can see their hands and faces are smeared with blood.

"The son got away," I say.

Weasel-face utters a string of curses, but the bear-man says calmly, "But the father is dead."

Weasel-face stops in mid-curse. He thinks a moment, then nods. "True. Let's back to the king and tell him what we've done."

Taking no notice of me, they hurry off. I am left standing there, staring at Lord Banquo's body.

"Don't be dead," I whisper. "Please, let this be a trick. Please move. Please, let this be your ruse to fool those stupid murderers."

But Lord Banquo does not move.

I kneel down and pull his cloak back. He looks as if he has been dipped in blood. There are more wounds than I can count. His eyes are frozen open. I hesitate, and then I gently close his eyelids. My throat is tight, and, to my shame, my eyes fill with tears. I would love to lie down on a bed of leaves and howl like a silly babe. I want to turn back time. I want to be stronger and wiser. I want to be a witch indeed so I can mumble a spell and bring him back to life.

"I tried," I whisper. "I tried to save you." I bite my lip. I hear a night bird give a mournful cry over in a thicket. The rest of the wood is very still. "I didn't know what else to do." I want to take his hand, but I can't stand to touch the body again. So I rest my fingers on a fold of his cloak. "I saved your son, sir. I saved your son."

If only you had killed Him earlier, then Lord Banquo would be alive now. Because you did not act, because you have not stopped Him, Lord Banquo is dead. Because of you, Lord Banquo is dead.

My life is an arrow . . . but I do not feel like an arrow. I feel like a small girl who is lost in a world that is much too big.

"I have made my life a weapon," I whisper, but I cannot remember the rest of the phrase.

I lower my head to pray, and then I see that around his neck Lord Banquo wears more wealth than I have seen in my entire life in the wood. A thick gold cross encrusted with rubies, nearly a hand's span from top to bottom, hangs there. *The king must have given it to him. It is the twin to one I have seen hanging around His own neck.* There is no one else here to claim it.

Around his neck, the dead Lord Banquo wears a happy fortune for Lisette and Pod. Around his neck he wears a small house and shop for them. Around his neck he wears their future.

"Forgive me, Fleance," I whisper. "I know this gold necklet belongs to you, but I did give you life. Surely this jeweled cross and necklet is but a small boon. Don't begrudge me this. With it I can buy a home and livelihood for Pod and Lisette."

I slip it around my own neck and slide it under my shirt. I do not let myself notice whether there is blood on it.

"Forgive me," I whisper to Lord Banquo. "I will trade you something for this fine gift." I slide off the cloak I wear. I know it is not mine—it belongs to the soldier in the kitchen—but I have nothing else. I drape the cloak over him.

"A trade," I say, though I know it is not a fair trade. I take a couple of steps away, and then I move back to the body. I pull my soldier's cloak off to his side, and then unfasten his own cloak. Its gold-and-cream-colored stripes are smudged with huge puddles of damp blood. I have to roll his body from side to side to pull it away from him, but I do. It is a costly garment. I have some dim notion of sending it to Fleance. *Even though I have taken the ruby cross, I will save the cloak for him.* Then I smooth my soldier's cloak back over the dead man and bundle his up in my arms. His striped cloak is heavy and smells of blood. It is awkward to carry, but I cannot bring myself to wear it.

As I step away from his body, Lord Banquo's cross bobs against my chest.

I know what I must do now.

THIRTY-SIX

I SCRAMBLE UP onto the back of Lord Banquo's horse. He shies a little. I wonder if he smells the blood on Lord Banquo's cloak. The horse is huge. I feel as if I am straddling a house. But the poor creature has a sensitive mouth so he responds easily to my guidance.

It is full dark by the time I approach the castle. At the bottom of the small rise to the castle gates, I slide off the horse's back and pat it.

"You poor thing. I well know 'tis hard to be adrift in the world."

I drop the reins to the ground. I have no wish to make His stables richer by the addition of Lord Banquo's beast. "Be free," I tell him, but the silly creature just stands there, nuzzling grass. I decide not to slap him on his rump and send him off. "Poor horse, you have had more than your fill of excitement this evening."

I rub my face against his neck. "Then wait here. I will be back before moonrise. For almost all my life I have been waiting to kill a man, but I will chase this vain bubble no longer. Tonight I cast this whole business aside. Tonight I throw the broken stick over my shoulder and let the world know that He has beaten me. Horse, I will be back in no time, and you will come with me as we leave this murky castle behind. There will be two others with me. They are called Lisette and Pod. You can travel with us as we leave this place forever."

I pull the jeweled cross out of my shirt and cradle it in my hand. "What I have in my hands, what I took from your master, this is my new life. I will fetch Pod and Lisette, and then the three of us will journey far away. Perhaps we will even leave this accursed country and . . ."

I look hard at the castle crouched in the dark like an awkward, frightened black beast, its bony spine made of the line of pikes holding cut-off heads. Their empty eye sockets stare down. They seem to reproach me, but I am done with this whole business. I am neither witch nor warrior. I am only a girl. Finally I understand—He cannot be defeated.

Time feels immense now that I will pursue my revenge no more.

Like lightning, a vision of Nettle and Mad Helga's faces flash into my mind.

"No!" I say, talking like a mooncalf to the empty night. "I cannot take everyone with me. They are safer in their wood than they would be in a village with us."

I run my fingers up and down the horse's neck. "Wait, horse. I will be right back."

I start to put Lord Banquo's cloak over the horse as a blanket, but he sniffs and whinnies and shies away from the scent of the blood. I can't bring myself to put the stained drape on him. I give him a reassuring pat. "That's all right, old fellow. I don't blame you for not wanting your master's blood on you."

I hurry into the castle. For once luck is with me. The guard at the gates is one who has spent many evenings spinning war tales around the hearth in the kitchen, and he recognizes me, growling a good-natured curse as I pass. Even from the courtyard I can tell that the Great Hall is filled with light and music. The banquet is well under way.

The courtyard is deserted. Everyone except the guard at the

gates must be at the revels. Then behind me I hear the guard call out, "Stop! Who comes so late to the feast?"

To my horror, I hear weasel-face's whistling tones. "Peace. We come on the king's business. Here is a token he has given us for admittance."

Quickly I step aside to the shadows by a rain barrel. The two assassins tramp past me.

At the foot of the steps to the Great Hall, bear-man gestures to the other to wait. Weasel-face hesitates, and then steps back into the shadows by the gates. Bear-man twitches his clothes into place. He seems nervous. Then he heads up the stairs to the Great Hall.

I should go straight to the kitchen. I have finished with this foul business. I am settled in my mind. I am going to find Lisette and Pod, tell them I have money enough to set us up in a small house and a small business, and—

Despite my decision to have no more to do with Him, I tiptoe behind the bear-man to the Great Hall, pausing only to stuff Lord Banquo's cloak under the seventh stair. *I will take only a few moments to see what happens. Just a quick peek at what is taking place in the Great Hall, and then I will collect Lisette and Pod, and we will leave His life forever.*

The hall is filled with all manner of Scottish lords and their attendants. It flames as bright as a Twelfth Night feast in paradise. All the folk are dressed in their best clothing, and I see the servers darting nervously about. Master Steward stands at the far end, rubbing his hands up and down his apron in an anxious gesture.

Then, in one corner, I see the bear-man chatting to Him. The bear-man looks afraid, and He looks angry. I edge through the crowd, hoping to get close enough to overhear their conversation, but suddenly I am seized by the back of my collar.

"Shirking your share of work, peasant!" It is Brude's voice. He gives me a shove and I slam into a nearby table. The soldier at the table shoves me backward, and I tumble to the floor. Brude looms

over me, his pretty face flushed with anger or heat or both. He holds
a heavy jug in his hands.

"By rights I should tell Master Aswald that you have been playing truant this evening while the rest of us labor like slaves. But perhaps if you're a good little serf and work hard tonight and give me
any coins you receive in laud, perhaps—just perhaps—I will refrain
from letting Master Cook know what a hop o' revels you are."

He aims a kick at me, but I see it coming and roll to one side,
almost all the way under a bench, and he misses me, unwilling to
kick the guests perched on that bench. Then he slams the jug down
on the floor beside me. It is a wonder that it does not shatter.

"Pour the wine, peasant boy. Let anyone grow thirsty, and I'll
personally see you're whipped."

First I crane my head to see if He and the murdering bear-man
are still talking, but Brude is in the way. So I hoist myself to my feet
and head up and down the narrow aisles between the tables, lugging
the heavy jug of wine, sloshing wine into any empty glass I spy.
Whenever I have a chance to look up, I try to find Him in the
crowd, but I do not see Him.

As I move from guest to guest, I hear them muttering, complain-
ing of their hunger and griping that Lord Banquo is not yet there so
the feast can begin. *He is dead,* I want to scream. *He has been murdered, and his bloody cloak lies under the seventh stair just outside this
door.* How they would gawk should I tell them that!

I see no empty chairs at the high table on the dais, saving only
His chair. This makes me angry. How arrogant He is—He does not
even make a pretense that Lord Banquo is truly coming. He does
not even bother to leave a seat at the high table for Lord Banquo,
the man who is supposed to be the guest of honor. Saint Colum's
eyes, are all the guests blind or so befuddled with drink that they
cannot see that He does not expect Lord Banquo to come?

Then I see Him, still standing in the corner, but the bear-man is
gone. I ease my way over toward Him. Before I get there, His witch-
wife calls something to Him, and He raises his goblet.

The room grows silent.

"Welcome, friends!" His voice rings strong and sure throughout the hall. "It little befits our hospitality that our chief guest is tardy." Several guests mutter in agreement. I am sickened by His hypocrisy. *Not only did He order Lord Banquo's death, but now He makes Lord Banquo himself the subject of blame.*

Then I get an idea as bright as the midsummer sun!

In a few steps, I reach the high table on the dais. I move along it, pouring wine, until I reach His empty seat. Then I slide Lord Banquo's cross out from under my shirt and hang it on the back of the one empty chair. *Let Him recognize this cross. Let it startle Him so that He reveals His deceit to the whole gathering. Let Him understand that nearby there is a witness to His cruel murder. Let Him know that somewhere in this hall there is someone who has seen Lord Banquo's slaughtered body and now comes for Him.* I jiggle the chain so the cross hangs smoothly down the chair's back. The sides of the chair's back hide the sight of the cross from the view of His lady and from the lord who sits to the left of the chair, but surely He will recognize it when He goes to sit down. *It will frighten Him,* I think gleefully. *He will wonder how that cross got there. He will wonder who is His enemy, who is the witness to the foul murder He ordered.*

Once again He silences the room. He raises His goblet higher. "Still, I drink to the general joy of the whole hall, and to our dear friend Banquo, whom we miss. I wish he were here!"

I step away from His chair, just as His lady rises.

"Please take your seat, my lord." Though her voice is soft, it is clear that she is giving Him a command.

"The table's full," He says.

The lord to the left of the empty seat rises to his feet. "Here's your seat, my lord." He gestures to the chair with the cross hanging down its back.

I hold my breath. *Let it work. For once, let my scheme work.*

And then I see His eyes spot the hanging cross. Almost immediately, His eyes jerk wide in horror.

"Where?" He whispers.

"Here," says the lord. He gestures again to the chair with the cross.

Then He screams.

Joy leaps in me higher than a spawning salmon.

From my place close by the dais, I see the startled faces of the guests.

Gasping like a landed fish, He raises a shaky finger and points it toward the chair. "Who did this?" His voice is harsh and ragged, like a torn shriek.

No one else seems to notice the cross. "What?"

"Did what?"

"What does your lordship mean?"

The guests stare at Him, bewildered.

Again He points at the chair. "You can't say I did it!" His outstretched finger trembles. "Don't shake your bloody head at me."

A lord at the end of the table calls out, "Rise, gentlemen, his highness is not well."

In fact He has fallen to His knees and shakes with fear.

Never have I felt more delight. *I have done it. I have injured Him. And, God willing, never will He be able to regain the respect of His people. Surely after this display of cowardice, they will snatch His kingship away.*

But His lady calls out, "Sit, worthy friends. My lord often suffers these fits and has done so since he was young. 'Twill pass quickly, and he will feel shame if you let him know you notice his suffering. And that will make his fit last longer. Please sit." She signals Master Steward to begin serving the food. Then she moves to the end of the table where He cowers, gives an angry frown, and takes His arm. She leads Him to the same corner in which He talked with the bearman.

I feel a sudden flash of fear. *Don't let her talk Him out of this terror.* She is skillful as the devil in coaxing men to do her will, no matter how difficult or outrageous. I cannot permit that to happen.

I must do something to prolong His fit. I must not let Him recover from this fit.

A fresh idea darts into my head. Holding the wine jug tight to my chest, I run out of the hall and clatter down the stairs. To my surprise, Pod, Lisette, and a few kitchen lads are standing there.

Lisette says, "We heard shouts."

Pod asks, "Gilly, what is happening in—"

"I cannot talk to you now!" I snatch up Lord Banquo's cloak and pound it as compact as I can. I do my best to hide it between the wine jug and my tunic. It is an awkward fit, but if I stay in the shadows, I pray no one will notice. I race back up into the crowded hall, shoving my way back to the dais.

Just as I fear, she has indeed calmed Him down. They are walking back to the table, arm in arm. He walks right to the empty chair. For a moment He stares at it in contempt, then He stretches forth his arm and snags the cross with two fingers. He lifts it in the air and laughs. Then He tosses it to the ground and grinds it hard beneath His heel. Rubies pop out and scatter like wheat on a granary floor.

There goes my chance to give a home to Pod and Lisette. But it was worth it. Surely it was worth it. I have made my life an arrow. . . .

His lady nods her approval. "My worthy lord, your noble friends have missed you."

He pushes back His chair and stands at His place. He calls out, "Worthy friends, do not let my fit upset you. I have a strange illness that is nothing to those who know me well."

His fingers close around a fresh goblet on the table. To my surprise, He thrusts out His arm to me.

"Boy! Give me some wine." His glance is hard and cold, like a magic stone that turns everything to ice.

As I move slowly toward Him, I ease the bundled cloak sideways till it is wedged awkwardly under my arm. My hand shakes as I pour the wine into His goblet, taking great care that the cloak does not fall. Some of the wine splashes onto the tablecloth, making a stain like spattered blood.

Does He recognize me? Simultaneously my bones dissolve into water and my blood hardens to ice.

I fill His goblet halfway so that I will spill no more on the white tablecloth. But He glances down at it, then thunders, "Fill full!"

I manage to fill the goblet to the top. Then I step backward, behind His chair.

"I drink to the general joy of the whole table."

His chair hides me from view. I must work quickly. I set the jug down on the floor.

"And to our dear friend Banquo, whom we miss."

I shake out the cloak. The bloodstains have caused parts of it to stick together. Some of the stiffened folds poke out at unnatural angles like broken wings, but there is no time now to separate the stuck bits.

"I wish he were here."

Now comes the tricky part. I have observed that no one seems to notice a servant if the servant is performing servant like acts. *Let me be steady. Let me be true.*

"I drink to Banquo and to all of you."

It is time. In the few seconds that they drink, I whisk the striped cloak over the back of His chair. It falls from the top to puddle on the seat and then spill onto the floor. In the bright torchlight of the dais, the gold stripes glitter, except where they have been dyed dark by blood. The knife slashes can be plainly seen.

I step back and wait.

He sets His goblet down and turns back to the chair, preparing to sit down. I watch Him as He sees Banquo's cloak.

He recognizes it.

The color drains from His face.

Yes! Yes!

THIRTY-SEVEN

LIKE A MAN who has been suddenly struck blind, He backs away, His hand fumbling across the table, sweeping cups and serving platters to the floor. He is screaming.

"Be off! Quit my sight! Let the earth hide you! Your bones have no strength. Your blood is cold."

At the same time, His lady calls out, "'Tis just the fit again, dear friends, but it spoils our festivities." Her voice is faint, like watered milk. I doubt anyone can hear it above His screaming.

"I am a man," He screams, "and I dare do anything a man does. I can face any form but this one. Bring on a tiger, a bear, a rhinoceros. Come back to life and I will face you armed with anything you choose. If I tremble before any living creature, then call me a baby girl! But to face the dead—"

Then His wife reaches out and tugs on the cloak. It catches on the chair and as she pulls harder and harder, the chair itself topples to the floor with a huge crash. The crash seems to bring Him to His senses. He begins to laugh, a loose gushing laugh like a nosebleed.

"Why, being gone, I am a man again!" He laughs again, and

many in the hall put their hands over their ears at the sound of His mad loud laughter.

Then the shaken guests begin to rush for the door. He turns to them, His face stiff with fury, and bellows, "Sit down!"

Like in the game of grab-the-chair, the guests quickly plant their rumps in the nearest seat and stare in fascinated horror. He steps backward, knocking over the jug of wine behind His chair.

A sick silence reigns.

His wife raises her hand. She looks controlled, but I am close enough to see her other hand gripping the edge of the table, gripping so hard that her knuckles are white. Her voice seems to tremble. "You have distressed our guests with your fit."

She stares hard at her husband, but He is righting his chair. He flings himself into it. "Wine!" He shouts.

Brude darts forward, but to my surprise, instead of serving Him himself, Brude thrusts another wine jug into my hand. I move forward nervously, looking for a goblet to fill, but He snatches the jug from my hand and takes a long drink right from the jug itself.

"How can all of you sit quietly when these sights turn me pale with fear?"

The guests' faces twitch into deeper horror, as terrified by Him as He was by the sight of the stabbed cloak.

All of this has fallen out even better than I could devise.

"What sights, my lord?" asks a guest with a cheek crisscrossed by an old scar.

"Do not speak," His lady cries. She seems close to tears. "He grows worse and worse."

"My lord—" calls out the Master of Arms, but the queen interrupts.

"Questions enrage him. Go. Please go. Go!"

Had a dragon flown into the hall, the guests could not have scrambled more frantically to be gone. They hurry out as if His madness is contagious. Some almost knock each other over in their eagerness to be away from there and talk about the events of the evening. Even the other servants run away.

I look out over the empty Great Hall. Tables and benches are overturned, and the floor is a trash heap of spilled food and drink, enough food to feed a village for a half a year. He and His lady look tiny in the midst of the huge, deserted hall.

Hoping not to be noticed, I drop to the ground and pretend to be picking up trenchers and cups, but I peek out at the lord and lady. My heart rejoices to see them so broken. She is clearly bone-weary and He looks to be in a trance. She leans down and plucks up Lord Banquo's cloak and then sinks down into her chair. She begins stroking the cloak as if it were a frightened cat.

For a long time they sit in silence.

When He finally speaks, His voice is thick as cold porridge. "'Twill have blood, they say. Blood will have blood. Stones have been known to move and trees to speak."

Has He gone mad? Can I be that lucky? *Let Him be mad,* I pray frantically. *Let Him be mad, and then this whole business will be well finished.*

His wife does not even turn to look at Him.

Then they continue to sit silently.

I squat in the shadows, moving slowly, pretending to tidy up but keeping them in my sight. No other servants return to the hall. They have all been well spooked.

The fire burns out, and He takes no notice.

My head begins to ache.

They go on sitting there.

"What is the time?"

My head jerks up. I realize I have fallen asleep. Now I see that the nighttime blackness in the windows has faded to gray.

She is still sitting in her chair, stroking the cloak.

"Almost morning," she says in a cold, dead voice.

He nods like an old man, as if He expected that answer. "Did you say that Macduff refused to join our feast?" He asks.

"Did you invite him?"

"I have spies in every household," He says, "and I hear He refuses to acknowledge me as the true and rightful king." He stands, knocking over His chair. The empty hall echoes with the sound of its crash. "Tomorrow, I will seek out those three weird women who first foretold that I would be king. I must know more about what is to befall me. No matter what it takes, I will make them speak."

He throws a goblet across the hall. It clatters on the floor. His wife flinches at the sound.

"From this moment forth," He announces as if He were addressing a battlefield full of troops, "for my own good, all causes will give way. There are strange things in my mind, and I will no longer consider whether they are right or wrong. Whatever I think, I shall do. Nothing must thwart my desires or will."

At that she looks up at Him, her brow puckered with worry. "You lack sleep," she says, and now her tone is gentle.

He laughs His ugly nosebleed laugh. "Yes, my love, 'tis time to sleep."

He closes His fingers on the cloak in her lap and pulls. For a few heartbeats she holds on to it, and then she lets go. He then pulls her to her feet and wraps the bloodstained cloak around her shoulders.

She draws her breath sharply and holds it.

He laughs again and then kisses her, hard, as she stands stiffly wrapped in that cloak stiff with blood.

"My love, we have only begun!"

She flings the cloak off. It slides to the floor. He laughs again, His harsh, mocking laugh.

She sweeps out of the hall.

I seize my courage with both hands.

"My lord," I say, and I am pleased that my voice does not tremble.

He turns to me, blinking with surprise.

I must do it. "My lord, you speak of three weird women who can foretell the future."

His fingers flutter to the handle of His sword. I fall to one knee and try to look meek.

"My lord, do you know that three such women who dabble in prophecy live in Birnam Wood, not two hours' journey from here?"

He strides across the floor and grabs my arm painfully.

"Do you spy on me, whey-face?" His fingers tighten. There is such strength in His hand. *He could rip me apart with His hands alone.*

It takes all my concentration to keep my voice steady.

"My lord, I came to the hall to tidy up and I heard you speak of the three weird women. All of us know that just outside the village of Cree live three witch women who claim to have encountered you once on a misty moor. Ride to that village, and anyone there can tell you where the women are to be found."

Stay calm. Stay calm. Let Him take the bait.

He stares at me hard for several heartbeats. I cannot read His intentions in His cold eyes. Then He flings me from Him like a broken toy and is gone from the hall.

I must to Nettle and Mad Helga. Though I am weary to the very bottom of my soul, I must away tonight if I am to reach them before He does. *The tide has finally turned my way! It would be false of me now to wade back to the shore.*

First I will run to the kitchen to bid farewell to Lisette and Pod. But immediately I push that notion away. *It would only upset them. They might want to come with me, and they would slow me down.* It will be the second time I left them with no word of leave-taking, but I must. After all, they are not my blood kin.

I pick up Lord Banquo's cloak from the floor. It is stiff with dried blood. But I harden my resolve and draw the cloak round my shoulders.

My one dream is about to come true.

I have made my life a trap . . . and now it is time for the fly to walk into my web.

THIRTY-EIGHT

THROUGH THE THIN early morning light, I hasten back to Nettle's hut. I ride Lord Banquo's horse hard. I am determined to reach the women before He does.

My body aches with every jounce, and I am so sleepy that I fear I will need to prop twigs in my eyes to hold them open.

Just before the village of Cree, I slide off the horse's back and head into the wood. I avoid looking at the leaves for too many of them are the color of blood. I lead the horse, making sure that the huge brute steps carefully over fallen branches and avoids snake holes. When I reach my old stream, I stop long enough to let the tired horse drink. He drinks for a long time. Although it is good to be back in my familiar wood, I hop from foot to foot, tired but impatient to reach Nettle's.

"We must hurry, horse," I say, patting him. "Old fellow, I know you are tired"—and a yawn cracks my jaw—"but we must hurry. I must reach Nettle and Mad Helga before He does. They must be warned!"

Then I pull his reins with one hand and push branches out of the way with the other as we make our way through the wood. Even though I urge the horse to go faster, faster, I am nonetheless a little anxious about how Nettle and Mad Helga will receive me. I am so very tired. *I feel like the walking dead.* I stumble a few times. Tiredness weighs me down like a heavy cloak, like Lord Banquo's cloak that is my only protection against the autumn chill. *I must reach the hut first. It will be disaster indeed should He find the women before I do.* So I force myself to go on until we reach the clearing of Nettle's hut.

The place has hardly changed at all. A few chickens scratch at a patch of dirt, and a skinny goat raises his head to stare at me with his eyes as blank as a black stone, but there is no other sign of life. The hut looks just the same as it did when I left it back in the tail of spring.

I fall to my knees and press my head to the ground, panting.

"Usually 'tis the horse that does the grazing." Nettle's voice is as clean and biting as spring greens.

Before I can stop it, a smile splits my face, but I am determined not to show Nettle how good it feels to be home, so I keep my voice gruff and douse my smile.

"If you were not such a contrary old woman," I say, "you would help me to my feet."

Nettle's skinny hand closes around my elbow, and—none too gently—she hauls me to a standing position. She looks older and more tired, near as tired as I feel. Her fingernails are split, and dirt hides in the cracks.

She pats my cheek, and her voice is as soft as ever I have heard it. "'Tis good to see you, Gillyflower. 'Tis empty here without you."

Then, as if she is shamed by her unusual gentleness, she says in a rough tone, "Though 'twould be even more a treat if you'd looked less like a charmbaby."

I rub my forehead with the back of my hand. "I must talk to you, Nettle, and Mad Helga, too. We have something important to do."

"You need to wash and sleep—"

I blow out my breath impatiently. "There's no time to wash, and I can sleep when I'm dead."

Nettle chuckles. "Oh ho! Oh ho! When I need you to hurry, you sneak off to duck yourself in the stream, but when you have need of me, no washing time—"

"Hold your prattle, Nettle."

"Gilly, let me get you some food and—"

"I have no need of food at this moment. What I need is to talk with you and—"

Nettle continues as if I had not interrupted. "There's last night's onion stew that needs only a bit of a warm-up—"

Home not a hundred heartbeats, and already I want to shake the skinny crone. "For once in your life, Nettle, be more Mary than Martha."

"Gilly—"

"Or if you must bustle, then find a bucket and give some water to this poor horse."

I brush past her and start for the house. "Is Mad Helga stirring?"

There is a flat-topped stone in the clearing. Its surface is half-covered with herbs left to dry in the sun. Nettle squats beside it, her knees making a kind of creak when she goes down. She carefully picks the herbs out of the cloth she carries and lays them flat on the stone. "I mistrust the glitter of your eye, child. There is a wildness in you that will not—"

I glare at her. "Come inside, quickly."

But she will not come until she has laid down every leaf and sprig of her herbs, even though I jiggle from foot to foot in impatience.

Mad Helga shows no surprise at seeing me. I wonder if she even realizes that I have been gone a long time. Quickly I tell them about His approach and what we must do.

"No," says Nettle.

"No?" My voice slides upward. "What means this no? 'Tis a simple enough plan."

Nettle presses her palms against her thighs. "'Help me this once,' you said, when we met him before in the wood. 'I shall not ask you again,' you said."

"I was wrong," I say.

Mad Helga says nothing. She rocks back and forth, making a humming noise like a drunken bee.

Nettle lets her breath out in a little angry puff. "Do you not see, Gillyflower? 'Tis not safe for us to pose as witches. Herb craft and woodlore are dangerous enough, but to set ourselves up as seers and spell weavers—Gilly, 'twould be the same as strolling into the dragon's mouth."

"We *are* witches," I snap.

Nettle rolls her eyes.

"The villagers see us as witches," I say.

"You could call a haddock a horse," Nettle says, "but woe betide you should you try to saddle it and ride to market."

"The king will be here any minute, old woman, yet you prattle proverbs like a granny in the sun. Stop your nonsense, Nettle, and—"

"'Tis you, Gilly, that prattles nonsense. As you well know, calling a thing by a name does not mean that the thing is that named thing."

"You have the double sight," I shout, "and I have witnessed your conjuring up the Old Ones. You know herb lore and woodcraft—"

Then Mad Helga begins to add words to her buzzing little tune.

> *A dragon came to Dunisferne,*
> *Sing ho, my lads, sing ho.*
> *And there it wed a lady fair—*
> *Hey nonny, hey nonny, hey—*

I kneel in front of Mad Helga and take her leathery hands in mine. "Please. Please, Mad Helga. Please pull your wits out of the fog, gather them, please be clear. I know I owe my life to you and Nettle and therefore have no right to ask more of you, but I do ask. I will pay you in any coin you wish. Do me this one last favor, and I will sign over to you my freedom, live as your slave for the rest of my life. Do me this last favor and I will steal for you, kill for you. I will take to the roads as an outlaw. I will wrestle a field from the wood. I will peel my skin from my arms and feet and cure it to make you slippers. Whatever you wish is yours if you will but grant me this one wish."

She seems to fumble to gather her wits together. Her eyes meet mine. As long as I can remember, she has looked old, but now she looks more ancient than the world. "What you ask will lead to death," Mad Helga says. "Nettle has told you that before, yet—"

"I know. His death is what I seek."

" 'Tis not of *His* death that we speak."

Nettle breaks in. "Would you sacrifice someone you love, Gilly, just to bring him down? Death demands death—death is the blood coin needed for what you ask."

For a moment I hesitate. *This does not feel right.* Then I say, "I do not love anyone. There has been death already and I'm owed His life. 'Tis my due."

Mad Helga says, "Those past deaths are stale. A blood spell needs a fresh death."

"Then I will be the one taken," I say. "I will give my life to cut off His. No one else need fear." Fine words, but inside myself I do fear. Inside myself I have pulled apart as if I were tied to two horses and they were whipped to gallop in different directions. One part of me urges, *Forward, plunge forward,* while a deeper part screams, *Turn back, turn back.*

Nettle says, " 'Tis not so simple to—"

Mad Helga holds up her hand and silences her. Then she leans close to me. She smells of old clothes and the dark, damp smell that many ancient people have. "Child, if you are wise, you will step away from all this."

I make my choice. "I do not wish to be wise or safe or loved!" I shout. "There is one thing I want, and you have the power to give it to me. Help me. I beg you, help me once more."

Mad Helga and Nettle look at each other.

"Just once more," I plead. *As we sit and mumble here, time slides away.* "He will be here any moment." I tune my ears to catch the notes of His arrival.

"Not till dusk," Nettle says in a reluctant tone. "He will not arrive until dusk. And 'tis not here that he will find us. At dusk we will find him at the ring of old stones that lies halfway to the village."

"Did you see His coming, Nettle?" I ask.

Nettle turns away.

"He seeks us out," I tell them. "We have the power to destroy Him."

Nettle sighs. "I can mix a potion, Gilly. We can drug him with herbs. As soon as he drinks, his mind will be troubled with strange fancies. For a pace, his wits and reason will go begging. He will see strange and troubling visions. Anything we say to him will gnaw out a home deep within his mind and haunt him as long as he lives."

Joy floods through me. *This is my right path.* "Make me that potion, and I will carry it to Him, Nettle."

Nettle drums her fingers against her lip in a worried gesture. "'Tis a misuse of the herb craft."

"Who cares a thorn for that?" I ask.

"Some minds stay damaged," Nettle says. "I cannot predict how he will respond. 'Tis a potion that could send a madness that will not fade."

I force a laugh. "He is mad already, Nettle. He sucks the blood of the country like some monster in a granny tale. He kills like a raging beast, slaughtering powerful and innocent alike. 'Twill be best for our country if we bring Him down. Poison is as good a weapon as any."

"'Tis not for our country you wish him destroyed, Gilly," Nettle says.

"No." I smile. "Now make me the potion."

"Make the potion," Mad Helga says.

I add, "And teach me to make it."

Nettle shakes her head. "It demands too many ingredients, Gilly. You would never hold it in your mind. But slice a beet root and boil it in the pot with a hand's worth of water till 'tis red and thick as baboon's blood.

"Work quickly," I say.

And yet a part of me, like a demented raven, screams, *Turn back, turn back.*

FOR THE LENGTH OF THE AFTERNOON, Nettle works, blending dozens of herbs together: lizard eye, cockscomb, frog toe, blind-worm thorn, dragon leaf, hemlock, tiger guts, ladyslipper, and many others, including some I've never seen her use before. The broth smells like a cesspool in the underworld, and, as it cools, it thickens into a porridge. Nettle looks flushed and exhausted. Finally she presses the smelly mess through a cloth, squeezing out a thin liquid, which she pours into a vial. She wedges a whittled peg into the neck of the little bottle and hands it to me.

"Here. 'Twill be up to you, child, to find a way to make him drink it."

She lowers herself onto a stool. I tuck the vial into the drawstring pouch under my tunic. "Now, Nettle, there's no time to sit and ponder. We have the potion—now we must be off."

"Gilly, I am faint with weariness—"

"You can sleep when you're dead. Let's be off to the ring of stones."

I pull Mad Helga up from the hearth, and then I pull Nettle to her feet.

"Come on!"

THIRTY-NINE

HE'S NOT THERE.

With an impatient hand I slap one of the stones. These stones are smaller than the ones in the heath to the north, more like sheep than giants, but there are seven of them spaced around a circle. All the villagers avoid this place, calling it haunted. This is a fitting place to meet Him.

Only He is not here.

Nettle frowns. "I told you that he would not be here till dusk."

Angrily I plop down on the ground.

The late afternoon creeps along like a lame snail. Nettle and Mad Helga doze, each leaning against one of the fat stones. I sit there, staring, wondering if it is true that the stones were put there by Merlin the Wizard. I decide it cannot be the case. There is no reason for Merlin to visit this out-of-the-way nubkin of the world. Sometimes I think God himself does not wander deep into these wild places.

Still He does not come.

I begin to pace. I feel blurred with weariness, but at the same time, prickly with anger. Nettle takes no notice. After a while I say, "Why doesn't He come? 'Twill soon be dark."

Nettle does not even bother to open her eyes. " 'Tis better for us in the dark. 'Tis easier then to put fancies deep into his mind."

I call to Him with my mind. "Come—rot your soul—come! Come now to me!" I fret and fight back my weariness that lays siege to my intentions.

At last it is dark. The stones feel cold, yet I curl next to the biggest one, Lord Banquo's stiff cloak wrapped around me as a blanket. Suddenly Nettle jerks awake. Her body tightens like a drawn bowstring. She looks at me and nods.

" 'Tis He?" I ask. I feel more anxious than triumphant. *Can we do this indeed? Will He recognize me?* Now that it is too late, I realize I should have left Lord Banquo's cloak back at the hut and found some other wrap. I quickly consider tossing it aside, but I decide the risk is greater that He recognize me without the cloak than that He recognize the cloak in the dark. *Perhaps if He does recognize it, He will think it part and parcel of the witchcraft.* Then with a shock, I realize I have not yet thought of a way to make Him drink the potion. *Think, girl, think!*

Nettle nods again, this nod sharper and more insistent.

I rummage in the drawstring sack I have brought and take out a small cup hollowed from smooth white stone, one of Nettle's greatest treasures. I pull out a small leather bottle of ale and empty it into the goblet. Then I add the contents of the vial. It bubbles for a few moments and then it is quiet. I set the goblet on the lowest stone, the one with the flattest top. I pull the hood of Lord Banquo's cloak low across my face. *Do not let Him recognize either me or it in this smudge-edged darkness.* I hear several horses gallop up and then stop nearby, just out of sight.

Then I hear His voice. "Stand back. I will face them alone."

How did He know to stop here? Then I catch sight of Nettle's face, rigid with concentration. In a flash I understand—*she summoned Him here.* I do not know how she did it, but her mind called to Him and He came.

He strides into the clearing, standing in the center of the ring of stones. For a moment He blinks at all three of us, seemingly unsure which of us He should address. *The arrogance of the man—assuming that we have nothing better to do than to wait here for Him to show up.*

Only—that's just what we did.

I keep the cloak low over my face. *Surely He will not recognize a servant so far from the castle.* My heart pounds so loudly that I fear He will hear.

Finally He selects Nettle as our leader. He points His finger at her and raises His voice. "I will have information! Speak to me."

I step nervously into the ring of stones to stand next to Him. I raise my chalice. "You are weary, your majesty. Drink first."

He whirls to me. "Damn you, I want no drink! Tell me—"

"We will see into your heart more clearly if you drink."

I hold my breath, waiting. I have staked everything on this moment. Oh, how I wish I had asked Nettle to poison Him instead. *Although death alone would not be enough. I do not want Him to have an easy death. I want Him to see His death coming. It is only fitting.*

For a long, hard moment He stares at me. Then he scoops up my goblet and drinks the contents at one go. He flings it to the ground and stands defiantly. All at once, one cramp seizes Him, then another. He reaches for His sword, then falls to the ground and begins to jerk in convulsions like a landed carp.

"I conjure you," He screams, "by that evil art which you profess, however you come to know it, answer me! Though you untie the winds and let them fight against the churches, though the foaming waves drown all the ships, though the grasses be blown flat and the trees blown down, though all castles topple on top of their dwellers, though disaster howls until even destruction itself grows sick— answer me! Answer me!" His speech trails off in an unearthly howl.

"Speak!" Nettle says.

"Demand!" Mad Helga says.

I sink to my knees beside Him. "We'll answer."

He gives another howl of pain. "Damn you!" He paws at the air. "Stand back! Or fight like a man!"

I should enjoy the sight of Him thrashing about on the ground, but I feel uneasy. The sight disturbs me. Nevertheless, I fall to my knees beside Him. I ask greedily, "What do you see?"

"A warrior," He gasps, his empty fingers paddling wildly. "A helmet—a head only—no body, just a head. What does it mean? Tell me!"

Nettle and Mad Helga wait silently. I must say something. "Macbeth, Macbeth—beware—" *What, what can I say?* Suddenly I recall His conversation with His wife back at the castle. *Frighten Him. Name an enemy.* I see Mad Helga watching. *Speak like Mad Helga. That should put Him into fear.* "Beware Macduff!" I croak in my best Mad Helga voice. "Beware the Thane of Fife. Dismiss me. Enough!"

"One word more—" He begins.

"We will not be commanded," I thunder. I clap my hands, right in His face, and He scoots away in terror. "Here's another more powerful than the first!" I flap my hands at Nettle. *Let her take over. She will know what to do.*

She understands, and she moves forward and kneels by Him. She strokes His forehead with her fingers. He gives a whimper and pulls His knees to His chest.

"What do you see now?" asks Nettle, her voice as soothing as a nurse gentling a dream-spooked babe.

He points a finger toward the invisible air. "A child! There's a child covered in blood."

Mad Helga steps forward and lowers herself on His other side. She rests her dry, wrinkled hand on the top of His head. In her age-cracked voice she croons,

> *Be bloody, bold, and resolute.*
> *Laugh to scorn*
> *The power of man*
> *For none of woman born*
> *Shall harm Macbeth.*

He laughs and rolls onto His back. "Then live, Macduff. I need not fear you!"

I am confused. *Did Mad Helga just countermand my own spell?*

Nettle strokes her bony hand across His eyes as if she is shutting the eyes of the dead. "What see you now?"

"Another child," He whispers. He reaches up and squeezes her hand. "A child holding a tree."

This stumps us. Nettle looks at me, but I bite my lip. How can we work this vision into our warnings? Then Nettle says, "Macbeth shall never vanquished be until Birnam Wood to high Dunsinane Hill shall come against him."

What a foolish thing to say! How can a wood come to the castle? But I cannot blame her. She had little time to think of aught to say, and I myself could think of nothing better.

Then Nettle begins to snap her fingers over and over in front of His eyes until he focuses on them. He squeezes her hand again. "Tell me—tell me—" And he begs like a castaway child—

"Yes?" Nettle asks.

"Will Banquo's descendants ever reign in my kingdom?"

Nettle stares deep into His eyes. Her gaze doesn't waver until He screams and scoots away. He flings His hands up like a shield.

"What is it?" I whisper.

Again He points at the empty air. "Look! Look! Don't tell me you fail to see it."

"What?" I ask.

"Look! There are a line of kings, all with looking glasses in their hands—and Banquo brings up the rear! Never!" He pulls Himself up to His knees. "Never! I have not done all this for Banquo's brats! This is my kingdom, mine. It does not belong to *his* children. It belongs to—"

"To whom?" I demand. *How dare He prattle of kingdoms unjustly stolen, usurper and master murderer that He be.* I shriek, "You have no children!"

He screams again, covers His ears, and cowers, rocking back and forth and sobbing. He is a revolting sight. My mouth turns down in disgust. I turn to Nettle.

"He sickens me."

" 'Tis the potion, Gilly," she says. "No one would be brave and strong—"

"No! This is His real self! The body of a bully and the soul of a terrified child."

He continues to sob. Nettle crouches by Him and strokes His hair.

"Sleep! Sleep! You have need of sleep."

"No!" I say. I kneel in front of Him and pull His head up to look at me. My fingers dig into His cheek. "You will not sleep! Sleep will desert you. You will become a ghost of the night, roaming your castle like a specter. You have murdered sleep itself!"

Nettle shakes her head at me. "What you say to him in this state, that he will believe."

"Good."

"This is soul murder that you do to him, Gilly."

"Good." I let go of His face and again He collapses to the ground.

For a long time, He sobs. Finally His sobs fade to little whimpers, no louder than the squeaking of a mouse. For the space of a hundred heartbeats, He lies sniffling on the ground. Then Nettle motions to Mad Helga and me to withdraw. We fade back among the trees, just out of sight.

We watch as He lies there, whimpering and sniffling. Then Nettle flings out a warning hand, and we hold very still.

There is the sound of horses clattering up and then stopping just out of sight. We hear a rumble of voices, and then the horses gallop away again.

Night spreads across the sky as smoothly as melting goose grease. Finally He raises His head. He looks drained by His experience.

"Where are you?" He calls. "Damn you, where are you?"

We do not move.

A young lord runs into the clearing. I remember seeing him at the feast for Lord Banquo, but I do not know his name. "Yes, my lord?"

"Where did they go?" He asks. His voice is still a little hoarse, but it has regained much of its strength.

"Who, my lord?" asks the young lord.

"The witch women?" He grabs the top of one of the stones and pulls Himself to his feet, hunched like a humpback hag and holding tight to the stone for support. "Did they go past you?"

"No, my lord."

"I heard voices."

"Messengers, my lord. They bring news that—" He stops and takes a deep breath. Even though he is little more than a shadow in the shadows of night, it is clear he does not wish to give this news to his lord. He swallows hard and then says, "—news that Macduff has escaped to England!"

For several heartbeats, He stands in startled silence. Then He cracks the night air with his curses. "Damnation seize him! The devil himself dye him black! Let him hang, burn, freeze, starve! Damn him and all his brood to the deepest bowels of hell for all eternity!" Then He puts a hand out, and the young lord helps Him to stand upright.

"From this moment forth," He shouts, "anything that comes into my mind will be put into action. Nothing will stop my will." He shakes back His bright red hair. "I have learned this night that Macduff is a danger to my throne. Therefore I order you, gather a group of soldiers together and leave immediately to attack Macduff's castle. Kill everyone you find there—his wife, his servants, his children—all! Tear the castle to the ground!"

No! No! I whisper to Nettle, "Your potion has made Him worse."

"I told you that it might," she whispers back.

His scream shatters the quiet of the wood. "If I cannot hold this land forever, then I will drown it in blood."

I begin to run back to Nettle's hut.

The horse is there. I have need of it.

Before His men reach Fife, I must warn Lady Macduff.

FORTY

I AM RUNNING AND RUNNING through the wood with an ache in my side. My breathing is like a rusty saw. When I can run no more, I stumble along until I catch my breath, then I run again. Branches whip at my face, vines catch at my feet, and still I run.

Lord Banquo's horse is waiting at Nettle's hut. I fling myself onto his broad back.

"Run!" I croak through a throat sore from panting. "You could not save your master, but now you can redeem your failure. Now you have the chance to save an entire family. Run!"

I dig my heels into his sides, and he takes off.

I am not sure whether I am talking to the horse or to myself.

ALMOST IMMEDIATELY we must slow to a walk. It is no easy matter to wend my way through a wood in the dark. There is an orange moon, but the branches play catch-as-catch-can with the light. Before we reach the stream, I must slide off the horse and lead him along, all the way to the road.

THE FULL MOON IS HIGH when we reach the road, and it gives good light. Tiredness has nearly dissolved my bones. It is my second night without sleep. I remember the directions the lady gave me, and I know I must ride south and east. I scrabble back onto the horse's back.

"Go," I say. And he does.

It is almost as if he is glad to race. I jounce along, his pace pounding my sitting bones hard against my shoulders. *Let me be in time, let me be in time, I will ask nothing else from life if only this once I may be in time.* Shadows loom across the road like ancient creatures risen from the grave to snatch at me, but we gallop past them, almost flying. Trees and fields swishing past, always moving. My head rattles with hoofbeats pounding, my breath pounding, the voice inside me pounding, *Go, go, go, go.* After hours of this, I hear the lady talk to me.

Come to Fife. We will find you a fine lad for a husband.

I hear her silvery laugh.

Then I am jerked awake, still pounding through the night.

A little while later, I jerk awake again. *Mama?* I call. *Mama, have you come back for me?*

Sometimes I get confused and wonder if all this is the dream, if I only imagined Him in the wood and His prattling about the bloody babe and such. The earth pounds and pounds about my ears and bones, the way a dead soul might pound on the gates of Heaven. The night swoops about my ears, and there is only the riding. . . .

THEN DAYLIGHT SLAPS ME in the face.

I am lying in a field. The grasses are sharp and stiff beneath me. I squint and sit up.

"Nettle?" I call out. "Pod? I have had the strangest dream—"

Then I see the horse nosing among the grasses.

"Oh, no!" I do not know how long I have slept. I jump to my feet. *How could I sleep? How long did I sleep?* Pray God that it will take Him some time to gather His army together—

A yawn cracks my jaws.

"No!" I scream. "You hound of hell, you will not get this one!"

I am on the back of the horse, a back warm from the sun, and we are moving fast, fast, faster. . . .

• • •

TWICE I ASK FOR DIRECTIONS, and then the castle itself stretches above me. It is a homey-looking place, perched on a hump of ground next to a fast-rushing river. It suffered damage in the recent war, for scaffolds girdle its walls. There is no sign of immediate danger. In a nearby field, peasants hack at the hay with curved sickles. All looks peaceful.

Thank God I am in time.

I see a richly dressed noble ride from out of the gates. A cross-shaped scar mars his cheek. He looks familiar, and then I remember seeing him at the banquet for Lord Banquo. This man sat at the high table. I wonder if he is one of His agents, but this man does not seem to be uneasy or wishing to hide.

Nonetheless, I wait behind a stand of birches for him to pass. Then I gallop full speed to the courtyard.

A grimy gooseherd stands in the courtyard, scattering grain among his greedy, squawking fowl.

I slide off the horse, my sweaty legs sliding easily along the sweaty flanks. "The lady of the castle—I must see her."

The gooseherd eyes me doubtfully.

I stamp my foot. "You fool! Take me to the lady at once. She will not thank you for making her wait."

I do not know whether it is my anger or my wild eyes that cow him, but he bobs his head, pulls his forelock, and motions me to follow him. He leads me to a light-filled room. I did not know that it is possible to have so much light in a castle. Then I see the lady, clean and dainty in a fragile gown the color of primroses and as airy as a spider's web. She is playing catch-ball with young Ninian. He is as bouncy as a pup, but she looks very frail and small. It is clear from her flat belly that she has given birth since I met her by the sea. Then I see a Moses basket on the seat by the window. Inside is a tiny babe fast asleep.

Lady Macduff and Ninian are calling jokes back and forth and do not notice me.

I drop to a knee. "My good lady!"

Lady Macduff whirls around, startled. "Who are you?"

"My name is not known to you, my lady, but you gave me mutton stew and invited me to your castle."

Then I hear horses approaching—a large company. I run to the window and look out. Up the hill rides a large group of armed men.

The lady pays them no mind. Instead she clasps her hands together, her face bright with joy. "Oh, then you have come, my little girl who dresses as a boy! What fun!"

Ninian jumps up and down, clapping his hands. "You will teach me to fight with sticks!"

I shake my head. I hear the horses gallop through the gates. "My lady, you must be gone. You and all your little ones. Danger approaches. Go!"

She blinks at me with a bewildered look on her pretty face. "But who would want to harm me? I've done nothing wrong."

I tug her sleeve, trying to pull her toward the door. "We must be gone! Come, lady!"

She pulls away, and I eye her doubtfully. She looks too delicate to survive much rough travel.

I hear the voices of men in the courtyard. "Where's the bitch who rules this castle?"

A woman screams in the courtyard. A dog begins to bark. Then it squeals once and is silent.

"Come!" I whisper.

Color drains from Lady Macduff's face. "This cannot be happening," she whispers, her eyes large and murky with fear. She sinks to the ground in a froth of pale silk.

"Lady, come," I beg. "I dare not stay."

She buries her face in two small hands. "Oh, I am in this cruel world in which to do good is no defense against evil." She holds out her arms, and Ninian runs into them. She hugs him tightly. In the Moses basket, the wee babe awakens and begins to cry. She looks over at it helplessly.

I hear the sound of boots on the stairs.

"Come, lady!" I command.

"There is not time. But I have done nothing. Surely that counts for something." She buries her face against Ninian's head, rocking him back and forth and whispering, "Shh, shh, shh." The sound of the boots grows closer. I see that the lady will not come, and now we have no more time. She does not let go of Ninian. I remember there are other children in the castle. I make my decision. Quick as a flash, I grab the Moses basket and hang it from my arm. Then I run to the far end of the hall. An elderly maidservant is cowering against the wall, her eyes wild, fingering her rosary beads and fluttering her lips in silent prayer.

"The nursery! Where is the nursery?"

The servant is speechless with terror. She stares at me with terrified eyes. I shake her.

"The nursery!"

She points a shaking hand up the winding stairway. I run up the stairs. Behind me I hear the men explode into the hall.

A rough voice demands, "Where's your husband?"

The lady answers, "In a place where none like you can find him."

"He's a traitor!" says the first voice.

I hear Ninian cry out, "You lie!"

At the top of the stairs, the passageway divides into two. The men's voices grow indistinct. I look back and forth. Which way is the nursery?

Behind me I hear Ninian scream.

I decide to go left.

Then I hear the lady scream, over and over.

I dart through several rooms until I find what I seek. Ninian's little brother and sister huddle together on a small bed, their arms wrapped tightly around each other. In a nearby trundle a toddler is crying.

I hold out my hand to the older children. "Come with me. Quickly."

From below come the sounds of screaming and the men shouting as if they are cheering on a race. The lady's screams grow fainter, like milk poured into a stream.

The children do not move.

Then the little girl knuckles her eyes and whispers, "Mama!"

"Come on!" I say.

Roughly I pull the children to their feet. Even though the Moses basket hangs from one arm, I scoop up the toddler and tuck him under the other arm like a new-baked loaf. With my basketed arm I shove the two older ones across the floor. The Moses basket swings back and forth. The little boy stumbles, so I kneel down and say to him, "Climb on my back."

He stares at me, confused.

"Your mama said for you to come with me."

He glances at his sister, and the little girl nods. He climbs onto my back. With the back of the arm I've wrapped around the toddler, I press his leg against my side. I feel as unwieldy as someone trying to carry a cow and two chickens to market. I say to the little girl, "Grab hold of my robe." Then we hurry out of the room.

I hear furniture crashing and the screams of women. I shift the toddler around to my front so he can cling to my neck, making it a little easier to carry him. I run down the passage away from the screams. Then we reach the end, a solid wall. There is nowhere else to go.

The noise behind us grows louder. I glance from side to side. *There must be some way out. I am an arrow, an arrow—*

Then I remember passing a ladder up to the roof.

I turn around and start back the way I came. The toddler and the baby are both crying, but I have no time to shush them. My arms are beginning to ache. We go back three rooms, and there is the ladder! I tell the little girl, "Climb up!"

She looks at me, her face puckered with worry and looking strangely like her mother.

"Go!" I shout at her. "Climb, rot you! Climb!"

Then the little girl bursts into tears and begins to climb. I start after her.

I am very slow, since I can use but one of my hands. I must set both feet on a rung before I can go up another. Still, I make it to the top. I consider whether 'twould be best to try to pull the ladder up after us, but I decide not to set the two little ones down. Instead I grab the little girl's hand and run to the far end of the roof. I have no clear plan. All I can think of is to get as far away as possible.

At the end of the roof, there is no place to go. *Think! Think!*

I hear cries below, and I glance down. I see a scene of horror. All is chaos. There are several rough-garbed men, running their swords into cornered servants who are begging for their lives. The murderers are laughing as if they play at a game.

Then a voice behind me calls out, "Stop!"

I glance back. One of the attackers is climbing through the roof. He is followed by several others—one of whom has Lady Macduff's veil wrapped around his neck like a trophy of war.

I look around wildly for a place to run.

"You are cornered!" the man calls out. I see another man climbing up behind him. "Give me the children and you can go free."

Down below in the courtyard I see a pile of straw. I bite my lip, wondering if it is deep enough for me to drop the children in, but I do not think it is fat enough to break their fall. Like a wild thing, I run to the far wall. Below is the river. I have no choice! I lean forward to pick up the little girl to toss her into the stream. *Dear God, let the water be deep enough.* But someone grabs me from behind. The little boy screams. He clings to me like a baby squirrel, but he is pulled from my back screaming and kicking. I scream too and twist around. Then someone else yanks the little girl away. She screams.

A man dangles her over the edge of the roof.

"Little bird, can you fly?" he demands.

Then a third man lunges toward me and grabs at the toddler. I pull him away, but someone else seizes him, and someone else is pulling on the Moses basket, and I am jerked backward by the neckband of my tunic, and then I am falling. . . .

Falling over the ramparts!

FORTY-ONE

THE CHILD KEEPS RUNNING to the window to peer down into the castle courtyard. She is too excited to stand still.

"Nutkin, never will I get your hair plaited, and your lady mother will skin me alive if you are not ready on time. Stand still, do, my little rosebud, my little millikin."

"I want to, Nurse, but my feet will not stand still. They're too excited. My papa's coming home!"

"Your mama wants you to look nice for your papa, my blossom."

"Papa will be riding up any moment, Nurse. Hurry, do!"

"Yes, lovey, but do stand still!"

And then she hears the clatter of horses down in the courtyard. The child breaks free of her nurse and runs back to the window. Down below a dark-haired soldier, tall and strong, leans down and takes a mug held out by a servant. He takes a long, deep drink. Then he lowers the mug and laughs.

"Papa!" the child cries.

She starts to run out of the room. The nurse grabs at her skirt, but the child shakes herself free and runs down, her hair half undone.

She runs across the courtyard, holding her arms up.

"Papa! Papa!"

The dark rider sweeps her up in his arms, his horse rearing and the little girl squealing with delight.

AFTER SUPPER, *the warm firelight flickers like fireflies on the faces of young soldiers who are gathered around the hall, listening to the tales of the dark man, their leader. The little girl tiptoes in, carrying a huge book with beautifully tinted drawings. She has been neatened up, her hair tidied into plaits. She shoulders her way past the soldiers.*

"Now what is this?" her father demands as she plops the heavy book down on his knees.

"I have been waiting and waiting—ages, sir—for you to finish my story."

"But I have been at supper for only—"

The child stamps her foot. "I do not talk about supper, sir. I am talking about your war. You were gone forever and ever, Papa. I think that if I had to wait another single day, I would shrivel and die."

Her father tosses back his head and roars with laughter. He shouts to his men, "Although the only whelp my wife has thus far managed to give me is this girlchild, my little chit here has wormed her way into my graces. 'Tis a clever wench, so I just might keep her after all and not drown her with that last litter of unwanted kitchen kittens." Most of the warriors laugh heartily at the joke, but toward the back of the hall, a tall, broad young man with a shock of reddish hair grimaces and bites his lip. Her mother, bright in her apple green gown, slides her slender hand into his and leads him from the hall.

The child frowns to see them go.

Her father tugs the ribbon knotted in her plait. "So you feel that reading this book is more important than the tales of war I have to tell these young soldiers, do you?"

She nods. "Your soldiers have had you for months and months, Papa. 'Tis my time now."

"And what would your mother say to your sneaking into the hall?"

The child sighs loudly and cuddles closer to her father. "I fear I am a sad disappointment to Mama. She longed for a tabby cat but gave birth to a lioness instead."

The whole hall rings with laughter, and she twinkles with delight at the success of her joke.

"Where is your mother, child?"

The girl glances toward the end of the hall, but her slender, beautiful mother has not returned. She senses that she should not mention the red-headed man with her mother. So she climbs onto her father's knee and pulls the book up onto her lap. "Now shall we finish the story?"

Her father looks out at his men. "I never thought anyone would value me more as a scribe than a warrior."

His warriors laugh again. She tilts her head to look around at him. "Now, sir, if you would teach me to read, then I would not need to bother you for these tales."

"But you can read."

"English, but not Latin, sir. I would like you to teach me to read Latin."

"Teach you to read Latin, chit? What a minx you are! You will grow up to be a great lady. What need have you to read at all, much less Latin?"

The child leans back against her father's chest with a contented sigh. "I will not be a great lady! I will be a girl forever and ever!"

Again the room rings with laughter.

Her father rests his chin against her warm little head. "You cannot be a girl forever."

"Then I will be a soldier like you."

"You cannot be a soldier, chit." His voice is cozy and kind. "You will grow and become a beautiful lady like your mother, but unlike your mother, you will give your husband many sons."

The child stiffens. "I will not be like my mother! I will not!" Her voice is pulled tight. She twitches out of his arms and slides to the floor.

The soldiers laugh again and her father ruffles the girl's hair and pulls her back onto his lap.

"All right, all right, I surrender for tonight, child." He opens the beau-

tifully illustrated books. "Pay heed, chit. This word is Deus—*it means* God. *This word is* stabat—*it means* . . ."

SEVERAL DAYS LATER, *the child stamps her foot.*

"I will not go with you, Mama. My father is home so seldom. I shall stay here with him."

The slender lady who left the gathering with the red-haired man closes her fingers on the child's shoulders. "That you shall not, my girl."

"That I shall, Mama."

Her mother shakes her till one braid tumbles loose.

"You will obey your mother!"

She hears her father calling her to come to the hall. As soon as her mother stops shaking her, she twists herself free and begins to run.

"I'm coming, Papa!"

But her mother is faster. She grabs the girl and pulls her back.

"You will come with me."

"Papa is to give me my Latin lesson."

"'Tis not a fitting business for a young lady. You will come with your mother."

"Papa said I might—"

"I do not care a fig what your father said. Now go to your nurse. Now, I say. Put on your old gown. 'Tis time you learned the tasks of a lady of a castle, not the frumpery-rumpery of Latin. You are not to be a priest, girl. Even your father would tell you to behave."

She eyes her mother with something close to hatred. Then she says, "And even your husband, madam, would tell you to behave."

Her mother raises a hand to slap her, but just then the nurse walks into the room. Her mother moves her hand to her hair and pretends to be tucking in a few stray wisps.

"Change my daughter's gown, Nurse. Then you and she and the other women will go with me down to the stream. The bed linens need washing, and we will gather flowers to fill the hall with posies to celebrate my lord's safe return."

Her mother swishes her way out of the room. The child hears her call out to her father, "My love, there will be no Latin lesson today. Our little wild beast of a daughter must be tamed this afternoon. She must come with me down to the stream . . ."

W HAT ANGERS HER MOST *is that her father will not say nay to her mother.*

"We were to have a Latin lesson," the child reminds him. The bevy of women, loaded with baskets overflowing with linens and small clothes, have started their march down to the stream. The child clings to her father.

"Do not make me go," she begs.

But her father laughs and crooks a finger in her tumbled plait.

"Your mama is right. We have a wild thing for a daughter. She must learn to be a fine little lady." He laughs at the sight of the child's cross face. "How else can I get a wealthy husband for you?"

He laughs again at her frown.

Then he slides his arm around his wife's slim waist and pulls her to him. "Teach her to be just like you, my love," he whispers.

The child scowls.

Her father rests his forehead against his wife's head. "I miss you every moment you are away from me, my beauty. Hurry back to me."

Then he kisses her, hard, and she kisses him back.

Out of the corner of her eye, the child sees the red-haired man watching them hungrily from the shadows.

T HE CHILD REFUSES *to admit that it is actually fun to be down at the stream.*

It is a different world when the men are not about. The women and girls of the castle spread the linens out on the rocks and pound stones and sticks against them, singing lively tunes together. Many of the tunes are comical, and she can hardly keep from laughing, especially when the fat henwife begins to dance around, a twisted bedsheet on her head.

After the laundry has been washed and spread to dry in the sun, the women sit on the rocks, their skirts kirtled high about their waists, and eat apples and dried figs. They take turns telling riddles.

As soon as she sees a chance, the child slips away and runs back to the castle.

I will have my Latin lesson, *she tells herself.*

It feels like a long time before the castle comes into sight. She is panting and sweat trickles down her face.

Papa will want me to look sweet. I dare not appear looking like a ragamuffin. *She plops down on a stump and fans herself with her hand, trying to cool down. She mops her forehead with the hem of her gown.*

Then she hears a thunder of dozens of horses. She falls on her belly and slithers down behind the stump. She peeks over the top. Sleek chargers pound their way past her, galloping toward the castle. A cart clatters along with them.

She hears the castle gates scrape their heavy way closed. She feels a moment of panic. I am too little to know what to do. Should I run back and get Mama? Should I stay hidden here? *She wants to whimper with fear. Instead she inches her way up to peer over the top of the stump.*

The riders gather around the gates. She can see that some of them have bows and arrows. Two of them stand beside the cart. It carries a strange machine that confuses her. Then one of them lifts the top off a metal pot. She cannot see what is inside until one man uses some tongs to lift something that shines like a hot coal. He places it in a little bowl at the end of an arm of the machine on the cart.

Then she notices the red-haired man is standing among the attackers. He seems to be their leader.

"Papa," she whispers. "Papa!"

Then the arm of the machine swings through the air. Something like a rock, a glowing rock, flies out of it and over the wall of the castle. In a few moments, she sees flames shoot up. The arms swings again. More flames.

Things seem to move slowly, like in a dream. She knows there must be sounds, but she hears nothing. Her ears feel stuffed with silence.

The machine keeps flinging its arm, and the fire-rocks keep flying over the wall of the castle. She knows the buildings inside are built of wood. She knows fire is an enemy worse than men.

The gates open. Through the gates she can see that the courtyard of the castle has become an orange and red mouth of flames.

But the war is over. Papa came home because the war is over!

Then when the men from the castle try to escape, the men outside fall upon them, slashing them with swords and clubbing them with sticks. So the men from the castle fall back inside and push the gates shut once more.

This is not happening. This is a dream. This cannot be real. My papa is in there. This cannot be real.

The red-haired man signals with his hand. Her hand flies to her mouth in horror as she sees what is happening.

The attackers pull long boards out from under the cart. Some of them hold them across the gates. Others nail them in place with long spikes.

Then the sounds begin. She thinks she hears cries and pounding from behind the gates, but maybe it is just the echo of the hammers outside.

This will stop soon. It will stop.

Something like an archangel from a picture in the Latin book appears atop one of the walls. Wings—golden and red—stream out from its arms and shoulders.

Then she realizes it is a man on fire.

He holds his arms out wide.

And then he jumps.

Another man—not on fire—leaps over the wall. He lies on the ground, his leg twisted at an unnatural angle. The attackers smash logs against him for a long time. When they move away, he is still.

And always it seems the red-haired soldier is in the thick of the fray.

Then more men, their clothes alight with flames, leap over the walls. To her horror, they still look like archangels.

Papa is not there. He cannot be there. My Papa must have left before all this began.

It is impossible that any of the archangels could be her father.

Toward the end of the afternoon, she can no longer see the tips of the flames, lapping like cats' tongues above the walls of the castle. After a while longer, the attackers rip off the boards they nailed across the gates. Then the red-haired man eases the gates open.

Everything inside the gates is black and ragged although overhead there is a lot of light. The buildings are all gone, replaced with a jumble of ash and burned lumber. No one is moving around.

The red-haired man and his soldiers disappear inside.

For a moment she thinks about running down there and nailing the boards back up. Then she will be the one to send the glowing rocks flying over the castle walls. The attackers can feel what it is like to burn inside a castle.

But she is too little to do anything.

So she waits.

Late in the afternoon, all the attackers come back out, laughing and strutting. They clap each other frequently on the shoulder and make loud jokes. She is glad she is too far away to hear them. Then they all ride away.

She picks her way carefully down to the castle. She feels like the charred castle walls. All her feeling has been burned away, and she is nothing but feet, hands, and eyes. She walks inside the silent castle. She can hear things grit and grate under her feet, but there is no other sound. Jagged black boards like dragons' teeth poke straight up to the sky. But it is a strange, unearthly landscape like a picture of one of the circles of hell. She does not recognize anything or even remember where the keep or the stable were.

She finds a hole underneath some tumbled rocks. She crawls into it, like a small, weak animal in a tiny den. She hears something making little mewling sounds. For a while she wonders if there is a kitten hiding somewhere, but then she realizes that the sound is coming from her own chest.

At dusk she hears someone ride into the courtyard. She peeks out of her hole. It is the red-haired man. He walks among the dark shapes that smell of smoke, poking at them with his sword.

After a while she hears another horse approach. He runs to the gates to meet it. It is her mother.

He reaches up to lift her mother out of the saddle.

"Well, my love? I see the deed is done," her mother says.

He begins to kiss her passionately. She kisses him back, but the child sees her kisses are not as passionate.

Then her mother pulls back to ask, "Quickly?"

He nods and tries to kiss her again, but her mother holds him back. "All dead?" she asks.

He nods.

Then her mother nods once before she asks, "My husband, too?"

He nods again. The child wonders if his voice has gone away. Her mother kisses him, but this time he is the one to pull back.

"He killed my father," he says, holding her at arm's length. "I would not be worthy to be his son if I did not right that murder."

Her mother gives his wrist a quick kiss. "He was a boor! Full of stories of high adventure and little to show for it."

The red-haired man releases her and walks away. He stands looking at the burned rubble, his back to her mother. She looks after him, troubled, and then approaches him from behind and slides her arms around his chest, resting her cheek against his back. "'Tis war, my dearest love. 'Tis war. Now you can claim me as your spoils of war. How will you use me, my love?"

He pats her hand, but he does not look at her.

Now her slender hands pull at him till he turns to face her.

"My daughter," she says. "We cannot find my daughter down at the stream."

The red-haired man stiffens.

"Did you see that child on the road?" She takes his hand in hers and looks deep into his eyes. "I cannot think where she might be." She gives a little laugh. "I have left the women searching for the little minx."

He lets her hand drop. For the first time, his face looks troubled. His voice is heavy with horror. "Lady, tell me, 'tis not possible that she came back here with her father. Tell me that—little as she is—she could not travel so far. I do not mind the killing of men, but to murder a child—"

"No!" her mother snaps. "Of course she was not here. Why do you fill my ears with such fantasy? She did not reach her father. She did not!"

She presses her palms against her forehead. She backs away from him, wobbles, and almost falls. The red-haired man catches her.

"You are not well, love. Let me fetch some water."

She begins to gasp and shake.

"Breathe, breathe, my love," he says.

"Was she here?" Her mother begins to beat her fists against his chest. "Was she? Did you kill my child?"

"It happened so quickly—"

"Was she in the castle with her father? Was she?"

"I did not see her—it all happened so quickly—"

"Was she here?"

"I did not see her—but I cannot swear 'twas not so—"

Her mother makes a sound like a wounded animal and sinks onto her knees, rocking back and forth, moaning. He scoops her up in his arms.

"My lady, my love, let us go from here. My dearest love, I would give my life for you. I will never do anything to hurt you."

After a while they ride away, leaving the child alone in the ruined castle.

EVENTUALLY, THE STARS COME OUT *and they fill the sky. They do not seem to care that the child's father is dead. The child finally crawls out from the pile of burned boards.*

Then she begins to run.

She runs for a long time. Sometimes it is day, and sometimes night. Sometimes she walks, and sometimes she crawls. She drinks water wherever she finds it, even in a ditch or a pond whose surface is sticky with scum. She does not eat. Whenever she hears the approach of people, she hides until there is silence again. Sometimes she wakes, curled in a patch of heather or a heap of leaves with no memory of falling asleep.

And then, she stumbles in the wood. She falls to the ground, the nub of a stick pressing deep into her cheek. She has no more strength to get up.

She smells the damp wool of a skirt that kneels near her face, and rough fingers stroke her cheek. Then the hands prop her head up, and water is poured into her mouth.

Nettle's voice comforts her. "There, child, there. You're safe here, child. I will keep you safe. 'Tis time to rest, my little gillyflower. The horrors are over, child. The horrors are gone."

BUT WHEN I OPEN MY EYES, the horror has only begun.

FORTY-TWO

I FIGHT MY WAY UP to the surface of the icy water. My chest feels as if it has cracked and is lashed into place with ropes of ice. I cannot breathe.

I thrash and paddle my way to the shore. I pull myself onto the bank. My gasps for air are greedy. My head aches and my stomach churns. For a long time I can't open my eyes.

Stand up! Stand up!

I roll over to my stomach. I cough, choke, and finally pull up to all fours. My head whirls from the effort and my breath comes out in little pants. Finally I manage to stumble to my feet, half-crazy from the pain in my throat and chest. My body feels like it's been beaten.

The castle is silent. I see a few twists of smoke rising above the walls.

With one hand on the wall to steady me, I limp my way toward the gates. My clothes are wet, heavy, and cold. When I come to the corner, I peep around it, but there are no signs of the attackers. I feel my way to the gates and enter the castle.

The courtyard is littered with heaps of bodies, their limbs

splayed out in all directions. Some piles are as high as my shoulder. These dead have surrendered even their dignity. They lie with their clothes disordered, their arms and legs all tangled with everyone else's. I do not see the lady or her children, but I do not search through the piles of corpses. It is clear that nothing has been left alive. Even the bodies of dogs, geese, pigs, and hounds lie silent about me.

I stumble my way to the keep. The door to the hall is closed. I put both my hands against the door to push it open. But the door is hot and burns my hands. I smell smoke and back away. I start toward the rear courtyard, but the smoke grows thicker.

It is clear that there is nothing for me here.

I stagger back to the front gates. I see no sign of Lord Banquo's horse. *Poor beastie. To have gone through so much and to have traveled so far. . . .*

I trudge out of the castle, cold and heavy. My mind is muddled—scenes pop into my head, but I cannot tell whether they are memories from the castle today or the one many years ago. As soon as I see a wood, I stumble my way over to it and hide among the trees. I pile leaves and branches around to make myself a nest and snuggle down into them, falling immediately asleep.

Until I am torn wide open by my dreams.

"No!" I scream.

Make me a witch indeed so I can have the power to change things. Let time turn backward. Let this day's misadventures unravel and then knit up again in a new tapestry, something pleasing and beautiful.

I am so sick of this world in which children are beaten and torn and damaged beyond all saving.

"No!" I scream again.

IT TAKES ME THIRTEEN DAYS to reach Nettle's hut.

When I am almost at the door, my legs give out and I fall to the ground. The frozen grass is stiff and scratchy against my back.

I hear quick footsteps, and then my head is resting in Nettle's lap. Her apron smells of wood smoke and dried herbs. Her rough hand is smoothing my forehead as if I am still a child.

"Hush," she says.

When I open my mouth to speak for the first time in thirteen days, I am surprised by my voice. It is cracked and dry, and there is a fierce soreness in my throat. "I have nowhere to go." My words sound like they were croaked by a toad.

"Hush, Gilly," Nettle says. "You're home."

I fumble my hand up and close my fingers around her stick-thin wrist. "Nettle, I'm done with revenge. I will have no more to do with Him."

Then all is darkness and silence.

Until I scream myself awake.

"Mama!" I am screaming. "Mama!"

I look around. I am safe inside the warm hut, wrapped in a soft, new, white woolen gown. My hands are bandaged, and my skin is clean. I am lying on a pallet filled with fresh-smelling pine boughs. I do not know how Nettle and Mad Helga managed to carry me into the hut.

Mad Helga is crouched on the far side of the fire, her cloak wrapped around her, the hood so low over her face that I see only her pointed chin with the few hairs growing out of it. She does not even lift her head.

Nettle stands over a small cauldron, ladling dark green liquid into a mug. She moves to me and kneels down, handing me the warm cup. She does not say a word. I sip it. Her potion is bitter but soothing. It smells like fresh grass and the husks of walnuts. When I have finished drinking, I set the mug down next to my pallet. After a while my eyelids grow as heavy as stones.

I sleep.

Through the winter, through the spring, I throw myself into work around the hut. Work that is hard enough can wash my memory clean, at least for a little while.

Nettle lets me keep the fine new wool gown. I boil it with onion skins and nut shells, and it turns a fine golden brown. One day I build a big bonfire in a corner of the clearing so I can make soap. It is dreadful work, but I offer to do it. I stand for hours over the hot kettle, stirring the stinking mixture of fat and ashes till my arms ache. When I take it off the fire, Nettle sprinkles the gluey mixture with dried chamomile and lavender and other sweet-smelling herbs, and we pour it into a wooden trough to cool. After she has gone inside, I throw my short tunic and other boy's clothes into the hot fire, poking them around with a stick until they burn to ashes. I do not want any reminders of my other life.

I haunt the wood, gathering the fresh shoots of lion's tooth and burdock for spring tonics. My hair begins to grow long again, tickling the nape of my neck until it is long enough to catch back with a bit of cord. When I go to take some dried herbs to the nunnery at Cree in exchange for a bit of dried fish, I wear a kerchief over my head.

"'Tis a fair age since we have seen you, Gilly," says Sister Grisel. She gives me a hunk of fresh wheaten bread and a sliver of pale sheep's cheese. The nunnery kitchen is clean and painted white.

I do not let it remind me of the kitchens in the castles.

Mad Helga sleeps most of the time. From time to time she still brings broken wild creatures home—toads with torn-off legs, birds with snapped wings, one time a tiny fox kit that cannot eat or drink. She rocks them in her arms and jabbers to them in a strange language, warming them in her ragged blankets. None of them survive, though, no matter how fiercely she nurses them. I notice she no longer bothers to boil their bones. She lets Nettle take the poor little corpses away, and she does not ask what Nettle has done with the bodies. On bright days, she chooses a sunny spot in the clearing. She brings out her little stool and naps sitting up, our two scarred cats curled on her lap or about her ankles.

My hands heal so that I no longer need to keep them bandaged, although the new skin is red and puckered. I weed the garden and gather fresh cress from the brook. Some days I go sit by the waterfall, but I no longer bathe in its waters.

I want there to be no trace of the old mad Gilly.

I scatter corn for our chickens and collect the eggs from their hiding places. I help Nettle make the goat cheeses, carefully turning them each day. I comb burrs out of the hair of our goats, and in the evenings I sit around the fire with the women, carding bits of wool.

Yet many nights I awake screaming from my dreams.

"In time," Nettle says, "the horrors will go away."

But when she tells me this, she does not look me in the eye.

From time to time, I wonder how Pod is doing, and Lisette. I miss them sorely, but I never speak of them.

Sometimes Nettle and Mad Helga play a game I used to love as a child. I suspect they do this to cheer me up. We call this game, Revenge.

One night Nettle begins it. She looks up from the wool she is spinning on a spindle in her lap. "When I took the elderbark tonic to the miller's wife today, her son called me a witch."

Mad Helga, who is awake for once, asks, "What will you do?"

"I'll make myself as small as a worm and crawl into his ear," Nettle says. "There I'll whisper such scary tales as will rid him of sleep forever."

We laugh. We have little power for revenge, but it is fun to fancy what we would do were we real witches.

Mad Helga takes the next one. "I went for a walk today."

I ask, "Who did you see?"

"Old Sven's second daughter, the one who wed the sailor. She was munching on a lapful of chestnuts. I asked for one, but she only said, 'Get away from me, you mangy old mare.'"

"What will you do?" Nettle asks.

Mad Helga answers us in rhyme.

> *I'll become a rat without a tail,*
> *And in a sieve I'll sail and sail*
> *To her husband's ship—*

"I'll conjure you up a wind," I offer.

Mad Helga nods. "I myself have all the other winds," she says.

> *And on her husband I'll cast a spell*
> *On which he'll sail to the ends of hell.*
> *For your insult, he will pay.*
> *Sleep shall neither night or day*
> *Hang upon his deep eyelids.*
> *He shall live a man forbid.*
> *Weary seven-nights, nine times nine*
> *Will he dwindle, peak, and pine.*
> *Though his ship cannot be lost,*
> *Yet it will be tempest tossed!*

Nettle grabs a dried bean pod and waves it in the air. "Here I have that sailor's thumb—"

I rack my brains trying to think of a rhyme. Then I call out, "Wrecked as homeward he did come!"

We all laugh at my rhyme.

I begin the next story. "When I walked by the church today, the parson spat at me and called out, 'Aroint thee, witch, I charge thee by all the saints in heaven.'"

Nettle asks, "So what did you do, Gilly?"

I love playing the Revenge game. It is a treat to see Nettle so lighthearted. In truth, I am glad to be lighthearted again myself. Even when Mad Helga's wits wander, it only adds spice to the game.

How splendid it would be if we could indeed do these things we imagine to make one another laugh.

Yet all the time I feel like an impostor, a monster dressed in the clothes of a peasant girl. Life in the hut no longer feels real to me. In truth, for seven years and more, no life has felt like my real life. I feel like an enchanted creature who lives caught between worlds with no real place of her own. I am a girl who passes as a boy, a mortal who is seen as a witch, a lord's daughter, a warrior who longs to right the wrongs done to those she loves but who seems only to make things worse.

One afternoon I offer to tell Nettle what happened back at Lady Macduff's castle. We are snapping sticks into kindling. I look sidewise at her and ask, "Would you like to know what came to pass, Nettle?"

Nettle looks down. She continues to break the sticks into smaller pieces. "There's no need to talk about what's done. What's done is done. The less said, the sooner rewoven."

I do not know whether she does not want to know, or if she is telling me that, thanks to her double sight, she knows already and there's no need to speak of it.

Yet I wonder all the time. I wonder if wise little Fleance and beautiful Prince Malcolm reached safety. I wonder if Pod is safe.

I do not wonder if He is still alive.

Although I am done with Him, I will nonetheless know in my very bones on the day He stops walking the earth. Although I do not have the double sight, I know that I will feel in all my being when His wife—she who was once my mother—begins her flight to the bowels of hell.

But I will have no more to do with them in my lifetime. It is a great relief to be free, finally free.

One afternoon, just before Midsummer's Eve, when I am milking the goats, Nettle comes back from her rambles in the wood. She has a basket filled with dark green leaves.

"Gilly, I found a whole patch of early adder's tongue. The good sisters will pay well for this. They use it to flavor their mead. Gilly, at the first rising of the sun, take this to the sisters. Remember to ask to see Sister Grisel. Do not accept less than a basketful of dried fish in return."

I reach the convent by mid-morning of the next day. I knock

boldly on the wooden gate. A very small, very young sister comes to answer my knock. She has pale golden freckles and the downy look of a newhatched duckling.

"I come to see Sister Grisel," I command.

The small sister inclines her head and glides away. In a very short time, the door is opened wide. Sister Grisel, plump and jolly as ever, stands there. She looks like a barrel with arms, legs, and head. Across one cheek is a large birthmark the color of berry juice. It sprawls out like a splayed flower.

Her face lights up at the sight of me. "Gillyflower, my child. Now what magic does my good Nettle send me from the wood?" She lifts the cloth from the top of my basket, and her face shines with delight. "Ahh, bring it into the kitchen, my girl. I have some fresh milk, still warm from the cow, and Sister Inge will have her bannocks cooling by the time we get there."

I perch on a stool in the kitchen, nibbling a warm bannock. I find the kitchen's tidiness restful. It is so unlike our hut in which things are all over the place. Sister Inge leans over the griddle frying bannocks. She is long and thin, rather like a heron or a broomstick in a wimple. Sister Grisel snatches up a second hot bannock and plops down beside me. "And how does the good Helga?" She bites off a bit of her bannock.

"Her wits wander more each day," I say through a mouthful of crumbs.

Sister Grisel sighs. "The poor thing has a heavy cross to bear."

Sister Inge adds, "The way the world goes, perhaps 'tis a mercy she no longer has to bear witness."

Sister Grisel sets her bannock down as if she is no longer hungry. "'Tis true. Scotland aches under the harsh hand of—"

"Hush!" Sister Inge raises a floury hand in warning. "He has spies in every household."

Sister Grisel nods. "True. And I am too old and too fat to be one of his sacrifices." She picks up her bannock again and takes a mournful bite.

Sister Inge frowns at her. "'Tis especial folly to speak this way today with him and his men just over the hill at the abbey."

I let my bannock drop to the table and sit bolt upright. "What? The king is at the abbey?"

Sister Inge sighs. "They say he comes to hold holy vigil at the bones of Saint Brendan, but there are those who claim he wishes merely to gauge the wealth of the good brothers."

In my chest excitement rises like a bubble of blood. "He is there now?"

Sister Grisel says, "The little lad who takes our cows to pasture said he had heard from the baker that the king was coming to these parts today. Why else would he come, if not to visit the abbey?"

I stand up abruptly. God has obviously given me one more chance—God or the devil and I don't care which. All I care about is that there is still time to avenge my father's murder.

Sister Grisel stares at me. "Why, what's wrong, child? You've gone all pale. Are you ill?"

"I must go."

Sister Grisel heaves herself up. "I have some old linens I would send to the ladies of your—"

"I cannot take them."

As I run out the door, Sister Grisel calls after me, "Gilly, I have not yet paid you for—"

I cannot believe it. He is coming to the abbey—not half a day's journey. The man who killed my father, who stole my mother and made her His wife, who burned my home to the ground, and who sent me forth as an orphan. *Forgive me. I lost faith. But He has been sent to this corner of the earth for a purpose, and it is clear that the purpose of His coming is so I can finish my revenge.*

He would not expect to find His wife's abandoned daughter in this part of the world.

My life is an arrow, and at last it is headed home.

• • •

By early afternoon, I reach the abbey. I have still not thought of a believable reason to request admittance. To buy time, I duck down to the pond that stands by the gate to splash water on my hands and face. I pull off my kerchief and try to smooth my hair. Finally I go right up to the gate and knock.

The window in the gate is opened by a young snub-nosed novice, not above twelve years old. I wonder if he is standing on tip-toe to see through the opening.

"May I help you?" he asks.

"The king—the good sisters at Cree said that the king would be here today."

"What business is that of yours?" The contrast between the fierce words and the tiny voice almost make me laugh.

"I—have a touch of Jupiter's rash. I need the king's touch to cure me." After all, a rightful king should be able to cure this rash with just a touch of his hands. Perhaps it is not the best lie, but it will have to do.

As the boy slides the window shut, he says, "You are too late. He has come and gone."

My heart sinks. My disappointment is as bitter as poison in my mouth. I turn away and begin to trudge home.

Behind me I hear the window slide open again.

"Girl!"

I do not bother to turn around.

"Girl!" he cries out again. "With luck, you may catch him yet. He stopped here but to enquire the way to the heart of Birnam Wood. He said he seeks three women there—three women who are witches. He said they have enchanted him. He is on his way to kill them."

FORTY-THREE

I DO NOT REACH HOME until sunset.

Or at least what was once my home.

All the way, my brain chants, *Faster, faster, faster.*

Sunset comes late in midsummer in our high lands. This evening the sky is ablaze with a hot fire orange light. The trees are black scratchings against the violent light.

Where the hut once stood, there is only a black pile of charred fire stubs and ashes. Nothing moves in the clearing. The clearing and the nearby wood are silent. I put a hand against a tree to steady me.

I have seen too much of burned homes.

The clearing is silent. My feet drag the last few steps. I gingerly touch one of the burned wooden beams in the pile of rubble to see how long it has been since it was ablaze. The beam is warm, but not hot. I reckon it was set on fire near midday, just as I started off on my will-o'-the-wisp chase to the abbey.

It was good fortune that the woods themselves did not catch fire. That is thanks to Nettle. She has always been scrupulous about keeping the grasses and undergrowth pulled around our hut as a fire break. Still and all, the nearby trees are smudged with smoke. Their branches dangle broken, snapped and twisted by the large party of armed men who must have tramped back here to destroy the witches.

"I'm sorry," I say to the broken trees. "I never meant you to be hurt."

It is easier to love trees than people.

I see no signs of our goats, chickens, or our two cats. "Please be hiding in the wood," I whisper. "Please don't be dead."

Finally I gather courage enough to call out, "Nettle?"

No answer.

"Helga?"

Silence.

I pick up a burned stick about the length of my arm. I ease my way around the remains of the hut, poking into the mess.

The light begins to drain from the sky like pus from a blister.

Halfway around the hut I stumble over something and fall to the ground.

The body of Mad Helga lies stiff on the ground.

I crawl to her. It is hard to see plainly in the fading light, but it is clear that she has not been burned.

She napped all the time. Let this be just a nap. Be napping, Helga. Be napping. I say her name. She doesn't answer. So I shake her, commanding her to wake. I had not realized how thin she had become.

But she stays dead.

I begin to sob. I pull her into my arms and cradle her as if she were the child and I the grown-up mother. Crying, I cradle her until night comes. From time to time I whisper, "I'm sorry. I'm so sorry."

Finally I lay her back on the ground. Her old ashwood stick lies next to her. I lay my burned stick down and take up hers. The sky is overcast, and the darkness feels very heavy. "Nettle," I call out. I use Mad Helga's stick to pull myself back to my feet. I move like an old woman. For one wild moment I wonder if we have changed places, she the young girl and I the madwoman of the wood. With the help of her stick, I work my way on around the burned hut, poking and listening. When I find myself back at her body again, I fall back to my knees. I use my hands to scrabble through the ashes, feeling for Nettle's body.

When dawn stains the sky, I am still pawing at the ashes. I feel the grit and soot thick against my face and skin.

But I find no trace of Nettle.

If I had a knife, I would cut out my own heart.

At full dawn, I crawl over to Mad Helga.

"Forgive me," I whisper. My voice is hoarse and raw. "Forgive me. Forgive me. I thought He would die. I thought perhaps I would die. But I never meant—I wanted to free the land from two murderers, and all that's resulted from my quest has been more murders. Helga, forgive—"

Then I hear a noise. I leap to my feet, holding Mad Helga's stick in front of me. Something large and clumsy is moving through the wood, drawing closer. I stiffen. With my free hand I reach for my broken dagger. I draw it, and then I let it tumble to the ground. I will myself to let death come. *I have caused too much death. Now it is my time to pay. I will not fight. I will let Him take me and finish the business begun so many years ago. Now is the time to end all this.* But just before the noise grows close enough to see who is coming, I snatch up the dagger again.

Sister Grisel and Sister Inge blunder into the clearing. They are seated, one behind the other, on a fat donkey. The freckle-faced girl who opened the door to me yesterday leads their donkey.

Sister Grisel gives a cry like a cheated cat. "God be our witness, it is just as we feared." She squirms her bulky body to the ground. She flings her arms out as if she would embrace me, but I stiffen and she lets her arms drop.

Sister Inge slides off the donkey's back. "Helga?"

Wordlessly I march around to where she lies. They follow. With Helga's own stick I point to her body. Sister Grisel, Sister Inge, and the freckle-faced novice make the sign of the cross.

"We must bury her," Sister Inge says. "Is there anything to dig with?"

"Should we not take her back to the convent and put her in sanctified ground?" Sister Grisel asks.

Sister Inge shakes her head. "She would not wish it so."

"Do you say that, Sister Inge, out of concern for her feelings or because you do not wish to face Mother Brighid?" Sister Grisel demands, her face red.

Sister Inge flushes but does not answer. She walks around the clearing, looking for something to use as a shovel.

I cry out, "What has this to do with aught? Why should you bury Mad Helga in the convent?"

Sister Grisel and Sister Inge look at each other. It reminds me of the way Nettle and Mad Helga used to look at each other. Is this a talent that women teach each other, these silent knowing looks that shut out the rest of the world?

In a gentle voice, Sister Inge says, "Helga was a bride of Christ."

Her words are nonsense.

Finally I say, "She was the bride of no one. Who would take her with that face?"

"Helga was a holy sister, a nun." Sister Grisel's voice is also gentle.

"'Tis a lie," I say. "For my whole memory, she has lived with us in the wood."

"Did she never tell you?" Sister Grisel makes a clucking sound with her tongue. "Many years ago she was a novice, apprentice to the herb mistress, far to the north, way up in the Orkneys."

"Then why is she not there still?"

The two sisters exchange another look, and then Sister Inge says, "The Northmen came."

I know of the Northmen. All who live in this kingdom of Scotland know of the danger of the Northmen, of their shallow-keeled boats that can slip into a bay or up a river silent as a whisper, of how in the space of scarce a hundred breaths they can lay waste an entire village. Folk in church regularly pray to God to protect them against the ravages of those cold-eyed, cold-hearted men of the north. I glance around the destruction in our clearing. "'Twas not the Northmen that did this to our hut." I look at Mad Helga's motionless body and my heart squeezes tight within me. "But your story still makes no sense. If Mad Helga was a nun, why is she not still with her sisters?"

Smoothing her sleeve, Sister Inge says, "The sisters of her order were all killed."

"You stuff these words into my ear without a shadow of sense," I cry out. "How came Helga then to be living?"

Sister Grisel reaches out for my hand, but I pull away. She lets her hand fall. She says, "I got the story from Helga's own lips. Fifteen or twenty winters before you came here—I do not recall the time exactly—she caught a chill and feared she was dying. Nettle sent to the convent, but no priest would come to listen to Helga's confession. I was no older than little Sister Margred here, but I came. It seemed to me a sin to let a woman die unshriven for no reason other than she chose to live in the wood. In her confession, she told me how she came here alone." Sister Grisel's face darkens. "She was younger than you are now—barely more than a child. She told of how 'twas her turn to keep watch in the tower by the sea, and how she had smuggled a book up there to read. Intent on the book, she neither saw nor heard the silent Northmen ship that glided in from the sea and up the river. 'Twas the screams of her sisters that brought her to herself."

Sister Inge makes the sign of the cross.

Sister Grisel continues, "She ran to the convent, but there was naught she could do. All were dead. The Northmen caught her and beat her and abused her, but it amused them to leave her before all the candles of her life had flickered out. She said she wandered for a long time and prayed to God for guidance. For a long time she was out of her wits, she said, but God guided her here where she made herself a hut and set about to heal the creatures of the forest."

Understanding breaks across me like a wave against the sand. I was one of the wild creatures she helped to heal. She and Nettle.

"I cannot find Nettle's body," I say, and my voice also breaks.

The little novice pipes up. "The king took her."

"What?" I wheel around sharply to stare at her.

"'Tis true." She nods so vehemently that her veil wobbles. "'Tis how we knew to come here. Mother Brighid was in at the village baker's and saw her being carried through the streets."

Sister Inge says gently, "Perhaps he will not hurt Nettle."

I grow impatient. "He hurt Mad Helga."

Looking up from where she kneels beside the body, Sister Grisel says, "I see no mark on Mad Helga. I reckon her heart gave out before the soldiers could touch her. 'Twas not the soldiers that killed her, Gilly."

No. It was my mad craving for revenge that did that. My heart feels like a bruise that beats, and my stomach cramps like a clutched fist.

Sister Grisel adds, "'Twas her own heart that betrayed her."

No. I was what betrayed her.

My mind skitters back to the night when we gave Him the potion that made Him see imaginary spirits. *If only it could have been poison then. If He had just died then, Helga and Lady Macduff and her brood would still be—* And then an understanding flashes through me like an eel through clear water. *How stupid I have been. How could my wits have all gone begging? It was true! All that nonsense we babbled to Him—all of it was true.* It is as if God himself is shouting in my ear. *Those silly things we told to Him, they were all true. How could I not see it? Our foretellings pave the way to end all of this.*

I grab my dagger and hack a tear in the skirt of my gown, just above the knee. I rip off the hem.

Sister Grisel cries out, "Child, what are you doing?"

But I am too busy unraveling my revelation to pay her any mind.

We told Him, *No man of woman born shall harm Macbeth.* How blind I have been. It is so clear—this means that I am ordained to be the one to kill Him since I am no man of woman born. First, I am a girl, not a man And second, I was not born of a woman. My mother was no woman—she was a heartless fiend in the guise of a woman, a fiend who plotted the murder of her own husband and abandoned her tiny daughter to almost certain death. Therefore it is as plain as summer weather that I—girlchild of a fiendish mother—am the one called to kill Macbeth.

I pull strands of my grown-out hair taut and begin to slash them short. Both the nuns call out, but I ignore them.

We said, *Macbeth shall never vanquished be until Birnam Wood to high Dunsinane Hill shall come against him.* How could I have missed the clear meaning of this statement? I am the one meant by this, too. It was in Birnam Wood that I was brought back from the dead and reborn. In Birnam Wood I was raised. *I myself am Birnam Wood.* Now it is the time for me to come against Him.

I saw off the last few long strands of my hair.

Beware Macduff, we told Him. Yes. It was not enough for me to seek revenge for my father alone. God would not favor my campaign until I had a cause greater than revenge for my plight alone. But the king's order to massacre Lord Macduff's family raises this affair from my personal feud to a holy campaign. Now I have a grand cause for which to fight. I must stop Him, not just out of my own hurt, but so that others will not suffer. I am the warrior of God himself.

Without my knowing it, we spoke true prophecy to Him.

What could be clearer?

I begin to run from the clearing.

"Gilly, where are you going?" Sister Grisel calls out.

Over my shoulder I call back to her, "To rescue Nettle."

And kill a king.

FORTY-FOUR

EVEN FROM AFAR I can see that Dunsinane Castle is preparing for war. Banners hang from the ramparts. I see soldiers drilling in the field in front of the moat, although their clothing is foreign to me. At the gates, the porter stops me. It is the porter from Inverness, brought south now to guard the gates at Dunsinane.

"Where be ye going, ye bag of bones and crap, ye hellborn brat who reeks like the stench from God's back teeth?" If possible, he looks even dirtier and stinks more than before. "'Tis not the time for Satan's misborn whelps to be sneaking into this maw of hell." Then his jaw drops, revealing the black rotted stumps that were once his teeth. "By Saint Peter the seafaring tar and his boatload of saints—you're the kitchen lad who went missing ten or twelve moons ago. The one who left his little brother with us—that addlewitted pup who hangs on the petticoats of the wafer wench."

"Let me pass," I say. I have no time to wait. I am on a holy mission.

His laugh turns to a belch and then a fit of coughing. At last he croaks, "By all that's holy and hellish, all the wise folk be sneaking t'other way, lad. Have you not heard? Prince Malcolm and his army of English folk be marching toward the castle. If you have a grain of sense, you'll show tail and hie ye t'other way. 'Tis like rats in a barn fire, the way folk be sneaking out."

"Then why are you still here?"

The porter lifts his jug of wine. "My lady of the grapes, the madonna of malmsey, she makes it worth my staying here. Besides, I have nowhere else to go, and I'm too old and ugly to be seeking a new lodging. But you, lad, if'n ye have a few more seeds of sense than that brother of yourn, you'd be best to get you and your brother out of this hovel of hell as quick as ye can and take that French wench with ye. She's a fine figure of a woman, she is, and I would fain she outlive the inferno that's certain to engulf us."

"When will Malcolm's soldiers be here?"

"Within the afternoon, they say." He scratches the stubble on his chin with a black, cracked fingernail. "The last messenger delivered his donkey's end of news not half an hour since. He sent your brother to tell the great lord."

"Sent my brother? Why did he not go himself? Why send my brother with the news?"

"That devil above—our cursed king—rages and roars like old Sam himself. None would—of his own free will—come near him. Your brother, poor innocent, had not the wit to say no."

I push past him and run into the courtyard. "Pod?" I call. "Pod?"

The courtyard is a jumble of frenzied activity. All around me, servants with bundled possessions are trying to sneak out of the castle. I grab at the skirts of a frightened laundry maid.

"My brother, Pod—apprentice to the wafer maker—where is he?"

She clutches her bundled possessions more tightly and shakes her head, her eyes darting about.

I let her go and push through the crowd that pushes back in the opposite way. "Pod?"

I start up the stairs to the Great Hall and the private chambers. Then above me I see Pod, half running, half falling down the stairs. Tears are trickling down his face.

"Pod!"

For a moment Pod stares at me in disbelief, and then he throws his arms around my waist and hugs me tight. "Gilly! Gilly! You've come for me. You're going to save me and Lisette. I knew you'd come back. I knew you hadn't forgotten us." He turns a tear-streaked face up toward mine. "Now, please, can we leave?"

I hold him tight against me. I am overwhelmed by how glad I am to see him safe. For a few moments I can't speak. For the first time in my life, I think that if things had been different, I might have liked to be a mother. Only I would have kept my children safe and loved. But as Nettle says, sometimes it is not till we lose a thing that we understand how much we love it. My entire soul senses that I will not survive this final meeting with Him. I hold Pod out so I can look at him. "You're so big, Pod. You've grown so big." I smooth back his hair and discover an ugly bump on his forehead. "What happened, lad?"

Pod hangs his head.

"Tell me."

He shakes his head, refusing to answer.

I harden my voice. "Tell me, Pod."

Shame floods into his face. His voice drops to a whisper. "A soldier, down in the yard, he told me to tell the king that he spotted ten thousand soldiers and they would be here by the crest of the afternoon. So I went to the king. I was so proud—a soldier wanted me to take an important message to the king. But then—" His lip begins to tremble. "But the king shouted and he hit me and he called me names. He made fun of the way I talk and—"

His voice fails him and he begins to shake. I pull him close. "That's all right, my lad," I croon. "You need not stay in this place any more. 'Tis time for you to be going."

Pod looks up at me with a suddenly radiant face. It is clear that he does not notice that I say *you* and not *we*.

"There is a convent in the village of Cree. Sister Grisel and Sister Inge, they'll take you—"

Pod's mouth drops open and his eyes widen.

I continue. "—and Lisette—they would take all of you. There is another lady, too. Her name is Nettle. She is down in the dungeon. 'Tis up to us to rescue her. We must get past the guards—"

"The dungeon guards are gone," Pod says. "I saw them run away before breakfast. No one wants to be caught here when the soldiers come for the king."

He does not know that I will make sure that the king will not be living when the soldiers arrive.

I hunch over so that my face is level with his. "Listen to me. Listen carefully. You must find Lisette. Do you heed me?"

He nods.

"Then the two of you must to the dungeon and find the woman who calls herself Nettle—say the name, lad."

"Nettle," he repeats.

"Good. Keep saying the name to yourself until you find Nettle."

Pod keeps repeating the name softly as I speak. "Find Nettle. Open the dungeon door and let her out. Then fill all the baskets you can with goods from the kitchen. 'Twill be a journey of the better part of a day to the convent. Nettle knows the way. Find a way out of the castle—the porter will let you pass—and head out for the convent at Cree."

I give him a quick hug, but he does not let go when I do.

He says, "But where will you be, Gilly?"

I rest my chin on the top of his fuzzy little head. "I will join you there at the convent."

But I know in my bones, I know with every bit of knowing I possess, I know more surely than I know my own name, that I will not survive my meeting with Him. This does not matter. What does matter is that He will not survive it either.

Pod clutches me more tightly. "I will not let you go. I do not want to meet you there. I want you to travel with us. If I let you go, perhaps you will not find us."

I let him hold on. To my disgust, I find I am not as willing to die as I had thought. *My father would be ashamed of me. I must be an arrow, not a reed.*

And yet I long to see this boy grow into a man. And I long to feel wind and the icy sting of water washing away the grime and to taste wheaten bread and to sit with Nettle, playing the Revenge game with her and Lisette and Pod, and to see that beautiful young prince again. What kind of unnatural monster am I? After all that I have witnessed—all that I have done—how can I still want to live in this foul and soiled world? In this world that can be so carelessly cruel?

Only now—now that I know that I cannot live—do I feel life screaming in me.

But I am good at closing my ears to things I do not wish to hear. I am skilled in smothering thoughts half born.

I give Pod a swift kiss on the top of his head. "Find Lisette," I say. "Find Nettle. Take food and strike out on the road before Malcolm's army gets here." I give him a little push. "Go, little brother. Go."

To my relief, he clatters obediently down the steps. I watch him go. At the bottom he turns back to wave to me, but I shoo him on.

"Nettle!" he calls out as if he is giving a battle cry, and he thrusts one small arm up into the air.

I raise my hand as if in triumph. He smiles that smile that is like a slash of sunshine and then disappears from my sight.

Something blurs my vision, but it is not tears. I will not cry. I take a deep breath. I straighten my shoulders.

It is time to find the king.

My only weapon is my broken dagger, but God has given the omens to show that it is my calling to kill the king, so I trust God to provide the weapon as well.

Resolutely I head to the Great Hall . . . and come face to face with my mother.

FORTY-FIVE

SHE HAS NOT CHANGED. So many years have passed, and yet my mother looks just the same.

But then I see she doesn't. Her hair is dirty and hangs in rats' tails down her back. She wears an undergown that is soiled and ripped like a sheet half torn for bandages. Her feet are grimy and bare. Up close I see her skin has grown a little soft and slack like a stocking pulled out of shape. Her bottom lip is gnawed and chapped.

Yet she is beautiful still.

"Come," she says, grabbing my hand.

She pulls me up the stairs to a fine bedchamber, hung with tapestries and banners of silk. I follow her in stunned silence. It is the most wondrous room I've ever seen—a fantasy kingdom of pale colors and sweet smells. A small, carved ivory table stands across from the bed, which is draped in heavy, embroidered, rose-silk coverings. The tabletop is a hand's-width deep in spilled jewels that glow like dyed fires: rubies, emeralds, sapphires, topazes, and others that I cannot name.

She pulls me to the center of the room and then lets go of my hand. She smiles at me and strokes my cheek. "You came back!" She gives a little laugh like a child on its name day. "You have come back to me. I knew you would come back," she whispers. "I knew you were not gone for good, that you were somewhere safe, waiting. I prayed to be released, and it seems that the good Lord has answered my prayers."

How can she recognize me after all these years? I had thought there was nothing left in me of the child I once was. Do I still resemble that child so closely? I open my mouth to answer, but she covers it with the palm of her hand.

"Hush," she says. "When I asked to be unsexed, I did not mean it. We must turn you back again." She lets go of me and hurries over to a chest and begins rooting through it, like a hound digging out a badger.

Turn me back? Her words make no sense. I was the one who unsexed, not her. What does she mean? Does she think she is some sort of witch indeed who can shrink me back to my baby form? She tosses out fine gown after gown until they are piled knee-deep on the floor, a witch's broth of jewel colors in velvets and silks. *How I would like to kill her now. I want her blood to flood out and soak these fine clothes that she wore while I was ragged and shivering all those years in the wood.* And to my shame, deep inside me, a little child's voice is bleating, *Hold me, Mama. Hold me tight. Don't let me go again.*

Finally she gives a little cry and triumphantly plucks out a gown. "This is the one I seek!"

She holds up an elegant gown of gold cloth, slashed with pine green velvet and embroidered with silver threads.

"Oh, my soul," she laughs, "throw off that guise and take your rightful place."

Rightful place? What does she mean? Does she wish to acknowledge me as her lost daughter, to proclaim me to all the court?

When I do not move, her face grows hard. "Now!" she screams, and her voice is that of a dying gull. She stamps her foot and gives an ugly, wordless scream that startles me. She begins plucking at my tunic. "I said, take off that silly garb and put on your dress. I will not have you looking like a ragpicker or a fishwife."

Dazed, I pull off the short, golden brown woolen tunic that Nettle made for me. My mother tosses her sumptuous gown over my head and pulls it down over my hips, twitching it into place. Her eyes then light up like those of a saint at her first sight of Jesus, and she claps her hands with pleasure. "Oh, thank you for returning. I knew you were not dead." She pulls a spangled scarf over my head. "That is more suitable as a headpiece till your hair grows out." With trembling fingers she smooths the spangled silk flat on my hair. *She is madder than Helga ever was.* Then she grabs a looking glass that lies on the table under the jewels, knocking them out of the way. They clatter to the floor like frozen tears. She thrusts the looking glass in front of my face. "Look!" she commands.

I look into the glass, and my knees grow weak.

I have disappeared.

Instead, two faces stare out at me. One is my mother years older, her hair and face as wild as a witch.

Then there is the other face, the face where mine ought to be.

This second face is also the face of my mother, her face from my very earliest childhood memories, peering out from under a spangled scarf.

No!

I throw the looking glass to the ground. I hear the glass break. I tear the spangled scarf from my head.

"I do not look like you!" I say. "I am not you. I will not be you. I will never be you!"

"What madness is this?" She laughs. "Not look like me? You *are* me."

I grab her thin wrists although I want to strike her. "Tell the truth! Who am I?" I demand.

"Who are you?" She stops and looks at me with wide eyes. "Do you not know yourself? You are the queen. You are Macbeth's lady."

"No!" I toss her wrists away. "*You* are His lady—His whore."

"Have you forgotten who you are?" she asks. "Do you need to look in the mirror again?" She kneels and scoops up one jagged shard of broken glass and holds it up before me. "See yourself as you truly are."

"'Tis you who have forgotten yourself," I tell her. "You are the queen. I am—"

"No!" She throws the shard of glass to the floor and I hear it shatter against the wooden floor. "After I married him, I went away for a while, but I knew I would come back someday. Now I have come back. And I have only been dreaming this nightmare of a life. Now I can truly start to live."

"'Tis no surprise, lady, that marriage to the king is a nightmare—"

"Not marriage to Macbeth, fool! Marriage to that other man— that villain who was my first husband."

"Villain! He was a good man, a loyal soldier, a noble—"

"Why do you lie?" she screeches. She looks furious. She raises her sleeve to her mouth and bites into the fabric. With her teeth she rips off a strip. She spits it out of her mouth. "I was but twelve when I came to him, innocent as the moon. Don't you remember? That first night I thought I would die of the pain. When he was angry or his wars did not go well, he would take out his pain on me." Then she laughs again and begins to dance around the room. "So I began to go away until a time would come in which 'twould be safe to come back again." She stretches her hands out to me. "Now I have finally come home." She stops dancing and whispers, "Had it not been for Lord Macbeth, I would have died forever." Then she flings her arms wide and begins to dance again. "Now my self has come back to me, young and beautiful again."

The memory of my father in the burning castle flashes into my head. *I will not feel even a drop of sorrow for her.* "You let your lover kill your husband," I said.

She stops twirling. She nods solemnly as a child. "I did. Had I not done so, my husband would have killed me someday."

"Nonsense!"

"My first husband died so I could survive," she chants jubilantly. "Once he was gone, then could I thrive." Then she stops, and her face grows sad. "But now my second husband has gone away and someone else lives in his eyes. I do not recognize the stranger who has taken his place." She leans to me and whispers, "He killed my first husband, you know, and I can see in his eyes that soon he will kill me. He has killed everyone else. I am the last person left for him to kill."

What do I care about her marriage. "And what of your daughter?" I ask.

She stares at me with haunted eyes. She sinks to her knees and begins to rock back and forth, singing in a thin voice, "I once had a babe, but she went to her grave." She flutters her thin forefinger at me, beckoning me to bend down beside her. When I do so, she grabs hold of my sleeve and puts her lips close to my ears to whisper, "She burns, you know. We all burn. Either here or in hell. She burned in her father's castle for the space of an afternoon, but I am burning through all eternity. Burning in flames the color of blood. Poor tiny babe. I had thought her a child, but she was just a twig, you know. Just kindling for the fire of my hatred."

She stares at her hand clutching my sleeve and then she lets go. She begins rubbing her hand, harder and harder, scratching it with her bitten nails, until it begins to bleed. She holds it out to me. "See? Her blood is the color of flames."

"'Tis your own blood, Mother," I say.

"No! 'Tis the blood of the king—one of the kings. I have married two princes, but I have only been one queen until now."

She looks around as if she fears the presence of spies. Then she whispers, "I said I would kill the king, you know. Leave it all to me, I said. I thought I could kill the king all by myself." She lowers her head, and I see a few threads of silver laced among her dark hair.

"You were going to kill your husband?"

Her face tightens like a clenched fist. "Do not play the fool with me. Not my husband. The other king—Duncan—the king that was. I told my husband that I would be the one to kill him, and that my husband need do nothing. But at the last minute, I could not do it." She rubs a ragged, soiled sleeve across her forehead. "He had too much blood, you see. Who would have thought that such a milky man could have so much blood?" She peeks up at me sideways from under her lashes. She looks sly. "I drown in blood, you know. Every night I drown in blood. First the knocking comes, and then the drowning." Her skinny fingers clutch my sleeve again. "I killed my father, you know."

"No!" I grab her shoulders and shake her. "You killed *my* father."

"'Tis just what I said. You and I are one. We are the same—"

"We are not the same! I am not you!" I pull free and stumble to my feet. "There is nothing of you in me."

For a moment she stares at me with the bewildered eyes of a child. Then she sniffs her hand. "Blood still." She begins to lick it.

"Don't," I say.

She turns her head like a raven and peeks up at me. "He spoke true. Blood will have blood. I pray God to turn me into a stone, but not one of the stones that speak."

In the ravaged body in front of me I see the ghost of the proud woman who faced all the warriors after Duncan's death and convinced them to name her husband king. I see the ghost of the beautiful mother I once loved. *I am so tired of this mad world stuffed with ghosts.* I stand to go, but she springs up and grabs my hand.

"You are my soul. I am the body so you must be my soul. I knew my soul had left my body long ago, and I did not think to see you again. But through God's grace, you have returned. So stay with me. Do not leave me again."

"I am your daughter!" I cry out.

Her face twists with anger. She draws herself up like a queen. "Do not lie to me, my soul. My daughter is dead."

"I am not dead. I did not die."

She tosses her hair back and gives a laugh like a saw blade scraped across stone. "Do not mock me. You and I are the same person—"

"We are not! I am your daughter."

She laughs again, this time triumphantly as if she caught me in a lie. "'Tis all the same. Mother and daughter are one flesh, so no matter what you call yourself, you are still me. We share one flesh, one soul, one name. I gave my daughter my very own name so she would have nothing of her father in her. So even if she were alive, she would be all me."

I dig my thumb into her hand, wanting to hurt her. "Tell me— did you ever love my father?"

"Did I love my father? How could I? He sold me to the highest bidder. I begged him on my knees to let me marry Lord Macbeth, the man I had loved since childhood, but my father told me I was his property, his cattle, lower than cattle, because cattle never cried and screamed when they were sent to the slaughter."

"Answer me! Did you ever love your first husband?"

"How could I? I was twelve. 'Twas on my wedding night when he tore me in two. 'Twas on that night my soul left my body. On that night, for the first time, I understood that I had become two people— the girl crying on the bed and the girl who floated above the room, watching everything that went on. But always I looked through the eyes of the floating girl—but you never let me see you until now. Why have you become flesh today, my floating self? Have I finally endured enough? Is it my time to be the one who floats and is it your time to look through my eyes? Are you a walking looking glass, or have I indeed been torn in two?" She brushes her arm across her forehead as if she is waving away a pesky bee. "Am I the ghost, or are you?"

I cannot believe how small she has become. Now I am much taller and stronger. I have hated her so long, but she had always been tall and strong, big enough to contain my hate. I say softly, "You are the ghost, Mother."

For a moment she is silent, and then she whispers, "The wife of Macbeth must go to her death."

My heart cries out for Mad Helga.

"You killed your first husband," I say in a voice cold as a January stone. "You left your daughter to die. She did survive that fire, but she has lived as an outcast in the world, poor, lonely, snatching crumbs where she could find them. This was your doing, Mother."

As if I'd cast a spell on her, her face changes. All of a sudden she looks old, older than Mad Helga. Her bones fold in till she looks little more than a bundle of rags and twigs. All the wildness drains from her eyes. Her hand shakes as she reaches it up and strokes my cheek. "I have done you much wrong, Roah!" Her voice is low and sounds drugged.

To my dismay, I feel a splinter of pity. But before I can speak, she jerks away. She blinks, and her mad self is back in her eyes. She leans toward me as if she wishes to embrace me, but instead she snatches my dagger. "Do you want me to kill myself? If 'twill drain off some of your pain, I will."

She holds out the dagger above her chest.

The Lord knows, it is what she deserves. If I say 'Kill yourself, Mother,' will she do it? Perhaps God has sent me to— But it is clear my mother is mad. I feel cheated by her madness. I would like to make her suffer, but there is no satisfaction in causing more suffering to the mad. There can be no joy in driving a lackwit to her death. I hold out my hand.

"Give me the dagger, Mama."

She pulls it to her chest like a baby she is protecting from assassins. She backs away from me. "You and I are just the same." She begins to laugh. "Since we are the same soul and flesh, then this is my dagger."

"I am not you," I tell her. "I am not Roah."

She clutches my dagger close to her thin chest. Her laughter swells like a flood tide. As her laughter grows, I back from the room.

"Run, Roah!" she shrieks, her laughter rising as wild as a tempest-tossed sea. "Flee the castle now, Roah, or die! Try to outrun your fate, Roah! 'Twill catch you in the end." She begins to twirl in a frantic circle, chanting, "Run, Roah! Run! Run!"

I do not know if she calls to me or herself.

FORTY-SIX

I RUN DOWN THE STAIRS, fleeing that laughter that now sounds like something small and delicate being shattered over and over. When I can no longer hear the laughter, I lean against the wall of the castle, gasping for air.

A serving man, lugging a heavy woven sack that bangs and clatters as if he is hauling a load of silver plates, comes around the corner. His mouth falls open when he sees me. "Beg pardon, my lady," he wheezes, and he falls to his knees. Then he tilts his head up toward me. He frowns. "Wait a moment! You are not the queen! Who—"

But I take off running before he can finish his sentence.

In the Great Hall I hide behind the tapestry in the same place I overheard Him arranging Lord Banquo's death. I squat there, panting. The castle has grown unnaturally quiet. *I must figure out what to do. Where I can find a weapon. Where I can find Him.* But my encounter with my mother has unsettled me. I glance down at the gown I am wearing. *It is not safe to race about dressed like a fine lady.* I curse myself for letting that fiend trade my short gown for this fancy dress. *I could cut off the bottom of the gown*, but even should I do so, this fancy garb would never look like the tunic of a manservant. Then I remember that my mother still has my dagger. *Think, think of a new plan.* But my meeting with my mother has turned my brain to sludge.

Suddenly the air is split in two by the sound of several women wailing. *Has Malcolm arrived already?* I listen hard, but I hear no sounds of invaders, and after a moment or two, the cries of the women cease.

I need a weapon. I need a disguise. I run back up the stairs and slink like a midnight cat from bedchamber to bedchamber, looking for anything that might aid me. In one chamber I find an abandoned cloak. I grab it and wrap it around me. At least it hides the gown. Its thick folds will make it hard for me to fight with Him, but He would laugh to scorn a foe in a fine silk dress.

It is time. I must find Him before Malcolm arrives. I move quickly and quietly through the deserted castle. All the serving folk seem to have vanished. I do not blame them for running away. I feel like a ghost, drifting through corridors, popping in and out of rooms and sheds. *Has Pod found Lisette? Have the two of them freed Nettle?* I hope by now all three of them are far away.

I move back through the Great Hall and hurry across the courtyard. I see a few of His Irish mercenaries waiting nervously for the attack, swords at the ready. Even in the courtyard there is no sight of serving folk. Or of Him. Then there is the crash of a log being pounded against the closed gates, over and over. The Irish soldiers move toward the front walls. *Not yet! The attacking soldiers must have reached the castle. Not yet! I need more time. I must be the one to kill Him, not the soldiers.* I dash up a stairway to the battlements, just as the gates crash in.

No! Let me find Him first. I hear invading soldiers swarming in below me, shouting, and I grab up my skirts with one hand to run faster. I hear the clash of swords below. *I must find Him. The omens made it clear that I am to be the one to defeat Him. This is my last chance.*

Faster and faster I dart around the corners and about the battlements. Once I see a man who seems to be one of the attackers, but I am gone before he even knows I am there.

My heart pounds and my breath saws the air. I am so frantic I feel almost as if I am the one being chased rather than the chaser. Yet time is running even faster than I. As I race around a corner, I wonder how much time there is to—

And I see Him ahead of me.

In front of Him a boy of maybe fifteen summers lies on the ground. I do not recognize the lad. *He must be part of the invading army.* The boy is spotted with blood, but he holds his head high and his jaw is clenched. *He wants to look brave.* It is as plain as day that He has fought with the boy and knocked him down. High above the boy's chest He holds His sword as if He is mocking the lad. Then He growls, "You were born of woman!" and He plunges the sword down with all His might. The boy gives a cry that turns into a gurgle, shudders a few times, and then lies silent and still.

At that moment, I realize that I have been so intent on finding Him that I have not armed myself. For a few heartbeats, I cannot think what to do.

Then I see a sword almost at my feet.

It is a sign! Like the omens, God has provided this sword because He wants me to be the one to bring down this monster.

The other part of my brain tells me that this sword probably belonged to the boy, dropped when he was knocked to the floor.

My mind becomes very calm and clear. Slowly, deliberately, I kneel down and slide my fingers around its hilt. It feels solid and alive in my hand.

"Turn, monster!" I cry out in a low voice. "Turn and face your death."

He whirls around. He looks both angry and confident. His red hair flames forth, but for the first time I see that it, like my mother's, is tinted with silver.

"Begone, child!" He growls. "You cannot kill me. Or if you will not turn and run like a little whipped pup, then prepare to die!"

I step forward.

He steps to meet me, His heavy sword raised, His eyes a little bored. *Like my mother, He has grown old.* But He is just as tall, His body just as strong as ever. The cloak is heavy about my legs and the hood has slipped too far over my forehead for me to see well, so with one hand I throw the cloak off so it will not impede me.

Then all color drains from His face. His arm trembles, and His sword falls to the ground. He makes the sign of the cross.

"Angels and ministers of grace defend me," He whispers. "They said you were dead."

I am surprised that He recognizes me. It was so many years ago that He last saw me, and I was a child then. Now I stand tall and strong, holding the heavy sword high.

He slides to His knees as if He would pray, His face as white as leprosy. "My lady, be you ghost or live flesh and blood?"

"I am neither dead nor a ghost," I say.

I step closer, my sword raised. *Could this be a trick?* My brain feels drunk with confidence. "I am your doom!" I tell Him. "I am the goddess of divine retribution, come to claim my due. I am Birnam Wood, come walking to meet you. I am no man of woman born. Macbeth, behold your death!"

"My lady, my wife, forgive me! I have wronged you—"

I stop. *He thinks I am my mother.*

"Stand and fight!" I command. "Or die like the coward you are!"

"Were those reports false? Are you still alive?"

What does He mean? Has He gone as mad as my mother? She is not dead. I spoke with her not an hour since—

"Or did you not die? Are you the phoenix, lady? At the moment you killed yourself, did you find yourself reborn young and beautiful, changed back into the girl of fifteen that I first loved?"

Then I realize *my mother is dead. My mother has killed herself.*

Those women crying—they must have been crying for my mother.

I don't feel anything at all. Not glad or sorrowful. Just hollowed of all feeling.

"My dearest and only love," He says, "never did I mean it to end in this fashion. Forgive me. Lady, forgive me."

I screw up my courage. "Stand like a man and fight."

"My lady, I cannot fight with you. All I have done, I have done for love of you. My dearest and only love, I—"

"Fight or die!" I say in a voice as heavy and cold as the leg of a corpse.

He stays on His knees, His sword on the ground at His side. He makes no movement to pick it up.

"How came you to be dead and then alive again, Roah? I have learned to my cost that this is a land in which the dead do not stay dead. What brought you back, my love?"

"Damn you! Stand and fight!"

God has brought me to this place where I can avenge my father, King Duncan, Mad Helga, Fleance's father, Lady Macduff and all her little ones, even the dead boy whose sword I hold tightly in my hands.

"I am your death," I say in a voice that is supposed to sound like the voice of doom, but to my ears sounds more like a fearful child's. "I have come to kill you."

"Then kill me now!" He says, His arms open wide, His chest open to me. "I will not kill you."

"Stand and fight!" Then I realize that this does not have to be a fair fight. In truth, I am no match for Him in skill and strength. In a fair fight, it would not be Him who dies. *After all, it was not a fair fight when my father was butchered. It was not a fair fight when Lord Banquo was stabbed, or Lady Macduff savaged.* I see that God has given me this opportunity to execute this monster, and this is the only way I can have advantage enough to stop this beast. If He will not fight, then I will slaughter Him like a trussed pig.

I raise the dead boy's sword as high as possible. It is heavier than

I expect, and my arm trembles as I raise it above His chest. He does not seem to see it. He stares only at my face.

Let my stroke be swift and deadly, I pray. *Give me the strength of arm to plunge the blade deep into His cesspit of a heart.*

Then I hear Pod cry out from nearby, "Gilly, save me! Save me, please!"

FORTY-SEVEN

*O*N THE SEVENTH DAY, *the messenger finds them.*

"I come from King Malcolm," he announces in the liquid tones of one who has been educated far to the south. "I come seeking the kitchen lad, Gilly, who saved the life of the king. The king commands me to bring the lad to court so the grateful king can shower him with honors. I was told I could find the lad here."

The pale young woman looks away. "There is no kitchen lad here," she says in a voice that is as flat as a stone.

Nettle explains that the kitchen lad was really a lass in disguise.

The messenger looks a little surprised, but his voice remains smooth. "Then let me bring the kitchen lass called Gilly to court so King Malcolm can shower her with honors."

"Gilly is dead," the pale young woman says.

Nettle looks at her with irritation, then explains that Gilly is not the girl's real name, that her real name is Roah.

"She bears her mother's name," the pale young woman says in her flat voice.

"Then let me bring the kitchen lass whose real name is Roah to court so King Malcolm—"

"She was not a kitchen lass. She was nothing, nothing at all." The pale young woman stands up and moves back to the clearing and resumes her work, setting up willow posts for the walls of the new hut.

Nettle explains that Roah is really the daughter of Queen Roah—she who was Lady Macbeth—and her first husband.

At this, despite all his years of training in schooling his features, the messenger looks shocked. "Then she's a princess," he blurts out. "She's the great-granddaughter of old King Kenneth." He looks around at the rubble from the fire and the frame of the new hut. "But what is a princess doing here?"

Nettle explains how she took in the child found wandering in the wood many years ago, right after the death of her father. "Her mother thought Gilly had perished in the fire along with her father. For the lass's own safety, we saw no reason to tell her otherwise."

The pale young woman does not even turn around.

The messenger walks over to her and kneels before her. "My lady, I must escort you to court. King Malcolm is overwhelmed with gratitude. Not only will he honor you for saving his life, but he can restore your name, your title, and your lands."

"No," she says.

Though he coaxes, wheedles, and cajoles until sunset, the young woman returns no other answer.

After he is gone, Pod creeps out of the wood.

"Where have you been, you vexing young scamp?" Nettle asks, but her tone is more worried than angry.

"I do not like kings," Pod tells her.

"This is not a king like the other one," Nettle assures him. "This is a good and kind king." She glances at the young woman. "And he wishes to honor Gilly."

"Gilly is dead," the young woman says. She stirs the cauldron of soup. "Besides, she should not be honored. She failed. She was too much her mother's child. Like her mother, she boasted she would kill a king. Like her mother, she left it to someone else to do the murder."

Nettle sighs, and the sharpness of her sigh seems to slice through the *soft summer air.* "We've gone through this nonsense a dozen times, child. Because of you, I am alive. Because of you, Pod and Lisette are alive. Because of you—"

The young woman whirls toward her, her face full of fire. "And I have told you a dozen times that because of me, Mad Helga is dead. Lady Macduff is dead, and all her children and servants. Lord Banquo is dead. 'Twas my desire for revenge that killed them!"

"No. You did not kill them. Macbeth did. Never forget that. You were not the murderer. He was."

The young woman goes on as if Nettle has not spoken. "I had made my life an arrow. Its only target was the killing of the man who killed my father. And I failed at that."

"He is dead, just as dead as if you had been the one to kill him. What does it matter whether 'twas you or Lord Macduff who did the deed? Lord Macduff's cause was at least as great as yours. Surely you do not begrudge Lord Macduff his revenge. And had you not gone to Pod's aid, Pod would be dead now, too. Be you daft, child? You saved Pod from that soldier who was trying to kill him. Because of you, Pod is alive. Because of you, Lisette and I got away safe from the castle. So what does it matter that Lord Macduff killed him 'stead of you? He's just as dead, either way."

"I have failed," says the young woman, and she says no more all the rest of the night, even when Pod tells her about the newborn fawn he saw down by the brook.

ANOTHER MESSENGER RETURNS three days later, and another one three days after that, and soon they begin to arrive every single day until it is clear even to the young woman that the king will not take no for an answer. So at last she agrees to go to his court. When the messenger asks how many attendants she will take with her, she tells him three. They fetch Lisette from the convent, and Nettle, Pod, Lisette, and the young woman set off.

King Malcolm's castle is much larger than Dunsinane. When she arrives at court, she is given a chamber of her own with two antechambers. Heaped on the bed in her room are many elegant gowns with head-

pieces and stockings and undergowns of the finest materials. She looks at them indifferently. When Nettle and Lisette try to get her to choose one to wear, she says, "Lady Macduff dressed in fine gowns, and where is she now? Mad Helga dressed in rags, and she's just as dead." The young woman lets her eyes slide over the piled gowns. "Tell me—which gown best flatters a failure?"

Lisette gives her a look that mingles pity and impatience. "Wearing a silk dress does not mean you mourn any less for your good Helga and the rest."

Even Nettle agrees that it would be a good thing for her to bathe.

"I do not need to bathe," the young woman says. "I am the walking dead."

Lisette pulls the young woman's shift off over her head. "Good," she remarks. "The dead do not put up resistance, so stand still while we wash you and comb your hair and dress you as befits a princess, little rose leaf."

On that dark night on their journey away from Dunsinane Castle, Lisette showed no surprise when she learned Gilly was a lass. Pod, too, accepted the change calmly. Neither showed surprise when Nettle told them of the girl's history—Lisette because she claimed she was too old to be surprised by anything and Pod because he thought Gilly so glorious that even being named an empress would not be honor high enough for her.

Both Lisette and Nettle cluck with pleasure over the young woman's appearance when she is washed and dressed.

"You look like a princess indeed," Lisette croons, and Pod's eyes shine with amazement and pride. But when they want to bring a looking glass to show her how fine she looks, the young woman shakes her head. "In the glass I would see my mother, not myself."

The Great Hall is filled with folk in their finest clothes. Jewels glitter on hands and around necks. The tables groan with an abundance of food. Lisette, Nettle, and Pod—also dressed in fine new clothes provided by the thoughtful king—nibble and whisper, but the young woman sits with an impassive face, not eating anything.

After dinner, one of the lords talks for a long while to welcome the king back to Scotland. The crowd cheers when he describes the suicide of the for-

mer queen. They cheer louder when he recounts the story of how Macduff chopped off Macbeth's head.

Then King Malcolm rises to speak. Even before he opens his mouth, the crowd cheers and cheers. Malcolm speaks for a long time, thanking different lords and announcing they will now be called earls, not thanes.

"Finally," he says to the crowd that has grown hoarse from wild cheering, "my deepest gratitude is due to a valiant young woman who saved my life the night I fled the assassination of my father and escaped through the wood. Would Roah—once known as Gilly—come forth to receive the thanks of her king?"

Like a sleepwalker, she moves to the dais. She pays no heed to the crowd that whispers to each other of her beauty and bravery.

King Malcolm looks older than the boy she helped escape from the castle, but he is still just as beautiful. He takes her hand in his. His heavy-lidded eyes are warm. "I owe you my life," he says. "No reward is sufficient for that. Because you saved me, you thereby saved Scotland. There is no reward great enough for that. All I can do is to restore to you your father's lands. You are now rightly one of the richest nobles in all our land. Henceforth you will be known throughout the land as the first princess of Scotland. And I deed you the rents from the following holdings . . ."

He rattles off the names of a dozen or more properties. The hoarse crowd manages to squeeze out a few more cheers.

When she thinks he is finished, she turns to go, but he keeps her hand in his. "My fair princess and savior," he says, his eyes twinkling, "I would ask one more favor of you. Do not bury your beauty in the countryside, Lady Roah. Stay in my court, as the first lady of the court. You have given me a fine new life. Let me give you one as well." He smiles and tightens his hand around hers.

"Nay, your majesty," calls out a voice in the crowd. Surprised, she turns to locate its source. Lord Macduff strides forward, shouldering people out of the way so he can reach the dais. He kneels in front of her and bows his curly head.

"My lady, I have heard how you tried to save my family. I was gone, but you risked your life to save theirs." He looks up at her with sad

brown eyes. "Lady, both you and I have families who were killed by that dead butcher. 'Twas the fondest dream of my wife and my oldest son that you come live at Fife. Let me become the father you lack. Let me adopt you as my daughter. No father could love or pamper his child more than I will love and pamper you. My child, for too long you have had to take care of yourself in the world. 'Tis time for you now to let someone take care of you."

"Gilly!" A young voice calls out above the crowd. "I mean, Lady Roah!" Her eyes widen. Fleance squirms through the press of bodies until he stands on her other side. "Don't listen to them. Come with me instead." He squints in the bright light. "I am not yet used to you in that dress," he says severely in his squeaky-growly voice, and for the first time in a long while, she smiles. "You and I have had enough of this cold land. My uncle is going to take me to the south, to France and Italy, where I can study science. We will spend the next year in Rome. Come with us. You will love life in the civilized south, far from this cold and wild place. When you are there, you will have no reminders of all the sorrows you endured in this harsh land. There are fine libraries and great scholars. Come with me and leave this land forever."

She looks back and forth from one to the other of the men kneeling in front of her.

"Be my fellow in travel," Fleance says.

"Be my daughter," Lord Macduff begs.

"Be my princess." King Malcolm squeezes her fingers.

The crowd seems to be holding its breath, waiting for her decision. She looks around, wondering what to do.

Which offer should she take? Any of these lives would be a good one.

Then she catches sight of Pod, Nettle, and Lisette at the back of the hall. Their faces look split open with delight at her good fortune.

Then the sense of King Malcolm's words sinks into her brain. I am a wealthy woman. I have lands and money of my own. That means I have the power to create my own place, a kingdom within this kingdom. I can make a place where Nettle can have a cozy cottage and practice her herb craft safe from the gossip of nosy, ignorant villagers who regard her as a witch. I can make a place where Pod will no longer be teased and tormented for his slow mind but will be honored for the loving, loyal boy he truly is. A place where Lisette can lord over my kitchen, a place where I can hire tutors and learn to read in dozens of languages, a place where I can have a library of my own, a place where abandoned children can come and be safe—abandoned children like Pod and me and—

The face of her mother flickers into her mind.

I do not forgive her, but she, too, was abandoned in her way. And whether I like it or not, part of her will always be part of me. But Nettle, too, is my mother, and Helga and Lisette. They are all my mothers. Yes! Yes! It is as clear as water—we all have many mothers—and many fathers, too, and parts of them are always inside us, but it goes the other way as well, for inside all of them is a small part that is an abandoned, frightened child, and more important than killing a king is making the world safe for all abandoned children, and now I have a place and the money and power to make a safe world within this world for those I love to learn and grow.

I smile affectionately at the three good men in front of me.

"I thank you, sirs, but I must refuse all your kind offers."

Then I direct my smile at my family in the back of the hall.

"'Tis time to go home."

AUTHOR'S NOTE

EARLY IN MY RESEARCH, I realized that I could be faithful either to history or to William Shakespeare's historically inaccurate version of Macbeth's story, but I could not be faithful to both. Because I was initially inspired by Shakespeare's play, whenever history and drama diverged I followed the path blazed by Shakespeare. In order to stay true to the world of his play, I took liberties with medieval Scotland's chronology, geography, customs, and characters. I apologize for all historically inaccurate details in this novel.

ACKNOWLEDGMENTS

THE BEST WAY to develop intimacy with a play is to teach it or direct it. Therefore, I want to thank the hundreds of students in my English classes at Providence and St. Xavier High Schools who accompanied me in my yearly exploration of William Shakespeare's *Macbeth*. Every time I taught the play, I discovered something new. In addition, I would also like to thank the casts of my four productions of *Macbeth*. Each set of actors brought new insights and enthusiasm to the play and helped me look at the script in a different way.

I also thank the Antioch Writer's Workshop for inspiring me to believe in both myself as a writer and my story. The wise observations of my editors, Greer Hendricks and Carolyn Caughey, strengthened my manuscript immeasurably while their warm enthusiasm strengthened me. Finally, I am especially grateful to my agent, Fred Morris, whose wizardry helped turn a few pages of possibility into a published book.